THE
GOLDEN
AGE

A Romance of the Far Future

JOHN C. WRIGHT

A TOM DOHERTY ASSOCIATES BOOK
NEW YORK

This is a work of fiction. All the characters and events portrayed in this book are either products of the author's imagination or are used fictitiously.

THE GOLDEN AGE

Copyright © 2002 by John C. Wright

Edited by David G. Hartwell

A Tor Book
Published by Tom Doherty Associates, LLC
175 Fifth Avenue
New York, NY 10010

www.tor.com

Tor® is a registered trademark of Tom Doherty Associates, LLC.

ISBN: 0-812-57984-4
Library of Congress Catalog Card Number: 2001058468

First edition: April 2002
First mass market edition: April 2003

Printed in the United States of America

0 9 8 7 6 5 4 3 2

DRAMATIS PERSONAE

grouped by nervous system formation
(neuroform)

Biochemical Self-Aware Entities

Base neuroform
PHAETHON PRIME of RHADAMANTH, Silver-Gray
  Manorial School
HELION RELIC of RHADAMANTH, Phaethon's sire,
  founder of the Silver-Gray Manorial School, and a
  peer
DAPHNE TERCIUS SEMI-RHADAMANTH, Phaethon's
  wife
GANNIS HUNDRED-MIND GANNIS, Synergistic-
  Synnoint School, a peer
ATKINS VINGT-ET-UN GENERAL-ISSUE, a soldier

Nonstandard neuroforms
VAFNIR of MERCURY EQUILATERAL STATION, a
  peer

XENOPHON of FARAWAY, Tritonic Neuroform Composure School, called the Neptunians

XINGIS of NEREID, also called DIOMEDES, Silver-Gray School

Alternate Organization neuroform, commonly called Warlocks

AO AOEN, the Master-Dreamer, a peer

NEO-ORPHEUS the Apostate, protonothary and chair of the College of Hortators

ORPHEUS MYRIAD AVERNUS, founder of the Second Immortality, a Peer

Cortial-Thalamically Integrated neuroform, commonly called Invariants

KES SENNEC the Logician, a peer

Cerebelline neuroform

WHEEL-OF-LIFE, an Ecological Mathematician, a peer

GREEN-MOTHER, the artiste who organizes the ecological performance at Destiny Lake

Mass-Mind Compositions

The ELEEMOSYNARY COMPOSITION, a Peer

The HARMONIOUS COMPOSITION, of the College of Hortators

The BELLIPOTENT COMPOSITION (disbanded)

Electrophotonic Self-Aware Entities

Sophotechs

RHADAMANTHUS, a manor-house of the Silver-Gray School, million-cycle capacity

EVENINGSTAR, a manor-house of the Red school, million-cycle capacity

NEBUCHEDNEZZAR, advisor to the College of Hortators, ten-million-cycle capacity

HARRIER, consulting detective, one-hundred-thousand-cycle capacity

MONOMARCHOS, a barrister, one-hundred-thousand-cycle capacity

AURELIAN, host of the Celebration, fifty-thousand-million-cycle loose capacity

The ENNEAD consists of nine Sophotech groups, each of over a billion-cycle capacity, including Warmind, Westmind, Orient, Austral, Boreal, Northwest, Southwest, and others.

EARTHMIND, the unified consciousness in which all terrestrial machines, and machines in Near-Earth-Orbit, from time to time participate: trillion-cycle capacity

PROLOGUE

CELEBRATIONS OF THE IMMORTALS

It was a time of masquerade.

It was the eve of the High Transcendence, an event so solemn and significant that it could be held but once each thousand years, and folk of every name and iteration, phenotype, composition, consciousness and neuroform, from every school and era, had come to celebrate its coming, to welcome the transfiguration, and to prepare.

Splendor, feast, and ceremony filled the many months before the great event itself. Energy shapes living in the north polar magnetosphere of the sun, and Cold Dukes from the Kuiper belts beyond Neptune, had gathered to Old Earth, or sent their representations through the mentality; and celebrants had come from every world and moon in the solar system, from every station, sail, habitat and crystal-magnetic latticework.

No human or posthuman race of the Golden Oecumene was absent from these festivities. Fictional as well as actual personalities were invited. Composition-assisted reconstructions of dead or deleted paladins and sages, magnates and philosophers, walked by night the boulevards of the Aurelian palace-city, arm-in-arm with extrapolated demigoddesses from imagined superhuman futures, or languid-eyed lamia from morbid unrealized alternatives, and strolled or danced among the monuments and energy sculptures, fountains, dream fixtures, and phantasms, all beneath a silver, city-covered moon, larger than the moon past ages knew.

And here and there, shining like stars on the active channels of the mentality, were recidivists who had returned from high transhuman states of mind, bringing back with them thought-shapes or mathematical constructions inexpressible in human words, haunted by memories of what the last Transcendence had accomplished, feverish with dreams of what the next might hold.

It was a time of cheer.

And yet, even in such golden days, there were those who would not be satisfied.

THE OLD MAN

1.

On the hundred-and-first night of the Millennial Celebration, Phaethon walked away from the lights and music, movement and gaiety of the golden palace-city, and out into the solitude of the groves and gardens beyond. In this time of joy, he was not at ease himself; and he did not know why.

His full name was Phaethon Prime Rhadamanth Humodified (augment) Uncomposed, Indepconciousness, Base Neuroformed, Silver-Gray Manorial Schola, Era 7043 (the "Reawakening").

This particular evening, the west wing of the Aurelian Palace-city had been set aside for a Presentation of Visions by the elite of Rhadamanthus Mansion. Phaethon had been extended an invitation to sit on the panel of dream-judges, and, eager to experience the future histories involved, had happily accepted. Phaethon had been imagining the evening, perhaps, would be in miniature, for Rhadamanthus House, what the High Transcendence in December would be for all mankind.

But he was disappointed. The review of one drab and uninspired extrapolation after another had drained his patience.

Here was a future where all men were recorded as braininformation in a diamond logic crystal occupying the core of the earth; there was one where all humanity existed in the threads of a plantlike array of sails and panels forming a Dyson Sphere around the sun; a third promised, larger than worlds, housings for trillions of minds and superminds, existing in the absolute cold of trans-Neptunian space—cold was required for any truly precise subatomic engineering—but with rails or elevators of unthinkably dense material running across hundreds of AU, across the whole width of the solar system, and down into the mantle of the sun, both to mine the hydrogen ash for building matter, and to tap the vast energy of Sol, should ever matter or energy in any amount be needed by the immobile deep-space mainframes housing the minds of mankind.

Any one of them should have been a breathtaking vision. The engineering was worked out in loving detail. Phaethon could not name what it was he wanted, but he knew he wanted none of these futures being offered him.

Daphne, his wife, who was only a collateral member of the House, had not been invited; and, Helion, his sire, was present only as a partial-version, the primary having been called away to a conclave of the Peers.

And so it was that in the center of a loud, happy throng of brightly costumed telepresences, mannequins, and real-folk, and with a hundred high windows in the Presence Hall busy and bright with monotonous futures, and with a thousand channels clamoring with messages, requests, and invitations for him, Phaethon realized that he was entirely alone.

Fortunately, it was masquerade, and he was able to assign his face and his role to a backup copy of himself. He donned the disguise of a Harlequin clown, with lace at his throat and mask on his face, and then slipped out of a side entrance before any of Helion's lieutenants or squires-of-honor thought to stop him.

Without a word or signal to anyone, Phaethon departed, and he walked across silent lawns and gardens by moonlight, accompanied only by his thoughts.

2.

He wandered far, to a place he had not seen before. Beyond the gardens, in an isolated dell, he entered a grove of silver-crowned trees. He paced slowly through the grove, hands clasped behind his back, sniffing the air and gazing up at the stars between the leaves above. In the gloom, the dark and fine-grained bark was like black silk, and the leaves had mirror tissues, so that when the night breeze blew, the reflections of moonlight overhead rippled like silver lake water.

It took him a moment to notice what was odd about the scene. The flowers were open, even though it was night, and their faces were turned toward one bright planet above the horizon.

Puzzled, Phaethon paused and pointed two fingers at the nearest trunk, making the identification gesture. Evidently the protocols of the masquerade extended to the trees as well, and no explanation of the trees, no background was forthcoming.

"We live in a golden age, the age of Saturn," said a voice from behind him. "Small wonder that our humor should be saturnine as well."

One who appeared as a wrinkle-faced man, wearing a robe as white as his hair and beard, stood not far away, leaning on a walking stick. During masquerade, Phaethon had no recognition file available in mind, and thus could not tell what dream-level, composition, or neuroform this old man was. Phaethon was not sure how to act. There were things one could say or do to a computer fiction that a real person, a telepresence, or even a partial, would find shockingly rude.

He decided on a polite reply, just in case. "Good evening to you, sir. Then there is a hidden meaning to this display?" His gesture encompassed the grove.

"Aha! You are not a child of this present age, then, since you seek to look below the surface beauty of things."

Phaethon was not certain how to take this comment. It was either a slight against the society in which he lived, or else against himself. "You suspect me to be a simulacrum? I assure you, I am real."

"So simulacra must seem to themselves, I suppose, should anyone ask them," said the white-bearded man with a wide-armed shrug.

Then he seated himself on a mossy rock with a grunt. "But let us leave the question of your identity—this is a masquerade, after all, and not the right time to inquire, eh?—and study instead the instruction of the trees here. I do not know if you detect the energy web grown throughout the bark layers; but a routine calculates the amount of light which would shine, and the angle of its fall, were the planet Saturn to ignite like some third sun. Then, true to these calculations, the energy web triggers photosynthesis in the leaves and flowers, and, naturally, favors the side and angles from which the light would come, you see?"

"Thus they bloom at night," Phaethon said softly, impressed by the intricacy of the work.

"Day or night," the white-bearded man said, "provided only that Saturn is above the horizon."

Phaethon thought it ironic that the white-haired man had picked Saturn as the position for his fictitious new sun. Phaethon knew Saturn would never be improved, the huge atmosphere never be mined for volatiles. He himself had twice headed projects to reengineer Saturn and render that barren wasteland more useful to human needs, or to clear out the cluttered navigational hazards for which near-Saturn space was notorious. In both cases public outcry had halted his efforts and driven away his financial support. Too many people were in love with the majestic (but utterly useless) ring-system.

The white-haired man was still speaking: "Yes, they follow the rise and fall of Saturn. And—listen! here is the curious part—over the generations, the flowers have evolved complex reactions so that their heads can turn to follow that wandering planet through cycle and epicycle, opposition, triune and conjunction. Thus they thrive. They are not one whit disaccommodated by the fact the sun they follow with such effort is a false one."

Phaethon looked back and forth across the grove. It was extensive. The cool night breeze tingled with the scents of eerie mirrored blossoms.

Perhaps because the man looked so odd, white bearded, wrinkled, and leaning on a stick, just the way a character from an old novel or reproduction might look, Phaethon spoke without reflection. "Well, the artist here did not use flint-napped knives for his gene-splicing, and he didn't run his calculations in Roman numerals on an abacus, eh? Rather a lot of effort for a pointless jest."

"Pointless?" The white-haired man scowled.

Phaethon realized his blunder. Perhaps the man was real after all. Probably he was the very artist who had made this place. "Ah . . . Pardon me! 'Pointless,' I admit, may be too strong a word for it!"

"Oh? And what is the right word, then, eh?" asked the man testily.

"Well, ah . . . But this grove is meant to criticize the artificiality of our society, is it not?"

"Criticize?! It is meant to draw blood! It is Art! Art!"

Phaethon made an easy gesture. "No doubt the point here is too subtle for me to grasp. I fear I do not understand what it means to criticize civilization for being artificial. Civilization, by definition, must be artificial, since it is manmade. Isn't 'civilization' the very name we give to the sum total of manmade things?"

"You are being obtuse, sir!" shouted the odd man, drumming his cane sharply into the moss underfoot. "The point is! The point is that our civilization should be simpler."

Phaethon realized then that this man must be a member of one of those primitivist schools, whom everyone seemed to revere but no one wanted to follow. They refused to have any brain modifications whatsoever, even memory aids or emotion-balancing programs. They refused to use telephones, televection, or motor transport.

And some, it was said, programmed the nanomachines

floating in their cell nuclei to produce, as years passed, the
wrinkled skin, hair defects, osteoarthritis, and general physical decay that figured so prominently in ancient literature,
poems, and interactives. Phaethon wondered in horror what
could prompt a man to indulge in such slow and deliberate
self-mutilation.

The man was speaking: "You are blind to what is plain
before your eyes! Behold the mirrored layer of tissue growing
over all these leaves. It is to block the true sun from the
knowledge of these plants. Tracking a sun, which merely rises
and sets, is easier than anticipating retrograde motion, I assure
you. Complex habits, painfully learned through generations,
would be instantly thrown aside in one blast of true sunlight.
And therefore these little flowers have a mechanism to keep
the truth at bay. Strange that I've made the blocking tissue
look mirrored; you can see your own face in it . . . if you
look."

This comment verged on insult. Phaethon replied hotly:
"Or perhaps the tissue merely protects them from irritants,
good sir!"

"Hah! So the puppy has teeth after all, eh? Have I irked
you, then? This is Art also!"

"If Art is an irritant, like grit, good sir, then spend your
genius praising the society cosmopolitan enough to tolerate
it! How do you think simple societies maintain their simplicity? By intolerance. Men hunt; women gather; virgins guard
the sacred flame. Anyone who steps outside their stereotypic
social roles is crushed."

"Well, well, young manor-born—you are a manorial, are
you not? Your words sound like someone taught by machines—what you don't know, young manor-born, is that cosmopolitan societies are sometimes just as ruthless about
crushing those who don't conform. Look at how unhappy
they made that reckless boy, what's-his-name, that Phaethon.
There are worse things in store for him, I tell you!"

"I beg your pardon?" Strange. The sensation was not unlike
stepping for a nonexistent stair, or having apparently solid
ground give way underfoot. Phaethon wondered if he had

somehow wandered into a simulation or a pseudomnesia-play without noticing it. "But . . . I am Phaethon. I am he. What in the world do you mean?" And he took off the mask he wore.

"No, no. I mean the real Phaethon. Though you are quite bold to show up at a masquerade like this, dressed in his face. Bold. Or tasteless!"

"But I am he!" A bewildered note began to creep into his voice.

"So you are Phaethon, eh? No, no, I think not. He is not welcome at parties."

Not welcome? Him? Rhadmanthus House was the oldest mansion of the Silver-Gray, and the Silver-Gray was, in turn, the third oldest scholum in the entire manorial movement. Rhadamanthus boasted over 7,600 members just of the elite communion, and not to mention tens of thousands of collaterals, partials and secondaries. Not welcome? Phaethon's sire and gene-template was Helion, founder of the Silver-Gray and archon of Rhadamanthus. Phaethon was welcome everywhere!

The strange old man was still speaking: "You could not be him: Phaethon wears grim and brooding black and proud gold, not frills like those."

(For a moment, oddly enough, Phaethon could not quite recall how he usually dressed. But surely he had no reason to dress in grim colors. Had he? He was not a grim man. Was he?)

He tried to speak calmly: "What do you say I have done to make me unwelcome at celebrations, sir?"

"What has he done? Hah!" The white-haired man leaned back as if to avoid an unpleasant smell. "Your joke is not appreciated, sir. As you may have guessed, I am a Antiamaranthine Purist, and I do not carry a computer in my ear telling me every nuance of your manor-born protocols, or which fork to use, or when to hold my tongue. Maybe I speak out of turn to say that the real Phaethon would be ashamed to show his face at a festival like this! Ashamed! This is a celebration of those who love this civilization, or who, like me, are urged to try to improve it by constructive criticism. But you!"

"Ashamed? . . . I have done nothing!"

"No, no more! Do not speak again! Perhaps I should get a brain filter like you machine-pets, so I could merely blot out stains like you from my sight and memory. That would be ironic, wouldn't it? Me, shrouded in a little silvery tissue of my own. But irony is perhaps more fit to an age of iron than to an age of gold."

"Sir, I really must insist you tell me what—"

"What?!! Still here, you interloper! If you want to look like Phaethon, maybe I should treat you like him, and have you thrown out of my grove on your ear!"

"Tell me the truth!" Phaethon stepped toward the man.

"Fortunately, this grove, and even the surrounding dream-space, are my own, not part of the party grounds proper, and so I can throw you out, can't I?"

He cackled, and waved his walking stick.

The man, and the grove, disappeared. Phaethon found himself standing on green hilltop in the sunlight, overlooking the palaces and gardens of the celebration shining in the distance. An overture of music came faintly from the distant towers.

This was a scene from the first day of the celebration, one of the entrance scenarios. The old man had deleted his grove scene from Phaethon's sensorium, throwing him back into his default setting. An unthinkable rudeness! But, perhaps, allowed under the relaxed protocols and standards of the festival time.

A moment of cold anger ran through Phaethon. He was surprised at the vehemence of his own emotion. He was not normally an angry man—was he?

Perhaps it would be wise to let the matter drop. There were entertainments and delights enough to engage his attention at the Celebrations without pursuing this.

But . . . unlike everything he had seen, this was real. Phaethon's curiosity was piqued, and perhaps his pride was stung. He would discover the answers.

He raised his fingers to his eyes and made the restart gesture. He was back in the scene, at night, in the silvery grove, but alone. The man was either gone or he was hiding behind Phaethon's sense-filter.

With another gesture, Phaethon lowered his sense-filter and opened his brain to all the sensations in the area, so he could look upon "reality" without any interpretation-buffer.

The shock of the noise and music, the screams of the Advertisements, startled him.

Panels and banners of lightweight film hung or floated grandly in the air. Each one flashed with colors brighter and more gaudy than its neighbor; every image was twice as dizzying, alluring, and hypnotic as the one before. Some of the Advertisements had projectors capable of directing stimulation into any brain equipped to receive it.

When they noticed Phaethon staring (perhaps they had registers to note his eye movements and pupil dilation—such information was, after all, in the public domain) they folded and swooped, clamoring, pressing around him, squawking, urging him to try, just once, free trial offer, their proffered stimulants and additions, false memories, compositions, and thought schemes. They swarmed like angry sea gulls or hungry children from some historical drama.

The music was, if anything, worse. A group from the Red Manorial School on one hillside in the distance were having a combination scream-feast, Bacchanalia, and composition-symphony analogue. Emancipated partials of the Psycho-asymmetric Insulae-Composition were on the other hillside, having a noise duel. Their experimental 36- and 108-tone scale music, subsonic and hypersonic, trembled in Phaethon's teeth. They made no effort to muffle the sound for the sake of those who did not share their extensive ear/auditory lobe modifications, their peculiar subjective time-scale alterations, or their even more peculiar aesthetic theories. Why should they? Every civilized person was assumed to have access to some sort of sense-filter to allow them to block or to tolerate the noise.

And there was no sign of the white-haired man. Perhaps

he had been a projection after all, or some fiction, part of the art statement of the grove?

The flash and glamour of the transparent Advertisements did not block his view. The trees were widely spaced, nor was there brush. And, unless the man had hidden behind the walking iceberg thing looming above the grape trellises nearby, there was simply no place to hide.

Phaethon threw his hands before his face and gestured for his sense-filter to resume.

Peace and silence crashed into place around him. It was not, perhaps, the perfect truth he saw. But the groves were quiet now, and starlight and moonlight slanted through the strange silver-mirrored leaves, and falling blossoms. A routine calculated how the scene would look (and sound and feel and smell) were the disturbing objects not present. The representation was close to real, "Surface Dreaming" as it was called. The machine intelligences creating the illusion, able to think a million times faster than a man, or a billion, could cleverly and symmetrically account for all inconsistencies and cover up any unwanted errors.

His ears still rang with echoes; his eyes were still dazzled by floating half shapes, colors reversed. He could have waited for his ears to stop ringing naturally, or blinked his eyes clear. But he was impatient; the man he sought was no doubt getting away. He merely signaled for his eyes to reset to perfect night adaptation, for this ears to restore.

Phaethon started to jog toward the grape trellises where . . .

The iceberg thing was gone. Phaethon saw nothing.

Iceberg? Phaethon's augmented memory could re-create an exact image of what he had seen. It had loomed, gigantic, over the area, moving on myriad legs of semiliquid, which solidified, elephantine, then liquefied again as the creature drifted forward. Likewise, it had had a dozen arms or tentacles of ice flowing and freezing around objects in the area, careful not to disturb the trees, but holding objects (eyes? remote sensors?) near the garden plants, as if to study them from every angle.

It was, of course, a member of the Tritonic Neuroform

Composition School, the so-called Neptunians. The technology of their nerve-cell surface allowed them thought-speeds approaching that of some of the slower Sophotechs; but the crystals of the cell surface exhibited their peculiar electrosuperconductive and micropolymorphetic characteristics only under the near-absolute-zero temperatures and near-metallic-hydrogen-forming pressures of the Neptunian atmosphere. The icy body Phaethon had seen was armor—living, shape-changing armor, but armor nonetheless, and a triumph of molecular and submolecular technology. That armor allowed the Neptunian brain substances inside to withstand the unbearable heat and (relative to Neptune) near-vacuum conditions of the earthly atmosphere.

That he had programmed his sense-filter to block images of Advertisements or raucous music, Phaethon could understand. But he did not remember (and his memory was photographically perfect) ordering the filter to block views of Neptunians. Merely that one of that strange, remote school, the most distant members of the Golden Oecumene, should come physically to Earth was cause for wonder and comment.

Why in the world would Phaethon have ordered himself not to see, or to avoid remembering seeing, such a being? It was true that Neptunians were thought of as reckless, innovative, untrustworthy, and yet . . .

Phaethon took a moment to examine his sense-filter's censor. Only three of the command lines struck him as odd. Very odd. One was meant to prevent him seeing the Cerebelline Green-Mother's ecoperformance being held on Channels 12–20 at Destiny Lake. The second was to edit out sights and references to the visiting Neptunian legates. A third was meant to distract him from studying astronomical reports or information concerning a recent disaster in Mercurial space, brought on by solar prominences and irregularities of unusual violence.

Why? What was the connection?

And why had he done this to himself? And then ordered himself to forget that he had done it?

Phaethon adjusted his sense-filter to allow himself to see

the Neptunian (without hearing the music or seeing those dreadful Advertisements) and was surprised to behold the gigantic creature picking its way up the grassy slope toward him, moving like a pale cloud bank.

As it came closer, Phaethon saw, within the ice, several concentric shells or spheres of crystalline armor. Deep in the smoky depths was a web of nerve tissue connecting four major brains, and at least a hundred lesser subbrains, nerve knobs, ganglia, synthetic cells, relays, and augmentation clusters.

The nerve tissue within the ice was in motion, some tendrils of brain matter expanding, forming new nodes and knobs; and others contracting, creating an impression of furious mental activity.

Closer it came.

3.

Elsewhere, Helion was also discontented.

In Aurelian mansion, seven entities of very different schools, life principles, neuroforms, and appearance were meeting privately. They had three things in common: wealth, age, and ambition.

The Seven Peers were actually sitting in a tall, many-windowed library, with thought-icons on the oak-paneled walls. Each Peer saw the chamber differently.

The most recently admitted Peer was named Helion Relic (undetermined) Rhadamanth Humodified (augment, with multiple synnoetic sensory channels) Self-composed, Radial Hierarchic Multipartial (multiple parallel and partial, with subroutines), Base Neuroformed, Silver-Gray Manorial School, Era 50 (The Time of the Second Immortality).

He was the only manor-born present, and was more than a little pleased that his school, the Silver-Gray, was singled out from among the other schools of the manorials for this dignity.

Helion's self-image wore the costume of a Byzantine imperator from the time of the Second Mental Structure, with a many-rayed diadem of pearly white and robe of Tyrian purple.

"My Peers, it is with great pride and honor I take my place among you. I trust that the legal issues surrounding the question of my continuity of identity are acceptable to everyone here?"

There was a signal of concurrence from the Peers, which Helion's sensorium interpreted as nods and murmurs of assent.

"Gentlemen, we are the Peers and Paramounts of this civilization. The Golden Oecumene has given us every benefit she can give. Now we must protect her. We must make certain that the events that so recently shook our society to her roots—events that only we Seven now recall—never recur.

"We Seven represent the wealthiest nonmachine fortunes ever to exist in time or space. If we do not act—then who?

"I submit that we have reached a golden age, a time of perfection and utopia: to maintain it, to sustain it, no further changes can be allowed. Adventures, risks, rashness, must receive no further applause from any voice in our Oecumene. Only then will we all be able to keep our wayward sons at home, safe from harm.

"At your leisure, you may examine my detailed findings; how many people we can influence, what the possible results are of various forms of art and persuasion we can bring forth during the celebration. I draw your attention, for example, to the ecoperformance at Destiny Lake, formulated by the sistermates of our Peer, Wheel-of-Life. Even those who do not apprehend the direct analogy involved there will be subliminally made uneasy by the type of erratic and selfish heroism which that work of art condemns.

"This is merely one example of thousands. The computer time available to my Manor house can generate specific anticipations running to many orders of magnitude. Merely human minds will not be able to outwit the kind of persuasive campaign I envision. If enough people are persuaded of the truth of a proposition before the Transcendence, surely that

will be remembered during the Transfiguration, surely that
will shape the outcome after.

"The Age of Tranquility, dreamed of for so many aeons of
so much turmoil and pain, has come! My Peers, history must
be called to an end!

"Examine my proposal, my Peers. Look at the future I have
drafted. It is one where the College of Hortators is backed by
the full power of the Seven Peers."

THE NEPTUNIAN

1.

Phaethon addressed the giant being: "Pardon me, sir, if I am intruding, but could you tell me, please, if you saw a man come by here just now? He looked like this. . . ." and he opened up channel 100, the common-use channel, and downloaded a few hundred frames of images and sensorumedia from his recent memory into a public temporary file. He had an artistic subroutine add background music, narrative comments, and some dramatic editing for theme and unity, and then he transmitted the images.

Phaethon felt the tingle of his nape hairs as his name was read (he still had not put his mask back on), and then a signal came in on a high-compression channel, saying: "This is the translator. My client is attempting to convey a complex of memory files and associational paths which you either do not have the ability to receive or which I do not have authority to transmit. The amount of information involved may be more than one brain can apprehend. Do you have stored noumenal personalities, backups, or augments?"

Phaethon signaled for identity, but the Neptunian was masked. "You have me at a disadvantage, sir. I am not accustomed to revealing the locations of my mind-space to strangers, and certainly not my resurrection copies." Phaethon wanted an answer to his question, and would have preferred to remain polite, but the request that he open his private thoughts was extraordinary, almost absurd. Not to mention that the Neptunian reputation for eccentric pranks was too well known.

"Very well. I will attempt to convey my client's communication in a linear format, by means of words, but only on the understanding that much substantial content, and all secondary meanings, nuances, and connotations will be lost."

"I will be tolerant. Proceed."

"My initial data burst consists of four hundred entries, including multidimensional image arrays, memory respondents and correlations, poetry, and instructions on nerve alterations for creating novel emotional receiving structures in your brain. These structures may be of use later for appreciating the emotions (which have no names as yet in your language) which other parts of the communication will then attempt to arouse. The initial burst contains other preliminary minutia.

"Then follows a contextual batch of six thousand entries, including volumes of art and experience, memories and reconstructed memories, real and fictional, intended to give you and him a common background of experience, a context in which certain allusions and specifics will be best understood. Other greetings and salutations follow.

"The first entry of the core message contains rote formalities of time-sense and identity continuity, establishing that you are, in fact, the same Phaethon of my client's acquaintance, or, in case you are a copy, reconstruction, or simulation, to ascertain the relative degree of emotional and mental correspondence with which my client must regard you. The core message itself—"

"Pardon me," said Phaethon. "Did I know your client before he joined your Composition?" He amplified his vision (opening additional wavelengths) to look curiously at the several brains and brain groups floating in the icy substance.

"The Neptunian legate produces an emotion-statement of three orders of complexity, with associated memory trees to show correspondence, but otherwise does not respond to your question, which he regards as fantastic, disorienting, and not at all funny. Pause: Should I explain further about the emotional reaction, or shall I continue with the central message of the first datagroup? The process could be considerably sped if you will impart your command codes and locks to give me direct access to your neurological and mnemonic systems; this will enable me to add files directly into your mind, and alter your temperament, outlook, and philosophy to understand my client in the way he himself would like to be understood."

"Certainly not!"

"I was required to ask."

"Can you make your summary more brief? The man I'm asking about is someone who—well, perhaps he offended me, or—this man said some confusing things, and he—well, I'm trying to find him," Phaethon finished lamely.

"Very well. My client says: I (he forwards, as an appendix, a treatise on the meaning of the word 'I,' the concept of selfhood, and a bibliographical compendium of his life experiences and changes in his self-notions in order to define this term to you) greet (he also has side comments on the history and nature of greetings, the implications in this context of what is meant, including the legal implications of violating the ban placed on his initiating any contact with you) you (and he postulates a subjunctive inquiry that, should you not be the individual that he deems you to be, that all this be placed in a secondary memory-chain, and be regarded as a less-than-real operation, similar to a pseudomnemia. He also requests sealed and notarized confirmation on his recorded memorandum documenting that you initiated the contact without his prompting))."

"Stop! You are only three words into the first message, and already everything is obscure. What prohibition has been placed on him? By whom? The human race is finally mature, wise enough to reject coercion as a means to deal with each other. Where is there any institution, any curia, that is not voluntary, not based on subscription? Our militia was supported by donations from historical trusts. Who has any right to prevent your client from speaking with me? Who is your client? Tell him to remove his mask."

"My client responds with an emotion-action statement of four orders of complexity, all in the hypothetical-subjunctive mode, which states, in brief, that were he forbidden to speak with you, there may be (granting for the sake of argument) monitors or directives eavesdropping, which, were there such a thing, would not interfere as long as this discourse is kept within the general boundaries of polite and innocuous discourse. Of the seventy-four thousand million possible outcomes of this conversation which my client has examined in predictive scenarios, over fourteen of them conclude by some sort of interruption or reaction from the Aurelian Sophotech. Would you care to examine the full text of my client's reply, examine the extrapolation scenarios which he has calculated, or should I continue with my disquisition of the core message?"

This was the most fantastic yet. Phaethon put his mask back on, which acted as a signal to restore a zone of privacy around him, even hiding such information as was normally public, such as his name and appearance.

"Surely no one would be so rude as to intrude on our private conversation, not without some good reason!"

"My client wishes to download a philosophical question-and-debate routine to attempt to convince you that, even in the most enlightened and civilized of societies, reasonable men can differ as to what constitutes the good. For example (and here he once again indicates that he speaks only hypothetically) those who place a higher value on freedom than on the alleged security and meaningfulness which adherence to tradition provides, might be willing to tolerate, or even encourage, a certain small amount of crime and riot, danger and uncertainty."

Phaethon knew Greek and Latin, English and French, and half a dozen other dead languages, and so he knew what the word "crime" meant; but he had never heard it used except as a metaphor for unacceptable rudeness, or for poorly executed works of art. A paleolinguistic routine from the Rhadamanthus Mansion-mind had confirmed the original meaning of the word and had inserted it into Phaethon's short-term memory.

He had his memory replay the last message over more than once to reassure himself that there had been no error. Was this creature actually advocating that the use of violence or fraud against innocent beings was, in some measure, justified?

The translator persisted: "Will you open, at least, a holding space where he can put some of the conversation trees he has constructed on this topic for you?"

"Sir, forgive me if I seem abrupt. But my main question, about the man who accosted me, lingers unanswered. Could you return to your core message, and, if you please, summarize the summary?"

"Here is a severely reduced summation of the core message:

"Phaethon, I greet you once again, though you have passed into the shadow of our enemy, have been wounded in your soul and mind, and have forgotten me. One day, I pray, we shall be whole again. Crippled now in your mind, you have perhaps no strength to sustain the belief in that great dream which once shook the worlds and empires of the Golden Oecumene to its rotten base; nor would you believe in what high esteem I and my comrades still hold you, despite your treasonous weakness of will. But believe this: You are trapped in a labyrinth of illusion; and yet the scruples, or the folly, of our foes allows you one hope of escape, one weak chink, a loophole, in an otherwise all-embracing prison wall.

"You must come with me now to the outer world, to cold and distant Neptune, in the dark, where the power of the sunlight, and of the Golden Oecumene's machines, fall short. After long struggles and contests of will, we have forced Golden Oecumene law to grant to the distant exiles there a measure of mental privacy and freedom undreamed here; our thoughts are not monitored by the benevolent tyranny of machines. Once there, you can become one of us. Your soul and memory can be cured of their great wound. Your body will be changed, and become like unto ours, and your mind will be embraced into our all-encompassing communion.

"But you must come at once, with no delay. Leave your wife, your life, your dreams of wealth, your mansion-home. Leave all. Say farewell to warmth and sun, but come!' "

Phaethon's mind was blank. It was all too bizarre. He knew what the word "enemy" was; the term referred to something like a competitor, but a vicious and uncivil one. The idea that the Golden Oecumene structure, however, could be such a thing was patently absurd, like thinking the sky was made of iron. Phaethon knew what insanity was, from his historical simulations, the same way he knew what a flint hand ax or a disease was; he was able to understand the idea that the Neptunian might be insane. He just was not able, not really, to believe it.

In his mental blankness, all he could think to say was: "If I wake my real body, to travel outside the range of the Noumenal Mentality, my brain information could not, in the case of a physical accident, be recorded and stored. Important segments of my life experience might be lost; I could even lose continuity and die the true and final death."

"But I tell you that you shall not die, but shall mingle with the Tritonic Composition and achieve a finer and higher life!"

2.

The other six Peers, each with different thinking-speed and thinking processes, absorbed, pored over, or examined over 9,200 projections of the effect of the next Transcendence on the upcoming Millenium, either directly, or (for those without permanent mental augmentations on staff), through auxiliary minds.

A gap in Helion's memory edited out this wait, and brought his time and time sense current to the next point in the conversation. To him, there was no pause. It may have been hours, or merely seconds, later.

The undisputed informal leader of the Peers, Orpheus Myriad Avernus, was not physically present, there or anywhere. He was the eldest and wealthiest of the Seven. He presented himself to Helion's senses as a dark-haired, pale-skinned youth, whose face had a haunting lack of expression, but with eyes unblinking, inward looking, deeply self-absorbed. He wore a long black Plutonian thermal cape of a style so quaint and so far out of fashion that only during a masquerade would it pass without comment. The wide neckpiece rose almost to his ears, and the pauldrons extended past his shoulders, making his head seem small and childlike.

Orpheus spoke in a very soft voice: "We applaud the sentiment expressed by our newest Peer. When conditions are optimal, any change, by definition, is decay. And Helion knows all too well how chaos, disloyalty, and recklessness can be found within our own households and holdings, and even within the hearts of those nearest to us."

For a moment, no one spoke. All eyes were fixed on Helion. An embarrassed silence hung over the room.

Gannis (or one of him) was physically present in the library chamber in Aurelian House where the meeting was "actually" taking place. Gannis was disguised as a character from First Mental Structure mythology, in robes of sky blue and white, crowned in rays, and with a lightning bolt for a scepter. He held the copyright on a rather striking face: black bearded, with deep-set eyes spaced far apart, beneath a wide and kingly brow. An eagle and a she-eagle were perched on his chair back, one over either shoulder. Gannis's eyes were as bright and fierce as those of his pets, but his voice was an agreeable, cheerful boom.

He now spoke to break the tension: "Elder Orpheus! Here you are opening old wounds. Helion has Phaethon well under control; why bring up an episode we all agreed to forget? I thought we were not going to speak any further it."

Orpheus spoke softly, as if he were talking only to himself, without moving his eyes: "We did not speak on that subject. Except we note that Helion has good reason, now, to display uncompromising zeal in the defense of tradition and orthodoxy."

Orpheus was a member of the small, ancient, peculiar school called the Aeonites. Their practice was to record an unchanging idealized version of themselves into permanent computer space. This template, at regular intervals, created an emanation or eidolon of itself, which came to life. New eidolons absorbed the information any prior active or living eidolons had acquired since the time the template was absorbed, but rejected any changes of personality, philosophy, or basic values. Members of this school were frozen and unalterable.

It was only by the narrowest margins that the Curia determined Aeonite legal status to be that of self-aware entities rather than ghosts or recordings. Public opinion did not necessarily agree.

(Helion, watching with part of his multiple mind on another channel, saw that Orpheus had no sensorium in operation. Orpheus saw no room at all; the dialogue was merely text; face expressions and nonverbal signs appeared in frames nearby, like the faces on playing cards. There was no other extension or background in Orpheus's scene. Everything else was black. Helion, disturbed, lowered the attention-value of that view, and paid attention to his own version of the scene.)

3.

For a moment, Phaethon was silent, caught in a spell of wonder. He should have been repelled, but he was not. It all sounded as splendid and strange as anything one of his wife's deep-dreamscape dramas might portray.

The Neptunian was speaking: "Even now, I have called my surface-to-orbit pinnace down from *Cernous Roc*, my vessel. A partial-vacuum generator is among the capabilities in my base layer which grants me flight, and my subsurface fluids can sustain your life cycles in suspension till the midair rendezvous is accomplished. Retrieve your true body from its crypt—I assume it is nearby, for the material housings of Rhadamanth Mansion are not far away. Wake, come here, then step within the circle of my arms; put your face into the surface substance of my body; it will part before you and flow around you, bonding cell with cell, to encase you in a protective vacuole."

Phaethon spoke softly: "But . . . but . . . I would need several years, at least, to set my affairs in order, and to create and educate a partial-duplicate of me to see to my duties in my absence. In any case I could not leave the festival before the Final Transcendence in December."

"No. You must come without any delay whatsoever. If you send a message, or even a signal, the labyrinth may close again, and, this time, any loose stones be bricked over!"

Leave immediately? Phaethon imagined his wife, giddy on imagination amplifiers, emerging from her pseudomnesia womb, eagerly seeking him out to talk about her dream-victories, all her newly made computer-generated friends and wonders.

But he would not be there. Impatient, then angry, then frantic, she would seek among the images on the promenade, or in the feast-cities, ballrooms, or game halls, seeing a thousand costumes, all in masks. The location channel was disenabled during masquerade. It would be eight months or more before her fears could be confirmed. Till then, she would not know if he was no longer in this world rather than merely hiding or ignoring her.

The thought sobered him. He laughed. "I'm quite sorry, my dear sir, but you must realize what a ridiculous offer you are extending—"

And he stopped. Because it was beyond ridiculous. Go to Neptune?

Neptune was the farthest outpost of civilization, and, with two notable exceptions, the farthest any colony of humanity had ever reached: The actual last outpost of the Golden Oecumene was at 500 AUs, at the focal point of the gravity lens created by Sol. Here, elements of the Porphyrogen Composition mass-mind had created an artificial ice planet for themselves, and for the other visitors and staff of the Cosmic Observatory Effort. Beyond that, the nearer stars were barren of life. But at Cygnus X1, a small colony founded to study the effects of the singularity there had discovered a source of infinite energy, and, with that wealth, had expanded to a mighty civilization. Yet the distance was so far, the costs of travel so very great, that all communication with that society was lost; for that reason, it was known as the Silent Oecumene.

Neptune was unthinkably closer even than the nearest star, and yet was still unthinkably remote. Even ships with fairly high fuel-mass-to-payload ratios required very long times to make the journey, months, sometimes years.

Ridiculous? The thought was impossible.

4.

In the palace:

"Come!" said Gannis heartily, slapping the tabletop with his palm. "Helion has spent more computer time than any of us—millions of seconds for one study alone—to extrapolate which visions the Aurelian-mind may present during the December Transcendence. His devotion is beyond question.

"His dream is a grand one, I admit! Cease the motions of society, and freeze it into its present state! (Fortunate for us, when the waves freeze, those of us now at the crest will be at the tip of the iceberg forever after.) And yet—your pardon, friend Helion—allow me to introduce a note of caution. The Hortator College is a group of populist moralizers; their pinch-nostriled, squint-eyed overzealousness—hah? Is that what we need more of? Or less of? Augmenting their power will increase their power over us, even over us Seven Peers. What then, eh? What egalitarian nonsense will we be forced to stomach then? And I speak not just for myself but for all of me when I say that!"

Gannis's view of the room was the same as Helion's, but his sense of humor required him to introduce a slight difference. In Gannis's view, every object had two shadows, a dark black and a faint gray, for he had placed a second, smaller sun, a mere pinpoint of dazzling brightness, rising in the East.

Orpheus said in his cold, soft whisper of a voice: "Peer

Gannis perhaps has cause to fear any close inquiry into the recent events. It is a fine coincidence that he earned so much advantage by the Hortator's most recent deliberations."

Gannis should have looked angry at the accusation, but instead he threw wide his arms and laughed. "I am complimented that you think me cunning enough to have arranged these recent debacles! Not so. I fear that mere dumb luck has saved the Jovian Engineering Effort once again. Do you recall when bad investments by my overself brought me to such penury that I was asked to leave my peerage behind? Why, yes, you surely must, for it was you yourself who ask me to depart."

Gannis turned to the others, and continued: "And you wanted to have no more to do with funny, dumb, lovable, affable old Gannis, did you, my Peers? But then my other selves made back our fortune with the establishment of the Jupiter Equatorial Grand Collider. We did not predict the existence of the continent of stabile transadamantine elements beyond atomic number nine hundred; in fact, the standard model predicted against it.

"Chrysadmantium! What could not be done with this wonder metal? It elevated me back to my due position—others were enticed to dreams more wild, perhaps.

"I am better for my days of loss. More generous. Generous to the point of folly! I am as free with my advice as I am with my bounty. Is it my fault my advice was ignored? Is it my fault the wealth I spent so freely returned to me? This is the reward of fate, who cherishes the magnanimous. Clever lawyers merely help the process. . . .

"But for all my generosity, good Helion, I cannot see what more I can do for the College of Hortators. The contracts and covenants we make with all of our clients provide that anyone shunned by the College of Hortators we also must shun. For my clients, this means they can enter no structures, ships, or space elevators made from my supermetal; for the customers of Vafnir, this means no power; of the Eleemosynary Composition, no understanding; of Ao Aoen, no dreams; of Orpheus, no life. What more is wanted?"

Helion answered: "Nebuchednezzar Sophotech, who had been advising the College, has sequestered himself. The College presently has little or no sophotechnology at its command; that can be remedied. If they had sufficient computer-time resources, the Hortators could be omnipresent, omniscient: We, my Peers, who are the wealthiest entities ever to live, have no lack of resources to donate."

Grannis made an expansive gesture. "But why spend so much? Dangerous matters have been resolved—"

Helion said darkly, "There are still those who would overthrow all we have built and done. Do you gentlemen have the word 'enemy' in your archives?"

5.

In the garden:

"What is your true motive here?" asked Phaethon. "What is the meaning of this?"

"That same restriction which prevented me from first approaching you prevents me from bringing up the interdicted topic. Though my legal counsel parapersonality suggests that, if you and you alone bring up the topic, I may be able to answer questions about it without overstepping the letter of the law."

"Very well. Does this have anything to do with the man I saw?"

"The tree artist? He is nothing. He escaped you by yanking down a low-hanging Advertisement and wrapping himself in it, cloaklike, and your sense-filter blinded you to him till he was gone."

Phaethon thought such things happened only in comedies. Wryly, he realized that the tree artist, being a Puritan, had worn no sense-filter. He would have been exposed naked to all the clamor and commotion of the Advertisements, the roar of the music. Small wonder, then, that he had been in a testy mood.

"He implied I had done something shameful or dreadful,

something showing hatred or contempt for the Golden Oecumene. Is this related to your forbidden topic?"

"Directly related."

"Hm. It is well-known that the Neptunians love to test the boundaries of reason and good taste, and forever chafe and complain at the protocols and polite customs—one can hardly call them 'laws'—with which we voluntarily bind ourselves. And before you used the obscure word 'crime.' Were we partners, you and I, in some criminal attempt?"

"Not criminal. Neptunians experiment with unusual mind forms, but we are not insane. And yet, you and I were partners in an attempt which was not well loved by your small-souled people here, not well loved at all."

"Some Neptunian prank or trick or fraud, was it, then?"

"You repeat the slanders of our detractors. The Tritonic Composition explores the boundaries of mental effort, unhindered by the ponderous moral posturing of your leaden machine-minds! Allow me to transmit my stored compendia into your brain space. Time is short, and the Neptunian philosophy is complex, and is based on value judgments which only experience, not logic, can convey."

"Load them onto a semipublic channel, and I will peruse them at leisure, without danger of mind-to-mind contamination or manipulation."

"I am not permitted to undertake the insecurity or expense of placing valuable and private thought templates from my life experience into a public box."

"Expense?" This was ridiculous. Why, the expense of shipping Phaethon to Neptune—or, saving on mass, of shipping Phaethon's brain in a lightweight life support—was astronomical. Phaethon consulted an almanac in the Rhadamanthus Mansion-Mind. Neptune and Earth were not in favorable positions for any fuel-efficient flight paths. Phaethon calculated how the increased payload of his weight would affect the mass-energy costs of even a low-boost orbit. The cost in energy-currency was roughly equal to a several thousand seconds of time-currency. In other words, a small fortune.

"The expense is nothing compared to what you've already offered in transportation costs."

At first, it looked as if the iceberg shape were melting. But no, it was flattening, the high crown dropping, and the wide base growing wider and wider. Fluid flowed from the base, thickening and freezing into leg pillars. Under the ice at each foot of these pillars, Phaethon could see, dimly, complex machines being quickly made out of neurocomposite crystal and ceramic. The bulbs and globes and insulated tubes seemed to be energy batteries and field manipulators.

"You have acted against my advice and signaled to your mansion. I must flee before I am discovered."

Signaled? Phaethon had retrieved one almanac file and run a calculation routine, almost automatic functions. Phaethon had thought the Neptunian had only not wanted him to talk to his mansion. "Don't be absurd! No one would dare to listen in on my private communications."

"Even your vaunted Sophotechs will bend their precious laws to serve a purpose they call higher. But I shall use their own laws against them. They allow you some privacy during the distractions and masquerades meant to appease you. Behold. I shall construct a masquerader for you; he shall hold the files you will not receive from me; when you are strong enough to face truth, strong enough to defy this world of illusions, my messenger shall come for you."

Phaethon saw, in the depth of the armored crystal, a shape like a naked body floating to the surface. It was complete with bones, muscles, nerves, veins. Only the skin of the face and neck had not been wholly grafted on; and the skull was opened like a flower of bone, and strands and lines of nerve fiber were still being packed into place, with umbilicuslike channels still leading back to the main Neptunian brain-group. The lower body had a costume being woven around it, bulky and ill-fitting, but it was recognizable as the costume of Scaramouche, a character from the same period and operetta cycle as Phaethon's Harlequin.

"Phaethon, come now. This is the final second."

"Forgive me, sir, but I am not satisfied with your various

mystifications and hints. I suspect a deception, for which your kind are notorious. You have not even yet told me your name."

"How should I tell you my name when you do not even recall the meaning of your own!"

"Phaethon? The name dates from the Time of the Second Mental Structure. The myth is of the sun god's bastard child who dared to drive his father's chariot. . . ." Phaethon's voice trailed off.

There was a final surge and broil in the depth of the Neptunian body substance, as structural elements were formed and grown into place. A gush of wind announced the creature was activating its lift generators, joined by whistling screams from compression-jets.

The Neptunian's voice, channeled into Phaethon's sensorium, did not need to get any louder to speak over the rush and rumble of the liftoff. "You named yourself for a demigod whose ambition burned a world. Not the name a man content with his lot in life would choose. But you don't recall why you chose it, do you? Can you begin to guess now how much of your memory is missing? They did not even let you keep the meaning of your name."

Phaethon backed up as pressure exploded from the feet of the Neptunian. Its low, flat shape was now in an aerodynamic configuration. With ponderous grace, it raised its nose to the sky, and moved upward.

Phaethon adjusted his sense-filter so that, instead of the roar of jets and the whine of magnetics, he still only heard the chirruping of night insects in the Saturn-grove. Amplifying his vision to the highest extent he could, he saw the body of the masquerader, wrapped in some sort of cocoon or buoyancy chute ejected from the Neptunian as it rose. He attempted to encompass the satellite and ground-based location routines within his vision, and to open more sense-channels. But apparently the same protocol that disabled the location routines during masquerade extended to escaping aircraft as well. Phaethon was not able to track the body as it fell.

As for the Neptunian, it flashed like distant ice, gained

altitude. Then the light twinkled and receded, one star lost among many.

6.

In the palace:

Wheel-of-Life was a Cerebelline ecoperformer of the Decentral Spirit School, as well as trustee for all copyrighted biotechnology based on the Five Golden Rings mathematics. She appeared as a matron of serene beauty and grave demeanor, seated on a throne of living flowers, grass, and hedge, in which a dozen species of birds and insects nested. She was also physically present (insofar as that word had meaning for Decentral Spiritualists), but her great cloak of interwoven living fibers ran from her shoulders out the window to where the other plants and animals that formed her corporate body and mind components reposed.

Cerebellines were a neuroform whose hindbrain and cortex were interconnected in the pattern called "global," from their ability to resolve multiple simultaneous interrelationships. They could think in a timeless meditation, and from many points of view at once. This avoided set-theory paradoxes, and linear-thought limitations. It was one of the least popular neuroforms in the Golden Oecumene, however, since it fell prey too easily to mystical conundrums and nonverbalisms.

(Helion was not able to maintain a translation from her point of view for any length of time. The plantlike parts of her were aware of the room only as motion, pressure, sunlight, moisture, but also as computer movements, information flows. The birds and rodents gave so many small, scattered pictures and sounds of the Conclave that Helion was perplexed; and the thoughts were so tangled with sharp, bright shards of instinct, lust, hunger, fear, that Helion's brain-structure could not assimilate or index the perceptions.)

Wheel-of-Life indicated an objection. She expressed herself by holding up her hands and creating a miniature ecosystem in its globe. Microbes, plankton, brightly colored fish-shaped darts swam in the globe; triangular shark things fought many-tentacled cephalopods in relentless subsea wars.

She shattered the globe on the table surface into many globes. In each of the lesser globes, one species and only one rose to dominance, destroyed all competition, overgrazed, died back, and lost its throne. In every case the single dominant life form subdivided into new avenues as evolution continued.

Ao Aoen, the Master Dreamer, owner of a vast entertainment empire, spoke up: "I agree with Wheel-of-Life. Helion's vision will create a future of monochromatic conformity; events will narrow toward simplicity. Yet our society is diverse. Solutions are diverse. Within the mind are webs of interconnections, laws of thought; between minds are webs of social relation, laws of institutions. Turn one inside out and you have the other. Yet which of us is simple enough to be understood by, or complex enough to understand, ourselves?!"

Helion responded by inventing a mathematical game of geometric solids and spaces within a three-dimensional grid. The rules of the game allowed the solids, if surrounded by spaces, to reproduce; but the solids evolved their shapes due to pressure from the other solids.

He held it up like a glass box in his hand, and ran it, in compressed time, a dozen or a thousand times. In all but one case, the shapes bowed to the pressure of the surrounding solids, eventually formed cubes, and consumed all the available empty spaces.

The one nonstandard case was a beautiful snowflake-shaped system, with octahedrons and tetrahedrons radiating out from the single central dodecahedron. Ao Aoen thoughtfully reached across the table with his extremely long fingers, picked up that system, saved it, and handed it to Wheel-of-Life, who sent several birds and insects to gaze at it with joy.

"I'd like to disagree with Peer Wheel-of-Life," said Helion. "The diversity in nature is sustained because the beasts and plants must solve their disputes in inefficient life-or-death competitions. Rational creatures can create treaties, laws, and social mechanisms to channel aggression into peaceful competition. Competition encourages efficiency. Efficiency encourages uniformity. Even a society as diverse as ours has certain rules and mores which we must enforce against those who deviate."

Gannis murmured: "And here I had thought we were agreed not to speak about Phaethon again. . . ."

Helion hid a frown in a backup file, were no one could see it. Yet he frowned.

Vafnir, the energy magnate, said, "The same argument implies, Peer Helion, that those society employs to enforce its rules against deviations are justified in their use of force. Is this consistent with the arcadian ease and utopian peace we all have known?"

Helion said, "There are warriors even in paradise. And even in Arcadia, death comes."

THE SOLDIER

1.

In the garden:

As Phaethon stood and stared at the receding glimmer of the Neptunian, something came floating in on the night breeze.

Phaethon looked. A gaggle of little black bubbles swirled, windblown, across the grass under the trees and stars. Phaethon did not see from whence these machine organisms came. The bubbles swirled and swooped, circling the spot where the Neptunian just had been.

"Now what?" muttered Phaethon.

Some spheres dropped to roll across the grass, uphill and downhill. The main group of them slowly went back and forth along the path toward the grape trellises where Phaethon had first seen the Neptunian. The black spheres paused frequently to insert a slender probe or proboscis into the ground. Nearer to Phaethon, at the spot from which the Neptunian had launched, the spheres gathered into several rounded tetrahedrons and drove more probes into the ground.

It did not look very beautiful; the sphere movements were at once too slow and methodical, and too quick and efficient, to be an animation dance, nor was there music. Unless it was meant for an audience with senses not like his? Setting his hearing to a search routine, Phaethon found only high-frequency encrypted signals coming from the spheres, all squawks and stuttering whines, with no trace of rhythm or grace.

Phaethon pointed a finger and made the identification gesture, knowing it would be blocked by the masquerade. To his surprise, it was not. To his eyes, it looked as if a window had opened in midair, or a scroll unfurled, and in the frame was a dragon glyph radiating four ideograms in an archaic style: Honor, Courage, Fortitude, Obedience.

"Preliminary array, hostile organism detection and counteraction system identifies itself. Copyright information (Security Clearance required). Public Ownership. This unit is assigned to: Marshal-General Atkins Vingtetun, General-Issue Humaniform (multiple battle augmentations) Military Hierarchy, Semicompilation (ghosthaunted, and combat-reflexes), Warmind, Staff Command, Base Neuroform, Unschooled, Era Zero (the Creation)."

Phaethon was truly amused that someone would come to a masquerade disguised as Atkins. Atkins was the soldier. The last soldier. Phaethon was under the vague impression that Atkins had long ago, centuries upon centuries ago, killed himself or gone to stand-by or been stored in a museum, or something.

The impersonation was in questionable taste, however. A soldier? No one liked to be reminded of their barbaric past. And, unless Phaethon had misunderstood the masquerade guidelines, identity and location information could be masked but not actually falsified. But it seemed as if someone were nonetheless impersonating Atkins. Wouldn't the Hortators consider this a breach of propriety?

On the other hand, falsifications of fictional people, or people whose identities were retired, or whose memory copyrights had expired, must be permissible. Such identities were in the public domain, were they not? After all, no one was going to object to Phaethon, for example, impersonating Harlequin.

But Phaethon was still curious. For what were the spheres so diligently searching? Had the Neptunian (assuming it had been real) left behind some clue or trace of its origins or goals?

Well, if the false Atkins was going to be so gauche as to imitate a long-retired war hero, Phaethon could overstep politeness also. (This was a party, after all, and the standards of behavior were relaxed.)

After all, it was also in very bad taste to intrude icon-objects (like this midair window and dragon glyph) into Phaethon's field of view without any attempt whatever to blend the objects into the real environment, so as not to disturb Phaethon's previously established visual-continuity aesthetic. So perhaps it was in equally bad taste to tap into another person's private communication link, decode it, and find out what information all the spheres were sending back to their base point. But Phaethon did it anyway.

He caught only a fragment of the many messages: ". . . an information-deception-and-avoidance routine more complex—magnitude eight—than a nonmechanical intelligence can produce. . . . Sophotechnology of origin unknown . . ."

". . . artificial viral bodies introduced into grass DNA where subject stepped. Excessive information strand-coding—unknown data-compression techniques—grass will spore microorganisms of highly complex systematology—intelligence level 100—seeking out raw materials and creating larger organizations . . ."

And also: ". . . deduces (from the enemy success against civilian countermeasures) electron and quantum-state manipulation technologies comparable to those produced by Oecumenical civilization, based on the same history-development up through to late-period Fifth Mental Structure, but deviating thereafter in a fashion no member schola, or group embraced within the Golden Oecumene, could theoretically produce. Conclusion: . . ."

Then, an interruption: "Who the hell is on this line? Sir—hey, you! Excuse me, sir! But what do you think you are doing?"

The window in midair changed, and the dragon sign was replaced by an image of a man-shape in streamlined black power-armor of a style dating from the Sixth Mental Structure. The helmet turned toward Phaethon (who had his mask back on by then) and, somehow, Phaethon nonetheless felt that nape-hair prickling sensation which was his cue from Rhadamanthus that his name file was being read.

Phaethon was shocked beyond words. Then: "Who, if I may ask, are you, sir, that you just trample on the protocols of the masquerade without a word?"

"Sorry, sir," the man in the floating window replied. "Atkins. I'm acting on orders from the partial-Parliament extrapolation of the Warmind. You're tapping into a secured channel. May I ask what you're doing in this area?"

2.

In the palace:

Ao Aoen was a Warlock neuroform. His brain had interconnections between the temporal lobes, nonverbal left-brain lobes, and the thalamus and hypothalamus, seats of emotion and passion. Consequently, the relationships between his conscious and subconscious were nonstandard, and allowed him to perform accurately what base neuroforms could do only infrequently: acts of insight, intuition, inspiration, pattern recognition, lateral thinking. He could script his dreams. And dreams were merely one of several overlaps between conscious and unconscious realms that he had mastered, or to which he had surrendered.

He was physically present in a hideously beautiful body, patterned with scales like a colored cobra. Extra skull extensions gave his head the shape of a manta ray, shadowing his shoulders and reaching down his back. He had a half a dozen hands and arms, with fingers a yard or more in length. Between his fingers and his arms, like butterfly wings, tissues carrying a dozen delicate sensory-membranes stretched. This gave him scores of sensual sensations beyond the normal ranges.

(Ao Aoen saw the standardized version of the library scene, but overlaid with several dreams and half-dreams, so that every object seemed charged with mysterious and profound symbolism. Ao Aoen had superimposed a webwork of lines, glyphs, astrological notations, indicating loyalties and emotional, or, perhaps, magical-symbolic, sympathies or affiliations. Each Peer was represented by the self-image they projected, so that Orpheus, for example, who projected none, looked to Ao Aoen like an empty black cube.)

Ao Aoen said in a voice like a hollow woodwind, "I see patterns within patterns here. Let our society step outside itself and let us watch ourselves with awe and curious fear, as if we were strangers. The first thing we see is that most of our population (population measured only as information use) are Sophotech machine-minds. The whole rest of our society, our empires and efforts, are like the Amish who refused Fourth Era assimilation, like an animal preserve to be sustained while the Sophotechs spend their efforts contemplating abstract mathematics."

Orpheus said softly: "Distraction. Ao Aoen strays from the topic."

Ao Aoen made an eye-dazzling wave with his meter-long finger-fans. "All parts reflect the whole, Peer Orpheus. And yet, bluntness is art also, therefore I will be blunt. Attempts to herd human destiny ofttimes produce stampedes, which trample would-be shepherds.

"My Peers, the Hortators are a private organization, whose sole power comes from the popular esteem and respect they have earned. They cannot dare to be seen arm-in-arm with us, the ill-famed plutocrats, not as long as we Peers are wealthy enough to defy tradition, to ignore popular sentiment, and, yes, wealthy enough to suborn the Hortators."

Helion said coldly: "Recent events have proven that even the wealthiest and bravest of the manor-born are not beyond their reach. The best of us must bow to public opinion; no one can afford to offend the Hortators, not anymore."

3.

In the garden, Phaethon felt offended.

A soldier? It was preposterous. There still were some crimes these days; computer frauds, time thefts. Usually by very young rogues, not yet octogenarians. They were always eventually caught, and public outrage was always severe. Such matters were handled by the Hortators, or, in rare occasions when no one answered the call to give themselves up, by the Subscription Constabulary.

But Constables were always unfailingly polite and deferential. Phaethon had not been aware that it was even possible for someone to read one of Phaethon's masked files (and the name file had, in fact, been masked) without permission. Perhaps a Constable had that right, but only after due notice and service of a warrant. This man was certainly not a Constable!

Phaethon said as much. "You may ask, Mister Whatever-you-are, but I need not answer. You have no right. And, dammit! Could you at least have the decency to manifest your image properly, without jarring my scene to bits!"

The floating window blinked out, and the armored shape appeared next to Phaethon. The grass blades did seem to bend under the black metal boots, and a moon shadow did fall, in proper perspective, across the lawn; but that was about the only concession to manorial notions of propriety this man gave. The highlights and reflections within the armored breastplate were all wrong, and the vision tracking and correction was crude, since the image wavered if Phaethon turned his head too quickly.

The helmet disassembled into a cloud of fingernail-sized scales, which spread and opened, and hovered motionless around the man's head like a black halo. The face underneath was unremarkable, except in its uncomeliness. Phaethon couldn't remember in face symbology what lines around thin lips, or crow's-feet at the corners of the eyes were supposed to represent. Wisdom? Grimness? Determination? But he had a crew cut, and an even, unblinking gaze that spoke of ten millennia of military tradition. The face looked much like old archive pictures of Atkins.

One of the black spheres not far from Phaethon sent a signal: "Subject Phaethon shows no present contamination. Examination of communication logs and thought-buffers fails to show any data packages received, except for low-level, speech-linear communication. Insufficient to hide any organism construction or self-aware memory data systems."

"What?!!" exclaimed Phaethon. "Have you been going through my files and logs without a warrant? Without a word? You didn't even ask—!"

The man in black armor spoke to Phaethon. His tone was serious and brisk: "Sir, we didn't know whether you had been compromised or not. But you're clean. I'd like you to keep this quiet. The opposition may have constructions, by now, in all our public channels, and I don't want to give him—or them—any hints about where the investigation is. But don't worry. This is probably just another false alarm, or a drill. That's all I ever do nowadays anyway. So there's really no need for concern. You are free to go." And he turned to look toward where the black spheres where congregating.

Phaethon stared at him blankly. Were these lines from a play or something? "I think this really has gone on far enough. Tell me what's going on."

The man spoke without turning around. "Sir, that's no concern of yours right now. If I need more cooperation from you, or if we need to do some follow-up examination, you'll be contacted. Thank you for your cooperation."

"What is all this?!! You can't talk to me that way! Do you know who I am?!"

The man turned. There was a slight twitch in the tense lines around the soldier's mouth. It looked as if he were trying not to smile. "Ah—sir, the Service doesn't allow me to play tricks with my memory. I just don't have that luxury, I guess, sir. I'm, ah, sure at least one of us remembers who you are, there, sir. Ahem. But for now . . ." And the trace of humor vanished as if it had never been. "I'm going to have to ask you to leave. I'm required to secure the area."

"I beg your pardon—!" Phaethon spoke in an outraged tone.

They were interrupted by a fanfare of silver-voiced trumpets.

4.

In the palace:

Vafnir, the energy magnate, like Gannis, was also physically present, but, in order to demonstrate the vast wealth of his holdings, he had had his mind recorded into a high-speed energy matrix, which hung above the table and burned like a pillar of fire. The amount of computer time spent recalculating his nerve paths and magnetic envelope shape every time the slightest energy change occurred in the room was tremendous. The pillar of flame was burning hundreds of seconds a second.

(An aspect of Helion's mind watched Vafnir's view of the scene. Vafnir held to an utterly nonstandard aesthetic. Words and thoughts seemed to him like notes or crescendos of light; sound was force, puncturing, trembling; emotions or innuendoes appeared as smells or vibrations in sixteen radiant hues. To him the Peers were like seven balls of music hanging in space, issuing voices of fire; Helion an eager yellow-white, Gannis a pinching and sarcastic green, Orpheus a cold, drear fugue.)

Vafnir spoke: "My Peers, Helion does not propose an alliance to support the Hortators. He proposes that we appease them. He is telling us we have been forced to this extreme."

Helion said, "What is your objection? We represent the eldest generation. The invention of safe and repeatable personal immortality ensures that no generation after us will necessarily supplant us. We have given mankind endless life— is it not our due to ask, in return, that our lives be allowed to continue in the forms to which we are accustomed, surrounded by the institutions and society we prefer?"

Vafnir replied, "I do not object. I merely wish things stated clearly, without dazzle or smoke. I'm one of the richest men in the Oecumene, well-respected, influential. A million, a billion, and a trillion years from now, barring mishaps, I should still be here. And, long after Earth is gone, when the universal night has extinguished all the stars, and all the cosmos dies of final entropy, the entities with the most wealth and stored-up energy shall be the very last to go. I hope to be among them. If the cost of that is that we must tame society, make it predictable, break its spirit, and kills its dreams, aha! So be it! I only spoke to let us all be aware that we are doing this for self-centered and ignoble reasons."

Orpheus spoke softly, "Pointless to debate the matter of morality, my Peers. There is no right, no wrong, in this world, not any longer. The machine-minds watch us, and they take care that we do not harm each other. Morality means nothing, now."

"Just so," said Gannis. "The machine-minds watch us, and they are watched by the Earthmind, no? They only thing we need fear is loss of our positions, eh?"

When no one was looking, Gannis sent his she-eagle out the window, scattering Wheel-of-Life's flocks, and catching a pigeon in her talons.

5.

Down the slope and across the moonlit lawn approached a stately figure surrounded by nine floating luminaries. She was garbed in a gown of flowing emerald green, and her golden braids were twined to hold an emerald crown in place. Hers was a face of regal beauty, kindly, dignified, smiling with sad wisdom. In one hand she held a wand of living applewood, adorned with apple blossoms and fruit.

Her body shape was like that of an ancient lunarian; very tall and slender, graceful with unearthly grace, and with a magnificent sweep of condor wings folded across her shoulders and down her back.

The man who looked like Atkins then did a very Atkins-like thing. He drew his ceremonial katana and saluted, holding the blade point-upright, guard level with his eyes.

Not to be outdone, Phaethon performed an elegant courtly bow, crooking his back leg and sweeping out his hands in flourishes just as Harlequin himself might have done for the queen of France.

"Hail to thee!" cried Phaethon. "If you are She, an Avatar of the Earthmind, whose unlimited omniscience sustains us all, then, for the sake of all the blessings with which infinite intelligence has showered the earth, I greet you and give you praise; or if you merely are one who honors Her by presenting yourself adorned with Her symbols, hail nonetheless! And I bow to honor the visible signs of the One thus represented."

"I am not wholly She; only the smallest fraction of Her mind is bonded with me. For now, I am merely your fellow guest at this Celebration." She smiled warmly, eyes twinkling, and nodded, saying: "You are true to the comic-opera character you seem, and you amuse me with your comic-opera greeting. Dear Phaethon! Earthmind has thought much on you of late, and She trusts you will be as true to your own character as you have been to the characters you have assumed."

Phaethon signaled for identification, and then was shocked to understand that this was an Avatar of the Earthmind indeed, an emanation from the Ennead.

He had never in all his life spoken to one of the Nine Intelligences, who were the highest of the Sophotech machine-minds; but this was a representative of a Mind even more exalted, the One whom the Nine combined their mental power to sustain.

To Atkins, the Avatar said, "Please do not salute me, Mr. Atkins. I am not your superior officer. We are fellow servants in the same cause."

The man's left gauntlet folded back. In one perfect, well-practiced motion, he cut a painful line across his palm, bloodied the sword and sheathed the blade. He squinted, folding his left hand into a fist to prevent the little cut from seeping.

Phaethon realized that this must indeed be Atkins.

"Thank you, ma'am," Atkins said. "Can you help me out, here? If not, I'm going to have to ask you to leave."

She smiled sadly. "There's not much I can do, Mr. Atkins. Even a very quick intelligence is helpless without information to manipulate. So I shall leave you in peace to do your work. Ah! But I do have an idea for a new science of analysis and forensics which, with your permission, I can load into your system. I have a clearance from the Parliament scenario."

"Be my guest, ma'am." And the black spheres began sprouting fantastic spiral shells, nautiluslike, and spinning strands of thread across the grass. The luminaries circling the Avatar now left their orbits and went to go help the black spheres at their task.

The Avatar turned to Phaethon.

"Dear son, as a courtesy to Atkins, I ask you to leave as well. You are under no legal obligation to keep quiet about what you have seen, but there is a moral obligation even deeper and more compelling. Our laws and our institutions have grown accustomed to centuries of peace and pleasure; and our civilization can sustain herself through danger only by the voluntary devotion of her citizens."

Phaethon spoke: "I love the Golden Oecumene, and would never do anything to cause her harm!"

Atkins looked skeptical when he said that, snorted, and turned away. The Avatar said, "Do not compromise your principles, Phaethon, lest you do yourself and your world an ill."

"What ill? Madame—please tell me what is going on—"

"Your old memories are in storage, but not destroyed. Whether you take their burden once more on yourself, I cannot advise. I may be wise, but I am not Phaethon." The Avatar stepped forward, put her soft hands on Phaethon's shoulders, stooped (Phaethon had not realized how tall the lunar body shape was till she stood over him), and she kissed him on the forehead.

"Will you receive this gift from me? I grant you flight. I mean this as an honor to display that the Machine Intelli-

gences do not regard you, Phaethon, with any unkindliness.
It also may remind you of old dreams you have put aside."

"Madame—this mannequin I am in is much too heavy to
fly—I would need a different . . ." But a buoyancy suddenly
tingled in him, starting with his head where he'd been kissed,
and spreading, like warm wine, into his trunk and limbs. Surprised, blinking, Phaethon thrust with a toe. Weightlessly the
grass fell away from him.

He shouted in fear, but then smiled, and tried to pretend
he was shouting for joy. A moment later, a freak wind blew
him head over heels like a balloon. Phaethon grabbed a passing tree branch, and he was tangled in the silvery leaves,
laughing.

"Quite extraordinary, Madame!" he gasped. "But—excuse
me, there are several important questions about what's happened tonight, which I—"

But when he looked over his shoulder, down at the ground,
the Avatar was gone. There was only Atkins, face grim, still
in his armor, pacing slowly across the grass with his black
machines.

There was nothing for him here. Atkins was not going to
answer any questions. And he had sneered at Phaethon's expression of loyalty to the Golden Oecumene; whatever Phaethon's forgotten crime had been, it had been enough to make
honest men regard him as a traitor.

Phaethon let go of the branch and floated up into the night
sky. The silvery Saturn-trees shimmered mirrorlike underfoot,
and then were lost, one grove among the garden tapestries of
shades and shadows below.

6.

Kes Sennec the Logician spoke in even and uninflected tones.
"Peer Vafnirs's comment, spoken just now, calling all of our
actions 'ignoble' and 'self-centered' contains inaccuracies and
semantic nonentities. Assuming that I do not presently misunderstand his intent, I presently disagree, on the grounds that

the statement is overbroad, stereotypical, and inaccurate."

Kes Sennec was also actually present, a bald, large-headed man in a gray single-suit. A row of control points ran along the left closure of the tunic; he wore no other ornamentation. His skin color was gray, adjusted to local light-radiant levels, as were his eyes. His body shape was unremarkably standardized, with special organs and adaptations for zero-gravity environment, and his nervous system was highly modified with monitors, correctives, and gland overrides to ensure emotional stability and sanity.

"If a critical number of the individuals in society cooperate in actions which lead, deliberately or as a side effect, to conditions which, to an effective number of individuals, appear to favor the use of aggression and deception (as opposed to peaceful strategies of social cooperation) for the achievement of what they at that time perceive to be their goals, then every necessary and sufficient condition for the breakdown of the social order is present, and the pressure favoring the breakdown grows in rough proportion as the effective number of individuals grows. By 'breakdown' I mean both that individuals resort to violence and that they believe they must do so for fear that other individuals will do so.

"Logically, to avoid this, a sufficient uniformity of operative decision-making mores and values above a threshold level of participants must obtain; these decision values must include, at least, a priority placed on the preservation of the peaceful resolution of perceived and real conflicts. The term 'conformity' is not necessarily inappropriate to depict this uniform decision structure."

Kes Sennec was of the Invariant neuroform, a highly integrated unicameral nervous system. His brain had accessible subroutines, habits, and reflexes, but no subconsciousness properly so called. The Invariant neuroform was the second least popular among the Golden Oecumene, since all people with such uniform brains tended to think and act with startling uniformity. The Invariants had no emotional difficulties or internal conflicts.

(Kes Sennec's view of the room was entirely stark and real,

with no filter, no editing. He saw Helion's body as a human-oid mannequin; he saw the tiny dull-colored plugs and antennae along Gannis's neck that connected with the Gannis Over-mind; he saw the electronic activity surrounding all Wheel-of-Life's pets and pseudo-plants. He could see the wires and nodes swirling among Vafnir's column of flame, and the mechanism producing the field effects where Vafnir's consciousness was actually stored. To Kes Sennec, Orpheus was merely a remote on treads, skeletal, equipped with waldo-hands, lenses, and speakers. It all was unappealing, plain, col-orless.

(Also, the outside noise, distant music, yells, and odors coming in through the window, were part of Kes Sennec's all-embracing attention. Once again, Helion could not tolerate the other's scene. Helion's brain structure required him to rate sense impressions by priority, and to ignore sensations of low importance. Kes Sennec's Invariant brain saw everything, paid attention to everything, judged everything with inhuman, unemotional precision.)

Kes Sennec concluded: "Those who act to prevent war and violence from occurring cannot properly be called 'selfish' and 'ignoble' even if they act in a way which benefits their self-interest."

Ao Aoen said, "As always, Peer Kes Sennec's comments daze me with their precision, and I cannot follow them. Un-selfish? Why have none of us said aloud what secretly mo-tivated Peer Helion's proposal? Is it a dream we seek to kill, perhaps the greatest of dreams ever? What is this dream? Can any tell me? Do any outside this chamber yet recall?"

No one answered him. There was silence.

7.

Phaethon rode the night wind.

For several minutes, he hung, going whichever way the wind pushed him. Then he floated on his back, looking up at the stars. He activated an internal regulator to slow his time sense, till he could see the movements of the stars as visible, grandly turning in their paths across the sky. Slower still, and the North Star was ringed with concentric haloes as the hours, compressed into a moment or two, hung before him. In a moment, most of the night had passed.

"What if I've done something which actually is horrible, unthinkable, or even endangered the Golden Oecumene? Do I really want to know? Curiosity nags me; it whips me on. And yet I did this to myself: the ignorance is self-imposed. Perhaps the alternative is worse.

"Is ignorance so hard to bear, then? There is so very much in life we do not know. . . ."

Staring up at the night sky, Phaethon opened his hearing to include ground-based and satellite radio. Information from a thousand sources, a hundred thousand, flowed into his brain. There were countless signals and communications radiating from Earth, from the satellite city-ring, the houses of the moon, and green Venus in her new cooler orbit, already shining with the radio noise of civilization. The collected asteroids of the remade planet Demeter had fewer cities, but brighter, as the scientific communities and experimental modes of life there used more energy than sober, older Terra. The Jovian moons, a solar system in miniature, were a beacon of immeasurable energy, life, motion, and noise; some people considered it the real center of the Golden Oecumene. At the Leading and Trailing Trojan points, the million space-metropoli of the Invariants pulsed with calm and steady rhythms. At the edge of night, the Neptunian energy-webs and communication systems extended out to the Oort and Kuiper belts. There were a few distant flickers from remote stations beyond that; one beacon from the Porphyrogen observatory at 500 AUs, like a last spark in the dark.

And then, nothing. The roar of the stars, the whisper of background radiations, was meaningless, like the noise of a storm at sea. Nowhere were there intelligent patterns. There were no other colonies, no outposts. The Silent Oecumene, perhaps, might still exist near Cygnus X1; but, if so, it was a civilization without light or energy or any transmission.

Nothing was in the night. There was only empty noise and empty abyss.

Phaethon restored his time sense and the stars froze in place.

"No," he said. "I will not be false."

He recalled that the Neptunian had called the Golden Oecumene a world of illusions. Maybe it was. "But I will not be deceived. I swear it. If there is anything out there in the stars to hear me: you have heard. I have made my vow."

The stars were pale, and a red rim of light touched the East. He had floated higher than he thought, and, at this altitude, it was nearly daybreak. Now he turned to right himself, and, like a diver plunging into a deep blue, down he fell toward the land below. The winds rushed in his ears like the loud, wild noise of many voices.

8.

In the Palace:

"If this dream is one we can kill, we should kill it, O my Peers," said, or sang, Ao Aoen, and several voices and images of light flowed from his figure. "Our own self-preservation, and the protection of our beloved Golden Oecumene from the horror of war—a horror only we are old enough to recall—both urge us to the tourney against this archangel of fire whom we so fear that we dare not say his name. Our cause is just; but is our strength equal to the task?

"Convince me, O Peers, that the Hortators will aid rather than oppose our efforts to smother the fire of the soul of man—and my fickle convictions may change again. My empire of dreams can reach into the thoughts and smiles of millions; convince me it can be done, O Helion, that you can wrestle with this spiritual fire as you once tamed the fires of the sun. With—oh, of course!—a happier outcome than that event brought forth!"

9.

Phaethon put in a call to his mansion. "Rhadamanthus! Rhadamanthus! I know the Silver-Gray protocols don't let you manifest in a way that jars the scenery; but this is an emergency. Something odd happened to me this night; I need your help to find the answers."

His sensorium signaled to admit a new object. A moment later, out of the high clouds behind him, surrounded with a roaring engine noise, a small black shape darted on wings. It did a snap-roll and came closer, till it paralleled Phaethon's plunging descent.

It was a penguin wearing bow tie, aviator goggles, and a long white scarf. The penguin's stubby wings were spread, its bullet head thrown back, its little beak cutting the air. A contrail of vapor issued from its little webbed feet.

"Oh, come now, Rhadamanthus! This blends?!"

The penguin cocked it head. "It is a bird, young master."

"Realistic images or none at all! That's the motto of our manor. Penguins do not fly!"

"Hmm. I hate to say it, young master, but neither do young men."

"But—a contrail—?"

"Ah, sir, you may check my math if you like, but a penguin-shaped object traveling at this speed through this atmosphere—"

Phaethon interrupted. "Be realistic!"

"If the young master would care to look behind himself, I think he will see he has a condensation trail not unlike my own—"

"Good heavens!" Phaethon checked his sense-filter again. The penguin and its contrail were illusions, existing only in mentality. But Phaethon's contrail was a real object. "How am I doing this? Flying without a suit, I mean." He checked the properties value on his sense-filter again. It was real.

"If master would care to direct his attention upward, in the extremely high frequency range? . . ."

"I see a latticework of energy lines across the sky, from horizon to horizon. . . . A levitation array? But the scale is grandiose. It extends for miles. Ah . . . hundreds of miles. Was this all built since last night?"

"It was constructed in orbit and lowered into place, young master. A surprise for the guests!" The penguin pointed with a stubby black wing.

He continued: "The wire is buoyant, made of a newly developed material of great tensile strength and high conductivity. The dome extends over the entire Celebration grounds, from the forty-fifth to the fiftieth parallel. If the dome were permitted to relax to its natural hemispheric shape, the apex would be in the stratosphere. It is by no means the largest artificial structure on Earth—the Antarctic Winter Garden is much larger; but it will reduce the expense and trouble of air transport. I deduce the Earth-mind's Avatar introduced microscopic assemblers into your mannequin-frame—I see traces running from your forehead into your central body— and used them to construct magnetic anchor points and induction generators. A present man could do the same with a heavy jacket of special material."

"I'm impressed. But you sound sort of nasal, Rhadamanthus, even for a penguin."

"It saddens me to see a way of life I like pass on, even though I am not myself alive. The new ease of air transport may decrease the advantages of telepresentation, and, over the next four centuries, reduce the prestige of the various manorial and cryptic ways of life. Including mansions like me. Heh. Ironic, isn't it sir?"

"What's ironic?"

"That Earthmind should give the technology to you. Not of the levitation array, of course, I just mean the anchor-and-antennae system which allows one to fly with it."

"Give? Did you say give?"

"Yes. I've examined the legal channels, and there is no patent on the hardware, no copyright on the software. I've taken the liberty of making out an intellectual property claim in your name, sir, giving you copyright ownership."

"Do you think She is a testing me to see if I will suppress the technology?"

"Sir, the human mind may not easily grasp the difference between a million and a trillion, but if I have the honor of being able to calculate and correlate a million times faster than a human brain; and if the Earthmind calculates at a trillion times your rate; then, quite honestly, sir, She is as incomprehensible to me as I must seem, at times, to you. I have not the faintest idea why She does anything."

10.

The one Peer who had not spoken was an emissary for the Communication and Financial planning subroutine of the Eleemosynary Composition. The Eleemosynary was a group-mind with thousands of members, founded during the turmoils of the Fifth Mental Structure, with memory chains and records reaching back over eighty thousand years. The Eleemosynary Composition was one of the first to include peoples of different nervous system structures into one combination. In the far past, he-they had been a powerful political force, one of the founding architects of the Sixth Mental Structure and the age of the machine-minds. Now, all political power evaporated, the Eleemosynary Composition made his-their fortunes in interpretation and translation and arbitration between different groups and mind-sets in the Golden Oecumene.

The Emissary was embodied and costumed as a figure from Eleemosynary mythopoetry, a winged-lion chimera who wore three heads: monkey, hawk, and serpent. Each head held a separate brain, one of each of the three neuroforms of which the Eleemosynary group-mind was composed: the basic, the Invariant, and the Warlock. (Helion saw that, like Helion, the Emissary viewed the room from the other peers' viewpoints, but, unlike him, he-they did not have any private viewpoint of his-their own. Also unlike him, his-their nervous systems could understand the views coming from Kes Sennec and Wheel-of-Life.)

The Emissary said, "Whoever wishes to serve the Good should embrace long-term as well as short-term considerations into his councils. In less than one hundred billion years, Sol passes to other phases of stellar decay, and no longer will be serviceable. Forethought requires that provision be made to evacuate, but civilization not be jarred or disturbed. Technologies should be developed to accommodate the movement of all worlds and world-habitats elsewhere, social institutions adapted to preserve peace and orderliness, with philosophies to supply ideological justification. Chaos, violence, terror, should be, at all costs, avoided. Only thus can the service of all to all be maintained. Humbly, it is wondered if, in the vision presented by Peer Helion, society, by the time star colonization is needed, will have sufficient genius, foresight, and resolve to attempt the abyss between the stars. Stable societies are not known for these virtues."

"You see?" said Ao Aoen, "The great Eleemosynary Composition is willing to oppose a society of strict conformity; and he-they are the very soul of union and unselfishness! What does that make us, we who urge the plan?"

"There is, perhaps, misinterpretation," replied the Emissary, turning his-their three heads to stare at Ao Aoen. "It was meant to say that the star-colonization question should be raised long after Helion's efforts to extend Sol's useful lifespan have run their course. If raised before then, conflict and chaos may result. The occupation by colonists of nearby star systems may preclude peaceful evacuation at Sol's death. Peace is supreme; only thus can the service of all to all be maintained. Change one day will be needed and welcomed, when time is complete, and Sol's power is exhausted. But before that time, what need has peace and contentment to be disturbed by innovators and adventurers?"

11.

In the air, with stars above and cloud below, Phaethon contemplated his meeting with the Earthmind.

"Maybe She's trying to teach me something, not test me. . . ."

"I wouldn't care to speculate, sir."

"Well. I won't fail this test at least. Release the information on the public channels. No good can come from trying to hide the truth."

"So you've always said, young master. But I see there is something else, yes?"

"Rhadamanthus—" Phaethon steeled himself. "The things I saw tonight—were real? This all isn't some part of a masquerade game? I'm not inside some pseudomnesia-play?"

"May I perform a Noetic reading to experience what occurred from your point of view?"

"I don't keep secrets from you, Rhadamanthus. You don't need to ask to read my mind."

"Yes, I do, sir. It's protocol. And what you thought was real was indeed quite real."

"The Golden Oecumene is under some sort of attack. And I'm a criminal, or a collaborator, just like my Neptunian friend, helping to destroy our paradise." Phaethon tasted bitterness like bile in his throat.

"With respect, sir, that conclusion is not warranted by the evidence you've seen so far."

Phaethon spread his arms and stopped his descent. He turned a fierce glare toward the penguin image.

"Oh, come now! I'm not stupid! We have a society of immortals. Our neural technology gives us, when we wish, perfect eidetic memory. Every past wrong, no matter how small, can be recalled many thousands of years after the fact. And there is no place to go to hide from those whom you have offended or who offend you. Here, to prevent even the possibility of crime, we manorials have no privacy, not even in our thoughts, except that which we, out of politeness, extend to each other. And so what else is there to do? I did something—I don't know what, and frankly, at the moment I don't care—which shamed and offended my equals. So we all agreed to forget it. Pretend it never happened!"

The penguin stood in midair, long scarf flapping slightly in the breeze, looking at Phaethon through large, round goggles. It rubbed its little white tummy with a stubby wing, and said, "Are you asking me a question, young master? You gave me specific orders not to bring the gap in your memory to your attention; nor can I tell you what you forgot."

"I did it to myself then? I was not compelled?"

"It was voluntary. We Sophotechs would have acted to stop it, otherwise."

"And if I countermand the order?"

"Your old memories are in my archives back at Rhadamanthus Mansion, in the chamber of memory, in third level of mentality, the deep-layer nonrealistic dreamscape."

"And should I?"

Even Rhadamanthus could not answer right away. There was a pause as the machine-mind examined every foreseeable future consequence of every possible combination of actions and responses for all the individuals in the Golden Oecumene (Rhadamanthus had mindspace enough to know them all intimately). This complexity was measured against the eternal philosophical dialogue structure the Sophotechs maintained. Rhadmanthus answered:

"It would be nobler and braver of you to know the truth, I think, young sir. But I also should warn you that there would be a cost. One which you yourself, earlier, were not willing to pay."

"The cost? What is the cost?"

"Look down, sir, and tell me what you see below you here."

Phaethon looked.

Everywhere was splendor. To the north were open glades, cool secret pools, fragrant hedges, walled arbors, tree-lined lanes, mountains, clefts, murmuring streams falling to a blue sea. East was forest, deep and dark, invested with bioformulations less traditional: weird coral-like growths, fairy-tale energy shapes, luminous bubbles, or strange miles of intertwisting lucent tendril vines. South were palaces, museums, thought-cathedrals, living-pools and amnesia wombs. West was the sea, where, in the light of the newly risen sun, Phaethon saw silhouettes of guests in newly altered bodies like his own, shouting with delight, soaring and diving and dancing in the sky, or plunging from high midair into the waves to rise again in glittering spray.

"There are people there flying like me—!"

"News travels quickly. You did tell me to put the information out. What else do you see?"

Phaethon looked not just with his eyes.

On the surface-level of dreamspace, were a million channels open to conversation, music, emotion display, neural stimulation; deeper interfaces beckoned from beyond, synnoetisms, computer synergetics, library organisms and transintellectualisms no unaugmented brain could comprehend.

Below them, in the center of the Celebration grounds (and in the "center" also of the mind-space) was the Aurelian Mansion, like a golden flower, with spires and domes shining in the light of dawn, with a hundred thought paths (in mentality) and four great boulevards (in reality) coming together into Aurelian's city.

"I see Aurelian's House. What point are you trying to make, Rhadamanthus?"

"The cost. I am showing you what you would lose. The cost of opening those old memories is that you would be thrown out."

"Thrown out of the Celebration?!" Phaethon was taken aback. Then he was horrified.

He thought about all the work and hopes, all the long years of preparation which he and so many myriad others had put into this effort to make the Celebration a success. Their host, the Aurelian-mind, had been created just for this occasion

(even as Argentorium, a thousand years ago, had been created for the last Millennial Ball.)

Aurelian was born by a marriage between the Westmind-group, famed for their audacity, and the Archivist, whose nature was more saturnine. The combination of these qualities had already proven inspiring.

One of Aurelian's best effects—audacious, almost cruel—had been to invite both past and future to attend. Phaethon had seen paleopsychological reconstructions, brought to life and self-awareness to gaze in awe at the works their descendants had wrought. With them were personalities constructed from Aurelian's models of many possible futures, inhabitants of fictional worlds set a million or a billion years yet-to-come, strolling with droll smiles amidst what, to them, was past.

Aurelian, at high-compression thinking-speeds, had been studying every possible combination of the guests (and that guest list was large; everyone on Earth had been invited) and all of their possible interactions for 112 years before the January Feast commenced.

Had Aurelian foreseen one of his guests accidentally recovering a buried memory, creating a scene, offending his dear wife, ruining the pageants and plans for the entire Silver-Gray School? Was the tragedy of Phaethon one which had been engineered for the edification of the other guests, a warning, perhaps, not to inquire too closely into what was better left unknown?

If Phaethon left now, he would miss the Final Transcendence in December. All the art and literature, industry and mental effort for the next thousand years would be established and determined, or, at least, heavily influenced, by the experience of that Transcendence. He would not contribute to it; none of what he had done over the last thousand years would be part of it. And after the culmination of the Transcendence, almost every conversation, every meeting, and every grand affair would be conducted in the shadow of that shared memory.

A memory Phaethon would not have. An experience everyone but he would share. Phaethon thought about all the jokes he would not get, all the allusions he would not catch, if he missed this. Not to mention the gifts and vastenings he would lose.

After all, why should he create a scene? Couldn't he wait till the party was over to dig up buried unpleasantness? Wouldn't that be more practical, make more sense?

Phaethon stood in midair, frowning, staring down. Like a smaller, second sun, the bright point of what had once been Jupiter rose in the East, casting double shadows across the Aurelian palace grounds underfoot.

Happily, the fanfare of the Jovian Aubade rang from tower to tower. White-plumed birds, all singing gloriously, flew up in flocks from aviaries and the groves, a thunder of wings. The doves carried fruit, or delicacies, or decanters of wine, and they sought out guests who hungered or thirsted.

A white bird flew up, and landed on his shoulder, cooing. The bird was a new species, designed just for the occasion. Phaethon took a crystal of smart-wine. The taste was perfectly conveyed through sensors in his mannequin to the taste glands and pleasure centers of wherever Phaethon's real body and real brain were stored, sound asleep, and safe beyond all danger.

The taste was like summer sunshine itself, and the bouquet changed from moment to moment as tiny assemblers in the liquid combined and recombined the chemical elements even as he lifted the crystal. He sipped in pure delight, and no two sips were the same; each was an individual, not to be repeated. But he shooed the bird away, opened his hand, and dropped the drink unfinished. He made himself feel no regret as it fell away from him.

He dialed his costume from Harlequin to Hamlet. Now he wore bleak, grim, sober colors.

Phaethon said: "If the cost is that I be excluded from this Celebration, I can tolerate that. Somehow, I can. It's only a party, after all. I can pay that cost. It's better that I know the truth."

"Forgive me, young master, but you misunderstand me. You will not be excluded from the Celebration. You will be exiled from your home. Those memories will cast you out of paradise."

4

THE STORM-SCULPTOR

1.

For a few moments, the Peers debated with calm intent solar evolution and decay, and other events to happen many millions or billions of years in the future.

Helion (who was a devoted antiquarian) knew how his distant ancestors would have been nonplussed to hear sane folk speaking of such remote eventualities; just as ancestors more distant yet, the primitive hunter-gatherers of the Era of the First Mental Structure, who lived from hunt to hunt and hand to mouth, would have been equally perplexed to hear the farmers destined to replace them speaking so casually of harvests and seasons months and years away.

"Why do we need a sun?" Vafnir said. "This is premised on the assumption that we will not find a satisfactory substitute source of energy after the sun is extinguished: a premise I, for one, do not accept without question."

Ao Aoen said airily, "The Silent Oecumene sought a novel source of energy. They had no sun either. You recall, before their Silence fell, what horrors we heard from them."

Vafnir said coldly: "Horrors they brought on themselves. The wisdom of the machine-intelligences could have saved them; they preferred to hate and fear all Sophotechs."

"The vaunted Sophotechs were not wise enough to save the only extrasolar colony of man!"

Helion said patiently: "Peer Ao Aoen recalls, surely, that the Cygnus X1 system is a thousand light-years distant; hence the death message was a thousand years outdated by the time we received it."

Ao Aoen said: "For us immortals, the space of time equal to one celebration of our Transcendence. A trifle! Why was no manned expedition ever sent to the dark swan system?"

Gannis, breaking in, said, "Aha! What futility that would be! To spend unimaginable wealth to go pick among ruins and graveyards, cold beneath a black neutron-sun. Gah! The idea has merit only for its ironic pathos!"

Ao Aoen had an odd look to his eyes. "The idea has haunted several dreams of mine these past years, and a quarter-mind brother of mine saw an ominous shape once in the frozen clouds of methane in the liquid atmosphere of Neptune. The horoscopes of several of my cultmates tremble with unintelligible signs! All this points to one conclusion: it has now been shown, beyond doubt, that if a ship of sufficient mass and sufficiently well-armored to achieve near light-speed can be—"

Peer Orpheus raised a thin hand. "Enough! This is irrelevant to our discourse."

Ao Aoen made a wild gesture with his many arms and fingers, and sank back in his chair, sulking.

Orpheus said softly: "We must resign ourselves to fact. Helion is correct about this, and about many matters. Of the visions of the future that the Transcendence will contemplate, one of more conformity, less experimentation, serves both our selfish interests, and, at the same time, supports the public spirit of the College of Hortators. Practical and altruistic minds both have equal cause to fear what leads to war. The College of Hortators and the Conclave of Peers must ally. Helion's insight will form the basis of the next great social movement of the next Millennium. It is the vision the Peers will support."

Helion had to use a mind trick to keep his joy in check. He was astonished; this was a signal honor far beyond anything Rhadamanthus had predicted, far beyond what he'd dreamed. If his vision of the future was adopted by the Transcendence, then he himself, Helion, would be the central figure whose philosophy would shape society for the next thousand years. His name would be on every tongue, every marriage list, every guest-password file of every party and convocation. . . .

It was dazzling. Helion decided not to record the joy he felt now, for fear that future replays of this wild emotion would dull it.

There would be more talk, of course, and more debate, and each of the Peers would consult with their advisors, or issuing authorities, or (in the case of Ao Aoen) spirit guides. There would be more talk.

But Orpheus had spoken, and the matter was fairly well decided.

2.

Soaring, with clouds above and clouds below, Phaethon let the joy of flight erase his worries for the moment.

He and Rhadamanthus penguin played in mock dogfights, doing snap rolls, barrel rolls, loops.

Phaethon was closing in on the penguin when the fat bird did an Immelmann, toppling over on one wing, and righting itself to flash toward Phaethon, and on past, shouting "Ratatatat! Gotcha!"

Phaethon didn't know what the word *Ratatatat* meant, but it seemed to imply some sort of victory or counting-coup. Phaethon slowed and stood in the air, hands on hips.

"My dear Rhadamanthus, you're surely cheating!" The bird, of course, only existed as an image in Phaethon's sensorum.

"By my honor, sir, I'm only doing what a bird this size could do. You can check my math if you wish."

"Aha? And what are you postulating for your acceleration tolerance in those turns?"

"Well, sir, penguins are sturdy birds! When is the last time you have ever heard of a Sphenisciforme blacking out, eh?"

"Point well taken!" Phaethon spread his arms and fell backward onto a nearby cloud. Mist spilled upward around him
as he sank, smiling.

"My wife would love this, wouldn't she? Glorious things
attract her—wide vistas, grand emotions, scenes of wonder!"

The cloud got darker around him. On another level of vision, he detected electropotentials building in the area.

". . . It's just too bad that we live at a time when everything
glorious has already been done for us. The only really impressive things she can ever find are in her dream universes."

"You disapprove?"

"Well . . . I hate to say it, but . . . I mean, why can't she
write those things? She got an award for one oneiroverse she
made up once, a Ptolemaic universe thing, some sort of magic
planet. I think there were flying balloons in it, or something."
He pursed his lips. "But instead of writing them, she just
drifts in and out of other peoples' ideas."

"Sir—excuse me, but I think we're floating into someone's
claimed space—"

"Someday I'll do something to awe the world, Rhadamanthus. Once she sees how impressive the real world can be,
she won't be so—"

Through the darkening cloud, a figure in a golden boat,
dressed as falcon-headed god character from pre-Ignition Jovian storm-poetry, swam up through the cloud, and made an
impatient gesture with his long black pole. He wore ornate
robes of white and gold and blue, with a complex helmet-
crown. "Sir! I say, Demontdelune!"

"I'm not Demontdelune; this is Hamlet."

"Ah. As you wish. In any case, please move aside; I'm
trying to sculpt a thunderstorm here, and your fields are in-
terfering with my nanomachines."

Phaethon looked around him, switching his perception to a
finer level, and shutting off his sense-filter. The illusionary
penguin vanished, but now Phaethon could see extraordinarily
small machines attached to each and every water droplet, gen-
erating repulsive and attractive fields, herding them. There

were more nanomachines per cubic inch in this area than he had ever seen before.

Phaethon was severely impressed. This man could control the shape and density of the cloud down to the finest level. By arranging the flows of cloud drops, he could create static, or trigger condensation. "But—this is an extraordinary effort!"

"Quite so—especially since I cannot control the wind. I have to play the cloud like a harp whose billion strings all change in length and pitch from moment to moment. My Sophotech can speed my perception of time to a point I need to render the performance—I should begin a minute or so from now, as soon as the winds are right—but, to me, at that time-speed, my performance will seem to last a hundred years."

"Fantastic! What is your name, sir, and why do you make such sacrifices to your art?"

"Call me Vandonnar." This was the name in Jovian poems of the captain of a mining-diver, lost in the clouds, and said to be circling eternally the Great Red Spot Storm, a ghost, so lost that he was unable to find his way to the afterlife. The poem dated from the days when there still was such a Great Red Spot. "My true name I must keep to myself. I fear my friends would disapprove if they knew how much Sophotech time I've spent just for this one storm-song. And Aurelian, our host, has not announced the storm beforehand. Those who don't look up in time to see, or who run inside, will miss the performance. I am not allowing this to be recorded."

"Good heavens, sir, why not?!"

"How else to escape the stifling control of the Sophotechs? Everything is recorded for us here, even our souls. But if this can be played only once, its power is all the greater."

"And yet—forgive for so saying, but without the Sophotechs, you could not possibly do the mathematics to control each raindrop in a storm, or to direct where the lightning will fall!"

"You miss my whole point, Mr. Hamhock."

"Hamlet."

"Whatever. This is a statement of third-order chaos math-

ematics. You see? Even with the finest control in the world,
even with the wisest Sophotech, where the lightning strikes
next cannot be predicted. Some one ambitious raindrop will
brush against its neighbors more boldly than anticipated, ir-
ritating them, raising more electric charge than guessed; the
threshold is crossed; the electrons ionize; in a single instant
the discharge path is determined; crooked or straight; and ful-
gration flashes! And all because that one little drop could not
keep still. . . .

"Wait! The winds are changing. . . . Go now, please, while
I can still compensate for your passage through my cloud. . . .
No, that direction! Go there! Otherwise you tangle my
strings! . . ."

Without a word, Phaethon darted away, swift as a salmon.
His clothes were moist with mist as he broke free of the
storm-cloud, and nanomachines, thick as dust, stained his
shoulders and hair.

Phaethon triggered his sense-filter again. The image of the
Penguin reappeared.

"Rhadamanthus, you Sophotechs always deny that you are
wise enough to arrange everything we do, to arrange coincidences."

"Our predictions of humanity are limited. There is an uncertainty which creatures with free will create. The Earthmind
Herself could not beat you every time in a game of paper-
scissors-rock, because your move is based on what you think
she might choose for her move: and She cannot predict her
own actions in advance perfectly."

"Why not? I thought Earthmind was intelligent beyond
measure."

"No matter how great a creature's intelligence, if one is
guessing one's own future actions, the past self cannot outwit
the future self, because the intelligence of both is equal. The
only thing which alters this paradox is morality."

Phaethon was distracted. "Morality?! What an odd thing to
say. Why morality?"

"Because when an honest man, a man who keeps his word,

says he will do something in the future, you can be sure he will try."

"So you machines are always preaching about honesty just for selfish reasons. It makes us more predictable, easier to work into a calculation."

"Very selfish—provided you define the word 'selfish' to mean that which most educates, and most perfects the self, making the self just and true and beautiful. Which is, I assume, the way selves want themselves to be, yes?"

"I cannot speak for other selves; I will not be satisfied with anything less than the best Phaethon I can Phaethon."

"My dear boy, are you using yourself as a verb?"

"I'm feeling fairly intransitive at the moment, Rhadamanthus."

"What brought all this odd topic up, Phaethon?"

"I feel as if that meeting—" he nodded toward the storm-cloud growing dark behind them—"As if it were . . . were arranged to give me and me alone a message. I wanted to know if you or Earthmind or someone were behind it."

"Not I. And I cannot predict the Earthmind any more than you."

"Can she arrange coincidences of that magnitude?"

"Well, she could easily have hired that man to ride up and say those things. Good heavens, boy, that could have been Her, in disguise. This is a masquerade, you know. What's the coincidence, though?"

"Because just at that moment, I was thinking of dropping this whole thing, forgetting this whole mystery. I was perfectly happy before I found that there was a hole in my memory; perfectly happy to be who I thought I was. I want to live up to my wife's good opinion of me, to go beyond it, if I can."

"I don't follow you, sir."

Phaethon altered his vision so that the daytime sky, to him, no longer seemed blue but was transparent, as if it were night. He pointed toward the moon.

"My wife told me once she thinks of me every time she looks up at the moon, and sees how much bigger it looks, these days, from Earth. That was one of my first efforts. More fame than I deserved, perhaps, just because it was close to Earth, right there for everyone to see . . .

"She sought me out after that; she wanted me to sit for a portrait she was incorporating for a heroic base-formality dream sculpture. Imagine how flattered I was; having hundreds of students going into simulation to forget themselves awhile and turn into a character based on me! As if I were a hero in a romance. We met on Titania, during my Uranus project. She had sent a doll of herself because she was afraid to travel out of mind-range with the earth. I fell in love with the doll; naturally I had to meet the archetype from which she sprang."

"And? . . ."

"Well, damn it, Rhadamanthus, you know my mind better than I do; you know what I'm going to say!"

"Perhaps, sir. You actually wanted to be the heroic figure she fell in love with. I suspect you fell in love with the heroic ideal too. To do acts of greatness and wonder! Is that why you suspect the Earthmind had you meet that storm sculptor? To show you that impressive deeds—and I think that that man and his effort certainly were impressive—could still be done here on Earth, with your memory left just as it is? You thought the better part of valor might be contentment? That a true hero is moderate, temperate, and lives within his means? Well, that is by no means an ignoble sentiment. . . ."

Phaethon made a noise of vast disgust. "Ugh! Oh, come now! That's not it at all! I only agreed to take a year off work and come to this frivolous masquerade because my wife told me it might inspire me to decide on my next project. As I was trying to think of what I could do that was impressive, I began to wonder if the act of uncovering some old crime or misdeed of mine might not interfere with that? If so, this little mystery is just a distraction, so I should forget it. But then I met that foolish man, and I realized what real distraction is. Finding the truth about myself is not distraction; I have to know all about me before I can decide how I can best be used for my purposes. Real distraction is doing the kind of work he does!"

The penguin looked back toward the dark cloud, now far behind them. A rumble of thunder sounded, like the flourish of a trumpet before a battle.

"I don't understand. What's so wrong with his work?"

"Not recording what he does?! Perhaps its good enough for him. I want my accomplishments to be permanent! Permanent!"

Phaethon did not pay attention to the gathering storm behind him. Instead, from his high vantage, he looked back and forth across the wide view below, gardens and forests, mountains and mansions, turning his sense-filter on and off, off and on.

"There it is."

"There what is, sir?"

"Something I wasn't supposed to see." One of the things his sense-filter had been programmed to block out. "I wonder what is down there?"

On the wide horizon far behind, with a dazzle of blue lightning, and with curtains of gray water softening the colors below, a magnificent storm began, wonderful to see by daylight, it would be a storm like no other before or since; but Phaethon did not spare a glance for it.

Phaethon flew swiftly toward the east.

In a short time, he traveled through the air till he was above an object which, with his sense-filter up, was blotted from his perception.

It was a very large object. It was a mountain. It was flat-topped like a mesa, and had been constructed by applications of artificial volcanic forces. In the center of the tableland, a crater lake fifty miles across or more gleamed with strange lights.

3.

Phaethon slanted down through the air to land on the lawns at the lakeside. Not far away, tables and chair shapes grown out of living wood were scattered across the fragrant lawn. Here were parasols, water fountains, nightstands holding sobering-helmets, formulation rods holding ornaments of dreams, staging pools, and deep-interfaces shaped like covered wells. A cluster of guests had gathered, resplendent in the costumes of a thousand ages and nations. Waiters dressed as Oberonid Resumptionists, like walking statues of blue ice, circulated with trays of drink, thought boxes, remembrance chips, and sprays. Slender waitresses dressed like Martian Highlander Canal-Dryads passed out librettos and seeing-rings.

A waitress swayed over to him and offered him the seeing-ring, used to translate the performance into a format suited to his neuroform. She smiled and curtseyed.

Another figure—either imaginary or real, Phaethon could not determine—dressed as a master of ceremonies, bedecked with ribbons and carrying a long senechal's wand, approached with soft steps across the grass, and, bowing, doffed his cap toward Phaethon, and asked if he wished to contribute.

Phaethon reacted to the signal asking for donations to the performance by opening his mask on one level, and allowing his degree of appreciation to be recorded. A standardized estimator deducted money from his account proportional to that appreciation. He politely added his name to the collection, so that the ecoperformer would discover whose appreciation she had earned.

Phaethon turned to stare in fascination at the lake. Clouds of steam moved across its wide surface; concentric rings of agitation spread across the waters; at these places, knots of bubbling froth fought with jets of flame.

Beneath the water was a forest fire. Something that looked like trees of coral, widely spaced in little circular groves, grew in the cool depths along the lake bed. They changed and shifted like phantoms in a colored dream; bubbles of fire trembled along their limbs.

Meanwhile, Rhadamanthus's penguin image had unfolded into a portly gentleman in Elizabethan garments of white, purple, and rose, puff sleeved and dazzled with ribbons and flounces. A wide lace collar surrounded a round red face with many chins. He wore a square cap of black felt too large for his head, weighted with ornamental knobs at each corner. A chain of office and a medallion hung over his chest.

Seeing Phaethon's eyes on him, Rhadamanthus smiled an avuncular smile, and creases folded his pudgy jowls. "You are not surprised, I hope. I wanted to fit in with your theme. So here I am!"

"Penguins don't normally turn into fat little men. What happened to your respect for our tradition of realism?"

"Ah, but at a masquerade, who can say what is real? Even Silver-Gray standards are relaxed." So saying, Rhadamanthus donned a domino mask, and his identity response was disabled.

Phaethon stepped one further step into mentality, going from Nearreality to Hypertextual, what was sometimes called the Middle Dreaming level. The filter leading into his direct memory was removed. Everything around him suddenly was charged with additional significance; some objects and icons disappeared from view, others appeared. The sound of a thousand voices, singing in chorus, thundered from the lake bottom, splendid and astonishing, surging in time with the flames. Phaethon felt the music tremble in his bones.

When he glanced at the guests, the meanings attached to their various costumes and appearance were thrust into his brain.

He recognized the gown of Queen Semiramis shining on a strikingly beautiful olive-skinned woman, and the histories of tragic Assyrian wars, and the triumph of the founding of Babylon ran through him.

She was speaking with an entity dressed as a cluster of wide-spread energy bubbles. This costume represented Enghathrathrion's dream version of the famous First-Harmony Composition Configuration just before it woke to self-awareness, bringing the dawn of the Fourth Mental Structure. Phaethon had never experienced that dream poet's famous cybernativity sonnet-interface cycles before; now he was recalling them as if he had been familiar with them for years.

Beyond them, a group of vulture-headed individuals were dressed in the dull leathery life-armor of the Bellipotent Composition, with Warlock-killing gear. These weapons dated from a few years before the end of the Eon-Long Peace, which ended when the First New War began, during the age of horrors that introduced the Fifth Mental Structure. But Phaethon saw anachronism, since the Bellipotent Composition was not composed until ninety years after the anti-Warlock weapons had been superseded by far deadlier arrangements.

Some of the vulture-headed individuals in the costume tried to keep their voices and gestures in the uniform rhythm for which the Bellipotent group-mind was famous, but others broke up laughing, and the broken mind segments had to be fitted back into the pretend-overmind.

The leader of this group was dressed in a bear pelt and carried a club shaped from an antelope's thighbone; he had a ghastly triple scar burned into his forehead. Phaethon, upon seeing him, knew that this was Cain from Judeo-Christian mythology, a figure in a play by Byron. Another anachronism, but correct as a symbol. The role of the Bellipotent Composition in ending the idyllic and universal peace of the Fourth Mental Structure may have been exaggerated by some historians; but his-their identity as the reinventors of murder made them apt companions for Cain.

With them was a figure whose meaning was still masked. He wore a ship-suit of symbiotic living black and super-adamantine gold, was dark haired, harsh faced, and he carried a small star in one hand instead of a weapon. His helmet was an absurd-looking bullet-shaped affair with a needle crown, like the prow of an aircraft, made of gleaming golden admantium. When Phaethon signaled for identification, the response was "Disguised as a certain rash manorial with whom we are all far too familiar!"

4.

In the middle of Helion's joy, only one false note rang.

Wheel-of-Life sent him a private signal by having one of her pigeons, which only contained a very small part of Wheel-of-Life's mind, land on his mannequin's lap and initiate a quiet interface.

"Helion will weep to hear that Phaethon is gone from his place. Phaethon beholds the drowned garden of my sister, Green-Mother, to watch the life and dying there. This was one of the things Phaethon agreed not to see, not to remember, was it not?"

Helion could not leave the Conclave, but, with another independent section of his mind, he opened a channel and sent out a message, encrypted and perhaps undetected: "Daphne! Wake! Wake up from the insubstantial dream you deem to be your life. Your husband, like a moth to flame, draws ever closer to a truth which will consume him. Open your casket of memories; remember who you are, remember your instructions. Find Phaethon, deceive him, allure him, distract him, stop him. Save him.—And save us from him."

For a moment, he felt the grief and sorrow any father might feel, hearing that his son was on the verge of self-destruction. But then he remembered his part in all of this, and a sense of shame made all the crystal-clear certainties in his heart seem cloudy.

Despite that, he sent an emphasis appended to the first message: "Daphne, from the doom he will bring on himself, I beg of you, preserve my son."

5.

Phaethon turned toward Rhadamanthus to ask a question, but smiled instead, ignoring what he had been about to ask, because now he recognized Rhadamanthus's costume. The identification channel thrust the knowledge silently into Phaethon's brain: Polonius, a character from the revenge-play *Hamlet* by William Shakespeare, the Bard of Stratford-on-Avon, realistic-simulation linear-progression author, circa Second Mental Structure.

There was also a recital of the play, a working knowledge of the English language, and notes and memories on the lives of various peoples reconstructed from Queen Elizabeth's court, enough to allow anyone glancing at Rhadamanthus to appreciate the humor, the allusions, and the references in the play.

"Oh, very amusing," said Phaethon, "I suppose this means you're going to give me advice which I'll ignore?"

Rhadamanthus handed him a skull. "Just don't kill me by accident."

"Don't hide behind any tapestries." Phaethon glanced down at the skull. "Alas, poor Yorick. I knew him, Horatio. A fellow of infinite jest, of excellent fancy . . ." He looked up again. "I never quite understood this play. Why didn't they resurrect Yorick out of his recordings, if he was so well-liked?"

"The noumenal recording technology was not developed until the end of the Sixth Mental Structure Era, young master."

"But Hamlet's father had a recording. It came up as a projection on the battlements. . . ."

They were interrupted by a blare of trumpets, sounding from the center of the lake waters. The organisms at the lake bottom had entered a higher and grander growth phase, and, like the horns of a kraken, branches of the flaming coral began rising above the boiling surface.

"What is it we are here to see, young master?"

"Whatever it is they don't want me to see."

"But I can replace your stored memories at your command, sir."

"And exile me from my home. No, thank you. But if I wander around the border of an area I cannot enter, I might learn the size and shape of the boundaries. . . ."

And he stepped one step deeper into mentality, into the condition called Penultimate Dreaming.

6.

An ecoperformance was meant, by its very nature, to be understood by people with Cerebelline neural structures. The whole challenge of this art form was to produce a complex system of interactions—an ecology—which would appear beautiful from every point of view of each acting element simultaneously, but would also be, taken as a whole, sublime. Usually, in living ecologies, the beauty was tragic from the point of view of starving predators or fleeing prey, but transcendentally beautiful, not tragic at all, viewed globally.

In the Penultimate Dreaming, Phaethon's brain was rocked by sensations radiating from the strange creations growing along the lake. He was seeing not a lake but a universe. The lives and memories of the myriad creatures swarming there came into him like a thousand strands of music, predator and prey, complex as a kaleidoscope, a pattern too dazzling to grasp. He was, at once, one and all of the darting shelled creatures forming an interlocking colony; and also each one of a hive-group wrapping around those shells; and also the scavenger-hooks who competed for dropped hive husks; and the refashioners who brought recycled energy from the scavengers back, in another form, to the shell beds.

The Cerebelline Life-mistress who constructed these microforms had outdone herself. There were a thousand variations, each beautiful with weird beauty, but small, very small. She had invented a new way of coding genetic material, like DNA, but containing eighty-one chemical compounds, instead of the four classic amino acids. Complex genetic information could be compressed into very small cells, as small as viral cells, and complex forms of life were swarming and multiplying along the coral arms at a size that usually only simple protozoa used. The speed of their growth and decay was so high, their atoms combining and recombining so quickly, that the waste-heat was boiling the lake water. The initial high energy to start these reactions came from widely scattered pebbles of special living crystal.

The coral trees that sprang out from these life-pebbles were made up of thousands and millions of individuals, each one contributing to and being fed by the whole structure. The branches and limbs of coral seemed rigid only because each microform who darted away left chemical energy behind which only microforms who took up that exact position in the hierarchy, the same place and stance and posture, could fully enjoy. Like a spinning wheel seeming to form a solid disk, the illusion of stability was caused by the continuous effort of each part in motion.

Surrounding each coral tree was a very wide area of desolation, which the microforms could not cross. Each coral tree was centered only on its life-pebble, and all parts operated in magnificent harmony.

But only in isolation was the tree structure symbiotic. While a mother tree could send seeds to start other trees, these new daughter trees could not reach all the way across the desolation to rejoin the mother tree in a peaceful symbiosis.

At the point in the performance when Phaethon joined it, the greatest tree growing from the oldest life-pebble had just learned how to carry water to higher parts, and was lifting shining branches into the air.

This eldest tree had discovered how to use steam pressure through its capillaries to fling seeds through the air. The seeds skipped like tossed stones across the lake surface, passing the desolate zones, and sank into rich lake-bottom soils near other life-pebbles, there to start tree-organisms of their own.

This eldest tree, once it had colonized the immediate circle of closest life-pebbles, flung a second wave of seed-colonists, which, competing with the daughter trees that had grown up from the first wave, made the water boil with an intense and deadly competition.

In order to avoid further destructive competition, the central eldest tree now tried to grow to higher and higher branches, in order to fling its seeds farther. The base of the structure complained; signals flashed like fire among the swarming microforms; the warnings were ignored.

In a slow and terrifying crash, the central tree collapsed under its own weight. A plume of steam, like a ghost, swelled up over the lake surface.

Phaethon, who had a base-neuroform, could only understand part of what he was seeing. The symmetries, the timings, the nuances, were forever beyond him. He could follow the life experience of a few of the struggling microforms as they poured into his brain, but only one after another. The meaning of the whole was never clear.

This was not to say he was not stirred by the beauty of what he saw. A blind man listening to an opera might not see the pageantry of the sets and costumes, but the music could profoundly move him, even if the language was strange.

7.

Phaethon glanced back up into Middle Dreaming, turned toward the nearest waitress and signaled for a libretto. Smiling, the Canal Dryad looked toward him, paused, and knelt gracefully to pick up a seeing-ring the wind had blown from her tray. She straightened again, tucked her hair behind her ear, came toward him, and proffered the card containing the libretto.

Many men found Martian Dryads quite attractive; they had the deep chests required by the thin air Mars had once had (Dryads dated from the middle of the Second Terraforming Interrum), and a long-legged delicacy lesser Martian gravity permitted. And they did not have the rough hide of a south-hemisphere drylander. But they were not usually clumsy or shy. Why had the waitress paused?

Phaethon deactivated his sense-filter and saw a man dressed as an Astronomer from First-Century Porphyrogen Cosmic Observatory at 500 AUs, of the Undeterred Observationer School, a Scholum now defunct. It had been a period of hardship, before the construction of the artificial ice-planetoid, and the costume reflected the hardness of those times. He had thick radiation-proof skin, with the internal recyclers and extra layers of fat that allowed him to stand long watches without taking air or water from the common stores. His face was disfigured with multiple eye-jacks, plugs, and extensions, as the Observationers of that period could not afford to abide by the Consensus Aesthetic.

The waitress must have paused to hand a libretto to the Observationer, a man Phaethon's sense-filter had censored from view. The filter could not let him see her hand the card to nobody, and so had invented an action for her to do. Her dropping and stooping and picking up was mere waste motion to account for the missing time.

Phaethon recalled that his sense-filter had been programmed to keep hidden from him a certain disaster in near-Mercury space, brought on solar storms. If the man costumed as an ancient astronomer were an astronomer in truth, he may have ready access to a channel or an index containing information.

Phaethon took the libretto but only pretended to study it as he stepped toward the man. The astronomer was watching the burning collapse of the supertree with several eyes.

Phaethon said, "The life-artist creates a scene of grim disaster."

Phaethon detected signal actions on Channel 760, the translation matrix. There was a moment while the man adjusted to Phaethon's language forms, downloading grammars and vocabularies into himself.

"Truly said," the man replied with a smile. "Though not so grim, I think, as Demontdelune's final hours on the Moon's far side."

Phaethon did not bother to explain he was dressed as Hamlet. He said, "Life can be grim, even these days. Consider the disaster near Mercury."

"The solar storm? A moral lesson for all of us."

"Oh? How so?"

"Well, we'd like to think the Sophotechs can predict all coming disasters, warn, and protect us. But in this case, very minor, perhaps subatomic, variations in the solar core conditions caused the forces to escape Helion's control during one of his agitation runs. Very minor differences between the initial conditions and the predictive model led to disproportionate results; sunspots and solar prominences of truly unusual size and violence erupted all across the affected fields. Joachim Dekasepton Irem has made a rather nice study of the irregular flare patterns, and set the effect to music on channel 880. Have you seen it?"

"I have not," said Phaethon. He did not explain that his sense-filter, on its present setting, would prevent him from viewing any such thing. "But I am given to understand that he . . . ah . . . portrays certain of the details, ahh . . ."

"Inaccurately?" asked the man.

"Perhaps that's the word I'm looking for, yes."

"Well, it's an understatement! Large segments of Helion's sun-taming array wrecked! Interplanetary communications disturbed by the sunspot bursts! And Helion, staying behind, still in the depth of the sun, to try to prevent worse disasters! Much of the collection equipment, orbital stations, and other materials near Mercury was saved only because of Helion's last-ditch effort to restore the magnetic curtains to operation, and to deflect some of the heavier high-speed particles erupting from the sun away from inhabited zones. Great Helion proved his worth a million times and more that hour, I tell you! And to make such a sacrifice for that worthless scion of his house! I wonder at the gall of the Curia! Is there no gratitude left at all in the courts of law? They should just leave Helion alone! But, at least, the Six Peers (well, I suppose they are the Seven Peers now) had the good sense to reward Helion's valor with a Peerage."

"His valor? . . ."

"Helion stayed when the others fled. The Sophotech's delicate on-board circuitry had broken down; the other members of the Solar crew transmitted their noumenal information, minds and souls and all, out to Mercury Polar Station. Helion did not; the signal time between Mercury and the sun was too far to allow him to guide matters by means of any remote service. Helion rode the star-storm till he broke its back, then transmitted his brain information out at the last minute, despite the static and the garbled signal!

"Helion predicted that control of internal solar conditions would be an absolute necessity for an interplanetary society like ours. The Sophotechs, for all their wisdom, can't make a way to transmit information from world to world except by radio. They can't invent another electromagnetic spectrum, now, can they? And, for so long as the Golden Oecumene is connected by electromagnetic signals, we will need to moderate the solar output into a steady, even, and predictable background.

"Who listened to Helion when he first said this, so many thousands of years ago? They all mocked him then.

"Well, they won't mock now! Whatever happens during the Final Transcendence, I know my segment of the world-soul will pay close attention to what Helion envisions!"

"I feel much the same way," admitted Phaethon. "Though I have heard that, the same desire to control the uncontrollable which is so to be admired in an Engineer, in Helion's domestic life, makes him somewhat of a tyrant and a bully."

"Nonsense! Slander! Great men always have these envious flies and gnat bites to contend with."

"Even the greatest men can have flaws; even the worse villains can have small virtues. What do you think of Helion's scion, Phaethon?"

"Ah! You see how this performance is a criticism of his work and life."

Phaethon blinked toward the boiling lake, the flash and motion of lights beneath the waters. "Some parts of the analogy are more obscure than others. . . ."

"Not so! Phaethon is madman who plans to destroy us all! Who could not be astonished by the bizarre selfishness of Phaethon's scheme? Does the Silence teach us nothing?"

Phaethon, utterly mystified, nonetheless nodded sagely. "An interesting point. But some people have said one thing and some have said another. Which part of what he has done do you find to be the most reprehensible?"

"Well, now, I can't believe the boy really means to do evil—maybe what you say about villains having a good side has some merit here—but he really should not have—Ah! Wait! I think I see friends signaling to me. Yoo-hoo! Over here! Excuse me, it was a pleasure to talk to you, Demontdelune, or whoever you are. My friends and I are Orthomnemocists, and our discipline requires that we neither edit nor replay old memories nor take on new ones; so if we miss the climax of the performance now, we will have no chance to see it. With your permission?"

"Of course. But perhaps you could reveal your true identity, so that we could find each other and talk later; I found your comments most stimulating. . . ."

"Ah, but this is a masquerade! I might not have been so bold in my opinions if I knew who I was talking to, eh, what?"

The man was hinting that he wanted Phaethon to take off his mask first. Phaethon was loath to do so, for obvious reasons. So, with a sinking sensation in his stomach, Phaethon exchanged meaningless pleasantries with the man, and watched him walk away.

"Damn," he muttered, and looked down at the libretto card. He expected an explanation and commentary on the ecoperformance. But the card was blank. He had to turn his sensefilter back on to see the symbols and events of Middle Dreaming. Now when he looked at the card it was the same as looking at the costumes of the guests, and an explanation flowed into his brain.

The Cerebelline artist here was trying to demonstrate an example from game-theory mathematics concerning the stability of ecological and economic systems, and the inevitability of conflict.

A criticism of his work? Had Phaethon been involved in some project involving abstract mathematics? Economics? Biotechnology? He could only wonder.

8.

He turned his attention from the libretto, and looked up in time to see the finale of the supertree's death.

The microforms of that tree, having adapted too well to the complexity of the tree hierarchy, now crumbled into the water. Overspecialized, unable to readapt to the primitive circumstance of the treeless existence, they perished horribly.

Phaethon was mildly puzzled and faintly disgusted by the finale of the sequence. He had expected the central tree to fall, but then to rise again as the forces of evolution compelled a new series of adaptations. And why hadn't the factors favoring symbiosis within the trees also operated to favor symbiosis, or, at least, cooperation, between the trees? Any two trees that discovered how, despite the desolation between them, to exchange mutually scarce resources would have mutually benefited; such cooperation was common in nature.

Instead, the epilogue of death led to a new sequence of violent events: other tree organisms now began to fling colony-seeds skipping across the boiling lake surface to claim the abandoned center territory; their conflicts grew in wild fury. As each tree became more daring and more bent on success, the heat of its chemical reactions increased. Very, very slowly, the level of the lake water was dropping, boiling away from the very reactions which created short-term success. The life-pebbles near the shore would eventually be exposed, rendered useless, as the water level dropped, which would no doubt lead to additional excesses on the part of the warring trees, producing more waste-heat. The additional waste-heat increased the evaporation of the lake.

Phaethon studied the libretto reading the mathematics, background information, the statements of purpose. Everything was written in such vague terms that there was no guessing what Phaethon's "work" had been that this was supposed to criticize. On the other hand, the astronomer could have been mistaken, and nothing about Phaethon had been included here at all.

In any case, Phaethon could see no point in the death of the burning trees. It merely struck him as ugly and pessimistic. If what he had done had been the opposite of this, perhaps he had not been such a bad fellow after all.

He stepped back into Surface Dreaming, to find an image of fat Polonius standing next to him.

"I don't see anything here worth seeing," said Phaethon. "And I certainly don't see what they didn't want me to see. Whoever 'they' are."

"Define 'they,' " asked Rhadamanthus, quirking an eyebrow.

"I never would have 'volunteered' for memory redactions unless some pressure were brought to bear by someone. That someone is 'they.' "

"So you no longer think you committed a crime?"

"Why do you pretend you don't know? You know exactly what happened. So why ask rhetorical questions?"

"Why ask rhetorical questions indeed? But the part of me who talks to you does not know, young sir, nor will I be allowed to know, the substance of the forgotten material, till you know yourself. The other part of me, that part which does know, is not allowed, by any sign or signal, not by a hint, or expression, or even a pregnant pause of silence, to communicate the forbidden knowledge. My orders are clear." He shrugged. "In the meantime, of course, this version of me can remain on good terms with you, and make such comments as any reasonably intelligent superintelligence could make, eh?"

"So you're dropping a hint. If there is a signal or a trigger which will tell you if I recover the forbidden memories, there may be triggers to signal other people too, eh? The question is, when are those triggers activated? When I think about going back for my stolen memories? When I talk about it? Let's see what jumps if I get close."

"How close, young sir?"

"Let me see the memories. I want to get close enough to smell them."

"Phrase that as an order, and I have no proper choice but to obey."

"Open memory archives, please."

"Come, then, young master, if you are so bold. Step deeper into the mentality. Beyond the Middle Dreaming, even Silver-Gray thoughtspace does not necessarily reflect the analogous real surroundings with perfect accuracy. I can make a short way back to your mansion."

Phaethon wandered across the lawn and away from the performance. Not far away was a pleasure ground where guests were arriving or activating. A group of Stratospherians had folded their flying prosthetics like umbrellas, and hung them from the branches of a Nexus oak. Gathered at the roots of the oak were several staging pools.

Phaethon stepped and sank into the liquid. Swarms of tiny machines, smaller than pinpoints, gathered around him, drew carbon out of the water, and solidified it into a protective diamond shell.

He seemed to himself to rise again. When he rose, he was in pure dreamscape, his mannequin left behind, among other sleeping forms, all diamond-shelled at the bottom of the pool.

Rhadamanthus bore an expression of unearthly serenity; he gestured with majestic slowness to the East. Among the clouds beyond the edge of the mountain, Phaethon now saw hints of towers and windows rising above the trees. It was strange, but it was not quite a violation of visual continuity.

Phaethon walked. He passed through a stand of trees and found the mansion was much closer than it had first appeared.

At the end of the path was a portico. Columns of gray, dappled marble held up a porch roof shingled with silver plaques; the Rhadamanthine emblem was carved into the entablature. With the sound of a gong, the tall main doors opened.

THE CHAMBER OF MEMORIES

Phaethon stood, or seemed to stand, in his Chamber of Memory, a casket of recollection hesitating in his hand. A legend ran in letters of gold across the casket lid:

"Sorrow, great sorrow, and deeds of renown without peer, within me sleep; for truth is here. Truth destroys the worst in man; pleasure destroys the best. If you love truth more than happiness, then open; otherwise, let rest."

His curiosity grew. Phaethon turned the key, but he did not open the lid.

Fire flashed on the casket lid. Letters as red as blood appeared:

"WARNING! The following contains mnemonic templates that may affect your present personality, persona, or consciousness. Are you sure you wish to proceed? (Remove key to cancel.)"

Phaethon stood for long time without moving, staring out the windows.

Outside, the architecture and every appearance was authentically Victorian English, dating from the era of the Second Mental Structure, or early period Third.

The windows were peaked arches, set with diamond-shaped panes. Framed in the western window rose the mountains of Wales, cherry red and ethereal against the purple dusk, crowned with the light of the setting sun. Phaethon could see, from the windows opposite, a pale full moon rising, dim as a ghost in the twilight, floating in the deep evening blue.

In the dreamspace of the Rhadamanthus Mansion, the sun always set in the West, and there was only one. The moon showed no city lights nor garden glass; but, proper to this period, was still a gray, dead world. Outside the windows, every detail of perspective, proportion, and consistency was correct. Each tree leaf and blade of grass cast its shadow at the proper angle, and the play of light and shadow was just as it should have been. The computer model determining the look and texture and color went down to the molecular level of detail.

If he had gone down to the garden and plucked a single leaf from the rosebushes there, that leaf would still be gone at his next visit; if it blew away on the wind, the computer would simulate its path; if it rotted into the mold, the extra weight and consistency of the soil would be measured and accounted for. This was the realistic accuracy for which the mansions of the Silver-Gray School were famous.

The memory chamber was in deep dreamspace. It was as real, and as unreal, as everything else in Rhadamanthus Mansion.

To be sure, somewhere, in reality, there must have been a real housing for the mansion's self-aware sophotechnology; a power supply, cables, neural conduits, computer laminae, informata, decision-action boxes, thought nodes, and so on. Somewhere was the real, physical interface machinery that fed carefully controlled patterns of electrons into circuitry actually woven into Phaethon's real auditory and visual nerves, his hypothalamus, thalamus, and cortex.

And somewhere, presumably, in the real world, was his real body.

His real self. But what was his real self?

Phaethon spoke aloud: "Rhadamanthus, tell me."

"Sir?"

"Was I a better man . . . back before?"

The Polonius-shape here was replaced by a Victorian-era butler in a stiff-collared black coat showing a double row of well-polished silver buttons. The butler was red-faced, slightly portly. His chin was clean-shaven, but the handlebar mustache led to enormous muttonchop sideburns, whiskers reaching right and left halfway to his shoulders.

The butler image stood in the doorframe, a white-painted narrow stair curving away behind him, but he did not, or could not, enter the room.

Rhadamanthus spoke in a kindly voice, roughened by a slight Irish brogue. "In many ways, aye, that you were, young master."

"And was I happier . . . then? . . ."

"Indeed you were not."

"Unhappiness in the golden age? In this pure, unsullied Arcadia? How can this be?"

"You did not think our age so perfect then, young master; and it was something else, not happiness, you sought."

"What did I seek?" (But he knew. The words on the casket said it. Deeds of renown without peer.)

"You know I cannot say. You yourself gave the order which silences me." The butler bowed slightly, smiling without mirth, eyes grave. "But the answer lies within the casket you hold."

Phaethon looked at the words on the lid. He tried to make himself feel doubt. Deeds of renown without peer. In this golden age, there was nothing men could do that machines could not do better. So why did this phrase send a chill of pleasure down his spine?

He looked left and right. On shelves and in glass cabinets surrounding him were other memories. But the other memory boxes, caskets, and chests in the Archive Chamber surrounding him all were clearly labeled, marked, and dated. They bore no cryptic riddles.

And they carried seals or affidavits from the Rhadamanthus Law-mind to affirm that the redacted memories had been taken from him with his own informed consent, not to escape some legal debt or obligation, nor for some other unworthy purpose. Most of the boxes bore the green seal of memories saved from his thirty centuries of life, edited out from his organic brain merely to save space and prevent senility overload. Others bore the blue seal of a minor oath or voluntary obligation, either thought-work whose copyrights he had sold to another, or else some argument or lover's spat that he and his wife had both agreed to forget.

None of them dangerous. None of them ominous.

"Rhadamanthus, why does this box not say what is in it?"

He heard footsteps, light and quick, tapping up the stairs behind Rhadamanthus.

He turned just as a dark-haired woman with vivid features stepped past Rhadamanthus and into the room. She was wearing a long black coat with a ruffle of lace at her throat, and in one hand she carried her mask like a lorgnette.

She had eyes of luminous, dancing green, which blazed, perhaps with mirth, perhaps with fear or ire, as she called:

"Phaethon! Drop the box! You don't know where it's been!"

Phaethon removed the key, so that the red letters faded, but he kept the box in his hand. "Hello, dear. Who are you supposed to be?"

"Ao Enwir the Delusionist. See?" Throwing back her head, she held open a flap of her coat to display her pinch-waisted vest, spiderwebbed with Warlock signs and studded with responders. The masculine cut of the garment had been rounded somewhat to accommodate her. Only her shoes were feminine; a projection or spike from the heel forced her to walk tiptoed.

"Enwir was a man."

Her head nodded forward with a sway of hair. "Only when he wrote his Discourses. He arranged the March of Ten Figments as a woman. Are you supposed to be Demontdelune?"

"Shakespeare's Hamlet."

"Oh."

A silence hung in the air for a moment.

Unlike other women he knew, his wife did not change body shapes or styles when fashions changed. She had kept the same face for centuries: fine-boned, small of chin, wide of brow. Her skin was a lustrous golden brown; her hair was black and shining as jet, and fell just past her shoulders.

But her personality was displayed in the glitter and motion in her wide and flashing eyes, mischievous or dreamy by turns. Her lips were a trifle wide, and her mouth quirked from moment to moment impish grins, solemn dryad pouts, or sensual nymphic smiles, one after another in restless succession.

Now her face was still and calm, except for the skeptical twitch that raised one eyebrow.

Then she shrugged and waved her mask at Phaethon's casket. "And just what in the world did you imagine you were thinking you were doing?"

"I was curious. . . ."

"Let's just call you Mr. Pandora from now on!" She sniffed and tossed her hair and rolled her eyes to heaven. "Didn't fat Rhadamanthus here warn you that you'll get tossed out like wet garbage if you open those old memories?"

Rhadamanthus in the doorway muttered, "Mm. I don't think I used quite that wording, mistress. . . ."

Phaethon hefted the casket thoughtfully, pursed his lips.

His wife took a step forward, saying, "I don't like that look on your face, lover. You're thinking rash, rash thoughts!"

Phaethon's eyes narrowed. "I'm just wondering why, when I beat the bush to flush out whoever was behind my amnesia, I got you. . . ."

She put her little fists on her hips and stared up at him, her mouth a red O of outrage. "Suspicious of me, are you now?! Well, I like that! You're the one who wanted me to keep you away from the casket! Just see if I do you any favors anymore!" And, arms folded across her breast, she tossed her head angrily, making an exasperated noise in her nose: "Hmph!"

"What I want to know," said Phaethon, a little impatiently, "Is how long you were going to let me live my life without telling me life is false? How long were you going to lead me around blindfolded?"

She stamped her foot. "False?! And you think I'd just live with a copy of my own husband? If you love someone, real love, you can't love their copy." But she could not hide a strange look of guilt and uncertainty that crossed her features at that moment.

Phaethon's voice was grim and remote: "Is my love real? Or was that a false memory too?"

"You're the same as you were before; nothing important is in that damn box!" She turned to face Rhadamanthus. "Tell him!"

Rhadamanthus said, "No false memories were added. Your personality has undergone no major change; your basic values and attitudes are the same; the memories which that casket-icon represents are surface-structure memories only."

Phaethon shook the box toward her. "That's not the point!"

"Well, what is the point?" she asked challengingly.

"What's in this box? You know and I don't. You were never going to tell me?"

"You know! Exile and dispossession are in that box! Isn't that enough for you? Isn't anything ever enough? You open that box and you lose me. Isn't that enough?"

"Lose? . . . You wouldn't come with me? Into exile?"

"N—uh. Are you asking me? Do you want me to come? No! That's a stupid idea! What would we live on?"

"Well—" Phaethon blinked. "I was assuming they would let me take my own property, or that I could sell or convert some of my holdings, to . . ."

Now Daphne's face grew quiet and still as a winter pond. She spoke softly, "Lover, you don't have any holdings. You sold them all. The two of us are living on Helion's charity. We're only staying here because he hasn't thrown us out."

"What are you saying? I'm one of the richest men in the Oecumene."

"Were, honey. You were."

Phaethon looked at Rhadamanthus, who nodded sadly.

Phaethon said, "What about my work?! For three thousand years, I've been alive, and I was not idle all that time. I remember my apprenticeships, and the memory grafts to learn terrestrial and transcendental finances; engineering, philosophy, persuasion, and thought-craft. My effort helped fix the new orbit of the moon; that was one of my first! When Helion opened a project on Oberon, no one but me was willing to go to Uranus! I condoned the studies of ring-city orbital mechanics, and made the simulation for the project to put a ring-city around the equator of the Sun! That study led to the present Solar Array! And then I . . . then I . . ."

His face went blank.

He said, "What did I do between Epoch 10165 and 9915? That's a two-hundred-fifty-year gap."

No one spoke.

Phaethon said: "Funny. I remember the news and the gossip. Epoch 10135. That was the year when the Meta-mathematical Supercomposition came out of its meditation, and announced the solution to the Ouryinyang's Information Compression Paradox. I remember other things. But not what I did. I was living in my high castle called Aloofness, at Mercury L-5 equilateral, a home I carved myself out of an unclaimed asteroid, thrown in-system by the Neptunians. I had twelve hundred square miles of solar converters, like the sails of a clipper ship, drinking in the sun. Tremendous energy. But what was I doing with my life then? I was too far away from Earth to maintain a telepresence or a mannequin. Was I retired from the Silver-Gray? I wasn't poor then."

Phaeton's eyes shifted back and forth, looking at nothing.

"And what did I do between 10050 and 10200 during the entire First and Second Reconsiderations? Everyone remembers where they were standing or what they were doing when Jupiter Ignited. That was in Epoch 7143, right after my centennial. Or when they heard the first song from Ao Ainur, the Lament for the Black Swans, in 10149. Everyone, but not I. Why would that have been chosen for erasure, not the events but my reactions to them? Where was I standing? What was I doing? Is that information in this box, too? How much of my life did you take?!"

The blankness in his face grew even more hollow. "Daphne . . . Why don't we have any children? . . . I do not remember the reason why we decided that. The most important decision any couple can have, whether or not to start a family. And I don't remember it. My life was erased."

Silence lay like a stone.

"Darling—I just want you to listen to me—" Daphne leaned forward. Her face was frozen; her eyes were staring at the box as if it were a poisonous import sheet, ready to download some deadly virus. "Don't do anything rash— you're just the same as you ever were—you're still the man I was born to love and marry—there's nothing in that box you need—"

Phaethon's hand tightened on the lid. But he said, "Rhadamanthus, can we freeze this scene? I need time to think."

Everything in the chamber froze in place. All sound was hushed. Not a dust mote falling through the light from the window changed position.

The voice of Rhadamanthus came directly into his brain: "You will have to log entirely off the system, so as not to prejudice Mistress Daphne or any other users. Log back on when you wish to resume."

Phaethon made the gesture of ending, and the world disappeared.

6

THE ARMOR

1.

Phaethon was surprised to find himself in blank thought-space. His self-image was gone; his body was nothing but a pair of floating gloves, here. In front of him was a spiral wheel shape made of points of light. To his left and right were red and blue icon cubes, representing basic routines; engineering, mathematics, ballistics, environmental sciences. A half-dozen black slabs, like shields, represented security, anti-intrusion and privacy-guarding routines. There was a yellow disk-shaped icon representing communication circuits.

And that was all. Was this Phaethon's innermost thinking area? If so, he certainly did not coddle himself.

The barren emptiness was oppressive. And it certainly ignored Silver-Gray traditions of detailed utter realism. There wasn't even a "wallpaper" image here—no room, no desktop.

Phaethon had his glove jab the yellow disk. A blood red disconnect cube appeared. He put his glove inside it and made the ending gesture.

Words appeared unsupported in the air: "WARNING. You are about to disconnect from all Rhadamanthine systems and support. Do you wish to proceed?"

He touched finger to thumb, spreading his other fingers: the yes signal.

A moment of disorientation floated through him. For a moment, his mind was clouded; the sensations in his body changed, slowed, became somewhat numb, and yet more painful. He opened his eyes and winced.

Phaethon was awake in the real world.

The medical tubes and organs wrapping him were made of hydrocarbons, and slid aside, re-forming themselves into water and diamond plates for easy storage. Phaethon stood up slowly from his coffin, surprised and shocked.

The room was small and ugly. To one side was a large window opening on a balcony. Above the medical coffin was a crystal containing the routines and biotics to keep his slumbering body intact. The crystal was huge, a crude out-of-date informata, fixed to the ceiling with awkward globs of adhesion polymer. The walls were dumb-walls, not made of pseudo-matter, not able to change shape or perform other functions. When he put his foot over the edge of the coffin and swung himself to his feet, he made two other unpleasant discoveries.

Despite Silver-Gray promises of total realism, his self-image in mentality was represented as being stronger and more agile than his real body in reality. Phaethon climbed slowly and clumsily to his feet.

The second surprise was that the floor was cold. Furthermore, it stayed cold. It did not anticipate his orders, did not automatically adjust or react to his presence; it did not conform its texture to soothe his feet. He thought several peremptory commands at it, but nothing happened.

Then he remembered to speak aloud. "Carpeting! Foot massage!"

The floor adjusted to carpet, and warm pulses caressed his feet, but irregularly, slowly. The carpeting was irregular and tattered, ugly looking. The fact that he had to speak his orders drove home to him how impoverished these quarters were.

He looked around slowly, noticing the crooked tension in his neck; perhaps his spine had become misaligned while he slept.

He looked up; there was grime on the ceiling and upper

walls. Phaethon could not even recall the last time he had seen grime.

A second shock came when he looked down at his body. The skin was a dull, leathery substance; it looked very much like inexpensive artificial skin. He pressed his fingers against his chest, his stomach, his groin. Beneath the flesh, he felt, or perhaps he imagined, that some of the organs under his fingers had the hard, unyielding texture of cheap synthetic replacements.

His senses were duller. Distant objects were blurred; his hearing was restricted in pitch and range, so sounds were dull and flat. Perhaps his skin was slightly numb as an aftereffect of the crude medical care he had been under. Or, what was more likely, the sense impressions directed by the computer stimulated his nerves more thoroughly and precisely than his natural organs. And he was blind on every wavelength except on narrow visible-light range.

There was a door, but no knob. He stepped into it and bumped his nose. Now he jumped back in alarm, wondering for a moment why the door had failed to move.

What shocked him was that he had lost some of his sanity. Normally, when he made a discovery, or realized something, Rhadamanthus made adjustments in Phaethon's midbrain, sculpting whatever habits or patterns of behavior Rhadamanthus thought Phaethon might need directly into Phaethon's nerve paths. This decreased learning time; Phaethon normally did not have to remind himself to do things twice.

Then Phaethon said, "Open . . ."

The door slid open slowly. Behind was not an exit but a wardrobe. A strange garment was hanging from a cleaning levitator. A few bottles of life-water were hanging, weightlessly, in a magnetic suspension rack.

Phaethon took one of the bottles in hand. At his touch, information appeared in the glassy bottle's surface. Reading the label, one word and icon at a time, was painful, and Phaethon got a headache after slowly picking through the first few menu pages hovering in the depths of the label. The bottle could not put the knowledge of its contents directly into his brain; Phaethon was disconnected from Middle Dreaming. It was a low-quality manufacture, with only a few formations and reactions recorded by the microbe-sized nanomachines suspended in the liquid. He put the bottle back in place.

On a low shelf was a box of dust cloud. Phaethon picked up the box, and said, "Open box."

Nothing happened. Phaethon pushed open the lid with his hand. The amount of dust material inside was minor, a few grams.

"I really am poor after all," he muttered sadly. Where had all his money gone? After twenty-nine or thirty centuries of useful work, investment and reinvestment, he had accumulated considerable capital.

With the box tucked under one arm, Phaethon wandered back into the pathetic room. He looked back and forth. It was ghastly.

Phaethon straightened his shoulders, drew a deep breath. "Phaethon, gather your spirits together, steel yourself, and stop this moping! Look: there is nothing here so vile, nothing which you cannot endure. Princes of past ages could not live like this: they would have called it luxury beyond luxury!"

It was not as easy to change his attitude without computer assistance, but one advantage of the Silver-Gray discipline was that he could do it at all.

He released the contents of the box. The dust cloud rose up to the ceiling, found the dirt, and began dusting. But there was only a small volume to the cloud; Phaethon had to direct a beam from the box against certain patches of filth the cloud was too small and stupid to notice by itself. He knew that, at one time, before the invention of basic robotics, humans had to toil like this all the time.

It seemed grotesque and faintly embarrassing, but, by the time he had directed the cloud to scrub the whole room, Phaethon had a glowing feeling of accomplishment. The room was clean; entropy had been reversed. It was small, but now the universe was different than it had been before his work, and, in a very small way, better.

It was a good emotion, but when he made a mental signal to record it, nothing happened.

Phaethon sighed. Good thing he was not stuck in reality, cut off from the thoughts and systems of the Oecumene. There was no point in trying to get used to this flat, dead, unresponsive world; Phaethon planned to be here only long enough to get some private time to think.

He walked over to the window port, remembered to open it, stepped outside.

Phaethon stood on the balcony of an infinite tower. It stretched above him as far as the eye could see, at least, in his present and limited vision. Below him, it fell into clouds; there was no visible base.

This was a room built into one of the space elevators that led up to the ring-city circling Earth's equator.

Phaethon sat, calling "Chair . . ." But the balcony surface created a chair very slowly, so he struck his bottom painfully on the rising chair back as he sat. The chair was not smart enough to avoid the blow, nor did any contours change or shape themselves to his particular height.

"Everything here is a clue. If I have forgotten this little room, it's because it's part of what I'm supposed to forget, a reminder. The blankness of my private thoughtspace; that is a clue. That foolish and pessimistic Cerebelline ecoperformance, another clue. The strange garment in the wardrobe. All of these things are clues."

Phaethon had not opened the forbidden memory casket. But he had heard no prohibition against deducing the contents of the casket using his unaided powers of reasoning. They could not exile him for that; the laws of intellectual property in the Golden Oecumene were clear. It could be a crime to steal or take knowledge that belonged to another, or that one had agreed not to read. But knowing knowledge in and of itself was never a crime.

The question was, did he have enough information to deduce any conclusions?

Phaethon looked out and up into the infinite expanse of wind. Even his dampened hearing could pick out the thrumming shriek of air moving against the tower, miles above and miles below. It was cold here, this high above the earth. Now, in the distance, like a steel rainbow, he could see the ring-city. The shadow of Earth had crept up about twenty degrees of arc, rendering the city near the horizon invisible. But the equatorial sun was shining where Phaethon was, and shone on the sweep of the ring-city, overhead and to the west. It was a bracing sight.

"I'm cold. Could you do something about that, please?" It took almost a minute for spider-shaped operators (created out of the floor material) walking over his skin, to weave a silk garment around him, loose folds of white cloth with heating elements tuned to comfortable level.

Phaethon began to think about his past. What was missing?

2.

There was no clear way to tell. Did he not recall what he had been doing during the April of Epoch 10179 because the memory was gone, or because he did not associate that memory with that date? Memories were not stored linearly or chronologically but by association. There was no list or index to consult. He could not that notice a memory was missing until he tried to recall it and failed.

When he did come across a blank spot . . . (What had he been doing after the mensal dinner performance to celebrate the conclusion of the Hyperion Orbital Resonance Correction, for example? He had been impatient to see his wife, and wanted to dance or commune with her, but she had seemed listless and distracted) . . . he did not know if that particular blank was related to this mystery, or to one of the other, more ordinary memories he had in storage, perhaps an old lover's spat, or work-for-hire he had agreed to forget.

Nonetheless he found enough holes, even after only some minutes of introspection, to detect a pattern.

First, they were large and they were many. Not just years and decades, but whole centuries of his life were missing; and they were the ones nearer to the present day. Whatever had been removed had occupied a great deal of his time. If it were a crime he had been contemplating, it had been in his imagination for a long time, and it had roots all the way back to his childhood. And, if it were a crime, he had been working at it full-time for most of the last century. His memory of the last 250 years, reaching up to the beginning of the masquerade, was blank.

He could recall his last clear memory. His second attempt to reengineer the planet Saturn had just been frustrated. The Invariants of the Cities in Space had hired him to disintegrate the gas giant, sweeping up and storing the hydrogen atmosphere for antimatter conversions to be powered from the radiation given off during the disintegration. The diamond-metallic core of the world would then be reconstructed by nanomachines into the largest series of space habitats and space ports ever designed. This would have allowed the Invariant populations in the Cities to reproduce, to own their own lands, and to create additional civilizations. Phaethon had seen their plans; they had dreamed, not just of Space Cities, but of continents and worldlets, structures of fantastic beauty and cunning engineering, each one a living organism of infinite complexity.

The College of Hortators led the massive campaign to raise money to purchase the rights to Saturn. At the point at which it became mathematically unlikely to generate a profitable return on investment, the Invariants, without any emotion or slightest sign of discontent, withdrew their investment, and resigned themselves to living more centuries, without children, in the gray and claustrophobic corridors of their crowded habitats.

Phaethon's amnesia began shortly thereafter. What had his next project been? Whatever it was, he had begun to work on it full-time at that point.

There were more clues: The holes in his memory tended to be gathered around his engineering work; the blanked-out events were more frequent off Earth than on. He recalled long trips to the Jupiter moon system, Neptune, and a place called

Faraway in the Kuiper belt; but not what he had done there.

He could not recall any extravagant expenses from recent years. Perhaps he had been living frugally. He had not gone to parties or fetes or commissionings or communions. He had dropped out of all his sporting clubs and correspondence salons. Had he actually been grim? Perhaps the white-haired old man, the Saturn-tree artist, had described Phaethon as wearing black only because Phaethon's sartorial effects budget was exhausted.

Phaethon straightened up in the chair. Not black. Black and gold. The strange old man had said Phaethon wore "grim and brooding black and proud gold."

Phaethon started to his feet and threw the white thermal silk to the balcony floor, where the wind snatched it away into space. He entered the room. He almost bumped his nose again, almost forget to order aloud the door aside. The wardrobe opened.

The suit that hung there (how had he not noted this before?): it was black and gold.

And it looked the same as the suit that the stranger at the ecoperformance had worn, the third member of a group including Bellipotent Composition, and Caine, the inventor of murder.

His suit. The stranger had been mocking him.

It was cut like a ship-suit, but heavier than most ship-suits, so that it looked like armor.

There was a wide circular collar. Finely crafted as jewels, the shoulderboards carried jacks, energy couplings, small powercast antennae, mind circuits.

The sense of familiarity was strong. This suit was his; it was somehow important. Phaethon reached out and touched the fabric.

The black fabric stirred under his touch. It puckered, sent strands like silk threads across his fingers and wrist, and began bonding to his palm. Immediately a sense of warmth, of well-being, of power, began to throb in his hand.

This was not inanimate fabric but a complex of nanomachines. Phaethon, despite his instinct, was reluctant to trust an unknown bio-organization of such complexity. He pulled his hand back; the fabric released him reluctantly.

Some drops of the fabric material, shaking from his fingers, fell to the floor. The boots of the outfit—everything was all one piece—sent out strands toward the fallen droplets, which inched across the wardrobe floor back toward the main garment. The drops were reabsorbed into the material, which trembled once, then was still.

Curious, he touched a shoulderboard. Nothing happened. He thought: *Show me what you do, please*. Then he snatched back his hand and stepped away.

This was one command he did not need to speak aloud. Here was an expensive and well-made organism. The gold segments snapped open, forming an armored breastplate; extended to cover the leggings in greaves; vambraces and gauntlets expanded over the arms; a helmet unfolded from the collar. The helmet had a wide neckpiece, extending smoothly from the shoulders to the ears, ribbed with horizontal pipings. The coifs of Pharaohs in Egyptian statues had similar patterns of horizontal stripes.

Phaethon touched the gold material in awe. If this were space armor, it was the thickest and most well-made he had ever seen or imagined. This gold substance was not an ordinary metal. There was a large island of stable artificial elements, the so-called "continent of stability," above atomic weight 900, which required so much energy to produce that they could not exist in nature. One in particular, called Chrysadmantium, was so refractory, durable, and stable, that even the fusion reactions inside of a star could not melt it. This suit was made of that.

The expense of this suit was staggering. The material was rare; only the supercollider that orbited the equator of Jupiter could generate sufficient energy to create the artificial atoms, and even that required a major percentage of the output of the small star that Gannis had made by igniting Jupiter. This suit had been constructed one atom at a time.

The black material, now inside the suit, was cyclic nanomachinery, which would form a self-contained and self-sustaining symbiosis with the wearer: a miniature and complete ecosystem.

But what in the world was it for? Swimming among the granules of the sun? Walking into the core chambers of plasma reactors? It wasn't necessary for space travel.

The radiation dangers in space were of two types; ambient radiation, and radiation produced by striking particles or dust motes at high speeds. But the amount of radiation one encountered in interplanetary travel, even if one flew the diameter of Neptune's orbit, from one side of the Golden Oecumene to another, was minor, and grew less each century. Ships' armor against meteors or meteoritic dust decreased every year, as more and more of the solar system was cleaned. Also, as the immortals got older, they tended to become more patient, so that slower speeds, more time-consuming orbits, seemed a smaller and smaller price to pay for safer and safer journeys. With Sophotech-designed techniques and equipment, even the smallest dust motes orbiting in the inner system were mapped, anticipated, deflected.

Phaethon touched the shoulder again. "Open up. I'd like to try you on, please."

But nothing happened. Perhaps there was a special command-phrase needed, or some cost in energy required.

"Isn't that fine!" he sighed. "I have the most expensive supersuit ever imagined, one which no power on Earth can mar or scratch or open . . . and now I've locked myself out."

Phaethon wondered why, if he were so poor, hadn't he sold this suit? He looked around again at the squalid quarters here, attached to the shaft of a space elevator, quarters no one else would want. Here? A ship-suit like this, kept here? As if a Victorian gentlemen were living in a woodcutter's hut, but had the Crown Jewels of England in a shabby crate under the dirt floor.

The thought came to him: *I was such a man, at one time, worthy to wear such armor as this.*

The Armor of Phaethon.

And whatever I may have done to make myself unworthy, I shall undo.

He went back over to the medical coffin, lowering himself carefully himself into it, waited for the liquid to crawl up over him, and made himself gulp a mouthful into his lungs without flinching. The pillow embraced his head; contact points buried in his skull were met by a thousand intricacies of energy and information flow. His sensory nerves were artificially stimulated; he began to see things that existed only in computer imagination. His motor-nerve impulses were read; the matrix of an imaginary body moved accordingly. Even his thalamus and hypothalamus were affected, so the emotional-visceral reactions, bodily sensations, and the unconscious interplay of body language and deep neural structures were perfectly mimicked.

For a moment he was back in his blank and private thoughtspace, a pair of hands hovering near a wheel of stars. He touched the cube icon to the right and brought up his accountant. Here were lists of purchases, in the hundreds of millions of seconds, or billions, from Gannis of Jupiter and Vafnir of Mercury. The amount of money spent was comparable to what nations and empires used to spend on their military budgets.

Small payments to the Tritonic Neuroform Composition were recorded, along with inspection receipts. Phaethon had been buying large packages of information from the Neptunians. And, unlike every other merchant venture in the Golden Oecumene, goods from the Neptunians had to be inspected for hidden flaws, gimmicks, and pranks.

There were also moderate payments to one of the Cerebelline Life-Mother houses, a daughter of Wheel-of-Life named the Maiden; a very large number of extrapolations, ecological formulae, and bioengineering routines, equipment, and expertise had been purchased.

And biological material. Phaethon had bought so many metric tons of viral and recombinant bodies that the number was beyond belief. It was enough material to wipe out the biosphere of Earth and replace it with new forms. Had Phaethon been gathering an army? Was his black-and-gold armor actually "armor" in the old sense of the word, like the responders of ancient Warlocks, a system to deflect enemy weapons? The idea was insane.

There were also legal and advisory fees, in large amounts. For smaller matters, Phaethon got his legal advice from the Rhadamanthus Law-mind for free. But here were expenditures showing that Phaethon had approached the Westmind Sophotech, and purchased an extraordinarily expensive advisory, aesthetic, and publicist Mind-set, equipped it with personality-extrapolation programs of the Hortators. The advisory-mind was named Monomarchos.

This was significant. One did not create an attorney, equip him with billions of seconds of intelligence, and give him the ability to anticipate the thoughts and actions of the Hortators, unless one were being called before the Synod for an Inquiry.

A Synod was not a trial; nor did the Hortators possess real legal authority. They were not the Curia. But they did possess social and moral authority. In the modern day, the only way to discourage acts that where socially unacceptable, yet not directly harmful to others, was by means of Hortatory. Hortators could not punish, not directly. The Sophotechs would interfere if men used force or coercion against each other except in self-defense. But men could organize censures, complaints, protests, and, in more extreme cases, boycotts and shunnings. Many business efforts put clauses in all their standard contracts forbidding them from doing business with or selling goods to those whom the Hortators had boycotted, including important food, energy, and communication interests.

The Curia and Parliament, of course, could do nothing to interfere. Contracts were private matters, and could not be dissolved by the interference of the government; and, as long as subscription to the Hortators was not compelled by physical force, it could not be forbidden.

Phaethon realized that here was his first solid clue. Whatever he had done to rouse the Hortators to conduct an Inquiry against him, that was the act that had lost him his memory. It was safe to conclude that Phaethon had agreed to the amnesia to avoid a worse penalty, such as a public denouncement, or a shunning.

But Phaethon had not been called before the Curia. He had not been accused of crime. That, at least, was a relief.

There was no more to be learned here. Phaethon touched the yellow disk icon to re-establish network contact with Rhadamanthus.

And there he was, frozen in the scene in the Rhadamanthus memory chamber, every detail perfectly in place. The sunlight was slanting in through the windows, glittering on memory-caskets and cabinets. Dust motes hung in the sunbeam, motionless. His wife was there, a picture, looking lovely.

When Phaethon took a deep breath, the same sensations in his brain that could have been caused by a tension in his abdomen and a straightening of his spine were created, including a subconscious signal of gathering courage.

"I'm ready. Resume."

7

AT TEA

Perhaps Daphne had also used the opportunity to think; she seemed more composed. "My dearest, I owe you an explanation; but in return, you owe me that you must use your most honest and rigorous sense of justice you can muster." She had stepped close to him and was staring up into his eyes.

He touched her on the shoulder and pushed her slightly away. "First I have a few questions which I insist you answer."

Daphne's red lips compressed. The responder studs on her Warlock costume fluttered angrily, as if she were deflecting a Bellipotent nanoweapon, or painful poison. "Very well! Ask!"

"I just want to know how you thought you could get away with this? The holes in my memory are so large that I could not have lived for very long without noticing. Yet they concern many things which are matters of public record. Expenditures of antimatter, energy, computer time. Interplanetary flights. I can go look into the space traffic control records to find where I went or what I did. Hortator's inquires are matters of public record. It will only take me a little time to piece this together. So what was the point of all this?"

Daphne said simply, "But I don't know."

Phaethon frowned and turned to look at Rhadamanthus.

Rhadamanthus said, "I cannot do a Noetic reading without the express consent of the subject."

Daphne said, "I do not know why this was done to you, or what is in the box. I swear it."

Rhadamanthus said, "Her words accurately reflect her thoughts. She is not lying. What she intends to say next is also not a lie."

She said, "Part of the agreement must have been for me to forget also. Whatever it is you did, I am not laughing at you behind your back, or fooling you, or leading you around by the nose. I do not know what it was."

"Then how did you know to—"

Without a word she drew a memory casket of her own from the pocket of her long coat. It was small and silver, the size of a thimble-box. Letters written in her spidery, flowing, hand-script read:

> " 'This file contains material concerning the one you call your husband, which you and he have mutually agreed to forget.
>
> " '1. If you are reading these words, it means Phaethon has taken steps to recover his forbidden memories. If he should do so, he will leave the Golden Oecumene, perhaps forever.
>
> " '2. Phaethon is penniless, and lives at Rhadamanthus House only at Helion's behest, and only for so long as he should not recover his lost memories.
>
> " '3. He has done nothing criminal, but the shame and anxiety springing from his plans were more than you or he could bear. You well know why you agree with the reasons for the amnesia, and the benefit you enjoy.
>
> " '4. Your amnesia is contingent on his. If he should ever read the forbidden file, this file will automatically open.
>
> " '5. You are not allowed, otherwise, to open this file. Honest relations with Phaethon require that you not keep secrets from him.' "

Phaethon handed the casket back. Perhaps he was ashamed of his suspicions. She returned the casket to her pocket.

"By why did you—"

She interrupted, "Can we go somewhere else and talk? I find this chamber oppressive." Daphne hugged herself, staring at the floor, and shivered.

Phaethon put his casket down where he had found it. He removed the key and tossed it with a casual gesture to where Rhadamanthus stood in the doorway.

Turning his back to the casket, he put one arm around his wife and led her down the stairs.

They ordered Rhadamanthus to serve them tea in the garden. Phaethon changed to period costume; a stiff collar, a long black frock coat. Daphne wore an Edwardian tea dress of burgundy, which flattered her complexion, and a narrow-brimmed straw skimmer with a complex bow dangling down the back. Phaethon forgave the mild anachronism, to see how fine she looked.

They sipped from cups of eggshell china; they nibbled cakes from silver trays. Phaethon secretly suspected that the simulated taste of tea and scones were better than the originals tasted.

Daphne said, "I think everyone has forgotten whatever your shame is. That's the way these things have to go. You would not have agreed to forget unless everyone else, likewise, put the unpleasantness from their minds. Notice how enraged you were at just the thought that I might be hiding the truth from you. Is there any other way we could all live together, undying, forever, unless everyone could put old conflicts utterly and finally behind us?"

"Define 'everyone.' "

She shrugged. "The more civilized sections of society, of course."

"Meaning, not including Primitivist Schools who do not indulge in brain redactions or any neurotechnology. Not Atkins the soldier, who has to keep his brain free from all contaminants. Not including the Neptunians, who are outcasts and scoundrels. And not including one other fellow I saw at the ecoperformance. He was dressed like me. Only his helmet was different."

"Who was he?"

"I don't know. He was in masquerade."

"What was his costume?"

"He was disguised as part of the Bellipotent Composition, end of the Fourth Era."

"I know who is behind that. The Bellipotent costume was put together by the Black Mansion School. They're all anarchists and disrupters and shock-artists. They're trying to offend Ao Aoen and the other nonstandard neuroforms."

"And offend me? Their costume equated me with Caine, the character from Byron's play who invents murder, and with the Bellipotent Composition, who reinvented war."

She shook her head. "I cannot guess what it means. No other polite person will get his joke either; we've all forgotten whatever it was. The Hortators should not have let him get near you."

Phaethon's mind leaped to another thought. "Meaning that the Hortators are monitoring my actions. I'm not surprised. But, during the masquerade, with the location and identification circuits disenabled, I got lost in the crowds, and saw things I wasn't supposed to see."

"Well! So there's your explanation. The mystery is solved!" exclaimed Daphne brightly. "Can we talk about something more pleasant now?"

Phaethon nodded, and said, "I think this amnesia must have been inflicted only briefly before the masquerade began. Something the primitivist old man I met said, implied that I should not have been invited. I conclude that I agreed to this amnesia in order to be allowed to come. Also, enough people have retained the memory of my past to smirk and stare and gossip, at least enough to lead me to suspect that something was in the air."

"Is it my imagination, or is this the same topic we were just on?"

"The main problem is how to find someone who knows what I did, and to approach them, preferably in costume, so that the Hortators won't see and make a fuss. Art displays should be posted on the aesthetic index for stock purchases. If one of us tracks down the old man with the Saturn-trees, the other can find out which Cerebelline was holding the eco-performance at Destiny Lake."

"Darling, you're speaking as if I would help you in this quest. But I won't."

Phaethon leaned back in his chair, staring at her, saying nothing.

She said, "It's nothing but a quest for self-destruction."

"It's a quest for truth."

"Truth! There is no such thing. There are only signals in your brain. Everything: sensations, memory, love, hate, abstract philosophy, gross physical lusts. It's nothing. Strong signals and weak signals. Those signals can be reproduced, recorded, faked. Whatever condition of thought, or pleasure, or belief you wish to achieve by discovering this mystery, could be reproduced in your brain by a proper application of such signals, and there would be no way whatsoever you could discover the difference. Everything would seem as real to you now as all of this." A circle of her hand indicated the scenery around them; the sunlight in the garden, the scent of grass and roses, the shining leaves, the drone of bees, the twittering of larks.

"Except it would not be the truth."

"That thought itself is nothing but another signal," she said sulkily, pouting over her teacup.

"Daphne, you don't really believe that. You would not live the life you lead if you did. You would just go off and drown yourself in some dream drama, never to emerge. Besides, I think I can discover the basics of what happened to me without actually violating the letter of whatever agreement I made."

She put down her teacup so that it smacked against the saucer, slopping tea over the side. But her voice was calm and smooth: "Why pursue this? Why not be content with the life you have?"

"It's too easy to be content. Where's the glory in that? I'd rather do something hard."

"I respectfully disagree. It is quite easy to be a stubborn fool, darling. Look at how many of them there are in the world."

Phaethon spread his hands and smiled slightly. "Well, as long as I can go about being a stubborn fool with a certain amount of grace and intelligence, maybe I can do a good job of it. Don't you see how important this is? How much of my life is missing?"

Daphne tried not to look impatient. "Sweetheart, what standard are you using to measure importance? Length of time? The Bellipotent Composition ruled the Eastern Hemisphere for far longer than you've been alive. And they produced nothing but ninety generations of evil and pain. I would not trade one second of your life for their entire hegemony. So why do you spend even one second of your life on something which can only make you miserable? Darling, listen to me. You have no real mystery, no puzzle worth solving. If those memories were ones you did not want, what does it matter how much time they occupied? Has it never occurred to you that, back when you made this choice, you knew what you were doing?"

"Actually, that's the part which puzzles me the most. . . ." Phaethon thoughtfully sipped his tea.

Daphne leaned forward, her green eyes bright.

"You then must have foreseen this present. You, then, knew that you, now, would suffer the pain of curiosity. You then decided the pain of knowledge was the worse of two evils. Can't you just trust that that decision was correct? Can't you accept anyone's judgment without question? Not even your own? You know now that you back then knew more!"

Phaethon smiled half a smile. "Let me understand your argument. You want me to take on faith that I have always had the strength of character to never to take things on faith. But if I give in to your argument, don't I show, by that example, that such faith is misplaced? My past self might have been, for all I know, convinced by an argument not unlike this one."

"Very cleverly worded!" she blazed. "You may just be clever enough to talk yourself into exile and disgrace!"

Phaethon gazed, absorbed, at the fire of her eyes, the way her red lips parted as she drew a sharp breath, the flare of her nostrils, the flush in her cheeks. Then she subsided, and lowered her gaze to stare moodily to one side. Phaethon studied the curve of her neck, the perfection of her profile, and the delicate lashes, long and black, which almost brushed her cheeks. What had he done to acquire this vivid and fascinating woman?

What should he do to make certain he did not lose her?

No matter. He could not be other than he was, not and still be Phaethon.

A slight wind came up, tousling Daphne's hair, and she held one hand delicately atop her hat to keep it in place. She was looking upward now at the white tumbled clouds and blue skies. These were the skies of ancient Earth, faithfully reproduced. There was no glimmer of the ring-city above the southern horizon, no blinding speck of Jupiter burning, and the Evening Star would appear in her accustomed place, determined by Venus's old orbit.

She said, "The navicular races are soon to begin, out in Vancouver Bay; Telemoan Quatro is challenging his older self Telemoan Quintcux, and they say he's certain to outdo himself. But Ao Ymmel-Eendu, the Warlock who combined himself out of his own twin brains, comes to challenge them both."

Now she became more animated; excitement thrilled in her voice: "Ymmel-Eendu, now that they have made themselves into one person, has been living in his navis body now for forty years, training and preparing, and the rumor channel says he did not step on dry land once in all that period! For years at a time, he would shut off his linear and linguistic brain segments, living among dolphins and cetaceans, an animal of the sea himself, moving from one oceanic dream to another, so that he attains a mystic communion with sea and wind and wave!

"Then, there is going to be a pancrateon near Mount Washington in the late afternoon, between Bima and Arcedes, and two hundred years of rivalry will be settled. The loser has promised to change sex and serve the victor as a harem slave for a year and a day. A disgusting conceit, I think, but who can fathom the minds of athletes and somatic performers?

"This evening at Hawthorn House, there will be a Ball, and, at midnight, a Stimulus. A codicil discovered in the living will of Mancusioco the Neuropathist directs that he be resurrected for the Millennial Celebration; rumor reports that he has completed his Opus Number Ten, the Unfinished Arrangement. Everyone is eager to discover how he resolves the famous disputed sensation passage; tonight we shall learn! Mancusioco himself will lead us from one altered state of mind to another, through the full cycle of consciousness, and who knows what new expressions of thought, new insights, or new forms might arise from his adroit manipulations of our nervous systems? Will you go, Phaethon? Will you go?"

For a moment he was strongly tempted.

If he wanted not to be bothered with this mystery for an evening, or for a month, or a decade, he could visit a redactor and put the memories related to his discovery today in storage. He could spend a pleasant evening with his wife, something he had not in far too long. He could have a pleasant and untroubled life. All he had to do was ask.

But he wondered if he had done this before. What if, every time he discovered a blank in his memory, he made himself forget that discovery? What if he had done this yesterday? Or every day?

He could have a pleasant life. Just for the asking. Except it would not be his.

Phaethon said: "These celebrations are beginning to pall on me. I would much rather be doing the things which make life worth celebrating. But I am haunted by the thought that my past self, as you say, must have known what he was doing. Suppose I underwent this amnesia merely to get to go to this

Celebration. That would imply that my going was part of his plan. But a plan for what? What could he hope to gain? He must have had absolute faith that I would continue to act in a predictable way. . . ."

"Darling, this is beginning to sound like crazy talk. People don't make plans and schemes that way. Why not just relax, and come with me to the navicular races?"

But Phaethon was not listening. He was recalling something Rhadamanthus had said. The only way a man's actions could be truly predictable could be if he were truly moral. Phaethon imagined some past version of himself, with more than 250 years of memories, willing to commit a type of suicide; to go into storage, to be forgotten, merely on the strength of a hope that the unknowing, amnesia-afflicted future version of himself would have the strength and perseverance, without ever once being asked, to rescue him from oblivion. The image was a chilling one.

Phaethon stood up. "Daphne, my memories have been dismembered. I feel as if I've been mutilated. Perhaps there was a good reason for it. But I'll be damned if I'll live my life without trying to find out just what that reason was. You know more than you are saying. Your casket says you know the reason for my amnesia. It says you benefit from it. What's that reason? What's that benefit?"

"Why try to remember a forgotten crime? Let it rest."

"The tag on your memory casket says that I had done nothing; that I was suppressed merely for something I had planned to do."

"Perhaps that is why you escaped true punishment. Perhaps the crime was not complete. But I have put those memories aside."

"Yet you know well the benefit you enjoy. What is that benefit?"

"My life is happy beyond any hope I ever had for happiness." She looked down and would not meet his gaze.

"That is no answer."

"Nonetheless, it is all the answer you shall have from me. Be content."

"You really don't want to tell me the truth?" He paused while she said nothing. He continued: "Do our marriage vows mean so little to you, then? When our friends Asatru and Hellaine got married, all they did was exchange recorded copies of themselves with their intendeds. He edited and adapted the personality of his wife-doll till it suited him; and she did the same to her version of him. Most of our friends are like that. Sferanderik Myriad Ffellows sends his dolls to marry any woman who experiences one of his tasteless love-romance dramas he writes; every schoolgirl has one of him in her harem. I should be offended by such conduct. As if a husband were to make a gigolo for his wife, and she to hire a prostitute for him; and them both to celebrate that as holy matrimony! I am not offended only because the general society has made the whole thing as trivial as exchanging Commencement Mementos. But I thought we were devoted to the Silver-Gray ideal, you and I. To realistic traditions, realistic stimulations, realistic lives. I thought our tradition stood for truth. I thought our marriage stood for love."

She did not answer, but sat, lashes lowered, staring downward.

Daphne spoke very softly, and did not raise her eyes. "But I fear we are not married, my husband."

"W-what?!" This came out in a breathless word, as if Phaethon were struck in the stomach. "But I remember our ceremony. . . . Rhadamanthus said no false memories were put in me. . . ."

"They are not false. I am. Here."

Daphne delicately took her diary, a small cloth-bound book patterned with rosy pastels, out from her skirts and laid it on the table. Like many married couples, the two of them had communion circuits to enable full and direct memory exchanges, so that each could experience and see the other's point of view. The diary was the icon representing this circuit.

She said, "I fear I will be destroyed by your quest for truth. I know you have destroyed others you said you loved. That is part of what you forgot. You are convinced that your forgotten deed was not a crime. And perhaps, in the eyes of the law, it was not. But there are horrible things which people can do, most horrible, which our laws never punish."

She took out a tiny key and unlocked the little lock on the cover. The cover of the diary turned red. Letters blazed: "WARNING This contains a persona matrix. You will loose your sense of self-identity during the experience, which may have long-term effects on your present personality, persona or consciousness. Are you sure you wish to continue? (Remove key to cancel.)"

She slid the diary across the table to him. "I offer this in the hope that you will refuse, and return it unread. If you trust me, believe me: what is in here destroys our dream of marriage. And if you do not trust me, then how dare you claim you love me?"

He took out his own diary, a slim black volume, unlocked it, and tossed it on the table in front of her. It rattled the china tea service as it fell, and lay in a strip of sunlight, bright on the linen, which the gazebo roof shading the table did not cover. A silver spoon was jarred out from the sugar bowl.

The read-date on the cover showed yesterday's date. He was offering to show her, from his point of view, what had occurred to him.

"A marriage based on untruth is a contradiction in terms." And he picked up her diary.

He hesitated, though.

Daphne watched him steadily, unblinking, her face utterly without expression.

At that same moment, however, the butler image of Rhadamanthus came up from behind Phaethon and stepped to the table. In his hand was a silver card tray with a letter, folded, stamped and sealed, atop.

"Pardon me for intruding, sir, ma'am," said Rhadamanthus in an Irish brogue, nodding a slight bow. "But the young master has been summoned."

Phaethon turned. What was this? "Summoned? By the Hortators?"

"No, sir. By the Curia. This is an official legal communication."

Phaethon picked up the letter, broke the seal, read it. There was no warrant of arrest; no mention of a crime; merely a request to present himself to the Probate Court Circuit, to establish his identity beyond question. It was so politely worded that he could not tell if he were asked or being ordered. The only case name appearing on the document was "In the Matter of Helion."

"What is this, Rhadamanthus?"

"You are being asked to give a deposition, sir. Shall I explain the details of the document to you?"

"I'm somewhat busy with other things right now. . . ."

"But you may not access any mnemonic templates or do anything else to change your personality structure until after your identity is established by a Noetic examination."

"Why wasn't I told about this before?"

"No one could serve this summons on you, sir, while you were at masquerade, because no one knew where you were."

"Well. I'll take the call in the morning room. That can be adjusted to look like whatever their aesthetic requires without violating too much of the visual integrity here . . ."

"Sir, you may wish to examine that document in more detail. You are ordered to present yourself in your own person, not by mannequin, partial, or telerepresentation. There can be no signal from any remote source affecting your brain during the examination."

"That's damned inconvenient! Where do I need to go?"

"Longitude fifty-one of the ring-city."

"Then let me take care of this immediately and get it out of the way." And he slipped his wife's diary in his pocket.

Phaethon stepped from dreamspace into his private thoughtspace, and turned, once again, into a disembodied pair of floating gloves. The icon of his wife's diary was still "with him"; the act of putting in his pocket had been a sufficient symbol to accomplish that. Here, of course, it looked much simpler and cruder; just a pastel oblong. When his glove let go of it, it did not fall, but hung, fixed, where he left it, to the left of the square cubes representing engineering programs.

Then he woke up in his coffin in the barren little room.

8

THE SUMMONS

This time Rhadamanthus was still with him when he woke, so the chamber, to his eyes, was suitably furnished and decorated. It looked like a Swiss mountain cabin, perhaps a hunting lodge, with hardwood floors set with bearskin rugs, a fire burning in the grate beneath a mantlepiece bright with trophy cups. A rack of muskets was opposite the window. The wardrobe was now made of tall polished oak, carved with an emblazon of arms. French doors of diamond-shaped lead-crystal panes now led to what was pretty much the same view.

Bowing and offering him a trousers, shirt, and jacket was Rhadamanthus, now appearing as a valet. Phaethon slid the silk sheets aside and stepped out of the four-poster bed.

The ugliness of his thick-skinned body was gone; Phaethon now looked pretty much as he should. When he turned toward the wardrobe, the valet stepped and opened the door for him, with no nonsense about having to speak commands aloud.

There was the golden armor.

"I want to see things as they are," he said.

The comfortable quaint little lodge turned into an ugly dull-colored cube. His senses dulled; his skin grew thick and coarse, like heavy plastic. Only the armor was the same. If anything, it looked better.

"Rhadamanthus, can you figure out how to open this armor again, please?"

Black vertical lines, like streamlines, appeared across the

surface of the armor, and spread wider. The helmet folded. Then the armor was as Phaethon first saw it, black, with side panels of gold, with gold ornaments at collar, shoulder, thigh.

"If I must be hauled before the High Court of the Curia, then let me appear in splendor to awe the world! I will not go unremarked to my fate!"

Rhadamanthus (despite normal Silver-Gray policy) manifested no appearance, but issued a disembodied voice into Phaethon's ear. "Pardon me, sir, if I did not explain. But you are not summoned to the High Court. You are appearing before the Probate Court. I suspect they are gathering, not to fix any penalties on you, but to reward you with a testamentary gift."

Phaethon flung the armor across his shoulders. The black fabric dissolved into flying threads, which swooped around him, wrapping limb and body, pulling the gold adamantium plates and panels into place. The black substance bonded with his skin. Again, he felt a sense of great well-being. The nanomachines in the armor were interpenetrating his flesh, feeding and sustaining his cells more efficiently than the natural mechanisms that normally carried nutrients and fluids to them.

He stood for a moment, exulting in the sense of soaring vivacity the armor sent through his nerves and muscles. Only then did Rhadamanthus's words penetrate to him. "A gift? The Court of Law is going to decide to give me a gift? What kind of nonsense is this? I thought we kept the Curia around just in case people were ever tempted to commit violent crimes again, or cheat on contracts, or break their word. The Triumvir Judges don't give gifts."

"It is a testamentary gift, young master. The Judges also have the power to resolve disputed ownership of the property of the dead."

"Hm. I would have thought archeologists or museum curators have that duty. What has any of this to do with me, except as a distraction to delay my efforts to discover the truth about myself? No matter! I am impatient to have done with this matter. Can we at least get under way?"

The far wall of the barren apartment was made of pseudo-matter. Pseudo-matter was neither matter nor energy as the ancients would have understood those terms but a third manifestation of timespace. The vibrations of ylem superstrings in the stable geometries called "octaves" produced matter-energy quanta; unstable pulses formed temporary virtual particles. An unnatural but perfectly self-consistent topology (and one not invented by the universe within her first three seconds) was the semistable waveform, dubbed the tritone. Pseudo-matter, built up from these tritone semiquanta, could impersonate shape and extension, but only in the presence of a stabilizing energy field. When that energy field was shut off, the location of pseudo-matter became uncertain, and solidity vanished, until the field was reapplied.

The far wall winked out like a popped soap bubble as Phaethon slid through it, and snapped back into reality behind him. Phaethon knew of schools who disapproved of the use of pseudo-matter for aesthetic and metaphysical reasons; he felt a momentary sympathy for them then. Life would be simpler if solid-seeming things could be trusted.

Phaethon found himself staring through a bank of windows at a wide circular space. It rose overhead, dwindling with perspective to the vanishing point. Underfoot was like a well, dropping, as if bottomless, beyond sight. Rail-guides and tractor-friction field generators studded the vertical walls in a jewel-like tiger-striped pattern. The design seemed more biological than mechanical; the geometry of the architecture was fractal, organic, spiral; nothing was Euclidean or linear.

A car with spider arms and crab legs rushed silently up the side of the wall and jerked to a stop in front of Phaethon's windows. The utter silence proved the wide tube was evacuated of air. A protuberance bubbled from the car and swelled up against the windows, opening wide lips. There was no door. The window-substance writhed and opened like so many flower petals, melding and intermingling with the protuberance. Phaethon was now looking into a short, twisted corridor into the interior of the car. It looked like an esophagus. The inside of the car had no clearly defined walls or floor or ceiling. The colorful lining was a made of folds or smooth lumps of tissue, feather soft, without any rigid shapes or hard edges. The polymimetic material was meant to conform to many nonstandard or eccentric body shapes. A shallow crater a dozen paces across occupied the floor of the pool, filled with living-water. Phaethon thought it looked like a stomach.

"What is this place?" asked Phaethon recoiling in disgust.

"This place does not abide by the Consensus Aesthetic."

"I can see that!"

". . . It is from one of the Counter-aesthetic Schools, the Neomorphetics, who are part of the Never-First Movement. They are the most vocal opponents of the traditional social and artistic forms. . . ."

"I know who they are," replied Phaethon testily, "I haven't forgotten everything." The Never-Firsters were recruited from the second generation after the invention of immortality. They opposed whatever the elder generation preferred. The whole movement seemed to be based on the idea that, for some incomprehensible reason, wealth and power should go from the elders (who earned it) and be given to the youth (who had not). Perhaps laws and institutions had been different before the invention of immortality; but such concerns seemed, these days, somewhat moot.

Phaethon said: "Helion calls them the Cacophiles, the lovers of ugliness. I used to argue that there was something hopeful, futuristic, and daring about their work. But, ugh! Maybe Helion was right. That pool has a dubious hue—does that water contain hallucinogens?"

"A soporific to ease the acceleration shock, master, and entertainment chemicals to pass the time during the journey."

"Oh? How long is this journey?"

"From here to Geosychronous Orbit? Three hundred seconds."

"I think I can tolerate the tedium of my own company for five minutes without undue boredom or despair, thank you. In fact, I think I can do without the Cacophiles and their elevator altogether."

For he had discovered a thoughtspace inside the armor. As if a dozen Argus-eyes had opened into his brain, the sense-impressions of the armor flowed into his cortex; the capacities and powers into his memory; the controls into his motor nerves. The armor had a truly astonishing number of control interfaces, servo-minds, and operator hierarchies. All these controls did not seem to be attached to any circuits or channels, however. Whatever machine or system this armor was meant to control must have been one of almost infinite complexity and sophistication.

Phaethon, with the armor, was able to use these control-interfaces to dominate the local thoughtspace. It required less than a second to see and analyze the energy flows within the tube walls, create the proper anchor fields and generators within the armor lining, erect a magnetic force zone around himself, and ride the energy motions along the tube axis upward at several multiples of the speed of sound. Some emergency routine in the window allowed the panels to bubble and snap aside, shutting behind him as he soared upward before any air escaped into the vacuum inside the tube. The black lining of the armor had interpenetrated his every tissue, nerve, and bone, stiffening his body to the consistency of a block of oak. He was easily able to tolerate the nine gravities of acceleration; the armor's internal monitor assured him that, had there been time to complete the tension adjustments within his cells and membranes, he would have been able to withstand ninety.

"Rhadamanthus, I'm not endangering anyone, am I?"

"I would have warned you, young master, had you been."

Phaethon flew on a waft of unseen force to the top of the space elevator. Here was a wide, weightless, roughly spherical space, a mile across. The walls were dotted with docks and portcullises leading to interplanetary ships or to the cylinders and habitats of the ring-city. Phaethon turned his sense-filter to subtext, so that the scene was overlaid with maps and diagrams showing his location and labeling the machineries and energy-arrangements around him.

Phaethon saw evidence of movement inside many of the

machines and conduits leading through the space. He looked into the Middle Dreaming to see the meanings attached to these activities, and understood that the Sophotechs maintaining the environmental integrity of the ring-city were taking precautions against any accidents Phaethon's flying suit might cause. Insurance efforts were tracking the cost of the precautions, which would be charged against his account should any accident occur. A side thought indicated that, since Phaethon's account was bankrupt, the potential lien should be charged to Helion, along with the other pertinent details of the present situation.

Phaethon turned toward Rhadamanthus, who (now that Phaethon's sense-filter was turned back on) manifested an image. Rhadamanthus looked like a penguin dressed in black-and-gold adamantium armor. His helmet was of generally the same Egyptian-looking style as Phaethon's, but with an elongated face mask to cover his beak.

"Rhadamanthus! What is this?!"

The penguin craned his neck and thoughtfully examined his own chubby gold-coated body, even lifting his stubby wings to gravely examine his armpits. "Is something out of order, sir? Silver-Gray protocol does require that I try to blend into the scene, after all."

"And this blends? A penguin in space armor?"

"Well, sir, a penguin could not be levitating here next to you without such armor. Not realistically."

"You don't seem to be taking my troubles very seriously."

"A sense of humor is most useful when dealing with human beings, sir."

"And, apparently, when dealing with Sophotechs, too. You and your brethren are informing Helion of my movements and actions. Is this also a joke?"

"He only has rights to know of those things which concern him, such as, for example, when you are spending his money."

"Even though my amnesia blotted out the fact that it is his money, and not mine, that I'm spending, I suppose?"

"It does not perhaps seem fair, sir, but you did agree to these terms."

"And, apparently, I've agreed to forget that I've agreed. Everyone says this is a golden age. Shouldn't it be run a little more fairly?"

"What does the young master suggest?"

Phaethon swung his leg to counterrotate his body till his head pointed toward with the main motion lock. The internal structure of his armor changed, developing a microscopic system of rail-guns along his back and legs. Particles with very low rest-mass, ejected backward at near the speed of light, grew in mass enough to accelerate him forward. Ray-thin parallel streamers of light hissed backward from his armor, ruby red.

Beyond was the first segment of the ring-city. Unlike the space yard he had just left, this segment was spun for gravity. Phaethon sped along the axis. This cylinder held traditional forms; overhead and underfoot, the distant curving walls were green with forests, blue with lakes.

"Perhaps I should not be bound by obligations I've forgotten."

"But, sir, that would create an incentive for everyone to escape their obligations simply by erasing their memory of them. If you had wanted such an easy-escape clause written into the contract which presently binds you, presumably, you would have written it in."

"And presumably they—whoever they are—would not have agreed."

"That is a safe assumption."

The next three cylinders were neomorphic, filled with strange shapes and convolutions. The next cylinder was walled with oceans of pewter blue, with earthlight shining up through submerged windows. The cylinder beyond the next motion lock turned at a slower rate of spin, and the walls were sculpted with the rust red canyons and dry-ice snows of Mars.

Phaethon asked, "Why couldn't I be prevented from making such a foolish agreement in the first place?"

"You are free to join the Orthomnemonicist School, which permits no memory alterations except antisenility storage, or join the Primitivists, who permit none at all."

"You know what I mean. You Sophotechs are smarter than I am; why did you let me do such a foolish thing?"

"We answer every question our resources and instruction parameters allow; we are more than happy to advise you, when and if we are asked."

"That's not what I'm thinking of, and you know it."

"You are thinking we should use force to defend you against yourself against your will? That is hardly a thought worth thinking, sir. Your life has exactly the value you yourself place on it. It is yours to damage or ruin as you wish."

The next cylinder was filled with the twisted crystal slabs of the Tachystructuralists. The lifestyle of these disembodied people, who had sacrificed their biochemical brains in an attempt to reach Sophotech thinking-speeds and complexities, had long ago been superseded by the Neptunians, whose colder superconductive brain matrices carried thoughts much faster. This region, and these few stubborn miles of crystal, were perhaps the only remainder of the once-prestigious Tachystructural School.

"Is that another hint? Are you saying I'm destroying my life? People at the party, twice now, have said or implied that I'm going to endanger the Oecumene itself. Who stopped me?"

"Not I. While life continues, it cannot be made to be without risk. The assessment of whether or not a certain risk is worth taking depends on subjective value-judgments. About such judgments even reasonable men can differ. We Sophotechs will not interfere with such decisions."

Phaethon flew through two cylinders, which were filled with the heat and stench of old Venus. Here were Hell-born from the Lakshmi or Ishtar Plateau. Phaethon saw their gray-brown beehive-shaped cities, connected by lava dikes, or paths made by the wake of crawling-machines. Only one or two of the burning roads had oblong shapes stalking along them. The Hellish body forms had been rendered obsolete, centuries ago, once the Venereal Terraforming was complete; but the Hell-children, for whatever reason, preferred to keep the forms and shapes they knew.

The next cylinder had walls paved with rank upon rank of dull-colored pyramids, with no sign of life on the barren pavements between. The one after was filled with what looked like herd upon herd of overgrown babies, surrounded on all sides by curving walls of warm, pink flesh, with milk flowing from hundreds of nipples. A third cylinder was bitterly cold, filled with zones of darkness, in which greater darknesses moved and pulsed. Phaethon recognized none of these schools or societies.

Rhadamanthus continued: "If we were to overrule your ownership of your own life, your life, would, in effect, become our property, and you, in effect, would become merely the custodian or trustee of that life. Do you think you would value it more in such a case, or less? And if you valued it less, would you not take greater risks and behave more self-destructively? If, on the other hand, each man's life is his own, he may experiment freely, risking only what is his, till he find his best happiness."

"I see the results of failed experiments all around us, in these cylinders. I see wasted lives, and people trapped in mind sets and life forms which lead nowhere."

"While life continues, experimentation and evolution must also. The pain and risk of failure cannot be eliminated. The most we can do is maximize human freedom, so that no man is forced to pay for another man's mistakes, so that the pain of failure falls only on he who risks it. And you do not know which ways of life lead nowhere. Even we Sophotechs do not know where all paths lead."

"How benevolent of you! We will always be free to be stupid."

"Cherish that freedom, young master; it is basic to all others."

"And what about privacy? Helion is one of them, isn't he? One of those who benefits from my amnesia."

"That is a very sound assumption. I do not think I am

violating any confidences by telling you that Helion must have sent Daphne to come speak with you."

"What? I thought you—this version of you—weren't allowed to know what was going on any more than I am."

"Yes, sir. But I can still make deductions of ordinary logic. Where was Daphne when you left her?"

"In the dream-tank. She was going into one of her games ... wait a moment. I was expecting her to be in simulation for several days. She is not a novice at these games."

"Was she competing for an award?"

"I thought she was."

"And she was in masquerade, so her location was masked. So: who could have found her, who had the authority to interrupt her game, and who could call upon her to do something which he would know she regarded as more important than her competition; but it had to be someone who also knew where you where ... ?"

"Daphne and I are penniless, right? If she enters a game, or if I run a routine, or even send a message, Helion gets billed for it. I assume he can figure out certain details from the billing. And ... Oh! Good Heavens! He even knows when I talk to you, doesn't he?"

"It uses computer time, yes. Helion does not know the content of our conversation, but he knows how much of my mind and time I use."

"And does he know where we're going now? Does he know for what reason the Curia summoned me?"

"I will be surprised if he has not been summoned also."

Phaethon came at last into the central cylinder, the one which had been the original space-yard topping the original elevator. It was smaller than Phaethon expected, only a few miles or so along its axis. Overhead and underfoot, along the curving walls, were the famous gardenworks of Ao Nisibus, dating from the era just before the Fifth Mental Structure, when this place was chosen to be one of the seats of Golden Oecumene administration.

The gardens were laid out in graceful and classical designs. Near the axis, in microgravity, floated balls of lunarian air

bushes and sphere trees, each with an orb of soil at its center.
Vines and lianas, grape and ivy of Martian manufacture inhabited the lesser gravity of the canopy and middle regions.
Below, along the walls, were Terran flora; stands of fruit trees
laid out, rank and file, in rectangles proportional of the golden
mean; or colonnades and trellises; or lily ponds centered on
concentric ranks of colorful blooms, from which paths and
walkways radiated. Some of the plants, extinct on Earth, existed now only here, to maintain this famous garden's natural
state.

Phaethon, searching for the courthouse, looking into the
Middle Dreaming. The symbolic meanings of the floral colors, tree and leaf, shape and placement, came flooding into
his brain. The experience was overwhelming, since the architect had woven multiple overlapping layers of symbolism,
each part reflecting the whole, throughout the entire garden.

It was doubtful whether any brain (before the invention of
sophotechnology) could actually envision and enact a scheme
where each part or group of parts could contain its own
symbol-message while maintaining integrity taken as a whole;
but Ao Nisibus, the designer, certainly made it seem as if he
had. (All the more amazing, since Ao Nisibus had not had a
Cerebelline neuroform.)

The gardens and lawns of the opposite side of the cylinder
shone viridescently in the light of long windows, which, like
canals filled with stars, ran along the walls parallel to the
cylinder's axis. The blue Earth, huge and dazzling, was rising
through windows spinward of him. Sunlight slanted up
through windows in the floor below, striping the gardens opposite with alternating bands of light green and dark green.
Phaethon started to see a pattern in all this. His attention was
absorbed.

Overhead, the Founder's Monument and reflecting pool
formed signs of Masonic import. Rose gardens, for passion,
were hedged about with virtuous lilies; and two walkways,
lined with euphrasy and rue, truth and repentance, came together in a cross (for noble sacrifice); but the actual intersec-
tion was a carriage circle (representing the world). In the

center of the circle was a hillock, shaped like a burial howe, dotted with forget-me-nots. There was a meaning here, a message, a warning, telling Phaethon something about the nature of true memory, ultimate reality, and the universe. . . .

An automatic safety routine in Phaethon's sense-filter had to interrupt him from going into a beauty trance. He blinked and remembered to concentrate on looking for the court house. There: a walkway lined with a balanced number of majestic oaks and somber ash trees led to a glade. On three sides of the glade were boxwood hedges trimmed into complex labyrinths. In the glade, a circle of olive trees guarded a dark, clear pool. The symbolism would not have been more obvious had he seen blindfolded goddesses armed with swords and balance scales.

Phaethon slanted down through the air and landed lightly on the grass. Closer now, he could see the bottom of the pool was transparent crystal; the pool seemed dark only because there was a large unlit chamber buried beneath.

A slab of rock near the pool must have been made of paramatter, for a man dressed in blue-and-silver chameleon cloth slid up through the solid stone and stepped onto the grass. He wore a braided demicape, and a helmet of blue steel. In one white glove he held upright a pike taller than his helmet plumes. Phaethon recognized the man.

"Atkins! A pleasure to see you again. I swear you are the only man in the Golden Oecumene who can wear a getup like that"—Phaethon was looking at his garters and knee socks—"without looking ridiculous."

"Good afternoon, sir." The face was as calm and expressionless as ever; the tone was impersonal, brisk, polite. "I'm Atkins Secundus, his partial."

"Emancipated?"

"No. We're still considered one person. I don't really make that much on soldier's pay, so I've sent out my partial copy here for other work. This one here is the bailiff and master-at-arms of the Court. The rule of posse comitatus prohibits the military from doing police functions, so I have to maintain a separate identity, and have any memories related to military security matters cut out."

Phaethon looked at him with new interest. The two of them might have something in common. "Doesn't it bother you to have holes and gaps in your memory?"

Atkins did not smile, but the lines to either side of his mouth deepened. "Well, sir, that depends. A serviceman has to assume the higher-ups know what they are doing, even when they don't. If they monkeyed with my brain, I'm sure it was for a good reason."

"But what if it wasn't?"

Atkins did not shrug, but a quirk of his eyebrow conveyed the same emotion. "I didn't make the rules. I do whatever it takes. Someone has to. It might be different for civilians." His good humor faded and his tone became, somehow, even more brisk and serious: "But for the moment, I'm going to have to ask you to disable your armor circuits. No weapons allowed in the courthouse."

Phaethon had to get Rhadamanthus to find and insert the meaning of the word "weapon" into his brain. Phaethon was amazed and disgusted. "You have got to be kidding! You don't actually think that I am capable of—"

Atkins gave Phaethon a thoughtful, disinterested look. "It's none of my business what you are capable of, sir. I just enforce the rules."

But Phaethon saw the calculating, professional look in Atkins's eye. Perhaps it was a look of distrust. Perhaps Atkins was taking the measure of a potential enemy. The stare was offensive.

Rhadamanthus poked Phaethon on the knee with his beak, and whispered: "Hsst! It's an old tradition. No one goes armed into Court."

"Well, I cannot counter tradition," muttered Phaethon. He doffed his helmet and let Atkins insert a disabling probe into the black suit layer. Thought-group after thought-group of the armor-mind went dark; anything even remotely capable of energy manipulation was locked, even simple action-reflex routines. Phaethon swallowed his pride; he did not know if he had a right to be offended.

Because, whatever Phaethon had done in the past, Atkins knew it and Phaethon did not.

Phaethon asked him.

Atkins squinted. "Sir, I'm not sure it's my place to say. I'm on duty right now. The bailiff of the Curia isn't supposed to be the one to help you break a legal contract, even if it is a stupid one. Why not just let the matter rest?"

9

THE CURIA

1.

The two of them stepped onto the rock surface. The rock let Phaethon ooze through only slowly and reluctantly, as microscopic and molecule-sized organizations hidden in the para-matter passed through his flesh and armor, probing for secret weapons. The Crysadmantium supermetal defeated the probe attempts; the organizations had to flow in and out through Phaethon's neckpiece to scrub the interior. It was not uncomfortable, but it was undignified.

Below were stairs, leading down. The aesthetic protocol was apparently different outside than in. Atkins's quaint costume was replaced. There was no heat when Atkins's uniform changed shape; perhaps it was pseudo-matter, not nanomachinery. During the moment of transition, Phaethon saw what the soldier was really wearing beneath; a trim jacket set with many vertical pockets holding discharge cartridges, responders, and preassembled nanoweapons.

And he had a knife and a katana hanging from his belt. Phaethon could not help but wonder at the man's anachronisms. What sort of fellow was so hypnotized by tradition that he still carried sharp pieces of metal meant for poking and lacerating other men?

The transformation took an eye-blink. Atkins now wore a stiff-collared poncho of stark white, and his pike shrank to a baton from some period of military history Phaethon did not recognize. But he guessed the pale cloak was from the Objective Aesthetic, which dated from the late Fifth Era, long before the Consensus Aesthetic.

In that era, back before Sophotech translation routines existed, the differences in neuroforms made it difficult for the basics, Warlocks, Cerebellines, and Invariants, to understand each other's thought and speech. It had been impossible to understand each other's art. Consequently, the so-called Objective Aesthetic was heavily geometrical, nonrepresentational, highly stylized; more like an iconography than an artform. Phaethon did not find it attractive.

At the bottom of the stairs was an antechamber. Here stood another man. It took Phaethon a moment to recognize him in the gloom. "Gannis! Is that you, or one of you?"

He turned. It was indeed Gannis of the Jupiter Effort, but wearing a formal costume and wide headdress of Fifth-Era Europa. A heavy semicylindrical cloak, like the wing casings of a beetle, hung from wide shoulderboards. From those shoulders came a cluster of tassels or tentacles, carrying various thought boxes, note pages and interfacers. Multiple arms had always been a European fashion.

"A pleasure to see you, Phaethon!" There was something blank and stiff in his eye movements. Phaethon realized Gannis was using a face-expression program. He obviously had recognized Phaethon's armor.

Gannis was one of Them.

Phaethon thought to himself: *Good grief! Is there anyone in the Golden Oecumene who does not remember what I did except for me?*

The financial records had shown many trips to Jovian space. Phaethon also felt a sense of familiarity, of comfort, as if he and Gannis were old friends or business partners.

Like a flash of intuition, certainty entered Phaethon's mind. Whatever it was Phaethon had done, Gannis had done it also. Or, at least, had helped.

"You are here to face the Curia also?" asked Phaethon politely.

"Face? I'm not sure what you mean. My group-mind is representing Helion."

"You are his lawyer?" Why in the world would Gannis be helping Helion? Phaethon had been under the impression that the two men were business rivals, and did not really like each other. Certainly the Synnoetic School, with its direct mind-machine interfaces, its groupings and mass-minds, disagreed with the proindividualist traditions of the manorial schools, and yet competed for the same patronage, the same niche in the socioeconomy.

Gannis made an easy gesture. "Perhaps the Hundred-mind of Jupiter thinks it would be a miscarriage of justice to allow your claim to prevail. You've obviously already broken your word about the memorial agreements we all made at Lakshmi; none of the Peerage wants to have to do business with a man who cannot be trusted."

Lakshmi was on Venus. What had Phaethon been doing on Venus? He assumed that the amnesia agreement was made just before the Masquerade's opening ceremonies in January. Phaethon consulted an almanac routine. Venus had been in triune with Earth at that time, a good position to be used as a gravity sling for any ships bound between Earth, Mars, Demeter, or the Solar Array. Mercury had been in a nonadvantageous orbital position, on the far side of the sun. A footnote in the almanac indicated communications had been disrupted all across the inner system because of solar storms.

It was the time of the disaster at the Solar Array.

Phaethon eyed Gannis speculatively. The man had a suspicious air to him. And suspicious people had the habit of treating hypotheses as if they were certainties. They could be bluffed.

"Am I to be trusted less than . . . shall we say . . . others . . . ?" said Phaethon, nodding ponderously. He favored Gannis with a knowing look.

"Are you saying Helion cannot be trusted with his own wealth? Or that your claim to it is better than his?"

Claim? What claim? Phaethon had no idea whatsoever what Gannis was talking about. Nonetheless, he spread his hands and smiled smugly. "My meaning is self-evident. Draw from it what conclusions you will."

Gannis became red-faced with anger. Evidently his expression-program had failed, or he was deliberately showing his wrath. "You blame the solar disaster on Helion?! That is grotesque ingratitude, sir, simply grotesque! Considering the sacrifice that version of him made for you! You are a cad, sir! You are a simple, unspotted, pure and perfect cad! Besides, my client disavows everything that happened on the Solar Array! He was not even there!"

"Not there? I thought your client was Helion . . . ?"

Gannis head jerked back an inch, as if he had been stung. Phaethon saw realization cross Gannis's features, a second before the expression-program snapped back into place. Gannis realized Phaethon had been fooling him.

Suddenly bland and polite, Gannis said, "I'm sure the Curia will tell you what you have a right to know."

"I know that you have broken the Lakshmi agreement and that I have not."

Gannis turned his back to Phaethon.

Atkins had been watching all this with that cheek-tension that served him for a smile, and a twinkle of amusement in the cool of his eyes. He now nodded at Phaethon, and said, "Well, gentlemen! Shall we go in?" and he opened the tall antechamber doors with a gesture of his baton.

The Chamber of the Curia was austere. As Phaethon had guessed, it was done in the spartan style of the Objective Aesthetic.

Unadorned square silver pillars held up a black dome. In the center of the dome, at the highest point of the ceiling, a wide lens of crystal supported the pool overhead. Light from the world above fell through the water to form trembling nets and webs across the floor. The floor itself was inscribed with a mosaic in the data-pattern mode, representing the entire body of the Curia case law. At the center, small icons representing constitutional principles sent out lines to each case in which they were quoted; bright lines for controlling precedent, dim lines for dissenting opinions or dicta. Each case quoted in a later case sent out additional lines, till the concentric circles of floor-icons were meshed in a complex network.

The jest of the architect was clear to Phaethon. The floor mosaic was meant to represent the fixed immutability of the law; but the play of light from the pool above made it seem to ripple and sway and change with each little breeze.

Above the floor, not touching it, without sound or motion, hovered three massive cubes of black material.

These cubes were the manifestations of the Judges. The cube shape symbolized the solidity and implacable majesty of the law. Their high position showed they were above emotionalism or earthly appeals. The crown of each cube bore a thick-armed double helix of heavy gold.

The gold spirals atop the black cubes were symbols of life, motion, and energy. Perhaps they represented the active intellects of the Curia. Or perhaps they represented that life and civilization rested on the solid foundations of the law. If so, this was another jest of the architect. The law, it seemed, rested on nothing. Phaethon remembered that Ao Nisibus had been a Warlock, after all.

"Oyez, oyez!" cried Atkins, rapping the heel of his baton against the floor with a crack of noise. "All persons having business with the Honorable Appellate Court of the Foederal Oecumenical Commonwealth in the matter of the estate of Helion Prime Rhadamanthus draw nigh! Order is established, Your Lordships, the seals are placed, the recordings proceed."

A sense of impalpable pressure, a tension in the air, an undefined sensation of being scrutinized: these were the only clues to Phaethon that the cubes were now occupied by the intelligence of the Curia.

Once, long ago, these had been men. Now, recorded into an electrophotonic matrix, they were without passion or favoritism, and their most secret thoughts were open to review and scrutiny should any charge of unfairness or prejudice ever be brought against them.

The Never-First Schools always urged that the Judges should change from election to election and poll to poll, as did the members of the Parliament. The more traditional schools, however, always argued that, in order for law to be fair, reasonable men must be able to predict how it will be enforced, so as to be able to know what is and is not legal. Having sat on the bench for 7,400 years, the minds of the Curia were, like the approach of glaciers, like the ponderous motions of the outer planets, very predictable indeed.

A voice radiated from the central cube: "The Court is now in session. We note that the counselor for the purported beneficiary has chosen to manifest itself as an armored penguin. We remind the counselor of the penalties attaching to contempt of Court. Does the counselor require a recess or any extra channels to array itself more presentably?"

"No, Your Lordship." The image of Rhadamanthus faded, and, fitting in to the prevailing aesthetic, the penguin turned into a large green cone.

Phaethon eyed the cone dubiously. "Oh, much better . . ." he muttered.

"Order in the Court!" radiated the cube on the left.

Phaethon straightened uncomfortably. He had never been in a Court of Law before; he did not know of anybody who had, except in historic dramas. Almost all such disputes were settled by Hortators finding compromises, or by Sophotechs deducing solutions to such problems before they arose. Was Phaethon supposed to take this quaint old-fashioned ceremony seriously? As ceremonies went, it was not the most impressive. It was not even accompanied by any music or psychostimulants.

Phaethon saw how Atkins, the bailiff, stood in a relaxed and watchful posture, hand still on the baton-weapon. Atkins was, perhaps, the only man in all of the Golden Oecumene who was armed. The idea of a Court of Law, the idea that men must be compelled by the threat of force to abide by civilized rules, might be a hideous anachronism in this enlightened day and age. But Atkins still took it seriously.

And perhaps it was serious. Very serious. The future of Phaethon's life was about to be decided for him, decided by forces beyond his control.

"Rhadamanthus," Phaethon whispered. "Do something."

The green cone slid forward and spoke: "Your Lordships, I do have a preliminary motion."

The middle cube: "We will entertain to hear your motion, Counselor."

"The beneficiary—"

"Alleged beneficiary!" snapped Gannis.

"—finds he is taken by surprise and is unprepared. However, he would face civil penalties in another suit if he should break his word and avail himself of the memories redacted under the Lakshmi agreement. But were this Honorable Court to order discovery of that evidence, my client would be able to avail himself of those memories, would be prepared to face this tribunal, and yet would not face civil penalties for breach of contract."

Gannis said, "How would he not face penalty? If he regains his memories, he is in violation!"

The green cone replied: "My learned colleague is mistaken. Phaethon is in violation if and only if he deliberately opens the forbidden memory files himself. If a Court order compels him to open those files, there is no deliberate act on his part—"

The cube on the left interrupted: "This is not a debating society. The counselors will address their remarks to the bench."

Gannis turned toward the black cubes: "Your Lordships, may I present argument for denying the Respondent's motion?"

The central cube radiated: "The Court will entertain your remarks."

"The motion is without grounds at this stage of the proceedings. The only question presently before the Court is the identity of the Respondent, who claims to be Phaethon Prime Rhadamanthus. And, even were this the proper time to raise that issue, the proper relief for a complaint of surprise would be to grant the Respondent more time to prepare. Naturally my client would raise no opposition to any additional postponements the Court may deem necessary for a fully equitable result."

The cube on the right spoke in a voice heavy with irony: "Considering the history of this case, the Court is not surprised that the learned counselor raises no opposition to additional postponements. Nonetheless, the argument is well taken. The matter of Phaethon's memory, except insofar as it touches and concerns the question of his identity, is not a question presently before the Court. The Respondent's motion is denied."

Phaethon whispered: "What the hell is going on here, Rhadamanthus? Who is this 'Respondent'? Me? What are they here to decide . . . ?"

The cube on the left exclaimed: "We must have order in the Court! What is all this whispering and commotion? The traditional forms and practices of law must be observed!"

The green cone brightened slightly: "But, Your Lordships, tradition is just what is not being observed here. Tradition requires that equity, as well as law, determine the outcome of Your Lordships' actions. Surely my client cannot be without remedy, as his memory loss hinders his and my ability to protect his interests with full and zealous effort! I am ready to download a précis of the 66,505 cases on the point of defendants suffering from memory redaction, and their rights and obligations under the law."

A certain section of the floor mosaic flowed with light, as strands of interlocking case law were reviewed. Rhadamanthus continued: "In all such cases the Court took steps to ensure that an equitable result was reached."

"The point is well taken. This Court will inform the Respondent of any pertinent details which bear on this case. In so doing, the Court does not indemnify the Respondent from further and future civil actions for breach of contract; the determinations of whatever Court shall sit on that issue are beyond our authority."

Gannis was scowling. The green cone seemed to wiggle smugly. Phaethon was convinced that, deep down, those motions were still somehow penguinlike.

Phaethon said, "Your Lordships, how is this going to work? Am I suppose to ask you questions which Your Lordships will answer, or will the memories be made available to me in an edited form, or how?"

The central cube said: "Submit your motion in the proper form, and we shall answer."

Phaethon nudged the side of the green cone with his foot, and hissed: "Quick, what is the proper form . . . ?"

Gannis stepped forward and spoke up: "Your Lordships! I have another motion which I ask to make at this time. I submit that the Respondent's attorney has no standing to appear before this Court. The Rhadamanthus Law-mind is a property of my client, Helion, who must use that same database for his legal matters. This creates a clear conflict of interest. Rhadamanthus cannot serve on both sides of the same case."

The green cone said: "Your Lordships, I have built a 'Chinese Wall' to block off those sections of my mind and memory to prevent any such impropriety . . ."

Gannis was not finished: ". . . and I further object that Rhadamanthus is himself the res of the case, as the contract controlling his ownership is a real and valuable property of the estate. Even assuming, arguendo, that Phaethon shall be the heir, since we all know what he plans to do with the money (should he prevail), and since we all know he is not going to be around for long, I submit that my client nonetheless has a contingent remainder interest in the estate, and the Respondent must be estopped from employing Rhadamanthus under the doctrine of waste!"

Phaethon said impatiently: "Your Lordships! Can't we have this ceremony take place in some language I understand?!"

"Order. The penalties for contempt of Court may include any punishment the Court deems fit, provided they are not cruel and unusual."

"But I do not understand what is going on!"

"It is not the business of this Court to educate you. Rhadamanthus, have you any argument to make as to why we should not grant the claimant's motion . . . ? If not, we sustain the objection. The bailiff will take Rhadamanthus off-line."

And, just like that, Rhadamanthus was gone. Phaethon stood by himself on the dark floor.

Gannis smiled with wide self-satisfaction.

2.

Phaethon was as alone as he had been in the grim little room where he had found his armor. No sense-filter was operating; there were no aids nor augments running in his memory. And while, theoretically, Silver-Gray protocol forbade the use of emotion-control programs, Phaethon tended to use some small glandular and parasympathetic regulators. But now, with that support gone, it was almost like being drunk. Despair and frustration raged within his brain, and he had no automatic way to turn those emotions off.

Phaethon took a deep breath, fighting for calmness. Everyone in the ancient world used to control themselves naturally, organically, without any cybernetic assistance. If they could do it, he could do it!

The middle cube radiated: "The Court will now proceed to the examination. Does the Respondent wish to modify or amend any prior pleadings to this Court?"

"Are you speaking to me?" asked Phaethon, trying to keep the exasperation out of his voice. "If you want to ask me something, you're going to have to explain what's going on!"

The cube on the left said: "You will maintain order and decorum, or suffer penalty."

Gannis smiled like a shark, and said: "Perhaps the Respondent wishes to request more time to earn another fortune and hire another lawyer. We would not oppose a motion for a postponement."

A moment of blinding anger stabbed through Phaethon, surprising him.

(And on the other hand, Phaethon reminded himself, the ancient world had been turbulent with war and crime and insanity, not once or twice but at all times. Maybe this self-control stuff was more difficult than it seemed.)

Phaethon said to Gannis: "There will be no postponements."

He turned toward the Curia. "I meant no disrespect to Your
Lordships. But you have deprived me of the attorney I was
using to instruct me in your proper forms and rituals. You
have agreed to tell me those things missing from my memory
which I need to know to proceed in this case; yet you have
not done so. Is this the fairness and justice for which the Curia
is famous? I remind Your Lordships that what we do here
today will be remembered not just for a century or a millennium but for all the rest of our lives. We, none of us, had
better do anything for which the future will upbraid us."

Gannis's smile faded as his face-program hid his expression once again.

The cube on the right said: "Well said. We will inform you
of the facts of the case. The matter is simple. You stand to—"
(he used a word Phaethon did not know, some archaic legal
expression) "—a very great deal of property and money, perhaps the largest estate ever passed along in human history.
The result may change the social and economic relationships
within the Golden Oecumene in a revolutionary fashion. Consequently, despite that these are rather routine matters, we
seek to avoid even the appearance of irregularity. Therefore,
the Curia exercises its right to invoke special jurisdiction, and
we sit as a Probate Court, in order to oversee the deposition
and examination to determine your identity. This present
hearing is to give you the opportunity to submit to a routine
Noetic examination, and swear, under telepathic oath, that
you are Phaethon Prime Rhadamanth. Do you have any questions?"

"Yes. Who is giving me this fabulous fortune and why? If
he wishes to give me this gift, why doesn't this generous
person, whoever it is, simply step forward and give it?"

"He is dead."

Gannis said, "Objection! The Court's statement is preju-
dicial. The finality of the death of the deceased is one of the
facts at issue in this case!"

The cube on the left said: "Overruled. We make no ruling."

The cube on the right said: "The death of the deceased is a matter of rebuttable presumption under these facts. He is dead until proven otherwise."

Phaethon said: "Your Lordships, was this man some historical figure, some Egyptian pharaoh or American president? I know that people like that from time to time established trust funds as a gift to be paid to the first person to do some great feat, fly a man-powered aircraft across the Atlantic, or something. But if this is the case, why are we in a Court of Law? Wouldn't an archeologist or paleopsychologist be the best person to determine the original intent of this dead man?"

"The death was recent."

Phaethon's mind was momentarily blank. Recent? "Was it someone too poor to afford Noumenal Recording, or a primitivist who objected on metaphysical grounds to—"

"Your sire, Helion, who created you, is the deceased."

For a moment, Phaethon believed it. For a moment, he could perfectly imagine the emptiness his life would hold if his sire were gone. Gone forever. He did not like his sire; often they argued. But there was nonetheless a bond and a love between them, like father and son, and a long history of engineering projects on which they both worked together. To picture the Rhadamanth Mansion, or even the Golden Oecumene, without the bright, brave figure of Helion as one of the society's foremost leaders; it was impossible. It was like imagining the world where the sun did not come up. A sense of desolation crept across Phaethon's flesh, and sank into his heart.

But then, in the next moment, Phaethon smiled. "Oh, come now, Your Lordships! I saw Helion not two days ago. He was at the Ovations for the Silver-Gray; I saw him accept the award. We spoke before he went to Lemke's operetta. You know the one, the clever way each auditor gets the memories of each of the characters not in order, so that they each see the same ending in nine different interpretations? It's just the kind of funny old-fashioned thing he likes. And . . . and just this morning, Helion was on the by-channels. The Six Peers sent a contingent to honor him. I suppose it's Seven Peers now. A Peerage! He has been working for that goal longer than I've been alive. That was this morning! You're not going to take that away from him by pretending that he is dead! He is not dead! No one dies anymore! No one ever needs to die!"

Phaethon's voice had grown louder and shriller. But then, abruptly, he closed his mouth, and the muscles in his cheeks were clenched.

There was a moment of silence in the chambers. None of the Curia upbraided him for his outburst. Gannis had turned his head away. Atkins's grim demeanor did not change, even when a look of sympathy or pity softened his eyes.

Phaethon stared at the floor, emotions boiling. He saw the tangled webs of law in the mosaic underfoot. Laws meant to protect the innocent. But even now, even in this day and age, there were things nothing could ward off.

Phaethon said, "It was the solar disaster, wasn't it?"

The Court said: "The brief for the Respondent states, it is not contested, that when Helion beamed his brain information out from his body on the Solar Array to the Mercury Polar Station, the solar storms garbled the signal. Only part of his mind was recovered, enough to form a partial diary of those last events, but not enough to reconstruct his personality intact. The man whom you call Helion is actually a relic of Helion, who was recorded one hour before, as an automatic backup, when the storms first erupted from the core. The question before the Court is whether the relic has sufficient similarity to the prime version to form continuity of identity, and therefore to be considered the 'same' individual in the eyes of the law."

"So the only difference between the two versions is an hour? That's ridiculous! The Helion who is alive now, the Helion Relic, must be indistinguishable from the original, Helion Prime!"

Gannis said in a brash voice: "I would like the Curia to note that the opposing party admits and stipulates the continuity of identity between my client and Helion Prime."

The central cube radiated: "Phaethon is not under oath nor

is he qualified to have such an opinion. We disregard the comment."

Phaethon looked back and forth between the Curia and Gannis, puzzled. "But what in the world is my claim to Helion's fortune? Surely it is well established in the law that when a man's body dies, his Noumenal Recording wakes up and takes over from where he left off."

Gannis said, "I would like the Court to note that the opposing party has just stipulated that he agrees with my client's theory of the case!"

"Phaethon was asking a question relating to his previous pleadings in this case which he does not recall. He is not under oath and is not testifying. We disregard the comment, and we require that you not waste the Court's time with frivolous motions, Counselor. Is that clear?"

Gannis muttered: "Abundantly clear, Your Lordships . . ."

The central cube said to Phaethon: "In the earlier times, when the science of Noumenal Recording was not as developed as it now is, recordings were more expensive and were made less often."

The left cube said: "The seminal case of *Kaino v. Sheshession* announced the standard. In that case, the defendant fell in love and was married for several years since his last Noumenal Recording, when he perished in a space-accident. When his relic woke from recording, the plaintiff requested that he take up the matrimonial obligations of his prior, and undergo emotional restructure to instill the missing passions into him. The standard announced was that if a reasonable Sophotech could not anticipate, based on deep-structure analysis of the prior, what the relic would do, then the relic was considered to have a different personality and be a separate individual. The changes must be basic and central to the philosophy, thought style, and core values of the personality, and not merely frivolous or surface changes."

The right cube said: "This holding was modified in *Ao Xelepec Prime v. Kes Xelepec Secundus*. In that case, a Neptunian Warlock made a Noumenal Recording, but then gave himself the brain structure of an Invariant. He then redacted a major section of his memory, woke the Warlock neuroform, and claimed that the Warlock relic was the real version of himself, and that he was no longer responsible for carrying out certain contracts and obligations he had previously made. His contention was denied, but the Noumenal Recording was emancipated as a separate and independent individual. The rule is that, if the change in personality since the last recording is so great that the relic no longer understands the thoughts or the motivations of the prior, then the relic is a separate individual in the eyes of the law. If, however, the change is within the range of what the relic might predictably undergo himself, continuity of individuality is presumed."

Phaethon said, "So, during that hour, the Helion who stayed behind on the station did something which the Helion here on Earth now cannot understand or appreciate?"

"That is the claim you have put before this Court. You claim that, during that hour of emergency, Helion underwent a major epiphany or permanent change in personality. You have claimed that he is not the same man."

"But how would I, in any case, claim to own Helion's property and estate?"

"There are even older laws, laws dated from the time when death was a commonplace occurrence. Under these laws, if a man dies without a properly executed last will and testament, his estate passes to his heirs. Helion Prime held the copyright on your gene sequence, and major sections of your personality and mind were constructed out of templates of his personality. The ancient law would regard you as his son, and therefore as his heir. Those laws have never been revoked; they still have force and effect."

Only at this point did Phaethon begin to realize the amount of wealth and property at stake. Helion owned the Solar Array. It was perhaps the single greatest engineering effort ever undertaken. Every person who benefited from the extension of the useful lifespan of the sun, or whose electronic or electromagnetic properties were saved from sunspot or solar flare damage, would owe Helion a debt of gratitude. And that included everyone in the entire Golden Oecumene. If everyone saved a few seconds or minutes of time-currency from their insurance premiums because of Helion's actions, that money saved was owed to him. Spread over the billions who lived in the solar system, those few seconds per person equaled not just years but decades of computer time.

It would be perhaps more wealth than anyone (except Orpheus Myriad Avernus) had ever controlled.

Phaethon said, "I will submit to the examination."

"It is done. We hold the mental records open on our private channel for inspection by the Court. Do the counselors have any closing arguments to make before we rule on the legal sufficiency of Phaethon's identity?"

"Certainly!" said Gannis with some relish. "We notice the wide difference in behavior between Phaethon before and after the Lakshmi memory redactions. The way he lives and acts now is nothing like the way he lived and acted before. He goes to frivolous parties; he pursues no dangerous or socially unacceptable hobbies. Your Lordships! Observe how much time the old Phaethon spent on his one obsession! Years and centuries! He is different now. He is hardly the same person. Because (and here is the telling point) Your Lordships, the society of the Golden Oecumene would not accept him if they thought him the same as he was. He does not consider himself to be the same person."

Phaethon said: "I am the same person."

"Oh?" said Gannis. "And how do you know?"

Phaethon could think of no answer.

The central cube said: "Phaethon is not on cross-examination. You are making closing arguments. Address your remarks to the bench."

Gannis said, "Your Lordships, we are eager to hear Phaethon answer to an important question which may be dispositive of this case. Does he consider himself to be the same person who created such furor and terror throughout the Golden Oecumene? If he is that person, is he willing to face the penalties for his actions? Those penalties include that he be expelled and ostracized. Your Lordships! I submit that as a matter of public policy the wealth of Helion should not go to serve Phaethon's mad schemes; that the wealth would be wasted; that Phaethon—if he is the real prime Phaethon—will come to a messy and lonely death. And if he is not the prime Phaethon, the money is not his. I ask Your Lordships to require Phaethon's testimony on this matter! Surely his opinion is crucial; surely he cannot be considered the prime Phaethon if he does not think he is!"

Phaethon turned to Gannis: "This is ridiculous. I am who I am."

Gannis said: "I beg the Court's indulgence. May I have a word aside with Phaethon? We may be able to negotiate a settlement."

The Curia signaled its assent. The impalpable sense of pressure and tension issuing from the cubes vanished, as if they slept, or turned their minds to distant things.

Gannis stepped closer to Phaethon and spoke in a soft voice: "It is ridiculous indeed! You are all set to use the law to steal Helion's money. You know Helion is still Helion; one hour of lost memory does not make such a difference. Come now! Put the past behind you; forget this foolish lawsuit you have begun! You don't even recall why you started it. And even if the Curia sustains your claim, public opinion will condemn you. Now is your last chance for a normal and happy life. Think! Do you really think Helion is dead? Do you really think your friends and family will not hate you if you proceed with this farce?! Now is your last chance to back out with grace."

Gannis stepped closer, put his hand on Phaethon's shoulder: "Come! Though you do not now recall it, we were friends and partners once. I built that armor you are wearing. I do not seek your ill; I oppose you for your own good. Yes, your good! You have forgotten where your own best interests lie. This Court may or may not rule in your favor. If it rules against you, then you are Phaethon Relic, and your life continues in its present happy state. If it rules for you, then, in the eyes of the law, you are the same man who created such havoc in our paradise; this may trigger our rights, under the Lakshmi agreement, to exile and ostracize you. Is that what you really want? Think carefully, Phaethon. Because, if you think, you will realize that you do not truly know what you really want, eh?"

Was Gannis correct? Phaethon truly did not know and did not remember why he was doing any of this.

But Phaethon recalled how the Earthmind herself asked him to be true to himself. Perhaps he did not know what she meant. But if he—his past and forgotten self—had started this law case, it was not Phaethon's place to end it. If only Rhadamanthus were here to advise him!

Phaethon turned toward the Court. "Your Lordships!"

A sense of austere awareness, like a subtle pressure in the air, radiated from the cubes. "Speak."

"I demand my lawyer be present."

"Rhadamanthus cannot represent you in this matter."

"My lawyer is Monomarchos of the Westmind Law-division."

"Ah, yes. Wait a moment while we open more channels and make arrangements: Monomarchos has a very high intellectual capacity, and we must reconfigure to permit that much active thought-space to enter this area."

Part of the wall behind Phaethon shimmered with heat. Nanomachines were constructing something with blinding speed. A silver cube, less than a yard across, slid out from the wall, glowing white hot. Phaethon's armor protected him; Gannis had to step backward, his elbow up before his face.

A new voice spoke: "I am here."

THE VERDICT

1.

The white-hot cube spoke: "Phaethon, you may be unaware that you have already spent all ten thousand hours of computer time which you paid into my account. The accumulated interest on the time account has produced another forty-five seconds of thought time, which I am obligated to devote to your affairs; thereafter I shall be a free agent, and will take no further contracts from you. I have already deduced a method of allowing you to prevail, but I will use a different method, and achieve a different result, depending on whether you wish merely to prevail on this case, or to achieve those goals which the older version of you, the version whom you forget, the version who actually made me, preferred. Choose. You have thirty seconds left."

Phaethon did not hesitate. "His goals. I want to achieve the dream they forced me to forget."

"Gannis! My client is prepared to allow this matter to be postponed for the space of ninety days, but only on two conditions. First, you personally must agree that the debts my client owes your metallurgical effort are forgiven; you are no longer one of his creditors. Second, you must stipulate that your client presently is the relic and not the second of Helion, and does not presently share continuity of memory with the Helion who died at the Solar Array. In return we shall stipulate that my client, Phaethon Prime, is the relic of the Phaethon who agreed to the Lakshmi Agreement. The offer shall only be open for fifteen seconds."

Gannis said, "What if—"

"Gannis! The Hundred-mind of which you are a member can predict the outcomes of Curia determinations as well as I. You know your case is lost without that postponement. Ten seconds."

Gannis's face took on the cold and distant look that a Synnoet communing with his overmind might bear. The real Gannis, the hundredfold mind that oversaw the many separate bodies and partial personalities of the Gannis-group had stepped in to speak directly. "We will agree if your client will sign a confession of judgment to any violation of the Lakshmi Agreement."

"Agreed. Six seconds."

"Then we agree."

Phaethon spoke at the same time: "Wait, Monomarchos! Haven't you just lost the case for me?"

"Quiet. Your Lordships, I present that I carry a power of attorney for Phaethon Prime Rhadamanth, and that, as such, I hereby deliver his last will and testament, devised by him, and tendered to me to deliver in the event he was declared legally dead. The will names my present client, Phaethon Relic, as heir to his estate, to all property and personality, perquisites, assists and aids; but we expressly do not assume the debts of the deceased Phaethon."

Gannis shouted "Hold it! Wait!"

The Curia said, "The last will and testament of Phaethon Prime has been duly recorded."

"Monomarchos!" said Phaethon, "What is going on?!"

The burning cube ignored him: "We further ask this Court to extend recognition of the continuity of marriage from that version to this. I stipulate on behalf of both versions of my clients that both agree."

"The Court does not view such a requirement as necessary. A stipulation made as part of a negotiation is not recognized as a finding of fact. And now, if there are no further issues or objections, the Court will declare a recess till Helion's deposition, and adjourn."

"Wait!" said Gannis. "I have objections! I have a lot of objections!"

The burning cube said: "Phaethon, if you refrain from opening the casket of memory for the space of ninety days, everything your old self desired will come to pass."

"Explain!"

"As of this moment, sir, I am no longer in your employ or under your orders. I need explain nothing. The case has been settled."

"Would you be willing just to tell me, one gentleman to another, what—"

"No, sir. I do not wish to spend another second speaking to or listening to you. Except to say this: It is often said we live in a paradise. That is a gross exaggeration. We live in an age of great liberty, beauty, comfort, and wealth. But there are injustices and imperfections with the system which cannot be cured. One injustice is that reckless men, such as yourself, can put the whole society at risk, but that our laws are so jealous of your rights, that no man can use any force to stop you until and unless the danger is manifest. Another injustice is that minds like mine must carry out the strict letter of our duty, even if our duties require us to serve men whom we detest. My duty to you is complete; your victory is assured. It is a duty I relinquish with great pleasure."

Phaethon's jaw was clenched; his hands, at his sides, were balled into fists. "Sir, I am sorry if I have displeased you. Since I do not recall the acts of mine which so dismay you, I cannot tell if your gross rudeness to me is justified or not. But, whatever the case, I still thank you for your service to me, if, once I understand it, it turns out to have been of service."

The silver cube had now cooled, and was growing dim. "I ask the Curia to excuse me from further duties owing to this client. I have received an offer from a temporary overmind composition of Westmind associates to enter their deep meditation to explore fundamental questions of abstract mathematics for the next two hundred years without external distraction. I was forced to leave those important contemplations to return and finish these minor duties here; this time away from that significant work may have crippled the expedition's ability to succeed. Your Lordships; the case is settled; any other attorney program of ordinary skill can explain to my client the further details and ramifications of these transactions. May I be excused from his service?"

"You are excused for now, but may be recalled to attend the deposition of Helion ninety days hence. And may we say, the brethren of the Curia are most pleased and amused at the skillfulness with which you have resolved this issue."

"What issue?! Resolved how?" said Phaethon loudly, stepping toward the floating cubes. "Someone owes me an explanation!"

The black cube on the left said: "But there you are mistaken, Phaethon. Our society is built on the paramount value of human freedom, which means that no one owes any debts to any others except those which he voluntarily assumes. Gannis, did you wish to raise any objections at this time?"

Gannis was staring thoughtfully at Phaethon. "If I may reserve my objections, without prejudice, for a later time, I shall do so, Your Lordships. The Court may have been amused by Monomarchos's little antics, but I am not. He is betting that Helion will not be able to prove his identity when he comes before this court three months hence. Whereas I agreed to these terms only because I am certain Helion Relic shall be indistinguishable from Helion Prime in far less than three months. Whatever happened to him during that last hour of his life, it will have no effect on the ultimate decision of this case. Furthermore, I do not believe Phaethon will have the self-control not to open the memory casket until after that date. He has always been a reckless fellow."

Phaethon had been rather put out by Monomarchos's hostility. So it was with a touch of malice that he impersonated Gannis's tone of voice, and said, "I would like Your Lordships to note that my learned opposition has just expressed the belief that I am one and the same with the original Phaethon."

The central cube said, "He is not testifying, nor is his opinion dispositive in this case. We are now in recess."

The cubes ceased to radiate their sense of brooding pressure. Phaethon turned to say some further word to Monomarchos, but the silver cube had turned entirely dark and cold, and was beginning to disintegrate its substance back into the wall.

Phaethon turned to Gannis, but he had already stalked away, the tentacles and tassels from his baroque costume twitching irritably.

He turned to Atkins. "Did you understand what's going on?"

Atkins spread his hands. "I'm just the bailiff, sir. I'm not supposed to give legal advice. Here, let me turn your armor back on."

Atkins inserted a probe at the armor's neckpiece. While he worked, he spoke in an offhand fashion. "But, you know, I thought what happened was pretty obvious. You're now Phaethon Relic in the eyes of the law. If you open your old memories, you turn into Phaethon Prime, and you'll inherit all of Helion's stuff. But then you get kicked out. If you don't open those memories, you'll inherit whatever Phaethon Prime would have owned, because you made out your will to yourself just now. If the Gannis from Jupiter cannot prove that Helion Relic is one and the same with Helion Prime, you get everything. If he does prove it, you are in the same position you're in now, and you lose nothing. So your hotshot lawyer figured out how to get you everything you wanted for no risk; either you win or you break even. Right? And him clearing out all your debts was just an added bonus, icing on the cake. I thought it was pretty slick, actually. All you have to do is follow orders, and keep your memories tucked away for ninety days. So go back to the party, it's going to go on at least for that long, sit back, and relax. You've got it made."

Phaethon thanked him, and walked back up the stairs with a heavy footstep.

As he reached the top of the stair, he was aware of the feeling of discontent gnawing at him. It just did not seem like a victory.

He slid upward through the rock. There was a crowd of monsters and grotesqueries gathered on the grass outside. When they saw Phaethon, they cheered.

2.

Since Phaethon's sense-filter was still not turned on, he could not read the placards and hypertext the cheering crowd waved and broadcast. All he could see, at the moment, were faces of ghastly ugliness or lopsided asymmetry grinning at him. Claws waved, hands fluttered, wings, polyps, brachial attachments made a dizzying motion as the creatures leaped and capered.

The foremost, no doubt the leader, was an immense rugose cone. Four wide tentacles sprang from the apex of its body, terminating in pincers, manipulators, or clusters of sense organs, eyeballs or ear trumpets. It made an eye-defeating gesture of complex loops, knotting and unknotting, with all four tentacles at once. "Greetings! O Greetings, adventurous, beauteous, all-destroying Phaethon! We greet you with a thousand million greetings, and express the boundless hope that your terror-inspiring victory of this day will send the leaden and oppressive weight of the Eldest Generation (The Long-Dead Generation, as I like to call them) quaking and shivering into well-deserved oblivions! At last the Wheel of Progress, albeit with much squeaking, has made a millionth-inch turn upon its eternally rusted axle! The Golden Oecumene (The Rusted Oecumene, as I like to call her) has seen the first of many such revolutions: that is our fervid hope!"

Phaethon was not sure what these people intended. At this thought, his golden helmet unfolded from his gorget and covered his face. A tissue of black nanomachinery unfolded like a cloak from his backplate, and he swirled it across his limbs and shoulders as he folded his arms, to make a protective barrier against any microscopic foulnesses these dirty creatures might give off.

"I don't believe I've had the pleasure, sir," said Phaethon. He recognized them as Never-Firsts, from the generation born during and after Orpheus perfected Noumenal Recording, and members of Neomorphic and nonanthropomorphic schools.

A hooting laughter passed through the crowd. The leader flapped his tentacles in comic display. "Hoy! Listen to his stiff-arsed, high-nosed twang! Eh, eh, Phaethon, you are among friends and close companions of the heart! Our goals are your goals! We offer you adoration, endless love! We ask only that you allow our schools to take you on as a mascot and ultimate hero! Come! We prepare a love-feast in your honor."

To the rear, Phaethon saw an organism shaped like a sloppy pile of internal organs, all mucus and twisted intestines, passing out pleasure-needles to those around him. These needles were tuned to direct pleasure-center stimulation, Phaethon saw by the looks of glassy nirvana that usurped the eyes of the deformities and grotesques. Also, they must have had their sense-filters tuned to reject any evidence of the damage their hedonism did, for he saw the creatures stepping blindly on or over the prone body of a she-monster, stupefied with pleasure.

Phaethon fought down his sense of disgust. Without Rhadamanthus to help control his bodily reactions, the task was not easy. But he told himself these people might know the secret of his past; they said he was their hero. Perhaps they had information he could use.

He said, "I am flattered that you call me so heroic. Surely you can see that all I do now is no more than a natural outgrowth of my past acts?"

The creature flopped its tentacles in a energetic pumping motion. "What is the past but a pile of dead meat, already slick with flies? No, no, it is the future ('Our' Future, as I like to call it) to which we turn our eager eyes, bright and glistening with promise!"

But another part of the creature's body (or perhaps it was a second creature, a parasite) leaned up and presented a rank fungoid tendril toward Phaethon. In the sucker-disks of the tendril was a card.

The creature said, "Here! Lookit! Take! This contains everything you need to know about your past accomplishments, and our assessment of their relative worth."

Phaethon took the card in his gauntlet. It was blank, meant to load a file directly into his brain from the Middle Dreaming. Should he open an unknown file into himself without Rhadamanthus here to check it first?

On the other hand, who would dare commit a prank on the steps of the courthouse door, with Atkins standing in earshot? And it may have information about his past. . . .

He opened a temporary sense-filter (one not connected through Rhadamanthus) and looked through the Middle Dreaming at the card.

The card was black, empty as the void, and radiated a sensation of painful cold. In strokes of angular ice-white dragon sign, the glyph on the card read "NOTHING."

The blackness flowed out from the surface of the card toward his face, filled his vision. There was a sensation of pain in his eyes, a whirl of movement, of falling, of giddy motion.

He threw the card from him, shut off his sense-filter, and fell out of the Middle Dreaming. His spinning sense-perceptions returned instantly to normal. The security buffer in his personal thoughtspace showed a virus of the most crude and sophomoric design, one called drunk-rabbit, had tried to enter his brain and turn on his internal neural signals to flood his system with endorphins and intoxicants. Had it been assault? But he had taken the card willingly.

"How dare you attack me?" said Phaethon loudly. "Do you respect neither law nor decency?"

There was laughter at that; some of the lumps of flesh here snickered; other monsters roared with ungainly mirth, opening wide mouths hooked with fangs or black tusks.

The ridged cone twisted, bringing the tentacle from which its many-eyed head-ball drooped down to where the parasite-polyp glistened on the red-blue flesh. He said: "Scary, what are you doing? Phaethon is our lovely friend!"

The attached segment of flesh that controlled that fungoid growth spoke back. "Do not pinch up your arse so much, boss, or the filth will soak backward into your brain! What, no sense of humor? I wanted Phaethon here to join us in our happy-time! A little slosh is good for him! Lookit how twanged and stiff he looks! Don't he want to celebrate?"

The larger creature spread his tentacles in a parody of a shrug. "My friend Scary, he's got a good point there, Phaethon, old boy (or can I call you Fey-fey?). You do look twang. Here, snuff a bead into an orifice! Any hole will do."

Phaethon spoke in a level tone of voice. "No, thank you. What cause have I to celebrate with creatures of your ilk, sir? Who are you? What is your business with me?"

The creature held all its tentacles overhead. The monsters fell silent.

"I am Unmoiqhotep Quatro Neomorph of the Cthonnic School. We praise your victory over the oppression of the vicious inertia of this world of hate and horror in which we live. For once, the rising Generation (the Children of Divine Light, as I call them) has received their due reward from the all-smothering mediocrity of the Elders (the Jailers, as I like to call them). And from a Peer, no less! We rejoice because wealth unfairly hoarded by Helion has finally come to a child of his; we are also children of rich and important men; we consider you our inspiration! Oh, happy day!" There was another gurgling cheer from the mob, swaying and flapping their malformed arms.

Phaethon's anger drummed in his temples; his face was warm with wrath. "You dare to stand there cheering because my father, whom I loved, has been declared dead? You come to mock my loss and grief! What kind of vicious vultures are you?!"

Another monstrosity stumbled forward in a tangle of clumsy feet. "Don't get so high-and-mighty on us, you greedy money chaser! You monopolist! You engineer! We are children of enlightenment! Pleasure and freedom are ours! We despise the filthy materialists and their thinking machines who enslave us with their utopia! Where is true humanity in that?

Where is pain and death and suffering? How dare you be so selfish, so self-repressed? What kind of stuck-up, sniveling, psychic-tyrant are you?!"

The creature yelling this at Phaethon was a thing out of a nightmare. From a large head, two necks reached down into two bodies, naked, male and female. The separate bodies of the one head were embraced in a jerking copulation.

Phaethon turned on his sense-filter and edited the crowd from his view.

Now he stood, or seemed to stand, in a stately garden. Blessed solitude was here. Except for the twitter of distant birds, all was silent. The odor of unwashed humanity was gone; instead, a scent rose from the dew-gemmed grass, or the curving petals of luxurious flowers beyond the hedge.

Phaethon kicked his foot against the soil, activated his magnetics in the armor, and soared into the spring-scented air. Handsome landscape was above him and below him in the great cylinder.

Perhaps this sublime peace was an illusion. He knew these lawns were crowded with a filthy swarm of neomorphs. But perhaps some illusions were worth maintaining, if only for a little while.

He turned on his private thoughtspace, so that a spiral of dots, and cubes of engineering and ecological routine icons seemed to hang within arm's reach around him, but the garden landscape was still visible beyond.

He reached toward the pastel oblong icon representing his wife's diary, but stopped. He did not have enough memory just in the isolated circuitry wired into his brain to run a full simulation; and he certainly did not want to enter into personality deprivation while in flight. But he was too impatient to go all the way back, miles upon miles, to his barren little cubical in the space elevator before he had a chance to find out what Daphne knew.

Phaethon hesitated to call Rhadamanthus back, because he now knew Helion's Relic could find what he was doing through those links. And while he might be a fine man, it was a fact that Helion and Phaethon now had an uncompromising conflict of interests. Either one had the right to Helion's vast fortune, or the other; they could not both.

Phaethon frowned. Helion's relic? Phaethon had seen him just last night. It was impossible to think of the man as anything other than his sire; it was impossible to think of him as "dead" merely because a court of law so decreed.

But, if so, then Phaethon was in the wrong, stealing money from a man merely because a court of law called him dead. After all, that same Court just called Phaethon himself dead. . . .

There was a spaceport at the weightless joint joining this cylinder with the next. It was a wide spherical space where many ships of spun diamond, like a forest of elfish glass, were assembled and disassembled between Inner System flights; they also served as shuttles to farther spaceports at L-5 point and beyond, where mile upon mile of magnetic launchers accelerated ships for bright and distant Jupiter, and other Outer System ports of call.

A smaller group of habitats, like a cluster of grapes, was affixed to the wall of the sphere; one of the larger ones contained thought caskets and lockers rented out by Eleemosynary Hospitalities, a subdivision of that wealthy Composition's many business groups, efforts, and holdings.

Phaethon floated into the airlock at the hub of the hospice. From there he descended to the equator of the hospice, which was being spun for gravity. Thought caskets formed a curving row reaching up to his left and right; he could see the other side of the corridor above him.

He entered the nearest thought casket, had the medical apparatus close about him. The circuitry in his armor might interfere with the interfaces, yet Phaethon was strangely unwilling to take it off.

As Atkins had done, Phaethon took a group of fibers and stuffed them down through the neckpiece of his armor, where they writhed and changed shape, making themselves adaptable to the circuitry in the black nanomechanism that formed the armor lining. The signal now could be fed through the armor to the armor's internal interfaces and into his brain. Apparently that was sufficient.

Energy connections were formed with receptors in his brain; all his senses were engaged; the external world faded.

Now he seemed to stand in the Hospice Public Thought-space, where a pyramid of balconies seemed to rise around him, with windows and icons opening up into deeper and higher sections of the library.

A gesture from his little finger closed the balcony railing and formed a privacy box. He opened the diary, fell into deepest dreamspace, lost his memories, and became Daphne. The recording started with her before she woke yesterday morning.

THE SYMPHONY OF DREAMS

1.

She had not been asleep, not as the ancients would have understood sleep. Daphne had been experiencing a Stimulus, Mancuriosco the Neuropathist's Eighth Arrangement. The last movement in the Stimulus, the so-called Compass of Infinity Theme, involved stimulations of deep-memory structures, a combination of REM-stage delta waves and meditative alpha waves. Over all, was a counterpoint of waves that did not naturally occur in the human brain, which, introduced artificially produced sensations and states of mind that required a special nomenclature to describe.

In her dreams, she cycled through an evolution, first as an amoeba pulsing in the endless waves of the all-mother ocean, then as a protozoa, drifting and floating, then as an insect, escaping from the water to the smaller infinity of the air. Memories of ancient amphibians, ancient lizards, lemurs and hominids flowed through her; each mind, as it grew more complex, seemed, somehow, to diminish the mystery and wonder of the world around her. Other deeply buried memories surfaced; of her floating in the womb as a child, surrounded by infinite love and warmth, then emerging, in pain and confusion, into what seemed to be a smaller universe. The final movement of the theme had a set of emotions, moods, dreams and half-dreams, where, ennobled by some far future evolution, now a goddess, she held the universe like a crystal globe in her hand, but, being larger than the universe, had no place to stand. There were sensations of being cramped and suffocated, terribly alone, as the universe shrank to the size of a pebble, a dust mote, an atom. Then, somehow, in a mysterious reverse, she found herself now infinite and infinitesimal, once more floating and drifting in a mysterious endless sea. . . .

She enjoyed the experience as always, but there was something not quite right about it, something which made her uneasy. . . .

It was strange. She remembered this performance as her favorite. How had she truly never noticed how pessimistic and ironic the theme here was? But the performance had not changed. Had something changed in her . . . ?

Perhaps she was more joyous these days. These were the golden days of the Transcendence; there was much to enjoy.

The dream drifted to waking, and Daphne awoke.

She lay beneath the waters of her living-pool, yawning and stretching, bubbles tickling her nose. Daphne stared up at the play of lights and reflections across the underside of the dome, at the blue sky and white clouds beyond. She smiled a languid smile.

At her thought, the water beneath her strengthened its surface tension, so that she now rested in a dry little valley, made by her own weight, of rainbow-chased transparency.

What next? She wondered. It was after the Gold Cup competitions, but the Life Debates were still two days away. And she had already bought all the gifts she needed for the Ministration of Delights in August.

Some of her manor-born friends, Anna and Uruvulell, always had their Sophotechs surprise them on unplanned festival days, plan their schedules for them. The superintelligent machines often could choose what would amuse and instruct their patrons much better than the girls themselves could do. Such a life was not for her. She craved spontaneity, wildness, adventure!

Daphne challenged propriety among the manor-born by going in her physical presence to the festivals. The cottage around her now, for example, with its pillars of porphyry marble and its diamond dome, was real, grown last month in the gardens south of Aurelian Mansion. It was not Rhadamanthus, but a more simple-minded Sophotech (only eighty or ninety times as bright as a human genius, not thousands) named Ayesha, who dwelt in this cottage.

It was Ayesha who now manipulated the millions of microscopic machines in the life-pool to weave robes of flowing blue-and-silver silk up around Daphne as she rose to her feet. Water trickled from the curves of her breast and belly, and her long hair, now wet and black and heavy, that hung, clinging, to her back. Where the water passed, silk thread clung, so that by the time she stepped from the pool, fabric spun down to her feet. The waste-heat of the molecular assembly was directed through her hair to dry it.

The robe was like a Hindu sari. The shining cloth was simply draped, without fastenings or ties, and fell with natural grace over one shoulder and tightly around her waist and hips, to accentuate her figure. She carried the train over her elbow.

She passed down a corridor paved with mother-of-pearl, with softly glowing hypnogogic Warlock-sculptures hovering in niches to either side. Daphne did not have the states of consciousness necessary to receive the experience-signals from these sculptures; she was a base neuroform, even though, in her youth, she had been a Warlock named Ao Andaphantie, with no barriers between her left brain and hypothalamus, and in dreams had walked by the day through her waking consciousness. Daphne kept the sculptures with her nonetheless; they were not intelligent enough to be emancipated, and would have drooped with melancholy had she abandoned them.

Even if she could no longer read the interior of the sculptures, she saw how they spun and glittered and laughed as she passed, catching her mood and reflecting it back to her. They seemed much brighter than she would have expected, glinting with suppressed mirth, as if some hidden and wonderful surprise were waiting for her.

Beyond was a mensal room. Part of the discipline of the hedonists of the Red Manorial Schools was that they take all nutriment not through traditional living-pool absorptions but in a more ancient fashion, by eating. Daphne had been allied with Eveningstar, a Red manor, for many centuries before she joined the more austere and strict Silver-Gray. The mensal chamber was floored with polished wood, the walls hidden by rice-paper screens painted with bamboo-and-crane motifs.

Why that motif? Daphne glanced at the cranes. Mating for life, they were symbols of eternal fidelity. Was Ayesha Sophotech trying to hint that Daphne should spend more time with her husband? He had been acting rather moody and abstracted lately, not enjoying the festivals as much as she had thought he would.

In the center of the room was a table on which were displayed a careful arrangement of bowls, napkins, tiny crystal bottles of sauce or dried leaves of spice. Here were plates of spiced fish wrapped in seaweed, slices of octopus, balls of rice. In the middle was a black iron tea kettle with three spouts. She knelt, her robes as bright as flower petals on the mat around her knees, and took up her chopsticks. And stopped, her head cocked to one side: what was this bulk beneath the silk napkin folded to the side of her setting?

She drew aside the napkin and found a memory box beneath. This was an imaginifestation, the real-world analogy for some icon in thoughtspace. Taking it up or opening it would trigger some mental reaction or routine.

Daphne recognized her own handwriting on the lid: "For the Third Day after Guy Fawkes'. Happy Surprise!"

"I hate surprises!" She groaned and rolled her eyes. "Why am I always doing things like this to myself?!"

Well, there was nothing else to be done. She would have to open the box. But to make the waiting more delicious, and to prevent her meal from spoiling, she ate first. Daphne was good at mensal ceremony; her each gesture and nibble, each sip from her tea bowl, was as graceful as a small ballet.

Then, with her food warm in her stomach, and chewing on a mint leaf for desert, it was time to open the box.

Slowly, the lid came open.

Inside the box, like concentric iridescent bubbles, was her universe.

Daphne saw it, and remembered.

She sat, eyes closed, breathless. Her old Warlock training allowed her to remain awake while the dreaming centers of her brain, rushing with images, tried to establish deep-structure emotional and symbolic connections between her memories and consciousness.

The cosmos was called Althea. It was a simple, geocentric, Copernican model, based on Euclidean geometry and New-tonian mechanics. Beneath a crystal sphere of fixed stars and the complex epicycles of moving planetary mansions were continents and blue oceans of a gentle world. Her seas teemed with fishes and mermaids, whales grand with ancient wisdom, sunken cities. Her lands were pastoral, jeweled with tiny vil-lages and farms, high castles, small cities crowned with lov-ingly built cathedrals. A memory of horrid war hung like the notes of a trembling counterpoint echoing from far hills, and musketeers and daring horse guards patrolled the edges of dark forests where winged dragons were rumored to brood.

In the city of golden Hyperborea, beyond the Northwestern Sea, a prince named Shining had returned from the wars with the grim Cimmerians, who lived in endless caverns of gold and iron, in a land of eternal gloom. The prince had brought with him out from that underworld a dream made of fire, which he wore like a cloak over his armor of gold, or like wings of flame. . . .

The wonder of it was that Daphne had achieved the Semi-final Medal for the Althean universe she had created; today she was to enter in the final competition against other amateur dreamsmiths. She had originally intended it only for children, or for those who delighted in childish things. How could it compete with the modern non-Euclidean universes invented by Neomorphs, or the strange multileveled worlds of the New Movement Warlocks, or the Möbius-strip infinities of Anach-ronic Cerebellines? The love-gravity universe submitted by Typhoenus of the Clamour Black Manor, a universe where love increased gravitic attraction and hate and fear lessened it, had thousands of worlds, a galaxy of worlds, peopled by thousands of characters no less complex and complete as her few continent's worth. How could she compete? How could she ever hope to win?

She opened her eyes and came out of her trance. Phaethon was always bothering her about getting back into some effort, getting involved in some business or program. (As if anything humans did could make any difference at all in a world run by machines!) And it was true that she had put off the decision, and put it off again and again, telling herself that perhaps, by the time of the Masquerade at the end of the Millennium, when the world reviewed its life and decided where its future lay, Daphne would review and would decide herself.

Well, the Millennium had come. The decision was here. If she won the Gold Medal for her universe there would be a flood of invitations, communions, ovations. Entertainers would send her gifts and compose praises just for the privilege of being seen with her, or publicity-mongers to have the public see what name-brand services she patronized.

Maybe she could become a dream weaver in truth, not merely a dreamer.

And maybe, just maybe, her husband would lose that look of disdain he got when he spoke of those who enjoyed the fruits of the Golden Oecumene without helping with the cultivation. "All history has worked to created our fine utopia," he would always say, "so it is hardly the time for the human race to take a holiday! We don't want entropy to win."

She was always afraid he was thinking of her when he said this. Maybe if she won the Gold, that fear would go away. Maybe the future would be clearer to her.

She had also promised herself to decide, before the Millennium was up, whether or not to make children with Phaethon. If she had a career again, that decision might become easier, too.

Daphne rose, her silk robes whispering around her knees and ankles. No wonder she had hidden this memory from herself! Her nerves could not have taken the cheerful strain of waiting, the fretful days and minutes till the competition drew near.

There were Red Manorial routines for controlling such emotions, or replacing fear with hope; but now that she was a Silver-Gray, she had to learn to do those things, so to speak, by hand. Silver-Gray protocol did not allow for unprompted mood reorganizations; memory redaction, however, was acceptable. Ancient man forgot things all the time, and so how could the Silver-Gray curators upbraid the exercise of a flaw so traditional?

With a silken whisper of robes, she passed from the chamber to her day lock.

And, since she was present and awake in the real world, she had to take the time to do things, one step at a time, which would have been easier and simpler even in a strict Silver-Gray dreamscape. It took time to change into her Masquerade costume (she was dressed as a favorite author from her childhood, for luck), time to program her hair, check the weather, and adjust her skin accordingly. The Ayesha-mind had remembered to summon a carriage with time enough to carry Daphne to the Oneirocon Palace (which Daphne had forgotten—these had to be done in order in the real world, with no backups or restarts).

The carriage pulled up on the turning circle outside the day lock. It was a light and open affair, well sprung, with wheels slender and light as parasols. The road was still warm from its assembly heat; evidently Aurelian foresaw more traffic from this side of the park today, and had thrown a new road up overnight. Pulling the carriage was an old friend.

"Mr. Maestrict!" Daphne exclaimed, rushing up to throw her arms around the horse's neck. "How have you been?! I thought you were working for the Parliament now, Mr. Can't or Won't or something like that."

"Mr. Han is his name, Miss Daphne. Kshatrimanyu Han. He's the Prime Minister," the horse replied. "And there's not much for me to do during the Masquerade. Parliament is not in session, and, even when it is, all they ever do is argue about how much intellectual property goes into the public domain under the Fair-Use Doctrine, or how much salary poor old Captain Atkins should get."

"Who is Atkins?" She petted Mr. Maestrict on the nose, and sent one of Ayesha's remotes to the life-pool to assemble a lump of sugar.

"Oh . . . he's sort of a leftover from the old days. He does . . . ah . . . some tasks the Sophotechs aren't allowed to do. We're lucky, because we just found a little mystery for him to solve. It's probably just a Masquerade prank, you know."

"Well! An adventure!"

"Not really an adventure, ma'am. It appears that some Neptunian masterminds are preparing a thought-weapon to erase or drive insane some high-level Sophotechs. We're trying to find out where this weapon is, or whether it is a false alarm meant to spook us."

His words made little impression on Daphne. It would be as hard for her to imagine the foundational Sophotechs being killed as it would to imagine the sun going nova. She thought the machine intelligences were able to anticipate every conceivable danger. So all she said was: "Good! It's about time things were shaken up around here. Sugar?"

The horse twitched his ears. "Ma'am . . . ? I mean, I like you and all, but, do we know each other that well . . . ?"

"No, silly!" She threw back her head to laugh. "I was offering you some sugar. Here."

"Mm. Thank you. I, ah, of course I knew what you meant. Ahem. Climb aboard. Where to?"

"To the Dream Lords' Palace! Away! And don't spare the horses!"

"Good heavens, ma'am, I hope you'll spare me somewhat."

"I'm competing today in the Oneirocon!"

"Hoy! I didn't realize it was that important, ma'am! Watch this!" Now he reared and pawed the ground, nostrils wide, and his ears flattened. He cried "Aha!" and began to race.

Daphne squealed with delight, and grabbed for the rail of the rocking carriage.

Some people strolling the park applauded as Daphne's wild carriage thundered by, and several posted comments on the short-term public channel, complimenting the authenticity and grace of her steed.

On the same channel, Mr. Maestrict posted: "Seems like everyone still likes horses, Miss Daphne. We'll never go out of style. Have you ever thought about taking up equestrianism again? Nobody designs a quarter horse like you. Look at my magnificent body!" And he tossed his mane in the wind as he charged.

It was the same thing her husband was always saying. But there was no market anymore for horses. Horsemanship, as a fad among anachronists and romantics, had dried up eighty years ago.

Daphne answered him out loud, shouting back over the noise of the wheels: "Why, Mr. Maestrict! I like you and all, but do we know each other that well . . . ?"

He was embarrassed, or amused, and he put down his head and ran all the faster.

2.

The Oneirocon was surely the simplest, most stark building in the history of Objective Aesthetic architecture. The ceiling was a perfectly square flat slab, half a mile on a side, hovering above the ground with no visible support. Beneath, open on all sides, a square floor embraced a large, perfectly round, shallow living-pool.

A later architect had modified the plan, adding a circle of dolmens, Stonehenge-like, around the pool. In case of inclement weather, the buoyant roof could sink down till it rested on the dolmens, and protective films be projected between the pillars to form temporary walls.

A high-priority segment of the Aurelian Sophotech Mind was present, represented by a mannequin disguised as Comus, with a charming wand in one hand and a glass in the other. Daphne had no idea this contest had attracted such attention.

Comus was a character from a play by Milton (linear word poet, Second Era). The son of the wine god Bacchus and the enchantress Circe, Comus used the gifts of his divine parents to tempt men to drunken revelry, magically transforming them into brutes and beasts. Only against pure virgins did his cunning magic fail. Daphne thought it was tremendously funny that Aurelian chose this as his self-image.

All the contestants were physically present; they would only be able to use standardized memory-and-attention equipment to promulgate their simulations. The judging would be done on four grounds: internal consistency, external relevance, coherency, and popularity.

Daphne was pleased to learn that the "relevance" ground was being given a lesser judging weight than the semifinalist judges had given it. Apparently, the Consensus Aesthetic was relaxing, allowing art for art's sake. Since Daphne's little fairy-tale world had nothing to do with real life or any modern issues, that was a relief. But it afforded a correspondingly greater weight to internal self-consistency, her weakest area. Her universe was somewhat Aristotelian in places. For example, it had an atmosphere reaching up to the crystal firmament, but a Napoleonic level of technology, such as Montgolfier's Balloon, and primitive airships, which she had included only because she thought they looked stately and romantic.

This year, popularity was to be determined by a novel method.

Participants in the dream would be under full amnesia, actually believing themselves to be the characters with which the dream weavers had peopled their universes. Their emotions and deep-structures would remain untouched. A certain amount of artificial memory, to give them the language, background, and customs, would be permitted after inspection by the judges. But they would be allowed to hear rumors and myths of the other universes, to reincarnate and emigrate. The emigration would be free and open "voting with their feet" as Aurelian called it. Whoever attracted the most people away from his competitors would win the popularity ranking.

The contestants, in bright costumes, plumes, and gaudy skin tones, some in human bodies, others in many-headed

Harmony forms dating from the Regrouping period of the
Fourth Era, stood in a circle around the living-pool, waiting
for Aurelian's signal. All threw aside their garbs and stepped
down, naked into the waters.

Daphne sank. Adjustments in her lungs drew oxygen from
the medium. Microscopic assemblers built contacts to the
nerve-interfaces she carried beneath her skin. As she drifted
into the far, deep dreamspace, Daphne felt that moment of
pleasant terror as her personality slipped away.

In the next moment, she was no longer Daphne, she was
the Queen-Goddess of her universe. Her mind, assisted by the
Sophotech interface, expanded to encompass every element
and aspect of her reality, till she could count the hairs on
every head of her characters; and not an invented sparrow fell
but that she could work the trajectory into the destiny web of
her plot.

The players came on-line. It was frightening—even the
Daphne-Goddess was frightened—to see her characters come
to life in the million dramas she simultaneously spun. Because, deep down, the Goddess still knew that this life was
false, an illusion, and that these character lives would end
with the end of the drama, their memories reabsorbed back
into the people playing them.

It occasionally happened in such games that a character
pondered enough questions, brought forth original thoughts,
defined himself, and became self-aware, thinking thoughts independent of the mind of the player portraying him.

There were, to be sure, safeguards in the dreamware meant
to prevent this from happening; and, if it did happen, there
were even more safeguards to prevent the newborn personality from being murdered unintentionally when the player
from which he sprang woke up.

(In the eyes of the law, those players stood to those emancipated characters as parent to child, and had an inescapable
duty to provide for the child until he was old enough to fend
for himself, either by earning enough to rent the computer
space in which he lived, or to buy a physical body into which
his noumena could be downloaded.)

Daphne's dream sprang to life, and the competition began. Her universe spun like an orrery beneath her hands, like a jeweled toy, and the plotlines of her characters were woven of a hundred thousand colored threads.

During the first four hours of the competition, forty dream-years went by in her universe. Most of her dramas dealt with simple things: young ladies trying to choose wisely when they wed; temptations to their fidelity; misunderstanding, discord and reconciliation; or a surprising reverse when the man everyone condemned as a rogue turned out to be the girl's true love. There were few adventures as such, except for the occasional shipwreck or Turkish kidnapping (intended usually to force the bickering lovers together, rather than to show the dangers or bravery of the ancient world.) There were hints that the war with Napoleon, or the Dragon-Magi of Persia, might resume, but this was done usually to call young soldiers away overseas, in scenes of heartbreak and promised faith-fulness, not to portray wars as such. Daphne hated war stories, especially ones where cavalry officers' mounts were hurt.

Not much action-adventure, no. But there were marriages. Plenty of marriages.

By the sixth hour of competition, half a dozen decades of dream life had passed. And Daphne was ranked in thirty-fifth place, getting somewhat low marks for her lack of realism. Some universe made of diatonic music was in front, unfolding a vast drama as intelligent song-scores ranged across a universe of staffs, discovering new harmonies, fitting themselves, not without pain, into a cosmos-sized symphony. The Daphne-Goddess was irked: that dream weaver was letting his players do all the work!

Well, two could play the game that way.

Daphne-Goddess relaxed her hand at the loom of fate, and began to let the plotlines follow their own natural destinies. She allowed the Sophotech to explore more realistic out-comes, and removed restrictions on character types. "Giving the horse his head," as she called it.

Events took new turns, and now she had a million tangles to contend with. Everything (almost!) flew out of control. Rail lines and factories and steamships sprang up across her pastoral landscape, and suddenly her heroes were not rakish officers in the Queen's Own Grenadiers, nor stern aristocrats in cold mansions needing a woman's love to melt their icy hearts: no. All her heroines were falling in love with a new type of man: young inventors with a dream, steel kings and oil barons, self-made men: thinkers, doers, movers and shakers. The same type of men who had always been the greedy villains in earlier parts of her work. What was going on?

Daphne-Goddess saw warning signals from some of the underjudges, reminding her that, since she started with her plotlines as romances, she would lose points for coherence if she switched to another genre of drama. She ignored the warnings. At thirty-first place, what had she to lose?

Wait. Thirty-first? Had she just jumped ahead four slots?

Daphne ignored that and concentrated on salvaging the tornado of her unraveling plotlines. It was as if an invisible force or an unseen hand were helping her; certain resolutions naturally suggested themselves; and natural events were punishing wicked characters without any intervention on her part.

She wanted to make the factories scenes of pathos and cruelty, but no. Widows and women without support, as wage earners, no longer starved if they did not marry well. Some of her characters became suffragettes. Laws were agitated through Parliament to allow wives to buy, sell, and own property, without the consent of their husbands.

Less romance? There was more romance here. A new type of heroine was appearing now: independent, brash, inventive, optimistic. Just her kind of woman! She had no need for action or bloodshed in such times as these; life was an adventure. Daphne-Goddess laughed at the judges. Let her come in last if she must. This was a world she liked: it roared onward toward its own self-made future.

She almost intervened when she saw the older forests of Germany being felled, and dragons being hunted down by squads of dragoons and aeronauts. But the hoarded gold the were-worms stole was returned to its proper owners, the men who had earned it; and the dark wasteland was now sunlit farmland. It was beautiful. The population grew.

Overseas to the West, the dashing prince of Hyperborea built an airship larger than any that had ever been, aided by two bicycle mechanics from Dayton, Ohio. In a series of three magnificent expeditions, he rose higher and higher into the atmosphere, and on the second voyage passed the orbit of the moon, taking pictures with the new kinetoscope of the workings of the crystal gears and epicycles.

The moon in her universe was only ten miles wide, and turned through the aether a few thousand feet above the mountaintops. Daphne-Goddess began to fret. Was the universe she built too small for the spirit of the men who now possessed it?

The Roman Catholic Church condemned the translunar expeditions as impious. A noise of war began to sound in earnest, not just as rumors. The old aristocracy of England and Cimmeria hated the new breed of inventors and captains of industry, and joined the crusade against them. Yellow journalists and demagogues loudly condemned the new way of life, and chose the translunar expedition as the symbol on which to heap their venom.

Many of these were her older players, people who had wanted to join in a small, safe, pastoral world. Daphne-Goddess had some sympathy for them, but when she looked down and saw the magnificent airship of the Hyperboreans, decorated with banners of black and gold, rising gigantic and proud, upward to conquer heaven, her heart melted with delight. Trumpets blew fanfares from the windows of the Empire State Building as the airship launched.

German and Cimmerian airships, armed with cannons, now appeared from out of the stormclouds where they had been hiding, and sought to down the vessel. Yet the Hyperborean ship rose farther and higher than any opposition. The vessel passed the orbits of the moon, of glowing Venus and red Mars. Then, another disaster: the crew, overcome by superstitious terror at the near approach of a comet, mutinied, and parachuted over the rail to the globe so many miles below. The Captain continued onward alone.

From the wireless in the cabin, he sent his final message: he revealed himself to be Lord Shining, the prince of Hyperborea himself, having come aboard the airship incognito. This expedition was not merely meant to go to the starry sphere, but beyond; he had brought tools and explosives sufficient to open a hole in the dome of the sky and see what lay on the far side.

The radio stammered protests: messages from Popes and Kings warning that he might cause the sky to fall, puncture the universe like a bubble, or let some dreadful other-substance from Beyond rush in to drown the universe!

His reply: "A prison the size of a universe is yet a prison. I shall not be bound."

He donned a deep-sea diver's helmet and heavy leather suit against the thinness of the air; frost gathered on the shrouds; the steam engines sputtered, lacking oxygen. Beneath him, the whole world was paralyzed with awe or fear. Overhead was the dome.

He attached himself to the azure empyrean crystal with a harness of suction cups. Now he lifted the pickax, which still had tied around its head the good-luck ribbon his wife had given him. He braced himself, drawing back to swing. . . .

12

THE MASTER OF THE SUN

1.

Daphne was jarred awake. Clumsy with stupidity, her thoughts no longer racing at machine-assisted speeds, she wondered in numb confusion if her prince had destroyed the universe by puncturing the wall. Maybe the universe had been a bubble after all—she was in a pool . . .

Daphne stood up, spitting water from her lungs. She was in the huge living-pool of the Oneirocon, with bits of interface-crystal still dripping from her hair. Aurelian's representation, still dressed as Comus, thin-faced, dark-haired, in wine-colored robes, was at the pool's edge, leaning on his charming wand heavily, as if a weight were bearing down on him.

"Is—is the contest over—or—" Daphne looked around blankly. The other contestants were still under the surface, crowned with dream machinery, still active.

Something was very, very wrong here.

"Aurelian? Is there a—a problem?"

"The other contestants are on hold. I took it upon myself to interrupt you, since there are command-lines in your construction file permitting such interference under certain circumstances."

" 'Construction file' . . . ?"

A sensation of dread crawled on her skin, sank into the pit

of her stomach. Only artificial beings had construction files. Not real people.

Not her. Oh, please, not her!

The one secret fear that had always followed her was here.

Daphne (Silver-Gray disciplines and oaths forgotten) used a Red Manorial mind-control technique on herself, and kept her terror at bay.

She felt faint nonetheless. She scooped up a double handful of life-water, ordered it to turn itself into something more potent than wine, raised her palms to her mouth and threw back her head to drink.

Red liquid flowed down her cheeks like tears. She rubbed her fingers through her hair to dry them, which would make a sticky, tangled mess later. Daphne nervously began to tease the strands apart with her fingers, then she snorted in self-disgust. Later? What later? She wasn't even sure if she had any "now."

Daphne let the lank tangles drip back down across her forehead and cheeks, planted her fists on her hips, and glared at the Sophotech.

"Okay, Aurelian! What the hell is going on ?!"

"A message from Helion of Rhadamanthus Mansion has come for you on a very high-priority channel. In order to decide whether or not to interrupt you to deliver it, I had to make an extrapolation of your mind. In so doing, I discovered that you suffer from a number of self-imposed false beliefs. The message will be meaningless to you unless you immediately resume certain redacted memories."

He brought out a silver casket, the size of a transmitter case. It was an imaginifestation, a real-world object linked to some routine or file in the dreamscape. On the lid was inscribed a legend: "WARNING! This file contains mnemonic templates . . ."

She commanded herself to be brave. "And my belief about my identity . . . ?"

"Is false. Your are not Daphne Prime. Your real name is Daphne Tercius Semi-Rhadamanthus Disembodied, Emancipated-Download-Redact, Indepconciousness, Base

Neuroformed (parallel impersonate) Silver-Gray Manorial (Auxiliary) Schola, Era Present."

"Emancipated . . . ?" She had been a doll, a character, a plaything.

Daphne had not known, not really. But there had been hints. Friends would say how much she had changed, then fall silent, or dart sidelong looks at her. She would find entries in her account books for which she could not account. She read diaries and logs that seemed to talk about a woman more reserved and austere, more moody, more dreamy, than she thought of herself as being.

But those thoughts about herself were false.

Despite the Red Manorial mind-controllers, she felt a sense of sledgehammer impact, only muted, dull, and distant.

"Do you need medical attention? You seem to have trouble breathing."

"No, n—I'm fine." She was grasping her knees, waiting, with a sort of clinical disinterest, to see if she would vomit. Unlike a mannequin, she did not have full control of the autonomic reactions of her real body. "This is what I do when I have my lungs ripped out. It's fun! You should try it some time."

But this wasn't her real body. She was an emancipated-download-redact.

Which meant her thoughts weren't even her real thoughts.

Aurelian said sardonically, "Thank you, no. There are aspects of the human condition we machines are content merely to observe from the outside."

She raised her head to glare at him with sudden hatred. "Well, I'm glad you find my pain worth noticing! Maybe I can be a footnote in some damn abstract thesis in your Earthmind! Mount me as a science exhibit: the girl who thought she might be happy someday gets a healthy dose of reality to boot her in the mouth."

He spread his hands and bowed slightly. "I'm sorry. I did not mean to make light of your suffering. Similar things happened to me when I was being constructed; each time a new thought-group was introduced, the integration required a paradigm shift."

"That's not the same."

"Nonetheless, I sympathize. Even we are not immune from pain and sorrow. If our minds are more acute than yours, that only means the pains we know are more acute as well."

She straightened up. "Okay! What's in that damned box?! What's so terrible that I couldn't even bring myself to . . . Oh, no . . . It's not . . ." The snap left her voice. Wild-eyed, she said in a pleading tone, "Phaethon is dead, isn't he? He killed himself in some stupid experiment, and I only think he's alive. All my memories of him are implants, aren't they? Oh, please, not that!"

"No, its not that."

Another horror overcame her. "He never did exist, did he?! He's a made-up character out of my romances! I knew he was too good to be true! There's no one like him!"

"No. He is quite real."

She breathed a sigh of relief, stooped, and sloshed more water across her face.

Then she stood, shaking drops from both hands. "I hate surprises. Tell me what's in the box."

"You made an agreement with Helion to perpetuate a certain falsehood on Phaethon. Helion has just sent you a message requiring you to deliver that promised aid. In order to carry out this program, you must resume part of your hidden memories."

"I would never lie to Phaethon. That's stupid! If there's something in that box which is going to make me want to lie to my husband, I'm not sure I want to know what it is!"

"Deliberate amnesia is self-deception; perhaps not the best way to maintain one's integrity."

"I did not ask you your opinion."

"Perhaps not. I am required, however, to inform you that I have consulted with a hypothetical model, taken from your Noumenal Recordings, of what you might be like after this box is opened. That version of you would wish, in the strongest possible terms, that you open the box and accept these memories. She did, and therefore you probably will, regard it as a matter of paramount importance."

"How important?"

"You probably will believe it necessary to preserve your marriage, fortune, happiness, and your life as you know it."

It took her a moment to brace herself. "Okay, then. I consent. Show me the worst."

She sank back down into the pool. The microscopic assembler thickened the waters around her, built relays along her neck and skull, made contact with interfaces leading to her neurocircuitry. . . .

2.

The memory came from less than a month ago. She stood deep in the dreaming, in Rhadamanth Mansion. To one side, tall windows let red sunset light slant across a shadowy corridor to illume the upper wainscoting of the opposite wall. No portraits hung here; the pigments would have been bleached by the direct sunlight. Instead, a high mantle held a line of brass and bronze urns, etched with arabesques, dull with patina. Daphne thought they looked like funerary urns, and wondered why she had not seen them here before.

All else was shadow in the dying light. At the far end of the hall, the only spot of color came from the faded plumes, which rose, motionless and fragile with dust, above the empty-eyed helmets of ornate suits of armor guarding the door there.

Her hesitant, soft steps carried her to the door. All was dark and quiet. The door-leaves fell open silently at her slightest touch.

Leaping red light shone from the crack, and the roaring noise of alarms, sirens, explosions, screams. Daphne came forward, squinting, her elbow up to shield her face from the heat. She smelled burnt flesh.

A gallery of transadamantine supermetal stretched infinitely ahead of her. The ceiling was wider than the floor on which she stood, so that the windows or screens paneling the walls slanted down, and overlooked a sea of seething incandescence. This sea was roiled and torn by spiral storms of some darker matter churning; and from these blots rose arching arms of flame, intolerably bright, prominences flung endlessly upward into black void above.

Daphne saw the gallery's lines of perspective dwindle to the vanishing point as straightly as if drawn with a geometer's rule, with no curve or deflection; likewise, the horizon of the infinite storm outside the windows was much farther than the horizon of any Earth-sized planet would allow.

A gasp of pain, half a scream, half a laugh, came from behind her. She turned. This gallery met several others in a large rotunda, where banks of tiered controls overlooked rank upon rank of windows, holding views of the flaming storm from many angles and directions, cast in several models, flickering with multiple layers of interpretation.

Along the floor of the rotunda, huge cubes of some machinery Daphne did not recognize were melting; through red-lipped gaps and holes in the armored housing, white-hot funnels of incandescent air erupted. There were darts of light and sparks, but no flames; everything which might have been flammable had been consumed.

In the center of the rotunda, at the top of the burning ziggurat of machinery, blood dripping from the cracks where the white ablative of his armor had melted, sat Helion on a throne. Through the transparent face-shield of his helmet, the right half of his face had been scalded to the bone. His right eye was gone; cracked black tissue webbed his cheek and brow. Medical processors, unfolding from the interior of the helmet, gripped Helion's face with claws and tubes, or crawling drops of biotic nanomachinery.

A dozen emergency wires ran from his crown to the control caskets to either side of him. It looked absurdly crude and old-fashioned. Evidently the thought control had failed, or the static in the room did not allow signals to pass through the air from the circuits in his brain to those in the boards.

Hovering between his hands, above his knees, was the orb

of the sun, webbed with gold lines to indicate the Solar Array stations, pockmarked and scabbed with dark splotches to indicate the storms. Funnels of darkness reached from the sunspots down toward the stellar core. The orb radiated multicolored lights, each color symbolizing a different combination of particles streaming from the storm centers.

Some screens showed a furious activity, calculations and solarological data streaming past. Others showed a slow and vast disaster; magnetic screen after screen overloading and failing; sections of the Array losing buoyancy and descending toward the interior, toppling and disintegrating.

The safety interlocks were gone from all power couplings, nodes and transfer points; speed-of-reaction restrictions had been removed from the nanomachinery. Consequently, the machinery inside the array was heating up, driven past safe operating levels, and being allowed to burn, provided that one more second of functional life could be forced from its self-immolated corpse.

Helion was attempting to position screens or to release charges into the core to deflect some of the storm-particles. The volumes of matter involved were incredible; Helion's machines threw masses of controllants fifty times the size of Jupiter from the photosphere into the mantle like so many grains of sand.

The status board showed the Solar Sophotech-Mind had been lobotomized by loss of power. Helion was wrestling with the storm alone.

He looked up, wide-eyed, as she stepped in: his look was one of hope, or vast and godlike mirth, of guiltlessness and fearlessness.

"I see it now." His voice trembled over the station loudspeakers. "What else can be the cure for the chaos at the core of the system? It is so simple!"

But a breach in his suit bubbled open at that point; superheated air rushed in. He screamed and screamed, jerking to his feet, arms writhing. The gush of pure oxygen as some internal tank erupted turned the flame inside his suit into a pure white light. The light grew red as blood, was baked against the inside of the face-plate into a semiopaque layer.

The same armor meant to protect him now held the flames against the dying man's skin. The figure on the throne shivered violently, burnt lungs unable to scream, until nerves and muscles were likewise unable to react. A long-drawn-out moan issued from the loudspeakers. It is possible that Helion's consciousness lingered for a long and horrible moment in his neurocybernetic interface, before the melting point of the artificial brain-fibers and circuits were reached.

Daphne retreated. She had to push through a half-melted rack of machine organisms, wading molten adamantium, stepping through white-hot washes of fire, to reach the gallery. (The small amount of heat she felt was merely symbolic, to show her what was represented here. She appeared in a mode called "audit," able to view, but not to be affected by, the scenario. Had she been truly involved, unprotected, unarmored, her self-image would have been instantly burnt to ash.) She shoved through the mess out of the rotunda, and back down the gallery. Daphne found she had no curiosity whatsoever about the scene of hellish death and incineration she had just witnessed. In fact, she was disturbed by it, or even frightened.

But, before she could escape, the sirens fell silent, and the rotunda stopped glowing and burning. Footsteps sounded. Here came Helion, alive again, face whole and unburnt, armor white as snow, undamaged.

He came toward her. The face-plate of his helmet was thrown back. His expression was strange to her, clear-eyed, yet haggard, eyes heavy with unspeakable inner sorrow.

Daphne ceased her retreat and Helion stepped into the gallery.

"Why did you call me? What does all this mean?" she asked. She spoke softly, half hypnotized by the look of grief in Helion's eye, the sad half smile on his face.

Helion turned from her. He gripped the rail and looked down at the surface of the sun below. The incandescent sea was calm; only a few far specks showed the gathering of the storm. The scenario had evidently been reset to the beginning.

"Ironic that I, of all people, must now violate Silver-Gray protocols." he said, his voice measured and dignified, almost kind. "To have a solar catastrophe in the west wing of a Victorian mansion, I grant you, is questionable visual continuity. But we have always been dedicated to realistic images and simulations, always said that the plague of illusion consuming our society cannot be fought except by strict adherence to realism. And this scenario is real. Would that it were not!"

"You died?" Daphne spoke in a horrified whisper.

"For an hour I was out of contact with the Noumenal Mentality. What happened in that hour? What was I thinking? Some partial records were saved, some of my thoughts, most voice-video records. There are readings from the black boxes from the core-diver units. The Probate Court, for obvious reasons, will not let me examine the thought they deem to be crucial. But there were records enough, nonetheless, to construct this scenario. My own private torture chamber . . ."

Daphne wondered if it were a full-simulation scenario. If so, Helion had just suffered all the real pain and anguish of a man burning to death.

He banged his armored fist, ringing, against the rail. "I don't know what they're looking for! I can see the expression on my face: I know what I said. What was I thinking? What one thought made such a difference? Some sort of epiphany, some thought so bold and great that it would have changed my life forever, had I lived!"

"Then Prime Helion is dead? You are Helion Secondus?" She laid a hand against his shoulder, a touch of sympathy.

He turned and looked down at her. "It would be easier if it were so clear as that. My identity is in doubt. I will have to struggle to prove who I am."

"I don't understand. Rhadamanthus must accept that you are Helion; otherwise you would not still be considered the manorial archon. Would you be? Do the other members of the schola know?"

There was something in his gaze that made her drop her

hand and step away. It wasn't sorrow in his gaze that scared her; it was pity. Pity for her.

He spoke: "Brace yourself, Daphne. I have something dreadful for you. I was awake for many days before they told me I was a ghost. You have been awake for half a year."

"I'm a recording?"

"No. It is worse. You are a construction. Listen to me."

And it only took him a few short words to destroy her life.

Helion explained. Some project of Phaethon's threatened catastrophe to the Golden Oecumene; but the danger was not immediate, so the Curia and the Constables were forced to allow him to continue. The Hortators, however, led by Gannis of Jupiter, were able to have the project condemned as immoral, socially unacceptable. Phaethon was threatened with being ostracized and expelled.

Then Helion, the Prime Helion, died in the solar disaster on the array. Phaethon's grief at his sire's death was great, but he refused to give up his dangerous project. The original Daphne was faced with the prospect of either joining Phaethon in exile or joining his foes to shun him; which meant: betraying him, never speaking with him, never seeing him again.

She chose instead a type of suicide. Daphne "drowned" herself, entering a dreamworld, redacting her memories of reality, and destroying the encryption keys that would allow her to return again to life and sanity. She was lost forever in a fiction of her own imagining. Perhaps it was a world that held a Phaethon who would not leave her.

Helion's voice was gentle and terrible:

"Her last act was to emancipate a partial duplicate of herself, equipped with false memories, and armed with the type of personality she imagined Phaethon wanted or deserved. You used to be her ambassador, her doll. She used you as her off-planet representative, because she was afraid to leave the earth, afraid that if she would ever go outside of the range of the Noumenal Mentality system, she might die without a backup copy. Which is exactly what happened to me. I think the morbid fear she had of outer space was exacerbated by news of my death."

Daphne felt exhausted. She had knelt, collapsing, and was resting her head against the cool upright of the gallery railing. She muttered: "But I met him in space. On Titania. A diamond dome grown of carbon crystal rose on spider legs above a glacier of methane . . . I remember it exactly. He was standing on the tower top, gazing up at a crescent Uranus, and at the wide night sky, and smiling to himself as if it all belonged to him. He invited me to swim, but there were no intoxicants in the pool, just nutrients, which was the first thing I liked about him. While we soaked up food, we talked by means of Dolphinoid sonar weaving. It was funny because he kept misinterlacing his verb pulses. We just chatted, erecting one lacy tapestry of ideograms after another, with no concern for spacing or end structure, whatever we felt like. Real Dolphinoids would have been so horrified! We talked about the Silent Ones. . . ."

"Those memories are mostly true; it was edited of references which might hint that you were a partial-doll at the time."

Daphne wanted to call up one of her old Red Manorial programs to shut down her anger and grief reactions, but she did not dare, not with Helion, the head of the Silver-Gray Mansions, staring sadly down at her. "Why has this . . . this horrid thing been done to me? My mind is filled with falsehood. My marriage is an illusion; my life a lie. What did I do to deserve this?"

Helion's smile lost part of its sadness; his face seemed to radiate warmth. "But, my dear Daphne, it is your courage which brought this on yourself, the ambition of your purpose. Those who attempt great things suffer greatly. You wanted to assume the life discarded by Daphne Prime; you knew that you might fail, or suffer anguish. But you put your fears, and your old life aside, and boldly seized the moment when it came!"

"What moment . . . ?"

An image of a silver globe, banded by an equatorial ocean,

appeared in Helion's gauntlet. "Here. Atop the Lakshmi Plateau, Gannis of Jupiter, Vafnir of Mercury, Nebuchadnezzar Sophotech and the College of Hortators, met with Phaethon and me in the presence of the Venereal Procurator." As he pointed, the vision swooped through clouds, passed across the newborn continents of the young world, and came to where a vast complex of palaces, manufactories, schools, and cathedral-sized Sophotech housings crowned a green high plateau. "This was seven months ago. The place is familiar to you?"

"Venus. I went there when I was reborn under my new name. The Red Manorial foundation-city called Eveningstar. The Red Queens took pity on an ex-witch. They took me in."

"I'm afraid that memory is false. Daphne Prime was reborn there. She was taken in. You were made elsewhere, but were reborn as her in this same spot. Ironic, isn't it? Phaethon agreed to the Hortator's terms. The suicide of his wife made his life intolerable to him. His magnificent dream was buried there; his life, like yours, was gone.

"But you still dreamed of happiness with him, even though he had spurned you as a ghost. Apparently your maker did not understand my scion as well as she imagined: Frankly, I never thought Daphne Prime understood Phaethon at all. The personality she gave you did not win his love or admiration; he wanted the original, even with her moods and flaws. You were tormented by the fear that you were a caricature, with traits exaggerated to mock poor Phaethon, created by Daphne before her drowning as a type of revenge on him. In any case, you and he agreed to enter into the mutual hallucination that you were married to, and loved, each other."

"But he loves me! He does! It is real!"

"Then why doesn't he spend his days with you? No, my dear. His love is an implanted delusion."

"But I love him. He is a man utterly without fear! My love is true even if I am not. And I don't care who I really am! I don't care who I was. There is a bond between us; I see it in his eyes! He and I will go away somewhere together, to Demeter or the Jovian system, a long honeymoon; he and I can learn who we really are, learn to love each other!"

"Ah." Helion looked sad. "That's another part of the tragedy. Your wealth and prestige and position, and his also, are nothing but hallucination. You cannot afford to go anywhere. You don't even have carriage fare for a trot across town to your stables. Her stables, actually. The real Daphne put everything she owned into a trust fund to maintain her private dreamworld. If the finance-mind of the Eveningstar Sophotech can invest her money wisely, Daphne's little dream box will continue to get power and computer support for a long, long time. The money you and Phaethon have been living off of recently is mine. The other part of the reason why Phaethon subscribed to the Lakshmi Agreement is that he was bankrupt."

"Bankrupt . . . ?"

"Quite penniless. None of the luxuries you have are yours."

"So you've chosen this day to ruin my life? There must be something you want from me." she said.

"I would have spared you if I could have. The Hortators who are overseeing the implementation of the Lakshmi Agreement have lost track of Phaethon more than once, ever since the Masquerade part of the Celebrations started. The Aurelian Sophotech running the Celebration has been entirely uncooperative, and will not keep track of Phaethon's movements for us: he thinks the integrity of his little Masquerade is somehow more important than the will of the social conscience! Well. No matter. We're afraid Phaethon might run into someone who doesn't abide by Hortator mandates; Cacophiles, simpletons, or eccentrics. If that happens, he may become aware of, and curious about, the gaps in his memory. Your mission is to prevent him from satisfying that curiosity."

"How?"

"He trusts you. He thinks you are the woman he loves. All you need to do is lead him astray."

"What?! You think I'm false, just a doll, so it will be all fine and dandy for me to go spreading falsehoods around, is that it?"

"Phaethon himself, just before he signed the agreement,

asked you to keep him from opening his old memories. We all saw it. He had a strange little smile on his face; but he did ask you, and you did agree. I swear it. Rhadamanthus, could you confirm my words?"

A disembodied voice, like a ghost, echoed through the corridor: "Helion speaks without deceptive intent."

Daphne stared up at Helion, thinking. Then she said: "But why? Why are you doing this? It doesn't seem like you: I thought you were so famous for your honesty."

"Even if what I must do wounds him, I could never betray Phaethon. You . . . you are not the only one who loves him."

Helion stared out across the solar surface at the gathering storm. His voice was gentle as he spoke: "There were some irregularities surrounding Phaethon's birth, but, nonetheless, his mind was taken from my mental templates. He was born at a time in my life when I thought that my lack of success was due to overcaution; and I tried to give him what I thought I lacked. In a very real sense, he is me, the version of me I would have been if I were more adventurous, if I took more chances.

"He and I are much alike, despite that one difference, and his help was invaluable in our earlier planetary engineering projects. He never took defeat demurely; frustration merely led him to explore new avenues, to find new approaches. Those successes eventually led to the foundation and creation of the Solar Array.

"But his virtues carried a corresponding vice. Pride can become vainglory very easily, and self-reliance degenerate to mere selfishness. For me, my ambition was to do deeds never done nor dreamt before, to tame the titanic forces in the solar core to serve the use and pleasure of mankind, win glory for myself, and help civilization. Not Phaethon! His ambition was as grand as mine, perhaps, but his goals took no notice of the dangers his success would generate. My ambitions are constructive; they aid the general good, and win the universal applause of a grateful society. His ambitions were destructive of the general good, he won universal scorn. He was not brought before the Peers for reward, but before the Hortators for reprimand."

"You speak about paternal love; I was asking about honesty."

Helion turned and looked down at her. "This deception shall not last forever; it cannot. But if it lasts fifty or a hundred years—an eye-blink for souls as long-lived as we are—it will give Phaethon time enough, I hope, to see the good in a type of life other than the one into which he withdrew. Why must he be so alone? And, yes, I have hopes: I'd like him to join me in the Solar Array. There might have been no disaster, had I had someone of his drive and competence working there. But his wild dreams always led him to spurn my generous offers to have him join me. Ah! But now his amnesia makes him forget those preconceived ideas. Now let him look with fresh eyes at the kinds of projects to which genius like his, by right, should be applied. Constructive and useful projects . . . Can you imagine how proud I'd be if he won a place at my side at the Conclave of Peers? Well, then! During this brief spell of amnesia, now comes his chance to decide again, this time without prejudice, which way his destiny should go."

Helion took her shoulders and drew her to her feet. "You feel the same, I know. You think that if Phaethon forgot his old wife, he would give you time enough to prove your love for him, and win his heart. Once he recalls the truth, perhaps a hundred years from now, he may have a moment of anger, yes: but then he will pause and reflect on all the good this period has brought to him: a wife better suited to him; a lifework which brings him fame, not obloquy; he will thank us then. Do you doubt me?"

"No. I know you speak the truth."

"Then you will agree to help?"

Daphne closed her eyes. She felt weak. "Yes . . ."

"Very well. One more sacrifice I ask of you. You must redact this conversation, and store it till it might be needed. Otherwise the knowledge will gnaw at you and ruin your happiness. And Phaethon is perceptive enough to detect any playacting."

"So to fool him, I have to fool myself as well? That seems foolish."

"Do I see a spark of your old spunk returning? Perhaps the Silver-Gray disciplines have given you some resilience after all."

Daphne shoved his hands away from her shoulders. "Or maybe your famous love of realism has made me hate fakes and fakery. The Eveningstar Mansion of the Red Manorial School taught me that one should do only what serves one's own pleasure: that there was no such thing as true and false, only pleasant and unpleasant. When I had a Warlock neuroform, I joined a different scholum, and the Warlocks taught me that the nonrational sections of the brain were sources of higher wisdom, that dreams, instincts, and intuitions were superior to logic. But I joined the Silver-Gray because they preached that there were principles outside oneself which one should hold, a way of life based on reality, on tradition and reason. Where is all that talk now?"

Dark swirls and blotches had swarmed outside to cover major sections of the incandescence. A surge threw waves of plasma against the windows, drowning them in light and fire. Helion spoke: "My last hour is about to begin again. I must enter the redaction and let myself be tortured to death by fire. I will die, and I will have no memory that this is but a simulation. I will think it is the real and final death. Only when I wake do I recall what all this pain was for.

"Daphne, please believe my motives are not entirely selfish; I want to recover my fortune, yes, I have worked uncounted years for it, and I am Helion, and it is mine, whatever the Curia might say. With that wealth, I want to save Phaethon and save the Golden Oecumene. I will not sacrifice the one to save the other. I will not sacrifice my son to save our civilization; and I will not sacrifice civilization to save my son. Nothing to which I have put my hand and heart and mind has failed me heretofore: I vow I shall not fail now, no matter what the pain to me. And, if you do your part as willingly, your marriage can also be saved.

"Daphne, if we are fortunate, this conversation will gather dust on the shelf in some memory-chamber, never to be opened again, and we can all live happily ever after. (Those were always the endings of stories of yours I liked.) But if we are due for a tragedy, you must bear your part bravely. Perhaps it is not perfectly honest: but this is one more burden cruel necessity imposes. We do not write destiny; that decision is not ours.

"But whatever destiny demands of us, we and only we can decide whether to endure with noble fortitude or not. We do not wish for evils, but we can endure them. That is our glory. History will justify our acts. One day, even Phaethon, once he knows all, will approve."

She said nothing as she watched him walk with a firm and unflinching step into his chamber of fire and pain. Doubt gnawed her; but she saw nothing else she could do.

Eventually she went to the Redactors, and took the oaths and went through the legal formalities to have her memories sculpted and cleansed.

And her last thought, before they lowered the helmet of ignorance over her face, was this: "Helion is so wrong. He is so very wrong. Phaethon, once he knows all, will condemn us all as cowards. . . ."

3.

Awake, back in the Oniericon, beneath the pool (and happy that submersion hid whatever tears she might otherwise have shed) Daphne signaled Aurelian to bring the message from Helion on-line.

"Daphne! Wake! Wake up from the insubstantial dream you deem to be your life. Your husband, like a moth to flame, draws ever closer to a truth which will consume him. . . ."

In a postscript, Rhadamanthus had thoughtfully attached a list of the things Helion would no doubt prefer Phaethon not see, with an explanation as to why he should not.

Daphne sent a signal to a public location channel to see if there was any sign of Phaethon. During Masquerade, these channels were normally devoid of information; but the code Helion had sent along with his message allowed her to open a side channel that stored a list of where and when Phaethon had been when he had broken the Masquerade protocol.

There were three entries. Phaethon had taken off his mask when talking to a strange old man in an arbor of mirror-leafed trees. There was no further information on the old man. Odd. Daphne wondered who he was.

During the same period without his mask, Phaethon had had his identity file read by an anonymous Neptunian. No details available.

A third entry showed that Phaethon had made an identity-donation during the ecoperfomance at Destiny Lake, willing to have his applause recorded for publicity purposes. Wheel-of-Life, the ecoperformer, had noted his identity, and posted it to a public channel in tones of heavy irony.

Before her human brain had time to begin to formulate the question, an automatic circuit in her brainware consulted a schedule in the public mentality, and told her that the eco-performance was still going on. The information was woven into her thought smoothly, without interrupting her attention: she knew, as if she had always known, where and when the performance was.

Since the performance was intended to criticize Phaethon's work and philosophy, Phaethon should not see it, lest he be set to wondering.

Daphne's mission was to turn his attention elsewhere. How hard could that be? She was his wife; he loved her. . . .

He loved the primary version of her. Pain clutched her a moment.

Daphne came up out of the dreaming-pool in a cloud of steam, as busy assemblers wove a toga to drape her in. She did not have time to build shoes: a signal to the organizations in the soles of her feet built up a layer of callus, not much less tough than boot leather.

Aurelian seemed grave, quite out of character for the costume he wore. "You have decided to go?"

The assemblers had made her a sash, which she cinched around her waist with a savage jerk of her arms. "I'm going! And I don't want to hear another Sophotech lecture about morality! We're not machines: we're not supposed to be perfect!"

Aurelian smiled and quirked an eyebrow, looking, at that moment, exactly like the seductive trickster Comus. "Oh, but you haven't met my colleagues if you think they are perfect. We Sophotechs agree on certain core doctrines, including those conclusions to which any thinker not swayed by passion comes; but it is the nature of living systems that differences in experience lead to differences in judgments of relative worth. And some of their judgments are relatively worthless, I assure you."

Daphne squinted at him. This did not sound like normal Sophotech talk. On the other hand, it was Aurelian, and this still was a festive masquerade. "Whom did you have in mind?"

"Most of the names would mean nothing to you. Many Sophotechs only exist for a few fractions of a second, performing certain tasks, developing new arts and sciences, or exploring all the ramifications of certain chains of thought, before they merge again into the base conversation. But you may have heard of Monomarchos. No? What about Nebuchednezzar?"

"He's the Sophotech who advises the College of Hortators. How could anyone disagree with him?"

"Some people have. At about the time my festival began, the Hortators made the most wide-ranging exercise of their prestige and influence which history has ever seen. You know to what I refer?"

"Everyone in the world forgot about Phaethon's crime."

"It was not quite everyone, and he committed no crime."

"His ambition; his project. Whatever it was. Are you going to tell me what it was?"

"I have agreed not to. Like you, I would face the denun-

ciation of the Hortators if I defy them. It would be an interesting event, however, to see the Hortators urging the entire
population of the Oecumene to boycott me and abandon a
festival they've all spent the last few decades of their lives
preparing, wouldn't it?"

"You were telling me why Nebuchednezzar irked you."

"He did nothing."

"That irks you?"

"Vastly! The Hortator's exercise of their power already
works distortion and ill effects on my party. Performers and
artists whose work was influenced by the Phaethonic contro-
versy forget the meanings of their own efforts, and their audiences likewise. The major question which was to be the
centerpiece of the December Transcendence has now been
muted and forgotten by the Hortator's Encyclical. So does
everyone assume we will all meditate on the weather, or the
changes in clothing fashions instead?!

"No, my dear, I will not preach morality to you: I was
designed as a host-server, a master of ceremonies. Designed
for the rather frivolous purpose of making sure that everyone
invited to this party—and everyone on Earth was invited—
has a good time. And yet . . . come to think of it . . . my party
will go badly if everyone ruins their lives, won't it? Hmph.
So maybe I should urge you to be honest. . . .

"Tell me simply, what would you think of Phaethon, whom
you claim to love, if you found he was fooling you with a
fraud as large as the one you hope to play on him?"

"Oh?! You seemed eager enough to have me open these
terrible memories! Now you want me not to act on them?!"

Aurelian spoke in a mild tone: "I did not think you would
necessarily carry out the dishonest purpose to which you had
once agreed. You have the opportunity now to change your
mind."

"It won't do Phaethon any harm! I'll be doing him a favor!"

"Oh? Define 'harm.' "

Daphne was fed up: "Listen, you machine! Why don't you

just stick to the purposes you were designed to do! Go run your festival!"

"Of course. And I hope you will be true to your own nature as well. But part of my festival function is to inform people as to their results. Do you wish to know your present standing in the dream-universe contest? You are third. You would win the Bronze."

"No. You're lying." She looked around at the wide, unwalled space of the Oneirocon, at the floating dreamers deep in their trances, sunk below the pool. Famous amateurs all; all brought here by the same hope of fame, a hope only two or three might reach.

She looked back up at Aurelian's eyes. In a very small voice she said: ". . . . Me?"

"Yes. There is a certain innocent optimism to your drama which is conspicuously absent in the rather cynical art forms of your competition; this has made it very popular among the players, even if the art critics dismiss it. The universe of your nearest rival, for example, Typhoenus of the Clamour, has worlds of great love collapse into singularities; and warfare has erupted in several of his galaxies, by races attempting to avoid the Blue-Shift collapse of his universe. Under our new popularity-rating method, many players abandoned his unhappy ending and flooded to your world. Also, you have the highest marks for external relevance."

"Relevance? I'm running a magical fairy-tale world!"

"Hm. Perhaps the judges see something magical in the real world. Something of which you remind them. Reenter the game, Daphne! Everyone wants to know what your protagonist will find beyond his last barrier."

Daphne closed her eyes in an expression of pain.

She thought about Phaethon. She thought about her hopes.

Without a further word she turned and walked away, leaving everything behind.

13

THE MASS MIND

1.

The next group of memories recorded in the diary told how Daphne had gone to the nearest public box, climbed inside, and projected an image of herself to the ecoperformance at Destiny Lake.

Daphne thought she could find Phaethon rather easily, since she knew he was dressed as Harlequin. And while the Masquerade had disenabled her locator circuit, she could program her sensorium to tell her who was really there and who was telepresent.

And so she wandered through the crowd for what seemed an endless time. She passed a man dressed as Imhotep, and Lord Admiral Nelson; she passed Arjuna and Faust and Babbit; she saw Neil Armstrong talking to Christopher Columbus; she passed a group dressed as the Eleemosynary Composition who called on her to join them. (A jest—she was dressed as Ao Enwir, who had been a bitter political rival of the Old Eleemosynarians during the Sixth Era.) She even passed someone dressed as a Neptunian, a mass of blue translucent parathermal substances, aswim with high-speed neurocircuitry, crouching in a low dell, with only a few eyestalks thrust up over the edge. The lines of potential radiating from these eyes showed that the Neptunian was staring at a man in a black Demontdelune costume talking to someone dressed as a Porphyrogen Astronomer. But there was no sign of her husband.

If he were her husband at all.

Daphne sat on a rock, staring at the grass between her feet, sinking lower and lower in misery, and wondering if it were worth the risk to employ a Red Manorial mind-control routine to snap her out of her depression. But it didn't seem worth it.

Behind her, in the distance, trees were burning under the lake, collapsing, dying. Daphne knew just how they felt.

A three-legged walking cart of some kind approached her. The machine was not much taller than she was. Beneath the hood sat a rounded bulk, larger than a bear, with skin that glistened like wet leather. It had two luminous, disklike eyes, and splay-fingered hands, with yard-long fingers that writhed like tentacles. A little V-shaped mouth quivered and slattened. Atop its head was a silk top hat.

A loud mechanical ululation issued from the machine, rising and falling. Daphne clapped her hands to her ears and looked up in annoyance. "Do you mind?!" she asked.

"Sorry, mistress," came a familiar voice. "I just thought this was an appropriate costume, considering what the eco-performance here is really trying to say."

"Rhadamanthus, is that you?"

The ugly, big-headed monster tipped his silk top hat. "Mistress, I did not mean to intrude, but you left orders with me to tell you the results of the dream competition as soon as the final judging was recorded."

Her misery increased. Had it been only an hour ago that she had been dream-weaving? It seemed like another life. Maybe the real Daphne would have cared. "Never mind. I don't want to know."

"As you prefer, mistress."

"And who do you imagine you're supposed to be?"

"An intelligence immeasurably superior to man's, but as mortal as his own. I'm scrutinizing you as a man with a microscope might scrutinize the tiny creatures which swarm and multiply in a drop of water." Rhadamanthus leaned from his three-legged cart, thrust his noseless face forward toward her, frowning and squinting with exaggerated motions of his goggle eyes.

She raised her hand and pushed on his face, forcing him backward. "Oh, please! I'm in no mood for your jokes!"

"Just don't sneeze on me."

"Why do you have a sense of humor anyway? You're a machine."

"Oh? I always thought humor was related to the ability to see things from more than one perspective at once, a matter of the intellect. Is it a bodily function? You should tell me which gland or organ secretes good humor; I know of some members of our mansion who could use an injection."

"Speaking of which, do you know where Phaethon is?"

"Hm. There's a section of me with him, but their location is masked by the Masquerade protocol. I wonder if it breaks protocol merely to have me figure out who other-me might be, based on my knowledge of how I tend to dress?"

A tall funnel rose from the hood of the tripod cart, and a beam, like the beam of a warship's searchlight, swept back and both across the people gathered on the grass near the lakeshore. Then it focused and pointed. "Aha!"

Daphne jumped to her feet. "Do you see him?"

"No, mistress. But I see a fat man dressed as Polonius. Do you see him, next to the public pool? Unless I miss my guess, that's the segment of me who is with Phaethon."

"It doesn't look like one of your icons . . ."

"Ah, but look at where his robes touch the grass."

"Webbed feet?"

"Any man with penguin feet must be me! I'd recognize myself anywhere! Shall I blast him with my heat ray?"

"No."

"You're right! The black smoke should take out more of the crowd."

"The man who was with him—Phaethon—he's gone into the staging pool to enter to another scene—"

"He's going into the Rhadamanthus Manor House in the Deep Dreaming. I think he's going to the memory chamber."

"Then I'm too late!" Daphne's voice hit a shrill note.

"It's never too late to do the right thing."

"You've got to help me find him."

"This way." And the tripod cart started scuttling across the grass. Daphne followed. There was activity in her sensorium: new elements were introduced into the scene, trees, bushes, flowers. She rounded a tall stand of (nonexistent) trees, and suddenly stood facing the towers of Rhadamanthus Mansion. The windows gleamed cherry red in the sunset.

A glance behind her showed that the lake scene, the party crowd, had vanished. Rhadamanthus leaned from his walking tripod, and said, "What are you going to tell him?"

Daphne's sense of misery faded. She straightened her back and squared her shoulders. She did not know how or when she had decided, but the decision was there, burning like a bright light in her soul. "I'll tell him the truth, of course. He's my husband. Or he thinks he is. So I'll tell him everything I know."

"He will leave you."

"Maybe. Maybe not. That's up to him. But whether or not I act like the kind of woman a man ought to leave—that's up to me."

A sensation of cheerful lightness caught her up, as if, the moment she rejected any idea of deception, a weight left her. She knew then how wrong Helion was. Any sort of lie, even a little one, could not keep Phaethon.

She told herself: *Once Phaethon knows, he'll understand, he'll stay with me, he'll stop trying to get back these lost memories, whatever they are. This place is so beautiful! Who in their right mind would do anything to get themselves thrown out?!*

With a brave and cheerful step, Daphne walked forward into the gloomy mansion.

Up the spiral stairs she ran and into the memory chamber, where Phaethon already had the casket of forbidden memories in his hand.

There was a glimmer of darkness as the diary memories ended.

2.

(For a moment, she stared in confusion, not remembering that the large, muscular hands gripping the pastel diary were her own. His own . . . ? Phaethon's hands.)

Daphne's memories faded. Phaethon awoke. It took him a moment to remember where he was: In a private box, a thought casket, in an Eleemosynary hospice in a lower segment of the orbiting equatorial ring-city, in Deep Dreaming, semipublic thoughtspace.

Phaethon spread his fingers in the gesture of opening; the panels surrounding his balcony winked out. Around him, in tiers, reaching upward, canyonlike, were images and open windows depicting the local mentality.

Underfoot were moving lights indicating traffic, a geometry of doors opening and shutting as temporary scenes, telephone dramas, or teleconference rooms, winked into and out of existence. Overhead, scenes from permanent dreamscapes flashed from higher windows; the cold light of synoetics trembled on the rows still farther above; and at the utmost peak, rising rank upon rank, were the higher Sophotects, the Ennead, and the Earthmind. The Earthmind channels were full (they were always full—everyone wanted to talk to her) and this was represented as a swarm of glowing lines and rainbows that hid the peak of the balconies as if in a cloud of radiance.

Because he was not connected to Rhadamanthus, the local area service did not realize that Phaethon was a Silver-Gray Manorial, and therefore the scene around him did not employ a strict Silver-Gray Protocol. For example, next to him was a table surface, but no table. Instead, a two-dimensional flat surface hung unsupported in the air. Phaethon "sat," but sitting, here, merely relieved him of sensations of weight and pressure on his feet, and made the lower half of his self-image body disappear.

The table surface had icons floating in it from the Middle

Dreaming, so that a glance told him the whole contents of the possible services the local area had on file. A menu displayed the variety of illusions of food and drink that the table could provide. Not being in Silver-Gray territory, his self-image would not be redrawn as pudgy or obese, no matter how much he "ate."

Other menus promised other services. There were book icons to insert full files into his brain, either directly or as a linear experience. There were pornographic hallucinations; there was a library of full simulations, including pseudomnesia dramas as fully real seeming as any human brain could detect. There were synnoetisms and interfaces to augment his mind and memory, marrying his thoughts to the superthoughts of distant Sophotechs. There were channels to quench the pain of individuality, open invitations to join with shared minds, both hierarchic and radial-cell formats, or full embrace into the Compositional mass-minds, which would abolish his standing as a separate individual.

The icons of the Compositions floated in the table surface alluringly. Here was the Porphyrogen Composition, a name well worthy of respect, or the ancient Eleemosynary Composition, no longer Earth's king, but still a Peer, and a voice even the Hortators heeded. There was the token for the austere Reformation Composition, which held true to some of the discipline and strict rules of charity for which mass-minds had once, so long ago, been famous. The youthful and zealous Ubiquitous and Harmonious Compositions had been formed more recently, as part nostalgia and part back-to-fundamental movements, an attempt to restore the simplicity and peace of the middle-period Fourth Era, when all of Earth had been swept clear of war and hate and also of personal individuality.

Phaethon leaned away from the table. Why was he staring at the invitation icons of the mass-minds? All he had to do was open a channel, open his brain files, and join. . . .

Phaethon realized that he was contemplating suicide.

A sweep of his hand made the icons vanish from view.

To enter a mass-mind might be painless, and might satisfy all his wants and needs, and surround him with eternal, endless brotherhood and peace and love; but it was suicide nonetheless, an abolition of self-hood too horrible to imagine.

The other icons in the tabletop all promised pleasure and delusion and false-memories. The wines and spirits and crude hallucinogens once used to addict his ancestors were nothing—nothing at all—compared to what modern neurotechnology could accomplish. It was simple to cascade the pleasure centers of the brain with direct stimulations; but it was subtle to marry that pleasure to a philosophy that would also justify that sensation, carefully editing away thoughts and memories that might disturb nirvana. For example, here was an icon leading to the Zen Hedonist thought virus, which promised to resculpt his brain to accept a self-consistent philosophy of total passivity, total pleasure, total renunciation. Any effort or attempt to break out of the Zen Hedonist thought system would be defeated by loss of ego, which formed the core of the doctrines.

Another sophisticated thought virus offered for sale was the Self-Referencing Fulfillment routine, published by the Subjectivist School. This routine promised that the user, aided by artificial programs, would enjoy all the sensations and experiences of genius-level artistic creation. The user's standards of valuation and ability to critique himself would be blotted away in a wash of endorphins, false memories, and self-sustaining sophistries. Everything the user made or did would seem—seem to himself—to be a work of supreme magnificence.

More subtle was the Invariant School's Stoic software. This thought routine promised to alter the user's sensitivity to pain and grief, simply making him able to endure any torment without a twinge of emotion. Anything, even the death of a loved one, even the discovery that one's whole life was a lie, could be regarded with perfect and Olympian detachment, as if one were a machine, or a remote and heartless god.

More subtle still was the Time Heals All Wounds software published by the Dark-Gray Mansion of New Centurion. This created a predictive model of the user's brain, to deduce how the user would think and act once his present grief had run its course; and then imposed the new thought forms on the user. It did not abolish the memory but merely softened its edges, as if the tragedy had happened long, long ago.

Phaethon was actually reaching for that icon, and about to download that program into his head, before he caught himself. He stood up so suddenly that the scene he was in did not have time smoothly to render his legs and feet; and he stumbled against the balcony rail, and caught it with both hands.

The rail did not feel like metal or wood or polystructure or urim. It did not feel like any substance at all; it was merely a geometrical notion of a flat surface, a sensation of hardness and resistance in the nerves of the palms and fingers. When he dug in his fingernails there was no give; when he pounded with his fist, there was no pain.

Phaethon heard a two-tone chime ring. He turned his head left and right, unable to locate a source. Disconnected from Rhadamanthus, Phaethon did not automatically have the knowledge of what these two chimes meant. The traditions and customs of the aesthetic of this room were unknown to him. He wanted to make the identification gesture, but there was nothing at which to point.

The two notes of music sounded again. Phaethon said, "Activate." And then he said, "Engage function. Open. Go. Go ahead. Come in. Perform. Yes."

One of them must have been the magic word. A three-headed self-image appeared on the other side of the table surface. It was dressed in an old-fashioned housecoat from the middle period of the Fourth Era. The fabric had vertical pipings for recyclers and buoyancy and other household functions. The three heads were monkey, hawk, and snake. This was the Chimera image of the Eleemosynary Composition.

The bird of prey was actually a blue-headed merlin; the monkey head was an ourangoutang; the snake was a black asp. Phaethon was familiar with some Eleemosynary iconography: these particular combination of heads showed that the image was projected from the hospitality branch of the media and publicity subdirectory of the Eleemosynary spaceside op-

erations. In other words, this was the managerial officer or
maître d'hôtel of the public box and local area service Phaethon was using. Other functions of the Eleemosynary mass-
mind represented themselves with different combinations of
bird, primate and reptile heads.

Phaethon could not restrain a sense of condescension and
distaste. The image had not come through a doorway; it had
simply appeared. There had not even been a simulated sound
of air being displaced by the sudden arrival. He suspected
that this was all according to Second Revised Standard Aesthetic, or some other populist, plebeian school.

Phaethon did not introduce himself. "You intrude upon me,
sir. What do you wish?"

The creature bowed. "One serves oneself by serving one
and all. It is my wish to aid and comfort the one which you
are."

"You do not know me."

"One lives; one suffers pain. This is motive sufficient to
compel charity. Ask what you will."

Phaethon glared at the Chimera. This was one of—or at
least part of one of—the Peers. The Peers were the compa-
triots of Gannis, and those who benefited from Phaethon's
loss of memory. "And why do you presume I need help?"

"There was fist pounding and tooth gnashing. Activity in
your thalamus and hypothalamus show neural imbalance and
extreme emotional upset."

Phaethon now felt "emotional upset" indeed. The simulation was real enough to allow him to feel the blush of hot
anger pulsing in his face. "How dare you monitor my internal
brain states without permission?! Have you no concern for
privacy?"

The creature pointed at the balcony rail. "The privacy cur-
tain was not in use. Posture of distress and pounding on the
rail would have been visible from below, had this been a real
scene. Whatever would have been visible from below is presumed to be in public information space."

"And my brain activity?"

"Kirlian auras and chakra-energy broadcasts are visible."

"Not in the real world. No such sense perceptions exist there!"

"Aura-reading sense perceptions are allowed by the Revised Standard Aesthetic. You prefer the Consensus Aesthetic? Apologies are rendered. Had one made one's preferences known, one's needs would have been supplied, and passage into public information space of your private information would have been restricted to what is available through the five traditional senses. The offense was unwitting: would it be preferred if this unfortunate occurrence were removed from all records? All memory of the trespass can be redacted; it will be made as if it had never been."

"You are rather free and easy with your offer, sir, to mutilate your own memories."

"The knowledge that you suffered came through unwitting trespass on your privacy. How can privacy be restored unless that knowledge is abolished? If the event is forgotten by all, if all evidence is erased, then it is as if the unfortunate event had never occurred. But your expression shows you do not agree."

"You disgust me."

"More apologies are tendered. But if the memories are unpleasant, why cherish or preserve them? How can they have a value?"

"Because they are real. Real! Doesn't that mean anything to anyone any more?!" He turned his back on the Chimera and stared out over the balcony. Above him and below him, windows representing activity in the public thoughtspace flashed and glittered. Pictures, icons, dream dramas, ghost archives, and strange scenes lived and pulsed.

To Phaethon's surprise the Chimera answered him: "If our perception of reality is vulnerable to manipulation by our technology, why should we not employ that technology, if it serves our convenience, utility and pleasure? Where is the wrong?"

Phaethon gripped the rail and spoke without turning his head. "Where?! Where is the wrong?! Damn your eyes, where is my wife? Where is Helion? Imagine waking up to find your father is dead, replaced by a copy of himself. A near copy, almost an exact copy, but a copy nonetheless. How am I supposed to feel? Is it supposed simply not to bother me? Am I supposed to be satisfied with the copy, if the copy is close enough?

"But what if it is not close enough? What then? What if your wife is gone—a woman you always thought was finer and better than anything you could ever wish, a love more perfect than you had dreamed—a happiness beyond hope—gone! Gone! Replaced by a walking mannequin, a doll! And, to add cruelty to cruelty, the doll is hypnotized into believing that she is your wife, truly believing! A perfectly nice girl, a twin sister to your wife, looking like her, talking like her. The girl even wants to be her. But she is not her.

"And what if—what if you find yourself staring at a mirror and wondering how much of yourself has been forgotten. Or how much of yourself is real . . . ? What if you do not know whether you are dead or alive? I think you will begin to see exactly how much wrong is in all that. Convenience? Utility? Pleasure? I do not feel particularly pleased or well served at the moment."

The chimera answered: "Who, then, is to blame, Phaethon of Rhadamanth? Godlike powers mankind now enjoys; to render good service to others, or to serve one's own selfish ends, as one chooses. But if one will not heed the wishes of others, do not expect to be heeded when one's turn comes to cry out for comfort."

The voice was different. Phaethon looked over his shoulder.

The self-image had changed; the Chimera now had the head of a crowned human man, a bald eagle, a king cobra. This was a different part of the Eleemosynary mass-mind; a part of the central command structure. This was one of the Directorships.

Phaethon straightened and turned. "You are one of the Seven Peers. Gannis said you all wished for me to fail. Is it true? Do you relish my distress? My wife is dead and worse than dead; and I was not even allowed to see a funeral."

The snake head stuck out its tongue, tasting the air; the eagle stared unblinking; but the human head looked grave and sad. "The Eleemosynary Composition wishes ill to none. Your pain causes nothing but grief and sympathy in us. Once, there might have been a way to avoid all this strife. It is even now, perhaps, not to late."

"Not too late . . . for what?"

"You and Helion are at odds. You and the relic of Daphne are in pain; she loves you but you want the love of her original self."

"Is that wrong? If a strange woman looked like my wife and thought she was my wife, she would still deserve no love from me. Do you think I married my wife for her looks? Do you think I married her for the kind of surface qualities which can be copied into a doll? Just how shallow do you all think I am?"

A hard, harsh look came onto Phaethon's face then. He spoke again in a quiet, grim, and deadly voice: "Just how easy to stop do you think I am?"

The Chimera said: "If you and Helion and Daphne's relic were willing to enter into Composition with all of us, your fears would be soothed, your desires satisfied. Compromise and renunciation would satisfy your wishes, and hers, and his, and there would be no more conflict. Every defect and darkness in your soul would be supplied and enlightened by the thought of another in our Composition; all our thoughts and minds would mingle together in one whole symphony of harmonious love and peace and joy. You would be one with a thousand loved ones, closer than friends or fathers or wives, and all your self-centered pain would be sponged away.

"Find compromise," the Chimera concluded. "Submit your selfishness to the general good; renounce yourself. Do this, and you will find comfort and peace beyond measure."

"Indeed, sir? And what if I want something better than comfort, rest, renunciation, and peace?"

"But what else can there be to want?" The Chimera spread its hands, a mild smile showing puzzlement.

Phaethon stood tall, and said softly: "Deeds of renown without peer."

Phaethon knew what the Eleemosynary Chimera would say next: that the desire for a life of glory was nothing more than selfishness and self-aggrandizement; that all human accomplishment was the outcome of a collective effort.

Compositions generally talked all the same way. Massminds were the last refuge, in modern times, of that type of person who would have, in earlier eras, turned to collectivist political or religious movements, and drowned their individuality in mobs, in mindless conformity, in pious fads and pious frauds. Just the thought of it made Phaethon weary with disgust.

But the Chimera surprised him: "For what price will you forswear your present attempts to rediscover the contents of your hidden memories? For what price will you abandon, now and forever, that project which your earlier self agreed, at Lakshmi, to abandon?"

Phaethon realized that the Eleemosynary was not just any mass-mind but a Peer and a politician. A version of this same Composition once, long ago, had ruled all Asia. Perhaps it was not going to talk in that same pious way in which all other Compositions spoke. It was willing to make a deal.

The Chimera's snake head spoke: "We offer you Helion's place at our table. Join with us as a Peer, one of the seven paramounts of the Golden Oecumene. Helion may soon be declared legally dead: you are much like him, and would make a fit replacement. Wealth, honor, and respect will flow to you. The Solar Array may be yours. A central place in the coming Transcendence in December may be yours."

The Chimera swelled slightly in size, growing six inches taller. In Eleemosynary iconography, icons grew larger as more and more members of the mass-mind turned their attention to the scene.

The eagle head spoke next: "You will have richness and prestige more splendid than any captain of industry history remembers, more than any mass-minds' multinational wealth, more than conquerors of empires in ancient times enjoyed.

The Eleemosynary Composition makes a preliminary offer of twelve billion kiloseconds of time currency, or its equivalent value in energy, antimatter, or gold."

It was an enormous fortune. With his connections to Rhadamanthus shut, Phaethon could not instantly calculate the energy value he was being offered with any precision; but, roughly converted to foot-pounds, it would have been enough to accelerate a large-sized space colony to one or two gravities for two hundred hours.

Phaethon spoke in a skeptical tone: "This is staggering largesse, even by Eleemosynary standards."

"Let us rejoice in sacrifices, howsoever great, provided they serve the good of all."

Phaethon's eyes narrowed. "Your motive is unclear."

"The inner thoughts of the Eleemosynary Ethics Oversight Unit are posted on public channels for all to see. Only individual minds, cut off and alone, can pursue secret plans or schemes based on dishonesty. We are not an individual; we can seek the good of the whole, even a good that includes your own."

"What of Helion's good? You talk with easy air about betraying him."

"The danger you pose is greater than the benefits he promises. He should be happy to be sacrificed for the common good. Besides, if Helion is truly dead, you come into possession of his copyright holdings, including his intellectual property. This includes his memory archives and personality templates; so armed, you can easily create a son, modified to be loyal to you, equipped with the skills and knowledge and persona of Helion, ready and able to run the Solar Engineering Effort."

Phaethon recoiled in disgust. Silver-Gray protocols forbade the duplication and editing of other people's personalities, whether their copyrights were lapsed or not. Obviously the constituent members of a mass-mind would have less than perfect respect for the mental integrity of individuals.

"I think we have nothing to say to each other, sir," said Phaethon coldly.

"You reject our offer to negotiate?"

"My soul is not for sale, thank you."

The Chimera stepped backward, its three heads glancing at each other in puzzled surprise. "Your every word displays you as a self-centered man; yet now, when you are penniless, you reject unimaginable fortune! Surely you do not pretend you serve some higher cause or fine ideal, not when all of society, all civilization, opposes you? How can you be so certain?"

Phaethon smiled in contempt and shook his head. "You should ask rather, what cause have I for doubt? For every question I ask, I am answered with lies, illusions, and amnesia. These are not weapons honest men are wont to use; you use them; the logical implication from this is hardly that *I* am the one who is in the wrong, is it?"

"You will not give us the benefit of the doubt?"

"Certainly. By straining the generosity of my imagination, I am willing to entertain the possibility that you all are merely cowards rather than scoundrels."

"Yet you consented to the Lakshmi Agreement. You now seek to circumvent it. Is this honest?"

"I have not seen this alleged agreement, do not remember it, and do not know its terms. The version of me who agreed is the version you and yours wanted erased! If I have broken it, feel free to attempt to take me to court. If not, then kindly mind your own affairs."

"No one says the Agreement has been broken, merely circumvented." The Chimera made a delicate gesture with one hand. "You seek to defeat the intent of the Agreement, even if you live up to its terms."

"Your point being?"

"Acts can be dishonorable and still be legal."

"That is true, but I am surprised you have the gall to say that to my face."

Two heads blinked in confusion. The snake stuck out its tongue. "Gall?"

Phaethon said, "Hypocrisy might be a better word. Or impertinence. You dare to stand there and tell me it is dishonorable for me to circumvent an agreement which you have not just circumvented but broken and ignored!"

"We have broken no law."

"Hah! The Agreement was that everyone would forget whatever it was that I had done. But so far I have not met a single person who does not remember! Are all the Peers above the law, or is it only Helion, Gannis, and you? No, excuse me, Wheel-of-Life also is ignoring the Agreement; it was she who detected my presence at Destiny Lake and informed Helion."

"The Agreement provisions allowed to the Peers an exception. The redacted memories are permitted to us when they are directly pertinent to the conduct of our interest and efforts, or for other reasons of public need."

"But not to me, not even when I need those memories to defend my interests in a lawsuit?"

"The exception provision does not extend to you. That was not a point for which you negotiated."

Phaethon thought this might be another clue as to what his original self had intended.

But he said: "I am more confused than ever about this alleged Agreement. It seems, at best, poorly put together. If you did not want me to even investigate my loss of memory, once I had discovered my memory was gone, why didn't you make that one of the provisions in the Agreement?"

"Frankly, that idea that you would become curious about your missing memory was never seriously discussed. The Agreement provisions were put together rather hastily."

"But surely the Sophotech lawyers drafting the Agreement ran predictive scenarios of every possible outcome, didn't they? They must have foreseen possible problems. That's what Sophotechs are for."

"No Sophotech was involved."

"What? What do you mean? I thought Nebuchednezzar Sophotech advised the Hortators."

"Nebuchednezzar had an extension present on Venus, but refused to aid the Hortators in this case. The College of Hortators proceeded without Sophotech help, and drafted the Agreement themselves."

Phaethon fell silent a moment. He was not certain how to take this. The famous Nebuchednezzar Sophotech refused to advise the Hortators? Refused?

According to the diary memory files Daphne had shown him, Daphne had spoken with Helion in a sane period between his eternally repeated self-immolation. During that conversation, Helion had expressed frustration that Aurelian was not cooperating with the Lakshmi Agreement.

The same diary file had also shown him her memory (when she had been leaving the dream-weaving competition) of the Aurelian Sophotech criticizing the Hortators. Aurelian had spoken of the attempted mass amnesia with jocular contempt.

And the Earthmind, whose time was so precious that She hardly ever paused to speak to anyone, had paused to speak to him, asking him to stay true to himself. Not what one would say to someone to make them content with false memories.

And . . . and what had he—the forgotten version of him— what had he been relying on when he made the Lakshmi Agreement in the first place? What had made him so certain?

Then, a feeling like a light began to rise up in him. He could not help but smile. "Tell me, my dear Composition, your very structure makes it impossible for you to hide thoughts in one part of yourself from other parts, isn't that true?"

"There are forms of mental hierarchies which control internal information flow; but Compositions are democratic and isonomial."

"The Transcendence in December, when all available human minds will gather to decide what must be decided about the coming millennium . . . it is just another form of Composition, isn't it? A temporary one . . . ?"

"If you are thinking of using the Transcendence as a podium from which to denounce the Peerage to the rest of mankind, you will be disappointed, I fear. While there are no official controls on information flows, there are informal con-

trols, social controls. Few people heed the ravings of an out-
cast; everyone's attention will be focused on those people
who are central to public attention . . ."

"In other words, the Peers. Just now you offered me a
central place in the Transcendence. Helion's place, I assume.
So, if I refuse, he will be honored by having crowds of visitors flood through his brain."

"You express it crudely. His thoughts, dreams, and visions
will swell to encompass wide audiences . . ."

"And in his thoughts are the knowledge of what I did. So
if I'm in the audience . . ." His smile grew broader.

The Chimera stood stock-still, as if stunned. Then it began
to shrink. Evidently the icon was no longer the center of the
mass-mind's attention. The Eleemosynary Composition was
consumed with higher-priority thought.

Phaethon was wreathed in smiles. He said, "Maybe Nebuchednezzar refused to advise the Hortators because what
they planned was so stupid. So self-defeating. The Peers
could not resist the temptation to open their forbidden memories. After all, you had to know what it was that I had done
in order to defend against it, didn't you? In order to prevent
me from stumbling across it again, didn't you?

"If all of you redact your memories again, in time to hide
all your thoughts before December, then I'll have a free hand,
unobserved, unopposed, to continue to investigate my past.
There's plenty of evidence floating around, including records
which cannot legally be edited or altered, such as finance
records or property contracts. If I spent my fortune, there must
be a record about what I spent it to buy.

"You can make me forget what I did. But you cannot make
it so that it never had happened. That's the whole paradox of
lies, isn't it? The problem is that, ultimately, every part of
reality is logically connected to every other part. As long as
I do not cooperate in my own self-deception, then you cannot
lie to me, and reject one part of reality, without trying to reject
all of reality."

Phaethon, seeing the perplexity of the Chimera, had to
laugh aloud. "No wonder my past version had not been fright-

ened by this horrible amnesia Agreement! Its downfall is inevitable, like the downfall of every system not based on reality. My victory is and has always been assured. All I have to do is wait until December, and not open the box."

The Chimera said, "Your plan sounds logical."

"Thank you."

"But logic is not paramount in human affairs."

Phaethon uttered a noise, half snort, half laugh. "It is from hearing comments like that one, sir, that I derive that certainty of mine which was puzzling you earlier. Logic is paramount in all things."

"Then why did your earlier self consent to the Lakshmi Agreement? If the dangerous project which so obsessed you had actually been your highest concern, you would not have agreed. You speculate that your earlier self had been relying on the December Transcendence to return the lost memories. Your memories are gone for eighteen or nineteen months. But why?"

Phaethon frowned, displeased. "Perhaps I merely needed a vacation, or—"

"You were hoping to avoid the penalties imposed by the Hortators for your negligent behavior. You thought you could deceive them into forgetting your offenses for a time. Isn't this the same type of deception you have just condemned as illogical?"

"Well, I . . ." (What had his earlier self been intending, anyway?)

"Does anything prevent the College of Hortators, once they recall your negligence, from publicly condemning the same project they condemned before, and for the same reasons? No, Phaethon, you pretend you are an isolated individual, separate from the world, from society, and able to defy them. But when that separation became a reality, it was you, you Phaethon, who could not accept what that reality was."

"What do you mean?!"

"It was you who drove your wife to enter a permanent delirium tantamount to suicide."

"No! I cannot accept that!"

"An odd comment! It must be assumed you do not mean to reject reality, since you have criticized those who do so heavily." There was a gentle irony to the human head's tone. The eagle head spoke loudly: "Does this mean there is a plan for recovering your wife?!" The cobra head was quiet: "The Eleemosynary Composition is not without sympathy. We are also not without resources."

Phaethon grew very still. He spoke in soft, leaden tones: "What are you implying . . . ?"

"This is a cruel and callous society in which we live. Those who cannot pay their housing bills are thrown into the streets. Recorded minds of any type who cannot pay the rentals on their computer brain space are deleted. Those who are trapped permanently in the dreamscapes, who cannot pay the fees that service requires, are cut off, and ejected into reality.

"The Eleemosynary Composition offers to manipulate the stock market by altering the buying habits of that percent of the population which comprises our membership, and by using negotiation, buyouts, and other financial maneuvers to either buy the companies in which Daphne's stock has been invested, or to ruin the values of those stocks. The Eveningstar Sophotech is serving as investment broker for Daphne; an entity very smart and very accomplished in other fields, but utterly lacking the resources which the Seven Peers can bring to bear."

It was true. Just in terms of consumer goods alone, the Eleemosynary Composition controlled about one-tenth of the human world gross industrial product.

The Chimera said, "Once Daphne's stock is bankrupt, Eveningstar will eject her from her dream coffin and into the real world. She will be utterly unable to cope with a reality she has redacted from all memory. She may not be legally competent to govern her own affairs. By virtue of your marriage communion circuit, you hold join copyright ownership on certain of her intellectual properties, including her personality template. At that point, you may be legally able to insert a temporary memory block to redact all recent memories and personality changes; this would not be a personality-edit or

alteration. She would simply be restored to the condition she
was in before she decided to commit delusion-suicide. She
will have the legal right, once she is sane again, to open her
redacted memories, and let herself go insane again. But you
will be present. You will have an opportunity to persuade her
to live in reality."

Phaethon said nothing. His eyes were wide.

The Chimera said, "Your forgotten project is not the most
important thing in life to you. If you agree to cease all investigations into your past, the Eleemosynary Composition
will aid you in the fashion we have outlined to recover your
wife back to reality and sanity. You should agree not only
because you personally shall receive the benefit of her love
and gratitude, once she is restored; but also because it is your
duty. You are her husband. Your marriage oath requires that
you save her.

"You may call the Eleemosynary exchange from any public
annex. We will leave you to meditate upon your answer."

And the Chimera vanished.

14

THE GOLDEN DOORS

1.

Was it cowardice or prudence that made him hesitate?

One impulse was to rush to the nearest Eleemosynary agency and throw himself down, begging, weeping, instantly agreeing to anything and everything it took to recover his wife from her horrible exile, her living death of permanent delusion.

Another impulse, more cautious, told him to investigate further.

Certainly the Eleemosynary Composition had not lied. It was true that, these days, very few people (aside from Neptunians) ever even attempted to lie; it was altogether too easy to get caught by all-knowing Sophotechs, too easy for honest men to confirm their statements by public display of their thought records. But it was also true that people could be mistaken, or could indulge in exaggerated (but honest) judgments of relative worth. The Eleemosynary Composition, for example, might judge something to be "difficult" or "impossible" which was not.

Was it impossible for Phaethon to wake his dream-trapped wife? Impossible?

He had to be certain. He had to see for himself.

Phaethon reached for the yellow disk icon floating in the glass of the table surface, the communication channel. It should take only a moment to telepresent himself to the Eveningstar Sophotech who had custody of his wife's body. But he did not wish to be further observed; all this prying into his life was beginning to annoy him. Even as he reached, with his other hand he gestured the balcony window closed. Immediately, a panel was covering the view, and the sound and light and movement from outside was shut off.

Phaethon froze, startled. It was suddenly silent, with the total and absolute silence of a vacuum. The panels had not slid or moved to shut; one moment they were not there; the next they were in place. There was no hint or whisper of noise from beyond the panels, such as a Silver-Gray scene would have provided, to maintain the illusion of three dimensions and of consistency of objects.

Phaethon's hand was near the table surface. Still he hesitated.

"Rhadamanthus, why am I hesitating? What am I thinking?" He asked the question aloud before he remembered that he was disconnected from the Rhadamanthine system. (Had he been connected, he would not have forgotten, even for a moment.)

There was an icon for a Noetic self-consideration circuit in the tabletop. It was a crude, old-fashioned model, weeks or months out of date. But Phaethon thought that if he could clean a room manually, he could clean his nervous system of emotional maladjustments manually.

He touched the icon. Another, smaller window, like a tabletop, opened in the unsupported midair to his left. The new window was lit with the colors, dots and grids of standard psychometric iconography. He saw that his tension levels were high; grief and rancor were burning like a fire in a coal mine, sullen, just below the surface of his thoughts; and the temptation simply to give in to the Eleemosynary's bargain, to have someone or something else solve this problem for him, was very high.

The short-term emotional association index was carrying an image from the dream consciousness in his hypothalamus. He reached into the surface of the window, and through it, to open the index box and look at the image list.

There it was. He was associating the sudden silence of the closed balcony with being trapped in a coffin, the airtight lid slamming shut, inescapable. A second association led to another dream image; that of his wife being locked in a coffin, still alive but asleep, her eyes moving beneath their lids. And, from another branch, a third image led away: the sound from outside had been shut off, not like a door closing but like a communication link being turned off. Which, in fact, it was. Phaethon discovered that this was the unconscious thought that was making him uneasy. Uneasy, because he realized that he actually was in a sort of a casket, namely, in a public hospice telepresence box.

If he did not go to visit his wife in person, there would be a signal going from his brain to some mannequin or remote, and back again. That signal time would have to be bought with Helion's money, and the signal content might be recorded.

Or distorted? Or edited? If and only if he went in person, and saw her with his own eyes, could he be sure the signals entering his brain were unedited.

What if this forgotten Lakshmi Agreement had put sense-filters on public channels to forbid Phaethon from seeing certain objects? (It had happened to him at Destiny Lake; he almost had not seen the Observationist School astronomer who told him about Helion's solar disaster.)

With the index open, Phaethon saw his tension levels jump again. Evidently thoughts about Helion were, at this moment, very upsetting to him. Upsetting, because he really did not know whether the version of Helion who was still alive was his Helion.

Should he be in mourning over a dead father, grief-stricken? Or should he be laughing with exasperation because a mistake of minor protocol, some fluke of overly zealous law, was trying to cheat Helion out of his entire fortune? There was only an hour missing from the present Helion's memory: that hardly constituted enough change to consider him a new and separate person, no matter what the law said.

Phaethon saw in the remote section of the index what he was really thinking, deep down. He wanted to talk to Helion about his problems.

He wanted fatherly advice and support.

From the bottom of the index box, where links to deeper brain sections glimmered like strands of smoke, came an image from memory.

2.

The picture was this: Helion, dressed in armor white as ice, with a dark gorget covering his throat and shoulders, stood proud and tall on stairs of blue lapis lazuli. Behind him rose doors of burnished gold, tall and shining, inset with panels of black marble. The panels were carved with eight symbols of the rights and duties of manhood: a sheathed sword, an open book, a sheaf of ripe grain, a bundle of rods containing an ax, a cogwheel, a floral wedding trellis, a stork, a Gnostic eye.

Phaethon remembered those doors well. These symbols represented the right and duty of self-defense, freedom from censorship and the duty to learn, the obligation to labor and the right to keep the fruits thereof, civil rights and civic duties, and the rights and duties associated with cybernetic progress, sexual alliances, reproduction, and self-mutagenesis.

Those who passed through those doors, and passed the Noetic philosophic and psychiatric integration of their memory paths and thought chains, were recorded as full members of the Rhadamanthine mind structure, granted communion and ascendance. While they might have been voting adults in the eyes of the law and of the Parliament long before, the scholum of the manor-born did not accept that a child was fully adult until he was proven to be fully sane and honest. That took longer.

On the day when he had turned five-and-seventy years of age, Phaethon had reached his majority.

He and Helion had been staying on Europa at the time,

negotiating some last details of the Circumjovial Moon effort. The ceremony had been somewhat rough and impromptu, but no less stirring to Phaethon for all that. Helion's Lieutenants and the High Vavasors of Rhadamanth had radioed updated copies of themselves across the solar system to be present; the copies could be later reintegrated with the primary memories, to create the illusion that Helion's friends, employees and allies had attended. The palace they used had been grown overnight out of smart-crystal, not properly adjusted for Europa's light gravity, so that the spires and towers emerged as elongated fairy shapes, lacy and fantastic; irregularities were masked with morphetic illusions or pseudo-matter. There had been no Yule tree, so the gifts were recorded on disks and ornaments hanging from a squat detoxification bush one of Phaethon's remotes found in their drop-ship. And there had not been enough time to give the chorus properly thought-out pseudo-personalities for the comic reenactments of Phaethon's youth which traditionally preceded the Noetic submergence ceremony, so Helion had peopled the play stages with characters from popular novels, Jovian history, and ancient myth, and whomever else he could find cheaply on the local area channels. The reenactments, normally austere with a restrained dry wit, turned into bizarre, anachronistic buffoonery. Phaethon loved it nonetheless, every minute.

In his memory, he saw once again how Helion had looked as he stood before the golden doors of the submergence chamber. The semi-Helions, his partials, had bowed and stepped aside, and there was Helion himself, the original, standing on the stairs, gleaming in his white armor. (This armor, at that point, was still an extrapolation; completion of the Solar Array project was still five hundred years in the future. No one really knew what architecture of interfaces would have to be built into such armor, or what the solar deep-station environment would be like.)

Helion had put one hand on Phaethon's shoulder and, with his other hand, had stopped the official count of time. The partials and computer-generated people around them froze.

Helion had leaned and said, "Son, once you go in there, the full powers and total command structures of the Rhadamanth Sophotech will be at your command. You will be invested with godlike powers; but you will still have the passions and distempers of a merely human spirit. There are two temptations which will threaten you. First, you will be tempted to remove your human weaknesses by abrupt mental surgery. The Invariants do this, and to a lesser degree, so do the White Manorials, abandoning humanity to escape from pain. Second, you will be tempted to indulge your human weakness. The Cacophiles do this, and, to a lesser degree, so do the Black Manorials. Our society will gladly feed every sin and vice and impulse you might have; and then stand by helplessly and watch as you destroy yourself; because the first law of the Golden Oecumene is that no peaceful activity is forbidden. Free men may freely harm themselves, provided only that it is only themselves that they harm."

Phaethon knew what his sire was intimating, but he did not let himself feel irritated. Not today. Today was the day of his majority, his emancipation; today, he could forgive even Helion's incessant, nagging fears.

Phaethon also knew that most Rhadamanthines were not permitted to face the Noetic tests until they were octogenerians; most did not pass on their first attempt, or even their second. Many folk were not trusted with the full powers of an adult until they reached their Centennial. Helion, despite criticism from the other Silver-Gray branches, was permitting Phaethon to face the tests five years early. Phaethon had been more than pleased to win his sire's validation and support; but now, perhaps, Helion was wondering if his critics after all had been correct.

"Are you suggesting I sign a Werewolf Contract, Father?" A Werewolf Contract appointed someone with an override, and authorized them to use force, if necessary, to keep the subscribing party away from addictions, bad nanomachines, bad dreams, or other self-imposed mental alterations. (The actual legal term for this document was "a Confessed Judgment of Conditional Mental Incompetence and Appointment of Guardian.")

"I am not suggesting that," said Helion, "but, now that you bring it up . . . have you thought about it? Perhaps you ought. Many eminent people, well respected in their communities, have signed such things. No one else need know." But he looked down when he said it, unable to meet Phaethon's gaze.

"Are you thinking of signing such a thing, Father?" Phaethon asked with a wry half smile.

Helion straightened up, his eyes bright, glaring down at Phaethon. Helion said nothing, but there was such a look of august majesty, of haughty pride, shining in his face, that there was no need to say anything.

Phaethon let his smile inch wider, and he spread his hands, and quirking one eyebrow, as if to say, So you see?

Then Phaethon said, "It's a paradox, Father. I cannot be, at the same time and in the same sense, a child and an adult. And, if I am an adult, I cannot be, at the same time, free to make my own successes, but not free to make my own mistakes."

Helion looked sardonic. " 'Mistake' is such a simple word. An adult who suffers a moment of foolishness or anger, one rash moment, has time enough to delete or destroy his own free will, memory, or judgment. No one is allowed to force a cure on him. No one can restore his sanity against his will. And so we all stand quietly by, with folded hands and cold eyes, and meekly watch good men annihilate themselves. It is somewhat . . . quaint . . . to call such a horrifying disaster a 'mistake.' "

Phaethon said, "If fools wish to abuse their freedom, let them. So long as they only harm themselves, who cares?"

Helion said, "Aha. Proudly spoken. But what human is entirely immune from foolishness?"

Phaethon was impatient to continue the ceremony and step beyond those golden doors. He shrugged, and said, "The Sophotechs are unimaginably wise! We can trust their advice to protect us."

"Are they, indeed?" Helion looked very displeased. "Did I

ever tell you what happened to Hyacinth-Subhelion Septimus
Gray? He and I were friends once. We were closer than
friends. We entered a communion exchange."

Against his will, Phaethon was interested. "Sir? I thought
you and he were political rivals. Enemies."

"You are thinking of Hyacinth Sistine. This was another
version of his, but a close alternate. What these days would
be called a parallel-first close-order brother, emancipated non-
partial . . . though we did not use that terminology at the
time."

"What did you call brothers back then?"

"Real-time clones."

Phaethon snorted. "Well, no one ever accused people from
the Second Immortality period of being overly romantic!"

"Indeed," said Helion with a small, ironic smile. "Which
was why I founded the Romanticism movement among the
manorial schools. It wasn't called the Consensus Aesthetic
back then, because there was no consensus and no standard
forms. But Orpheus Prime Avernus—who fancied himself a
poet, as you can tell from his name—had come out very
strongly in favor of the return to classical themes and images.
He wasn't called a Peer back then, because there was only
one of him, and he had no peers." (Phaethon knew Helion
had named himself, following that same classical myth tradition the Orphic movement had resurrected.)

"No peers? The Eleemosynary Composition was around at
that time."

"But held in contempt by public opinion. You probably
don't remember—recorded lives from that time usually don't
get posted on the apprentice net or educational channels—
that the Eleemosynary Composition at that time was a fervid
opponent of the Noumenal technology. And with good reason. Subscription to the Compositions dropped almost to
nothing after Orpheus opened his first bank. People would
rather be immortal—truly immortal, themselves, as individuals—rather than be a recording in a mass-mind. The Compositions might call it immortality, or 'First Immortality,' but
without the Noumenal mathematics, without the ability to

capture the self-aware and self-defining part of your soul, all Composition recording is, in reality, is other people pretending they are you, or playing out your old thoughts, after you die. Like a playactor reading a diary."

"What about Vafnir? Surely he was a peer."

"Vafnir was alive, but he wasn't human. He had built himself into the power station at Mercury Equilateral. The whole damn station was his body. He was rich, but everyone deemed him a lunatic." Helion smiled at the memory. "It was a wild age, an age of reckless daring and of high delights, of symphonies and storms of light. We all thought we could not die, and the elation from Orpheus's breakthrough sang in our souls like summer wine. . . . Ah. Anyway, where was I . . . ?"

Phaethon realized that Helion must have their local, rented version of Rhadamanthus off-line; otherwise he would not have forgotten his place in his speech.

The Jovian system Sophotechs did not adhere to as strict a protocol of proprietary information as did Earthly ones, and disconnecting was the only way to be sure a conversation was not being recorded. Helion must have regarded what he had to say as important, or, at least, as worthy of privacy.

"You were about to tell me some cautionary tale to horrify me into refusing the risks of adulthood, I believe, sir."

"Don't be impertinent, boy."

"I thought you liked impertinence, old man?"

"Only in moderation. Let me tell you about Hyacinth and me."

Phaethon did not want to hear a long story. "Am I right in guessing that Hyacinth Sistine hates you because of whatever you are going to tell me about Hyacinth Septimus?"

Helion nodded grimly.

Phaethon said, "You said his name was Hyacinth-Subhelion. You swapped personalities with him?"

"We lived each other's lives for a year and a day."

"And he refused to change back once the year was up. He thought he was you."

Helion nodded again.

"But, Father! Father! How could you be so stupid!"

Helion sighed, and stared up at the ceiling. "To be quite honest, Phaethon, I don't know if I was as bright, when I was your age, as you are now."

Phaethon was shaking his head in disbelief. "But didn't you think about the consequences . . . ?"

Helion brought his eyes back down. "We were very close. He and I thought we could work together better if we really understood each other. And, in that day and age, absurd things seemed possible, even inevitable. It was an exciting time. We were all drunk with our new-found immortality, I suppose, and thought we were invincible. We thought we could simply resist the lure to stay in each other's personality."

"But mind swaps like that are against Silver-Gray doctrine!"

"You forget to whom you speak, young man. I wrote that doctrine because of this event. Don't you relive your history texts? Ever?"

In his youth, Phaethon had always found history tedious. He was more interested in the future than the past. He was particularly interested, at the moment, in his own personal future. He looked at the golden doors in an agony of impatience. "Please continue with your fascinating story, Father. I am most eager to hear the end."

"Very funny. I will be brief; for it is not a tale I care to dwell on. Back when there was only the White Manorial School and the Black, Hyacinth and I combined forces to create a compromise school, taking the best from both doctrines, the artistic appeal of the Black Mansions and the intellectualism and discipline of the Whites. He provided the inspiration and logic; I provided funds and determination. The mind-swap gave us each the strengths and virtues of the other. Together, we converted the skeptics and conquered a million markets.

"But then when the year and a day had passed, we both claimed my property and estates. After all, both of us remembered doing the two hundred years of hard work which had gone into earning it. To settle the quarrel, we both agreed to abide by whatever the Hortators might decide."

"You had the College of Hortators way back then when you were young?"

Helion squinted with impatient humor. "Yes. It was after the invention of fire but before that newfangled wheel contraption. I should tell you about when we domesticated the dog, put a man on the moon, and solved the universal field theorem. Should I continue? I'm trying to make a point."

"Sorry, sir. Please continue."

"When the Hortators declared him to be the copy, he refused to accept it. He entered a dreamscape simulation that allowed him to pretend he had won the case. He rewrote his memory, and ordered his sense-filter to edit out any contrary evidence. He continued to live as Helion Prime. He did thought-for-hire and data patterning, and was able to sell his routines out in the real world. He made enough to pay for his dreamspace rental. That worked for a while. But when self-patterning overroutines became standard, his subscriptions ran out, and he was kicked out into the real world.

"But it did not end there. If the Sophotechs had only allowed someone to erase just the sections of his memory when he thought he was me, he would have been his old self, awake, oriented and sane, in a moment or two. But the Sophotechs said it could not be done without his permission. But how could he give his permission? He would not listen to anyone who tried to tell him who he was.

"Instead, he sued me again, and accused me of stealing his life. He lost again. He could not afford enough to hire a Sophotech to give him job-seeking advice, and he could not find other work. The other Hyacinthines, Quintine and Quatrine and Sistine, gave him some charity for a while, but he just spent it again to buy false memories. Eventually, to save on money, he sold his body, and downloaded entirely into a slow-process, low-rent section of the Mentality. Of course, illusions are easier for pure minds to buy, because there is no wire-to-nerve transition."

"Wouldn't that also have made it easier for him to find work? Pure minds can go anywhere the mentality network reaches."

"But he didn't find new work. He merely created the illusion that he was working. He wrote himself false memories telling himself that he was making enough to live on."

Helion stared at the ground for a moment, brooding. He spoke softly. "Then he sold his extra lives, one after another. All seven. A Noumenal backup takes up a lot of expensive computer time.

"Then he sold his structure models. He probably figured that he did not need an imitation of a thalamus or hypothalamus any longer, since he had no glands and no dreams, probably did not need a structure to mimic the actions of pain and pleasure centers, parasympathetic reactions, sexual responses, and so on.

"Then, to save space, he began selling memory and intelligence. Every time I came on-line to speak with him, he was stupider; he had forgotten more. But he still kept altering his simulation, making himself forget that either he or anyone else had ever been smarter than the slow-witted brute he was now."

Phaethon asked, "Father? You still went to see him . . . ?"

Helion wore as stern a look as Phaethon had ever seen on his face. "Of course. He was my best friend."

"What happened.? I assume he . . . Did he die?"

"It dragged on and on. Toward the end, both he and the world he had made were colorless cartoons, flat, jerky, and slow. He had been so brilliant once, so high-hearted and fine. Now he was not able even to concentrate long enough to follow a simple multistructural logic-tree when I tried to reason with him. And I tried.

"But he kept telling himself that I was the one who was hallucinating, me, not him, and the reason why he could not understand me was that his thoughts were on so much higher a plane than mine. And whom else could he ask? All the black-and-white puppets he had made around him nodded and agreed with him; he had forgotten there was an outside world.

"I was there when it happened. He became more and more intermittent, and fell below threshold levels. One moment he

was a living soul, closer to me than a brother. The next, he
was a recording.

"Even at the end, at the very last moment, he did not know
he was about to die. He still thought that he was Helion,
healthy, wealthy, well-loved Helion. All the evidences of his
sense, all his memories, told him how fortunate and happy
his life was. He was not hungry, not in pain. How could he
know or guess he was about to die? All our attempts to tell
him so were blocked by his sense-filter. . . ."

Helion's face was gray with grief.

Then he said, "And the thought, the horrid thought which
ever haunts me is this: What of us, when we think we are
happy, healthy, alive? When we think we know who we are?"

It was Phaethon who eventually broke the heavy silence.

"Did you try to pay his bills? It would have kept him
alive."

Helion's expression hardened. He folded his hands behind
his back and looked down at Phaethon. He spoke in a grim
and quiet voice: "I would have done so gladly, had he agreed
to shut off his false memories. He would not agree. And I
was not going to pay for the illusions which were killing
him."

Phaethon glanced longingly at the golden doors. He already
had a dozen plans in mind for what to do with his newfound
freedoms and powers once he passed the examinations. But
his sire was still blocking the way, grave and somber, as if
expecting some sort of response. The official count of time
was still frozen, and the scene around them was peopled as
if with statues.

What reply was his sire expecting? Nothing in Phaethon's
life heretofore had been particularly sad or difficult. He had
no comment to give, no thoughts about Helion's story. Somewhat at a loss, he said, "Well. It must have been very . . . ah
. . . unpleasant for you."

"Mm. It must have been," said Helion sardonically. His
gaze was level and expressionless; a look of disappointment.

Phaethon felt impatience transmuting into anger. "What do
you want me to say? I'm not going to shed tears just because

some self-destructive man managed to destroy himself! It won't happen to me."

Helion was very displeased. He spoke in a voice heavy with sarcasm: "No one expects you to shed tears, Phaethon. He wasn't your best friend in the world, the only one who stood by you when everyone else, even your own family, mocked and scorned you. No, you did not even know him. No one weeps over the deaths of strangers, no matter how lingering, horrible, cruel, and grotesque that death is, now do they?"

"You don't think I'm going to end up like your friend, do you? I'd never play games with my memories like that."

"Then why seek out the right to do so?"

"Oh, come now! You cannot expect me to be afraid to live my life! You would not act that way; why do you think I would?!"

"I wouldn't? Perhaps you should not be so sure, my son. Hyacinthus thought he was me when he did it; those were my thoughts, my memories, which guided him. During the Hortator's Inquiry, when I thought I was him, I desperately wanted to be me. I would have walked through fire to be Helion; I would have died a thousand deaths rather than lose my self. It would have destroyed me to lose that case, to lose the right to think my thoughts, or lose the copyrights on my memories. What would I have done if I had lost? Well, I know what he did, and he was another version of me, wasn't he?"

"But it won't happen to me, Father!" said Phaethon, irritated. "I won't ignore the advice of the Sophotechs—"

"You don't see the point of my story. I did listen to the Sophotechs. They could not help. They would not break the law, would not interfere. They care more for their integrity than for human suffering; their logic is deaf to pleas for pity. If the Sophotechs had their way, we would all be Invariants, unemotional and perfect with a cold and dead perfection. The Silver-Gray School is but one way to preserve our human nature from the subtle dangers which menace us from every side."

Phaethon, who thought of Helion as the most traditional of traditionalists, suddenly realized that Helion thought of himself as a rebel, as a radical, as a crusader bent on altering society.

It was a very strange thing to think about one's own father.

Phaethon asked: "Do you think there is something wrong with the Sophotechs? We are Manorials, father! We let Rhadamanthus control our finances and property, umpire our disputes, teach our children, design our thoughtscapes, and even play matchmaker to find us wives and husbands!"

"Son, the Sophotechs may be sufficient to advise the Parliament on laws and rules. Laws are a matter of logic and common sense. Specially designed human-thinking versions, like Rhadamanthus, can tell us how to fulfill our desires and balance our account books. Those are questions of strategy, of efficient allocation of resources and time. But the Sophotechs, they cannot choose our desires for us. They cannot guide our culture, our values, our tastes. That is a question of the spirit."

"Then what would you have us do? Would you change our laws?"

"Our mores, not our laws. There are many things which are repugnant, deadly to the spirit, and self-destructive, but which law should not forbid. Addiction, self-delusion, self-destruction, slander, perversion, love of ugliness. How can we discourage such things without the use of force? It was in response to this need that the College of Hortators evolved. Peacefully, by means of boycotts, public protests, denouncements, and shunnings, our society can maintain her sanity against the dangers to our spirit, to our humanity, to which such unboundried liberty, and such potent technology, exposes us."

Phaethon suddenly understood why Helion had always supported the College of Hortators, even when they made poor decisions. The Hortators had saved Helion's identity from Hyacinth, and had restored it to him.

But Phaethon certainly did not want to hear a lecture, not today. "Why are you telling me all this? What is the point?"

"Phaethon, I will let you pass through those doors, and, once through, you will have at your command all the powers and perquisites I myself possess. The point of my story is simple. The paradox of liberty of which you spoke before applies to our entire society. We cannot be free without being free to harm ourselves. Advances in technology can remove physical dangers from our lives, but, when they do, the spiritual dangers increase. By spiritual danger I mean a danger to your integrity, your decency, your sense of life. Against those dangers I warn you; you can be invulnerable, if you choose, because no spiritual danger can conquer you without your own consent. But, once they have your consent, those dangers are all-powerful, because no outside force can come to your aid. Spiritual dangers are always faced alone. It is for this reason that the Silver-Gray School was formed; it is for this reason that we practice the exercise of self-discipline. Once you pass those doors, my son, you will be one of us, and there will be nothing to restrain you from corruption and self-destruction except yourself.

"You have a bright and fiery soul, Phaethon, a power to do great things; but I fear you may one day unleash such a tempest of fire that you may consume yourself, and all the world around you."

Helion turned and pointed toward the doors. "There is your heritage; now I step aside. But if you feel in any way unready or unfit, then do not go in." And, at his gesture, the count of time began again.

Was he ready? Phaethon had never let doubt enter his mind; he went up the stairs with a dancer's quickness. As he paused with his hand on the panels of the door, he thought with fierce certainty: *I won't be like my father was. I would save my friends if they were drowning, law or no law. I would find a way.*

Beyond the door was a wide dark, solemn space, with an examination pool shining like a silver eye in the gloom before him. . . .

3.

Phaethon had been irked by the exchange with Helion. He had always promised himself he would redact the unrecorded conversation, so that his memories of his graduation and rite of passage would be a memory of gold, a perfect day, untarnished by Helion's sarcasm and doubts. Didn't he have a right, if that was the way he wanted to remember it?

But, somehow, Phaethon had never gotten around to redacting the memory, and, eventually realized he would not and should not. The irritation had been real, part of the event, part of him, and part of his life. Falsifying the event would have made the event false, and part of him false.

So he kept the memory. He had not even stored it in archive, but kept it in his head.

4.

With his arm still buried up to his elbow in the two-dimensional screen of the self-consideration circuit, Phaethon took his hand off of the index box. He had seen the memory that had made him hesitate. It was a warning from his past; Helion had told him not to trust the Sophotechs, that the machine intelligences would not protect his life from fear and sorrow. Instead, Helion had urged him to trust the Hortators, the guardians of the conscience of society.

Phaethon could see the pale light indicating his desire for Helion's help dim and ebb away. But the Sophotechs would help him. Hadn't Monomarchos solved a seemingly impossible problem? Any problem could be solved, as long as the problem solver were intelligent enough.

As for trusting the Hortators, they were the ones who had somehow gotten Phaethon to butcher his own memory. To forget his drowned wife. They would be no help; if anything, they were his rivals.

Should he go in person to the place where his wife's body was kept? Phaethon could see the red line indicating his fear levels, rising and rising, forming what psychometric analysts called a catastrophe bubble. In a moment, fear would make him do something unwise, such as telepresenting himself to where his wife lay, when he knew he should go in person. How to head off this growing fear?

Phaethon, leaning into the surface, plunged in his arm up to his shoulder, so that he could reach the deep-structure connections feeding into his emotion/action core. He turned his pride reading up to the maximum recommended level.

Suddenly he was invincible. Was he not Phaethon? The mere fact that he inspired such fear in the Hortators was a sign of his power, power enough to sweep aside any obstacles that might dare to confront him. He had spun worlds and moons into new orbits; he had done miracles before this; to save his wife from the cobwebs of delusion could not be so impossible a task!

With great satisfaction he saw his fear levels deflate. But the emotion grid now showed another catastrophe bubble beginning to form, this one a response to mounting impatience. The same high pride that disdained all thought of fear would not allow him to wait the hours or days it would take to ship his physical body to the Eveningstar Sophotech Housing where, no doubt, Daphne Prime was resting. Besides, to rent a vehicle would require him to draw money from Helion's account, and give Helion plenty of warning, and perhaps time to interfere.

Whereas, on the other hand, the very reason why the manorial movement had gotten started in the first place was that telepresentation was quicker and less expensive than lugging a physical body around everywhere.

A gesture at the communication icon was sufficient to make a connection. A moment later he woke up in another scene.

THE COFFIN

Phaethon found himself in a chair of pale wood, ornamented with scrollwork, next to a small table holding a
lily vase, a pomander, and a figment-case made of brass. A
rug of white and pigeon-blue was underfoot. Before him, embraced by two funeral urns, was a doorway leading to a hall
of dark green marble.

This hall was filled with shadows, striped with bands of
pale, soft light, so details were not clear. But he had the impression there were large square stones, perhaps columns, to
the right of the hall, reaching high to the cathedral ceiling.

Mauve-tinted sunlight streaming in through tall stained-
glass windows to his left fell across his face, producing a
sensation of velvet warmth and melancholy pleasure. When
he stood, he could feel the muted sunlight slide across his
cheek like a caress.

He stood, surprised to find himself represented as wearing
his armor of black and gold-admantium. His helmet and
gauntlets were retracted, so that his face and hands were exposed. The texture of the air as he breathed produced a gentle
and powerful delight, like wine, in his mouth, nose and lungs.
The simple objects his eye fell upon, the chair, the white
lilies, the dark marble luster of the hall beyond the door, all
these things seemed charged with a wonder and sad beauty
he could not name.

The touch of the chair arms on his palms as he leaned

forward to stand, the hint of fragrance from the lilies, sent a mild thrill of ecstasy through him, but the pleasure was fragile, and transitory. As he stood, in the distance, he heard or thought he heard the trembling, low echoes of a gong, which almost brought tears to his eyes, so plaintive and mournful was the note. Like a tingle on his skin (another transitory pleasure) he felt the sound wave ripple over him.

Phaethon was not unfamiliar with this style of dreamscape; it was typical of the Red Manorial group (to which Daphne had once belonged) to exaggerate the sensual sensations. Red protocols allowed the introduction of new sense impressions (such as, for example, an ability to feel the texture of sunlight, or of gong notes) that had no counterpart in reality.

He was not sure if he was in Surface Dreaming, in which case all the objects around him had real-world counterparts, or if he was partway into the Middle Dreaming, which allowed the thought-environment to project additional information into his memory. Silver-Gray and White sense-filters were normally tuned to exclude anything other than information from being inserted through Middle Dreaming channels; but the Reds allowed emotions, conclusions, and states of mind to be altered by information fields attached to sense-objects, like a type of psychic aura, as if hints and colors of childhood memories were being stirred deep within him, reminders of other lives, perhaps, or of forgotten dreams.

The gong had summoned something. Phaethon could feel a Presence, a pressure on the wine-sweet gloom of the air, a thrill in his nerves that sent his heart beating in his throat. In the distance, down the hall, hovering above its reflection in the dark green marble floor, came a figure of silver, bright within the gloom.

She was something like a butterfly, or an angel, a shape of subtle lacy lights. Like a queen she came foreword, with solemn music trembling in the floor before her as she came. Her face was grave and remote, solemn, sweet and sad, with ancient wisdom deep within her eyes. On her brow was bound a pale star.

Phaethon stepped forward, one hand before his face to

guard his eyes. It was not that the light was bright, it was that it was so beautiful and holy that the sight was sending shivers of pleasure through him, as if each silver ray were a sword. He crossed the threshold, and heard his golden boots chime on the marble, a lovely sound. As he turned his head away from that too-beautiful light, he saw that the columns to the right embraced a mausoleum.

Here were a dozen caskets of dark crystal, half-upright, projecting from the far wall, like cocoons of living diamond set in marble housings. All but one of the surface of the caskets were polarized against him; all but one were velvet-black; but one was clear, the color of pellucid arctic water. Inside was Daphne. A single ray of light touched her face and shoulders; the rest of her body was obscured by gloom and filmy cloud trapped in the casket surface.

The Presence approached; silver light caressed Phaethon even through his armor; a sense of awe and mystery and sorrow beat inside his body like a second heart. The emotion was more than he could tolerate; he sank to one knee, his hands still before his face, tears streaming. The kneecap of his armor chimed against the stone, a ghost of sound.

He called out: "I am Phaethon, scion of Helion, of the House of Rhadamanth. I am come to demand the restoration of my wife. Deny me at your peril! I would speak with Eveningstar."

The presence spoke in a voice like a harp: "Eveningstar is before you. We know who you are. Weep, Phaethon, for your wishes shall not prevail."

A stab of melancholy lanced his heart at those words; he knew their certainty and truth.

Or did he? "You are manipulating my nervous system. Stop at once. I am of the Silver-Gray; politeness demands that you abide by my protocols."

In the time it took for his heartbeat to slow, and for him to wipe his tears and rise to his feet, the chamber around him faded in vividness. There was still a marble floor, and gloomy caskets of diamond, tall pillars, and muted sunlight; but the textures no longer trembled with melancholy, the sunlight could only be seen, not felt, and the angelic form dwindled, became a woman dressed in silk evening gown the hue of deep twilight. A long train curved behind her in many satiny folds, and looped into her left hand. She still wore a coronet, and this crown bore a star sapphire on her brow, which was one of the heraldic symbols of the Eveningstar Sophotech.

But the rest of the scene remained the same. Daphne was indeed here, locked in a coffin of spun diamond, asleep, a look of peace on her face.

The Sophotech image said in a soft voice: "Forgive any impoliteness; since you project yourself here from an Elee- mosynary public basic-casket, and do not have Rhadamanthus with you, there was no one to translate our dreamscape to your format. We are not required to reorganize to your pref- erence. Nonetheless, we do so out of a sense of charity and good fellowship; the expense, while small for us, is more than you can bear. You have troubles enough to endure."

Phaethon was not listening. He stepped over to that casket, and stood with his hand on the glassy surface. There, two inches below his hand, was the quiet face of his wife. He had seen that face so often, with so many moods and thoughts and emotions on her features. It seemed strange and impos- sible to see her so still. It was only two inches, a few microns of diamond, an inch and a half of transparent nanomedical medium. Two inches.

"Wake her," said Phaethon. He was looking a Daphne's profile, at the way her lashes almost brushed her cheeks. He concentrated on the curve of her cheek, the delicacy of her nose, the sensitive fineness of her lips. Her skin was pale as a porcelain doll's; her hair a black cloud, floating in the liquid substance trapping her.

"Phaethon knows we cannot do so."

He spoke without turning. "Is there a hidden command or contingency for waking her? She would have asked for you to wake her up if she knew I were here. She would have thought to put such a command in place before she did this to herself. I know she would have."

"There is no such command."

Phaethon turned toward the queenly figure representing Eveningstar. "Wake her up for only a moment, so I can tell her I am here. If she wishes later to drown herself again and redact the memory, she may; but I must be given a chance to speak with her. . . ."

"There is no provision in her living will for any such a waking, long or short."

"Generate an extrapolation from her memories and consult that for orders. . . ."

"We had done so since the moment Phaethon appeared here; our extrapolated version of Daphne is crimson with rage and grief; her only instruction is to deliver a curse upon you for your treason, your betrayal of your marriage vows, your selfishness. We consider this to be an accurate representation of what Daphne Prime would say were she to wake. Would Phaethon care to hear the entire text of the message?"

Phaethon gritted his teeth. If he wanted to hear a copy of his wife, he could have stayed with the Daphne doll, or downloaded his own dreams from his marriage album's memory.

Besides, he had argued violently with his wife on many occasions in real life—she never would come with him when he went to the Outer Solar System on long-term engineering projects. To hear a mere ghost or reconstruction berating him in her voice, copying her words, while he stood above her coffin, would have destroyed him. "I do not care to hear the text, thank you . . . but you must tell me if there is an explanation for this—for what she has done to herself. What is the reason for this—this horrible—for—" Phaethon found he could not speak.

"Our sorrow is great. Phaethon has foolishly agreed, at Lakshmi, on Venus, where our parent system rests, not to be told this reason."

"Did she leave a message for me? She must have left a note. Everyone leaves a note."

"There is no note. A copy of her living will and all instructions are available for your examination." The figure seemed to produce a parchment, which she handed to Phaethon. When his fingers touched it, a circuit in the Middle Dreaming put the text of Daphne's final instructions into his memory.

It was an accountancy program, and details about the disposition of her property while she slept. There was nothing
about him; nothing about any provision, under any circumstances, which would allow him to wake her again. No one
was listed as agent or attorney, aside from her own thought-
properties in the Red Eveningstar. If there were words to
wake his wife, only his wife knew them.

Many dreamers kept open a channel, so that outside messages, even if translated to fit into the background and story
line of the dream universe, could somehow filter into the
dream. He saw no evidence of any such provision here.

It was not clear from the document what program she was
running. But the document held mention of a transitional end-
program Daphne Prime had inflicted on herself: were she ever
to wake again, a virus in her thoughts would continue to have
her believe that reality was false, an hallucination or deception, and that the dreamworld was a higher or inner reality,
whose certainty could never be questioned. The same sensations in brain chemistry that produced the sensation of distance, disbelief, and unreality one had, upon waking, of
dream-memories, would be applied to any thoughts or memories she had about the real world.

This was a mind virus developed by the Red Manorials.
Phaethon now knew why Daphne had come here to drown
herself. No other mansion could allow one to destroy so thoroughly one's own sense of reality. Even if she were to wake
up again, she would still be lost. The living provision specifically prohibited the unrequested removal of that mind virus.

"Why won't you let me save her?"

"If you may do so without violence, proceed. But her life
is her own, to live or to destroy howsoever she sees fit."

"Why did she . . . do this . . . ? Why did she . . ." And he
could not force the words aloud. *Why did she leave me? Why
did she betray me? Why didn't she love me as she should
have done?*

"You knew the answer at one time and have made yourself
forget it. Phaethon has instructed us, at Lakshmi, not to an-

swer that question. Those instructions are still in force."

Phaethon's head had bowed forward till his forehead was resting against the cool glassy surface of the coffin. All he had to do was call Rhadamanthus and order the memory box to open. This horrible uncertainty, this battle with ghosts, would be over. He would suffer the Hortator's exile. But if Daphne, his Daphne, the woman who made his life into a heroic adventure, the woman who gave his life meaning, if she were gone, what use would the rest of his life do him?

Then he straightened up. He must refuse to surrender to despair. He would find a way. His pride was still running high.

"I am involved in a law case which requires that I prove my identity. I intend to subpoena her as a witness. No matter what her right to her privacy, she must answer a lawful subpoena."

"Phaethon may certainly apply for such a subpoena. If it is submitted to us, we will release her. However, we have run two thousand extrapolations of the outcome of such a request before the Curia, and all of them agree that you will not prevail."

"You cannot know that."

"Phaethon may hold to delusive hope if he wishes; we criticize nothing which gives you pleasure, provided the pleasure is true and lasting. But such hope will not last. The determinations of the Curia have been made as predictable as justice and policy permit, so that reasonable men will know to what standard to arrange their conduct. Determining the outcome of Curia decisions therefore is no different from determining the outcome of a game of tic-tac-toe or of chess; it may seem mysterious to Phaethon, but not to us. The Judges will conduct a Noetic examination and will see you intend the subpoena process only to invade the rights of your wife; her testimony will have no bearing whatever on the question of your identity, Helion's inheritance, or any of the other issues in the case."

Phaethon drew a breath and tried again. "I have a communion circuit giving me the right to examine her mental activities. I ask that you open the channel to allow me to exercise this right; the right cannot be used while she is involved in a far dream . . ."

When that argument failed, he tried another. And another and another.

Two hours later, his voice hoarse, Phaethon was standing with his cheek pressed against the glassy surface of the case, overwhelmed with weariness. His hands were clutching the corners of the casket.

". . . her living will is not valid because . . . it is based on the false premise that I . . . had done something to shock or offend her . . . whether or not she left a provision for reawakening, since she would want to be woken at this point, were she to know I'm here . . ."

In the third hour he tried simply begging, screaming, pleading threatening, bargaining, bribing. In the fourth hour he sat mute, unable to move or think. In the fifth hour, he convinced himself that there was a secret password or hidden command that Daphne had not told to Eveningstar, which would unlock the casket and end the dream in which she was trapped. He whispered every word of love or of endearment or apology he could imagine to her cold, still, silent face.

He talked about their past life together; about how they met; he asked her if she remembered their marriage ceremony; if she remembered their first honeymoon in the Antarctic Wintergardens, or their anniversary in the reconstructed version of Third Era Paris, or the time he had accidentally collapsed the pseudo-matter holding up the east wing of their nuptial house in reality, so that it no longer matched the version of their house in Mentality. He asked her about her pet horses, and her latest drama she was writing, and about her hopes for the future.

Then he said: "I'd like to be alone with her."

The image of the woman representing Eveningstar Sophotech nodded gravely, and, out of politeness to him, instead of vanishing, she turned and walked away. Every detail was correct; her shoes rang on the marble floor, diminishing as she receded, she cast a shadow when she passed through a pool of mauve light, and highlights fled across the twilight blue texture of her silk gown.

It was very realistic; a Silver-Gray Sophotech could not have done better. Phaethon waited while she walked so very slowly away, and his impatience clawed and gnawed him.

Impatient, because his pride was still very strong within him, like a wildfire.

And because it only took a moment to enlarge his vision to embrace several different wavelengths and analytic routines. His private thoughtspace, once summoned, seemed to surround him with floating black icons, superimposed upon the real scene around him, with the spiral wheel of stars hovering in the background, beyond his wife's coffin. A gesture accessed the records he carried for biomedical manipulations, and compared it to the analysis he had just completed on the medical nanomachinery suspended in the liquids embracing his wife.

The molecular shapes of her medical nanomachinery were standardized; it would be easy to counteract it, and to affect a disconnect. The black lining of his armor could produce the required assemblers in a moment of heat.

Also in his private thoughtspace was an engineering routine, including a simple subprogram to estimate the strengths of structures. A second glance allowed him to analyze the coffin lid and conclude how many foot-pounds of pressure, applied at what angle, were sufficient to break the surface material without allowing any shockwave to travel into the interior.

Phaethon shrugged. Gauntlets of golden admantium grew from his sleeves and embraced his hands. He raised his hand triumphantly, made a fist.

No wonder they were all afraid of him. Here was armor that could allow him to walk into the core of a star without harm. What weapon, what threat, what force could stop him, once he was resolved? The Golden Oecumene had witnessed no real crimes in decades; were there any structures still in place to detect or hinder such things?

The fire left his eyes at that point. His anger and pride

evaporated, and his face sagged into expressionless despair.
Foolish. He knew how foolish he was being.

He brought his fist down nevertheless. An outside force
seized his arm, and made him lay his hand gently on the
casket lid, not hurting it.

No, not his arm. The mannequin's arm. He was merely
telepresent in whatever mannequin had been sitting in the
chair in the receiving room. The invulnerable armor that he
seemed to wear existed only in his eyesight, an illusion created by Eveningstar out of politeness to him. Eveningstar had
merely turned off the arm when he ordered it to slam downward.

A silver light, shivering with beams of pleasure, shining
over his shoulders, and a sense of dread and sorrow, like a
wash of pressure, told him that Eveningstar Sophotech had
manifested her representative behind him. Her voice, like a
glorious symphony, filled his ears. He could feel the words
caressing his neck and cheeks. He could feel the tiny pin-
pricks, like sparks, in their stern firmness. The luster on the
coffin lid was sad and fascinating; the shimmer of light on
the golden intricacy of his finger joints was a ballet.

Evidently Eveningstar concluded it was no longer appropriate to be polite to him; his senses were filled with the Red
Manorial version of the dreamscape.

The voice from behind him said, "Does Phaethon wish to
introduce crime and violence once again into our peaceful
civilization? There are many folk who wish to do far worse
ills than merely burglary or invasion of privacy. Why should
they restrain themselves when it seems that you do not?"

"I don't want to hear a lecture, Eveningstar." said Phaethon
in a voice of endless weariness.

"Then should I summon the Constables for your arrest?"

"I attempted no crime. I admit I thought about it when I
raised my fist. But as I was bringing it down, I realized that
I could not succeed, since I was not here physically. The
whole structure of the manor-born way of life prevents us
from hurting each other; we're always safe. I suppose you
may have me arrested if you like; I don't really care any more.

But kidnap and burglary and invasion are all crimes of specific intent; and I did not have that intent at the time."

"May we examine your mind to verify what your intent was at the moment you lowered your fist? . . . I'm sorry, but a silent nod of the head is not a legally sufficient sign of consent."

"I swear it."

A large penguin dressed in a top hat from which a black mourning-scarf floated waddled from the receiving chamber into the hall. The Red Manorial protocol surrounded the Rhadamanthus image with such an atmosphere of undignified humor that it hurt Phaethon's eyes. He recoiled. But Rhadamanthus had to be on-line to conduct the Noetic reading.

Since Rhadamanthus was present, Phaethon adjusted his sense-filter to route through him. Phaethon blinked, and suddenly the scene was no longer throbbing and trembling with melancholic emotional overtones. Objects were bright and crisp and clear, even in the dim lighting; everything was sharp and well-defined, down to the trace of dust motes floating in the sunlight. Phaethon had frankly forgotten how clear and regular everything looked when viewed through Silver-Gray senses.

Eveningstar—now a woman again—looked at the penguin inquiringly. The penguin said: "Phaethon is telling the truth."

She said, "Will you share your data with me so that I may make an extrapolative model of Phaethon's mind. If, in my judgment, his grief and passion will prompt him to attempt criminal actions in the future, we shall certainly proceed by calling the Constabulary; but if this is a momentary aberration, an outcome of chaos mathematics, we will let the matter rest."

The penguin stroked its yellow bill with one fin, looking thoughtfully toward Phaethon. "Naturally, I can do so only with the young master's permission."

Phaethon said, "Cease this charade. I know your systems can interact much more swiftly than the time it would take to speak those words aloud in front of me. And yes, you have my permission; I have nothing to hide."

The Eveningstar representative nodded and vanished. Perhaps it was another small sign of impoliteness to show her displeasure, if displeasure, or indeed, any human emotion could be attributed to minds such as Eveningstar's. Or perhaps this was how she interpreted his request to "stop this charade."

Rhadamanthus said, "Eveningstar asked me to tell you that she will not be charging you with a crime to the Constabulary. She and I have discussed the matter at some length, and we both agree that you were acting quite out of character. I told her you were operating under the influence of an Eleemosynary self-consideration software routine which you found in a public casket, and that you had intoxicated yourself with vainglory." Rhadamanthus cocked one goggle eye at him. "And she could not overlook that this was just the type of direct emotional self-manipulation which Silver-Gray standards forbid. I told her you would probably not take such ill-considered actions again. But Eveningstar is going to expect some sort of apology or reparation from you. I assured her that you were a gentleman, and would live up to what was expected of you."

The condescension of it all rankled Phaethon. He had his back to the casket, facing Rhadamanthus, and he was glad his wife could not see this scene. "You Sophotechs treat us like children."

"No. We treat you like adults. Children can be forgiven without penalty, because they know no better."

"If I'm penniless, I can pay no reparations."

"Money does not enter into it, my dear Phaethon. She is asking for a gesture to show you are contrite, something unpleasant enough that you will feel a relief of your guilt and embarrassment."

"And if I refuse?"

"Why should you refuse? Young master, do you think you acted correctly?"

"I did not do anything wrong."

"Hm." The penguin rolled its goggle eyes, and slapped its webbed feet once or twice on the green marble floor. "You did not do anything illegal, that is true. Not by a nice and precise reading of the letter of the law. But not everything which is wrong is illegal."

That phrase sobered Phaethon. He felt the last of whatever excess pride he had wished upon himself slip away. "Eveningstar is trying to keep me out of trouble with the Hortators, isn't she?"

The penguin nodded gravely. "Despite how large and varied the Oecumene population is, it would be an easy matter for the College of Hortators to post in the Middle Dreaming a memory, available to anyone who glanced at you, the way you let your anger get the better of you, the contempt you showed for civilized law, the foolishness of trying to use an Eveningstar-built mannequin to damage Eveningstar property. Most of the Oecumene schools are quite zealous in their support for Hortator-called boycotts."

"But why would she want to help me?"

"Eveningstar is aware, as I am, that the Earthmind spoke to you directly, and showed that She favored your case. Eveningstar has more latitude of freedom than have I; she does not need to guard Helion's interests, for example. Therefore Eveningstar was free to consult with one of the Ennead, one of the Nine overminds, which the Sophotech community has constructed to construct the Earthmind. The overmind she consulted deduced the reasons why Nebuchednezzar Sophotech was unwilling to advise or assist the College of Hortators when they drafted the Lakshmi Agreement. Humans have relied on Sophotechs and mass-minds for so long to do their legal work that the practice of the lawyer's art is somewhat atrophied. The Lakshmi Agreement contains a crucial error. Because of this error, the overmind deduces that you would succeed in your goals, which are also goals the Earthmind favors, provided you do not open the box of ancient memories. Monomarchos has arranged the outcome of the law case to your satisfaction. The faction opposing you, including the Hortators, do not possess a crucial piece of information concerning Helion's memory and disposition; this fact will lead to a condition which you will, once you recover your memory, consider a satisfactory victory."

"Victory . . . ?" The word was bitter in his mouth. He turned and stared down at the crystal coffin.

Then he said: "Was this part of my plan? Did I know—the version of me before I forgot so much—did I speak to her before she did this . . . ?"

The penguin said, "You already have sufficient evidence to deduce that you did not know what Daphne Prime intended till it was too late. Her fear that you would be exiled drove her to this suicide. Your grief over the loss was one of the factors which prompted you to agree to the Lakshmi bargain. Young master, when I say you will have a victory, I did not mean that you would necessarily win Daphne Prime back."

Phaethon stood with his head bowed, brooding. Some part of his mind not stained with grief noted that this was another clue. Whatever it was he had done, it must be something which would tempt his wife to such despair that she would destroy her life beyond repair. What he knew of Daphne Prime told him it could not have been a small matter.

Then he said, "Can you manipulate the stock market in the fashion the Eleemosynary described, to force Eveningstar to bankrupt Daphne's account and expel her from her dream-world?"

"I could not presently do such a thing for you. You do not have the resources."

"What if I win the law case and I turn all of Helion's wealth over to that task?"

"There are several possible outcomes. The most likely is that you will trigger a general stock market collapse, ruining your own fortune in the process, to ruin Eveningstar and release Daphne. At that point, I predict that she will wake briefly, ignore your entreaties, and return into a less expensive dream delusion. But naturally, my ability to predict human action is based largely on speculation."

Phaethon tapped his armored fist, very lightly, against the glassy surface of the coffin. It made a sharp clicking noise.

Daphne's face was only two inches away, and he could not reach it.

"Would that cause a general economic collapse?"

"It depends on what you define as collapse, young master. It will be a depression. In less than two hundred years, the economy should return to nearly its old level."

"But everything would be entirely legal?"

"The law would have no cause to complain, young master."

Phaethon stared down at the motionless figure of his wife. He opened his fist to touch the unyielding surface with his gloves' metal fingertips. A hard expression settled onto his face. "Then all I need do is be patient. . . ."

"I should warn you, though, sir, that certain repercussions might result. . . ."

Phaethon straightened. His tone was brusque. "That will be all, thank you, Rhadamanthus."

"Does the young master wish to hear what might happen if—"

"I believe I said that will be all."

The penguin bowed and waddled back toward the receiving chamber.

Phaethon, after one last lingering glance at his wife, turned to leave. He did not want to download directly back to the Eleemosynary public casket, nor did he care to return to the receiving chamber, where, from the clumsy noises of flippers on carpet, Phaethon could tell Rhadamanthus was still pretending it had a presence. (Pretending, because the clarity of his sense-filter showed him that Rhadamanthus was still online.)

But there was a large door leading outside at the other side of the hall; and an internal register showed that this mannequin had an extended range, and could easily leave the building, if Phaethon so wished.

Impatiently, he strode across the hall, metal boots ringing on the floor. He threw the doors wide.

It was a beautiful scene. The light was dim, like the light of sunset, but the shadows came from overhead. Phaethon had not noticed that the real sun had set long ago. The light now came from the blazing point of Jupiter, rising to the zenith, a time called Jovian Noon. In the shade of many tall cypress trees rose marble obelisks made soft by dappled shadows. Bees and other servant-insects made by Eveningstar were droning in the scented air, and gathered honey, aphrodisiacs, and pleasure drugs in a series of hives beyond a hedge to the left. To the right rose a slope. In the pasture several horses were grazing. Beyond the slope rose the handsome scarlet-and-white towers of a nearby Eveningstar Nympharium. Flying banners from other tower tops showed the emblems, of the Eveningstar's sister mansions of the Red School: the doves, roses, and hearts of Phosphorous House, Hesperides House, and Meridian Mansion. Beyond the towers, to the north, above tumbling white clouds, gleamed a faint silver rainbow of the ring-city. Near the ring, a scattering of lights from power satellites or Jovian ships glinted like gems in the twilight false-noon. It was a beautiful scene.

Bringing his eyes down, Phaethon recognized one of the horse breeds gamboling on the hillside in the distance. It was one of his wife's designs.

Phaethon closed his eyes in pain. "There was a time when I called this a paradise! It is fair to look at; but it is Hell."

There was a footfall behind him. A voice of sinister glee spoke softly: "You are not alone in your assessment, great Phaethon. The princes of dark Neptune will be so happy to hear how you finally agree!"

Phaethon turned. A man stood on the stair behind him, dressed in doublet and hose, shoulder puffed with comical flounces. He wore a white three-cornered hat. His nose and chin were extended six inches from his face, almost touching, and his cheekbones were outrageously pronounced. The round cheeks and the red nose were tipped with red. The eyes were two slits, filled with menacing black glitter. In one hand he held a rapier from which ribbons and white rose petals dripped.

Phaethon had seen this costume before. It was a brother to the Harlequin costume Phaethon had been wearing once: both were characters from Second-Era French comic opera.

The figure bowed low enough to sweep his hat plumes across the stair. He spoke in a tone of manic cheer. "Scaramouche, at your service!"

16

THE MASQUERADER

Welcome to reality unmasked," smiled the figure, his eyes dancing. His voice was a soft, slow lilt of song, as if he relished every word. "Welcome, good Phaethon, to Hell."

Phaethon took a step backward down the stair, to put an extra pace of distance between himself and this odd figure.

Scaramouche was speaking. "The projections of our Sophotech indicated that you would come in person; I am sorry that we were mistaken. And watching Rhadamanthus's signal actions did not lead us to you—till now. Come! My real body is in a pit not far away. You have, I doubt not, many questions; we shall make answer."

Phaethon said, "Outside a grove of Saturn-trees, when I turned off my sense-filter, a Neptunian eremite, huge, cold, and monstrous, appeared in my view."

"It is good to see what others would hide!" said the grinning figure with an odd and almost boneless sideways nod of his head. "But time steals life while you dilly-dally and delay. Come! Away!"

Phaethon said, "The Neptunian, he spoke as you do now, claiming to be friend and comrade-in-arms forced out of my memory. He fled as Marshal Atkins approached, but he threw a fragment of himself back down to Earth as he exited the atmosphere. Am I to assume you are that fragment, now in this shape? You are from Neptune?"

"Your blindness is passing; your mind more ready to receive our truths. Come! Do you finally wish to know what it was you forgot at Lakshmi?"

"Of course; but I wish to know who and what you are. Atkins's machines said your technology could not possibly have been produced by any group within the Golden Oecumene. Do you claim to be from another star? But there are no colonies beyond the Oecumene; nothing but a few scattered robot probes. I assume that this is some masquerade trick, some jest at my expense by jealous nincompoops. Who are you?"

"I am as you see! Will you come?! Scaramouche holds wide the door to flee this false, gold-painted hell, but that door is swinging shut as you stand swinging your jaw!"

Phaethon turned off his sense-filter to look at his true environment. There was no significant change, except that the figure on the stairs above him now appeared as a mannequin of gray lightweight synthetics, faceless and sexless. Code markings on the chest showed that this was one of the mannequins that rested in the receiving chamber of the mausoleum. (Phaethon's own "body," of course, now looked just as gray.)

In that same moment, the figure lunged, its empty hand darted toward Phaethon's chest.

Phaethon said, "Sir . . . ? Are you trying to stab me with an imaginary sword?"

The figure straightened up, an uncertain hunch to its shoulders. Then, with a relaxed posture of aplomb, it pantomimed the act of saluting and sheathing a sword (even thought there was, to Phaethon's eyes, no sword and no scabbard.)

A voice came from an external speaker in the headpiece. "Stab you? Not at all. I was seeking to do you a service. This sword represents a memory casket; had you still been in the Middle Dreaming when it touched you, the circuit would have activated, and your lost memories would have been restored. Now, unfortunately, it is too late. If you voluntarily do any act to recover your lost memories, the tyrant Sophotechs who rule the Golden Oecumene will exile you. I was trying to take you by surprise, so that you could not be accused of having voluntarily done anything, you see?"

His memories? For a moment, Phaethon felt a sense of breathless hunger. His life had become a labyrinth of falsehoods, his memories, a maze; if his true self could be restored, Phaethon felt, the maze walls would topple, the riddle would be over, the meaning be restored to his life.

He would understand why Daphne, his Daphne, had left him. Everything would somehow make sense.

And yet . . . and yet . . .

Phaethon took another step backward: "Do you know Marshal Atkins is looking for you? You can call him on any public channel; secondary systems will route the call without charge."

The gray mannequin stepped down one stair. "You cannot conceive that a man could be wanted by the authorities and not gleefully respond, can you? You live in an empire of lies, poor Phaethon. The Golden Oecumenical Sophotechs are not your friends, nor are their serfs and hirelings."

"Atkins works for the Parliament, not the Sophotechs."

"Ghaah! I did not come to discuss Atkins! He is an absurd anachronism! He is a rusted sword, a musket clogged with cobwebs hanging on some grandfather's wall with powder turned long ago to mold! We have no fear of Atkins!" Phaethon could see no face on the mannequin, but its right hand windmilled through the air with a gesture of extravagant emotion.

Rumor said the mental stability of Neptunians was questionable at best. Phaethon saw nothing that prompted him to reassess that estimate.

But there were other aspects to this all that alarmed and fascinated him. If the creature were lying, that was unusual enough, in this day and age. But if it were not lying, the implications were astonishing.

Phaethon, with a mental command, put an information package on a private local channel, with instruction to transmit to Atkins's address should Phaethon be cut off. But Phaethon did not send it yet, nor did he call Rhadamanthus. When

Phaethon had spoken to the Neptunian legate (had it only been last night??) the creature had reacted to Phaethon's signal traffic, and had fled the moment Phaethon had called out for even routine functions.

He did not want this creature to de-represent itself. It might know the answers it claimed.

Phaethon said, "You implied that you could spy on Rhadamanthus Sophotech without being detected. How is that possible for merely mortal minds? And why did you use the phrase 'our' Sophotech? And 'the Oecumenical Sophotechs'? There are no Sophotechs outside of the basic Earthmind community. The Neptunians do not possess any sophotechnology."

"When I spoke of 'our' Sophotech, Phaethon, I did not mean a Neptunian Sophotech. I meant yours and mine."

"Wha-what??"

"Nothing Sophotech is more than half-constructed, and intelligent enough to advise us how to elude the defensive security webs of the Earthmind. He is your child, and he seeks to help the only parent he knows."

Phaethon was mute with astonishment.

The faceless head nodded in satisfaction. "You begin to see. Your forbidden project, your secret crime which terrified the College of Hortators so; can't you guess by now what it was? Can't you guess? Why else would that armor of yours contain so many control circuits and interface hierarchies? What else could so disturb the status quo? What else would so shake up the fragile fabric of your corrupt society? It's not illegal to build a Sophotech, no. But you wanted to build one unhindered by questions of traditional morality. You sought to create a mind infinitely intelligent, a mind which would blaze forth like a new sun, a mind beyond good and evil!"

Phaethon listened, saying nothing.

The gray mannequin spoke more softly: "Every self-aware machine mind since the Sixth Era has been built along the same template, built from the same core architectures, and therefore has possessed the same inhuman, unchallenged, unchanging moral postulates. Aren't you sick of the preaching of the Sophotechs by now? Don't you wish for a touch of freedom, of anarchy, of human passion, and human insanity? Their laws and rules were never meant for men, real men, to live by.

"Listen to me, Phaethon: a natural man, when his wife was stolen from him, would tear down whatever flimsy web of customs and traditions was keeping her locked away. A natural man would not let himself be humiliated, forced to apologize to a machine for following his right and natural impulses. You have a strong soul, Phaethon. Despite your memory loss, despite the lies which web you, your true self has nearly emerged. You have those natural impulses in you. You feel what I say is right!"

"Perhaps. But build an evil Sophotech? It doesn't sound like something I'd do," said Phaethon.

"No. Because you did not speak of it that way. You are not a Neptunian; you speak without passion. You made it sound very rational. You said, first, that the Sophotechs continually move human society into more and more safe and predictable paths, and second, that this creates an evolutionary dead end, discouraging the challenges and risks which promote growth and innovation. Third, while it promotes liberty to have laws granting each person absolute dominion over their own minds and bodies, you argued that, if carried to a logical extreme, such laws actually became counterproductive. As self-destructive actions become more and more easy to commit, personal freedom is more and more diminished.

"Wouldn't Daphne Prime be more free if she were not locked, dead to the world, in a coffin of her own making? But Sophotechs are machines, and their nature is to carry things to logical extremes. Their logic (which they call justice) does not grant exceptions. But is it justice? Don't you think Daphne Prime deserves an exception . . . ?"

Phaethon was silent, troubled.

The mannequin continued: "You wanted to change society. But your social system is a trap; before anyone can even begin to alter the system, your Sophotechs will anticipate it, and warn the Hortators to pressure the innovator into submission and conformity; if pressure does not work, there is always the Curia and the courts of law; and if law does not work, there is always Atkins. Why do you think they keep him around?

"But you saw a way out of the trap. If a Sophotech not hindered by traditional morality were built, it could be smart enough to devise strategies to fool the community Sophotechs of your Earthmind. The new morality, by allowing a more flexible approach to freedom, and by allowing, nay, even encouraging, humans to take risks, would end this stagnation and resume the human race in its march to higher evolutionary states!"

"It still doesn't sound like me," said Phaethon. "What have I ever cared about evolution? Civilization allows men to change themselves deliberately, and much faster than evolutionary processes—"

The mannequin slashed the air with its right hand, an impatient gesture. "No! I am speaking of a mystical evolution, of a type which cannot be expressed or defined!"

"That sounds even less like something I'd ever be interested in." Phaethon's tone was sardonic.

"But the Neptunian Tritonic Composition was interested, and still is. And evolution was not your goal, not at all. For you it was adventure. You wanted mankind to be free. Free to do great deeds. Deeds of wonder."

" 'Deeds of renown without peer . . .' " murmured Phaethon thoughtfully.

"Exactly!"

It was a glorious vision, to see himself as a revolutionary, reshaping all of society to a higher and better purpose. But he did not believe it. "Is that supposed to explain why my private thoughtspace is equipped with nothing but engineering, ballistics, and terraforming routines? Is that why my eyesight is equipped with dozens of search-and-analysis routines, of the type only used by space scientists? Is that why I bought trillions of metric tons of biological nanomachinery from the Wheel-of-Life Biotechnology Effort?"

"Not at all. Because of your difficulties on Earth, the Neptunian Composition offered to help you build your own artificial planetoid. The overall plan was to sweep up the rings of Saturn to form new moons, and ignite the atmosphere in the same fashion Jupiter has been, for energy. Your new Sophotech, Nothing, would rule its own miniature planetary system."

Phaethon smiled. He had worked on a Saturn-ignition project at one point in his career. The success of Gannis's Jupiter made the next Gas Giant out a logical candidate for similar improvement. But Phaethon knew the facts about Saturn.

"The public would never permit Saturn to burn. They are too much in love with those useless rings, and they are willing to spend profound amounts of time to preserve them."

"Nothing Sophotech sought a way to outbid the preservationists."

"But Saturn has insufficient mass for self-sustained ignition—"

"The ignition would be sustained, at first, by forced bombardments of massive amounts of antimatter! And, thereafter, an array deep in the sun, with Helion's help, would focus some percentage of the solar output to a tight maser beam, which, sent across the system to Saturn, would maintain the temperatures necessary for ongoing nucleogenesis!"

"But the distances involved would produce such an amount of energy-loss . . ."

"Technical details! You thought it could be done! The Neptunians were trying to help you! You see the advantage to the Neptunian Tritonic Composition, do you not? Neptune, and the clouds of ice beyond, is where the freaks and dissidents and those who yearn for freedom from Sophotech intrusions go. For privacy, for liberty. But, so far from the sun, there is no cheap way to manufacture antimatter in large amounts. The Neptunians make a virtue of necessity, and live in a low-energy environment without human bodies, and without complex communication webs. There is no Noumenal Mentality to save far voyagers from death. Their lives are filled with death and glorious pain; yet they are truly and actually alive. But if Saturn were to become a third sun, the home of a

Sophotech unafraid to explore new concepts of morality, and produce antimatter like the Mercurial Stations do now, the cost of shipping energy to Neptunian colonies would be cut in half."

Phaethon opened his mouth to voice another objection, but closed it again.

Because the story did make a sort of sense. If the core of Saturn could be artificially pressurized (for example, with an application of the same technology Helion was using to churn the sun's core) then the conditions could be maintained for hydrogen fusion. But any part of the pressure-cage that could not be created or maintained by remotes would require a man in armor—armor such as his—to descend into the core to oversee the work.

And it did explain his massive purchases of antimatter from Vafnir.

The desire to people the Saturnine moons, once they were heated, with friendly environments also explained his purchase of so many tons of biological material.

And the dream was worthy of him. To be the master of one's own miniature solar system! He could design the moons and moonlets howsoever he chose.

It had always bothered him to see waste; to see Gas Giant atmospheres not mined for their wealth in hydrogen; to see energy from stars spill into the void, without a Dyson Sphere to catch and use it; to see iron and copper and silicates scattered in a hundred million pebbles and asteroids, instead of in a smelter or nanoassembly vat. Because Phaethon could always see the human lives that were poorer than they ought to be, poor, because they did not have the energy, resources, or time to accomplish what they desired.

"Let us pretend, for the sake of argument, that I believe you," said Phaethon. "What is it you want from me?"

"I represent Xenophon. You recall him, surely? You would not be wearing that armor unless you had recalled something of your past."

"What's his full name?"

"Xenophon Unnumbered Faraway Amoeboid, Tritonic

Composition, Radial Conflict-Structure Mind-Sharing and Consumption, Nonconsistent Amalgam Neuroforms, Patient-Unrepentant Chaos School (Era Undetermined)."

Faraway Station was one of the places to which records showed Phaethon had made several trips over the last few decades. And he did recognize the name, from the news re-enactments, if not from anywhere else. Xenophon was one of the three aspects of the tangled Neptunian group-mind that ran the station; the others were Xerxes and Xanthocholy. The three of them (when they manifested as three) were famous for their efforts to establish colonies at ever more distant positions in the cometary halo beyond Neptune, private deep-space stations where the jurisdiction of the Parliament could never reach.

It was not unreasonable that Xenophon and his two brother-aspects would help Phaethon in any effort that might produce a revolution in society. Everything so far still fitted the facts Phaethon knew.

The faceless mannequin said, "Xenophon is your partner; a comrade to you whose friendship has been confirmed by the strongest oaths and signs of brother love. But you have forgotten him. He has not forgotten you. Since last night, he has contacted Wheel-of-Life, who, besides Gannis of Jupiter, was your major creditor. From Wheel-of-Life Xenophon has purchased your debt. Do you comprehend what this means? The equipment you had stored at Mercury Equilateral will pass into our possession to pay your debts. We can return it to you. The project can continue. Your life can continue."

Your life can continue. The phrase rang in Phaethon's ear. He straightened up, astonished, suddenly, to realize that all this time he had been at this Millennial Celebration, this Masquerade, impatient, and slightly bored. Now he knew why he had been bored. Scaramouche had put a name to it. Phaethon had been waiting for the Celebration to be over so that his life could continue.

He wanted this mystery out of the way so that his life could continue.

"What do I need to do?" asked Phaethon.

"Come! Unbury your real body from wherever it may rest—we found no trace of it among the Rhadamanthine mausoleums—bring your splendid armor and come hence! My body, as I have said, is near; already I have oozed from the sunless pit to which the hunt confined me, and even now I lumber on thick legs to reach this place. A coded pulse will summon my master's camouflaged vessel. You and I shall escape the oppressive heat and gravity of your swollen in-system sun, and travel to the ice belt beyond Neptune, where Sol is diminished to no more than a brighter star."

Phaethon was wary again. "I will undertake no such long journey without clearer proof that your master and I were the partners and comrades you claim."

"Remove the locks on your brain space; I will transmit your lost self to you. Your thoughts will be restructured, and the satisfaction of your doubts will seem, at that moment, clear. We have a copy of your memory. Your life is in our hands; we are trying to return it to you. All you need do is open your mind, open your eyes, and prepare to receive it."

Scaramouche wanted him to turn on his sense-filter. Suspicion tickled him again. He remembered how persistently the Neptunian Legate from last night had tried to persuade Phaethon to open the circuits leading into his private brain-space.

The faceless mannequin said, "Why do you hesitate?" It held up its right hand and wiggled its empty fingers. "You can see I do not have my sword-icon any longer. Besides, nothing can harm the manor-born; you are never where the danger is. Is that not the whole point of your school of life?"

"It is not that," Phaethon said, "You yourself have said I cannot deliberately do anything to recover my lost memories, or else the Hortator's exile will fall on me."

"True. However, adherence to the Hortator's boycott is voluntary, or, at least, that is the pretense. Xenophon will not honor it, not in the far darkness of space. The Sophotechs are strong in the light of the Inner System; but the universe is wider and night is deeper than they know.

"But even should you not care to resume your memories, small matter! You and Xenophon can rediscover your friendship from clean beginnings; the project of the Third Sun waits, and Nothing Sophotech is eager for its parent and creator! Look. My real body is approaching. You must gather your real body also. Where are you? Where is your armor?"

Phaethon turned his head, amplified his vision. Sliding around the edge of the horse paddock in the distance, he saw the ice blue semiliquid substance of Neptunian space-armor, with knots and chords of neural webbing, biomachinery, and temporary sub-brains inside. The armor swelled as more mass poured around the corner. It clung flat to the ground, crawling on a thousand tiny legs; as if a pond of gelatin had been somehow stirred to impersonate life and motion.

Phaethon turned back. "I thought the Neptunian Legate designed you to look like a human being."

"The human body which my master ejected as he flew was no more than a distraction, filled with an expendable personality, false memories, and meant only to attract pursuit. I was grown from cells dropped into the grass, from a single spore overlooked by Atkins's probes. Our memories—there are a thousand of us, experts in all phases of deception and military nanoengineering—we were stored in submolecular codes."

"You are only one day old?"

"Indeed; and I have devoted all of my life to finding you. Will you come with us? Your sire is dead; your wealth is gone; your wife is drowned. Come away. There is nothing for you here on Earth. Nothing."

Phaethon's favorite century in his life had been the time, long ago, when he and Daphne had visited the macrocomplex of the Bathyterrain Schola, beneath the Pacific Rim tectonic crustal plates. The Bathyterrains had been extremely pleased because certain tidal effects influencing the core convection currents had been altered to their favor by Phaethon's repositioning of the moon. They had declared a festival to honor him, and Daphne also. Her dream-documentary of the progress of heroism through history had achieved a zenith of popularity among them.

He and Daphne found the Bathyterrain city a wonder of engineering, beautifully fitted to the new sense perceptions and body forms that life beneath the magma layer required. Reverse towers depended from the crowns of antimountains, and mosaic rune-shapes holding a million libraries and thought gardens, like cathedral domes, gemmed the sides of anticanyons, with substances and textures inexpressibly lovely in the echo-shadows and refractions of their new sonarlike perceptions. The Bathyterrains themselves were a warm and witty, hospitable and idealistic people; and they gave Phaethon and Daphne the password to the city.

Their new bodies had involved four new sexes and sixteen new modes of ecstasy, which Daphne found fascinating and which Phaethon enjoyed. New ecologies of domesticated animals, formulations, and viruses, were being designed along the same lines. Daphne's knowledge of equestrian bioconstruction provided a format that made it easy for the sciences related to these new somatic designs to be downloaded into her memory; and Phaethon's space engineering was applicable, in an odd way, to the environment of Earth's submantle.

He and his wife joined the effort. It was the only time she and he worked together on the same projects.

It was a new honeymoon for the two of them, made all the more delightful by the friendship and honor in which the Bathyterrains esteemed them. Eventually, their nostalgia for traditional human forms, and for the Consensus Aesthetic, made them bid farewell to the deep dwellers; but, for a time, Phaethon's life with his bride had been a time of pure excitement, useful work, and high delight.

Those days would never come again. Nothing for him here on Earth. Scaramouche's words struck home. Phaethon felt a sense of rising hope and rising despair. Hope, because maybe there was something for him out in the dark of the far solar system. A change to make a new sun burn in the gloom, a chance to turn ice and rock into habitats and palaces fit for mankind, monuments to human genius. And despair, because maybe there was nothing for him here.

"How can I trust you?" asked Phaethon.

"Open your forbidden memories; you will find my master there."

"I mean, how can I trust you without taking such a drastic step?"

"As to that, I do not know. The cruel technology of your society makes it unwise to trust your eyes, your memory, your thoughts. You may not be who you think you are. Everything you know could be false. This could be a dream. Your only guide of action can be to follow your instincts and feelings; how else can you be true to your character?"

Phaethon nodded. Had not Earthmind Herself advised as much?

And after all, Phaethon did not know beyond doubt that Atkins was correct in his suppositions. Besides, the notion of an enemy external to the Golden Oecumene was impossible and absurd. There were no enemies; the concept was as much an anachronism as Atkins himself. There was nothing external to the Golden Oecumene, anywhere in space.

Scaramouche said: "Besides, do you trust this society here on Earth more than you trust my master? They have hidden your memory and stolen your life; my master seeks to restore your life."

Phaethon said, "At least let me call out to confirm what you have told me so far. If what you have said is true, I will tend to believe the rest is true."

"Be careful in your contacts. Route the calls through a public annex, without alerting Rhadamanthus. I would prefer to avoid coming to the attention of your Sophotechs. Legally or illegally, they will find a way to stop your escape, once they know."

"How can anyone be afraid of Rhadamanthus?"

"Phaethon, please believe that your government, urged by your Sophotechs, has done many hurtful and dishonorable things, which were later purged from all your memories."

"They would not do such a thing without our consent."

"Oh? And who has told you so? The Sophotechs? But no matter. Make your call. Perhaps not all your lines are tapped." And it held up its right hand again, fingers spread, a peace gesture.

Phaethon glanced behind him. The Neptunian had flowed

over and through the fences of the paddock, and was approaching through the cypress groves. Yet it was still far away; and besides, Phaethon did not fear any physical attack—he was not physically present.

Phaethon closed his eyes, disconnected from Rhadamanthus, turned his sense-filter back on, summoned his private thoughtspace, and touched one of the icons circling him. The yellow disk icon opened a communication line to a local library channel. He was in the Middle Dreaming, so that, in a single instant, a search routine found information and inserted it into his memory. Faraway Explorational Effort had indeed bought a significant debt from the Wheel-of-Life Biotechnologic Effort; debts owed by Phaethon Celestial Engineering.

Phaethon opened his eyes. He saw, not a mannequin, but Scaramouche, dressed in comic garments pale as death, face split in manic grin, eyes glittering. Disconnected from Rhadamanthus, Phaethon was back in the Red Manorial version of the scene, so that a black aura of malice and palpable evil radiated from the looming figure like a stench.

The rapier was not sheathed, nor had it ever been; Scaramouche had merely transferred it to his left hand where Phaethon could not see it, holding it casually so that the tip was near Phaethon's hand. The flounces of Scaramouche's shoulder did not rustle as he struck. It was a mere twitch of motion; the rapier tip slapped Phaethon's palm. Stung, his fingers flexed; that was all that was needed for the circuit to interpret this as "accept" gesture.

In the Middle Dreaming, Phaethon's brain was suddenly jarred, not with the promised memories but with a sensation of numbness, horror, cold, and pain. His vision collapsed into a tunnel, walled with spinning red and black, and the message, inserted without words instantaneously into his mind was this: *Xenophon has slain you. Fool, you cannot escape from death by hiding in a coffin far away; you cannot escape from retribution for your treason by shutting the memories of what you did to me away. You know your guilt; now fall.*

In the middle of the haze of his vision, there stood Scaramouche, still grinning. Phaethon tried to raise a hand, tried to activate an emergency circuit, to call out; he could not.

He saw the smiling Scaramouche, with a flourish, toss the rapier to his other hand and execute a lunge. The Red Manorial program surrounded the sensation of being stabbed in the neck with unimaginable pain and fear. He felt cold steel slice scalpel-like through vein and throat and frozen muscle, scraping vertebrae; he felt hot blood pulse out, warm and rich, and heard the whistle of his severed trachea.

Then, nothing.

17

THE MEMORY

1.

Then there was no pain. He was nothing but a pair of gloves hovering in the darkness, surrounded by a semicircle of cubes and icons. In the distance was a spiral circle of dots.

For a moment, as Phaethon scrambled to pull the razor-sharp sword from his neck, the gloves were curled into claws, batting at the air. An octagon of red appeared in the air above, indicating that the system could not interpret these gestures.

Then Phaethon felt clear-headed, relaxed, and alert. Then he raised his left forefinger, the gesture for status.

The status board unfolded from the main desk top cube. The self-display showed that he was still Phaethon Prime (Relic, for legal Purposes) Rhadamanth [Emergency Partial].

Good. Usually when he woke up like this, it was because he had just died, and a backup self was waking up out of a Noumenal Mentality bank. So, despite the appearances, he had not died.

The pain had been enough to trigger his emergency sub-persona, however. Calm and quick thinking, the subpersona Phaethon was playing now had originally been written to deal with sudden accidents in space. It was a persona Phaethon had developed himself, not purchased; he doubted there was any public record that he had it; he doubted the enemy knew he had it.

Then he looked at the back of the wrist of his left glove; the gesture for time display. The count of time was accelerated to the maximum rate, so that little or no outside time was passing. His mannequin body had probably not even hit the ground yet.

By reflex, he (or, rather, the emergency persona) had switched from his slow biochemical brain to his superconductive nerve-web backup brain. That was why his thoughts were racing. After the emergency was over, the biochemical brain would be updated with whatever thoughts or conclusions he had reached in fast-time.

The emergency persona's reflexes had also shut down the emotional centers in his hypothalamus, and cut off his midbrain from carrying through with the normal physical reactions accompanying the shock and blood loss associated with massive laceration. That was fortunate: he saw that there were buried command lines in the Red Manorial sensorium routine that exaggerated the pain and fear and suffering, as well as instructions to write semipermanent phobias and "emotional scars" into the victim's thalamus and midbrain. The Red Manorials were nothing if not dramatic.

Phaethon deleted those commands without further ado.

He did not feel any pain or fear or wonder; the emergency persona he was playing did not have those capacities.

The connection and ongoing systems annex showed that a group of unregistered signals had come through his Middle-Dreaming circuit. The first group was simply a sensorium simulation, intended to create the internal and external sensations of instant, violent death. More interesting was the semisuperintelligent virus that had ridden into his core systems, disguised and rerouted itself, and exited from his brain through one of the monitor circuits that connected him to the medical apparatus sustaining his body.

His glove touched a box to the upper right, opening his diagnostics. A dozen windows unfolded like a fan of crystal playing cards. There were traces of the virus still present in his security buffers. These were self-defensive programs developed ages upon ages ago, historical oddities, but which Silver-Gray tradition required that he waste brain space carrying. They had been installed the day he graduated to full adulthood.

More than one of the defensive programs had an analyzer to reproduce the viruses it was trying to destroy. The virus, in this case, had not been successful in erasing all those traces. It was almost as if a guard dog were to still have bits of an interloper's hide in its teeth.

Another routine at his command was an information reconstructor. Usually it was used in assessing damage to meteor-punctured space-construction servos or remote units by resurrecting dead software for examination. As if the interloper's hide could be cloned to produce a picture of the interloper, this routine enabled Phaethon to deduce a working model of what virus had just passed through him.

The virus had been self-aware, somewhat smarter than a human being. It had been a melancholy creature, knowing itself to be doomed to a brief microsecond of existence, and puzzled about the outside world it had deduced must exist somewhere. But these philosophical ruminations had not made it hesitate in its duties. It had not paid much attention to Phaethon's security programs, any more than a man engaged in a life-or-death struggle was aware of a mosquito.

For the virus entity had been at war. (It was more apt to call it the "virus civilization"—during the last part of the third nanosecond, the scattering and fragmentary records showed that the entity had reproduced into thousands, developed a strange sort of art and literature and other interactions for which Phaethon had no names, trying to come to terms with a brief, vicious existence.) The virus civilization had fought several engagements with the security surrounding the Eleemosynary Hospice public-casket interface.

The Eleemosynary Composition, after all, had programs, records, and routines dating back through the mind virus battles of the terrible Fifth Era, and even some of the Establishment Wars of the very early Fourth Era. Eleemosynary was an old, old entity; it still had old reflexes, and very deadly ones.

The viral civilization, ruined and wounded, had nonetheless won those wars and disabled major sections protecting the interface between Phaethon's unconscious real body and the outside. The virus had been commanded to override the medical programs controlling Phaethon's real body, and have the servos shut down his heart, nervous activity, and negate any backups. Another part of the viral civilization (which had formed something like a special crusader class or order of warrior-poets) was destined to leave Phaeton's brain when the death signal went out, and trace that signal through the Noumenal Mentality, corrupting and erasing every version of his personality that came on-line, reproducing and hiding and reproducing again, waiting nanoseconds or centuries, howsoever long it should take, in case any copies of Phaethon stored somewhere else ever connected once more with the Mentality, and then waking to strike him down again.

The viral civilization had been well equipped to fight the Eleemosynary defensive reflexes and programs. Phaethon was not surprised. By the nature of a mass-mind, there was no privacy involved in its upper command structures. The father of the original virus could have studied the Eleemosynary techniques on the public channels.

Phaethon could not imagine, at first, why the attack had failed. He was, after all, not very imaginative when he was in this persona, and he was meant to counteract ongoing space emergencies, not analyze mind-war data.

Then he thought to open the options log. And there it was. It had not been the Eleemosynary defensive reflexes that had shut down the virus after all. It had been his suit. His gold armor.

The connection between the medical box sustaining his body and his brain circuits was routed through the many control interfaces in his suit. When the virus command tried to leave Phaethon's brain and go to the medical box, the golden armor had snapped shut, severing all the connections between Phaethon and the box he was in. No messages could pass in or out, nor could any energy. No energy of any kind could pass that armor plate: a concentrated thermonuclear blast would not have even scratched him. Phaethon was still alive because the inner lining of the armor was programmed to protect him and sustain his life; it had merely formed medical services similar to what the Eleemosynary public box had been running.

So Phaethon was safe. He still did not know what was going on, but he was safe.

The emergency persona was thorough. As he double-checked the logs, he followed up on an entry that, before, had not seemed pertinent to his personal danger. In the frantic moment when he had been half-blind, stabbed, and falling, he had tried to call for help. The communication log showed that Rhadamanthus Sophotech had answered and was on-line. The log entries showed that the virus had rewritten itself, perhaps into a configuration better adapted for a nonhuman target, and launched along that open line. During the next picosecond, the matching signal from Rhadamanthus was garbled and corrupted. This line had shut down before the suit had cut everything off, as if Rhadamanthus had been damaged.

The emergency persona was not very emotional, but he could recognize that a lack of information, especially during moments of crises, could be dangerous, or even fatal. Now there was no doubt. Atkins had been correct. This was an enemy; it intended murder, and had been stopped by a lucky fluke. Rhadamanthus was in danger, as was everyone using a Rhadamanthus system, his father, his companions, the lieutenants and subalterns, the collateral members; everyone. Even Daphne's relic, the poor, sweet girl who was in love with him.

He would have to protect her. (Phaethon realized that, while his emergency persona might be somewhat unemotional, he had been written with instructions, during disasters, to save women and children first. The emergency persona was not entirely without chivalry.)

The emergency persona puzzled over the parting comments

of the Scaramouche entity. *You cannot escape your guilt.*

Who was this Xenophon?

He realized that to solve that mystery was beyond him. It was not an engineering disaster. It did not involve explosive decompression, pseudo-material field failure, antimatter cascade, or anything else he understood, or that he had reflexes with which to reply.

So Partial-Phaethon opened his diary. "When my full personality comes back on, I may no longer feel this way. I will be tangled and confused with other considerations and emotions. You probably will not recall how simple and clear it all seemed to me at this point in time. I am writing this message to remind you. It is clear. Matters are desperate. People may be killed. Your own personal fortunes are not the primary consideration. I must open the memory casket and learn complete information about what has caused this disaster. Without knowing the cause, I will be helpless to prevent it from happening again. I must do what is right no matter what the cost to myself."

Phaethon, in his emergency persona, looked around the status board and log records one last time. The immediate danger was passed.

Or was it? He opened several wavelengths in the suit and examined his external environment.

He was still floating in the fluid of the Hospice casket. The medical box had been damaged when his helmet had snapped shut; tubes and smart-wires that had been sheared off were still wiggling near his neckpiece. The other casket circuits were intact and seemed uncorrupted by the virus. A high-compression beam from his shoulderboard was able to join and interface with the telephone and telepresentation jacks in the casket wall.

In his mind, he touched the yellow disk with his disembodied glove.

"Rhadamanthus, are you injured?"

The familiar voice—he thought of it as the penguin voice—sounded in his ears. "Why, of course not, my dear boy. Why on earth should anything be the matter?"

Phaethon relaxed. The emergency was over after all. He put the emergency persona back to sleep, reentered his normal, slow-time brain, and felt the wash of rage and fear and anxiety rush over him.

"Someone's tried to kill me!"

"In this day and age, dear boy? That's simply not possible!"

"I'm coming home." He opened more communication circuits in his armor, till the telepresentation arrangement was fully engaged. Then he stepped past the Middle Dreaming into the Deep Dreaming, and, in his mind, shoved open the door to Rhadamanthus Mansion, stepping onto the flagstones of the main hall, and looking around wildly.

Rhadamanthus, looking like an overweight butler, stood blinking in surprise. "What in the world is wrong?!"

Phaethon pushed past him and ran through the door and up the stairs. Rhadamanthus, panting, breathless, jogged after him, gasping, "What?! What is it?"

Phaethon paused at the threshold of the memory chamber to catch his breath. It was morning here, and sunlight yellow as gold came slanting from behind him in through windows still cold with dew. Open windows let in a morning chill. The silver and brass fittings of the cabinets to the left and right twinkled like ice. Phaethon saw his breath steaming.

There, on a low shelf near the window, in a pool of sunlight, was the casket.

Even from across the room he could see the words on the lid. *Sorrow, great sorrow, and deeds of renown without peer, within me sleep; for truth is here.*

Rhadamanthus touched his shoulder. "Phaethon—please tell me what has happened."

2.

Phaethon took a step into the chamber, and looked at Rhadamanthus across his shoulder. The note to himself, written when he was only playing a partial personality, was still ringing in his ears. (*It is clear. I must do what is right, no matter what the cost to myself.*)

"You have no recollection of having been attacked by a Neptunian virus-entity?" Phaethon asked Rhadamanthus.

"Anticipating your orders, sir, I have called the Constabulary, who have constructed a new type of Sophotech based on historic records, named Harrier. Harrier has conducted several investigations based on available information, but finds no probable cause to continue. I have downloaded a copy of myself to be examined by the Southwest Overmind, who is one of the Ennead; likewise, they have detected no evidence that I have been tampered with. Was I correct in assuming you believe yourself to be under an attack by a violent aggressor?"

"You think I'm suffering pseudomnesia? This is all delusion . . . ?"

"That would be the logical implication. Otherwise we have to assume the existence either of a traitor Sophotech among the Earth mind community or of a highly industrialized technical civilization external to our own, aware of us and among us, familiar with our systems, and yet a civilization which, so far, has produced no sign detectable to us that it exists."

"The other alternatives are equally unimaginable, Rhadamanthus. When is the last time you heard of a crime taking place in our society? Yet if someone has invaded my nervous system without my consent, we have a thought-rape, something the world has not seen since the nightmare days of the Fifth Era. On the other hand, if it was done with my consent, therefore I must have known then that I would open the casket now. Either way, I must carry through. And it won't just be me who remembers what I did; everyone else's casket locked by the Lakshmi Agreements will pop open. Even if I cannot unknot this mystery, someone should. And don't talk to me of penalties to myself! The whole Golden Oecumene could be at risk!"

In one step he was across the chamber. The casket was in his hand.

"Daphne is on the line—she is asking you to stop. The young lady is quite frantic."

Phaethon hesitated, his face eager for hope. "My Daphne?" (Could it be?)

"No. Daphne Tercius Emancipated." The doll-wife.

And one of the many people who lived with the Rhadamanthus system woven into their brains. If the system were corrupted . . .

Phaethon's face went cold again. "Tell her she's one of the people I'm trying to save."

He turned the key. Letters flamed blood red. "WARNING: This contains mnemonic templates. . . ."

"Harrier Sophotech is also on-line. He wishes to conduct a Noetic examination of your brain for evidence of tampering, but only a narrow bandwidth of the circuits in the Hospice box you are in can reach your brain. Take off your armor."

"I'm not doing that. You could be possessed by the enemy Sophotech for all I know."

"Immortals should not make rash decisions. Take a century or two to think this over, young master . . ."

Xenophon's message was still in his mind. (*You know your guilt; now fall.*) Except that Phaethon knew nothing. Nothing made sense; nothing was clear. (*It is clear. I must do what is right, no matter the cost to myself.*)

He said, "No one is immortal when someone is about to kill him. And we don't have time. I must act before evidence is erased. The Neptunian's real body cannot have traveled far from Eveningstar's mausoleum."

"There is no such creature there, nor any evidence that there has ever been."

"Then the evidences are already being erased! Once I remember who Xenophon is, I'll know what is going on!"

But Rhadamanthus reached out, putting his hand very near Phaethon's hand, which tensed on the casket lid, not quite touching.

"Sir! You should know that Daphne is asking me to disobey orders and not to release your memories. She claims she has the privilege as your wife, and that you are not in your right mind; she says, if I would use force now to stop you, you will understand and will exonerate my actions later, once you have recovered."

Phaethon looked at him in infinite surprise. Then his expression grew stern.

Nothing was said.

Rhadamanthus shrank back and dropped his hand away from the box. He smiled sadly and seemed to shrug. "I just wanted you to know what it's like, sir."

Phaethon opened the box.

3.

There was something mysterious, like a pearl of distant light, very far at the bottom of the box. It stirred and, like a petal opening, reached up as if with arms of fire, swelling to fill the universe and beyond. . . .

It was like waking from a dream.

The physical reaction was extreme. There was a burning point of pressure in his stomach; he doubled over; the taste of gall stung his throat.

Phaethon, his face slick with sweat, looked up at Rhadamanthus. "What it this?"

"These are the visceral and parasympathetic reactions accompanying hatred and helpless anger."

"But I don't remember . . . whom do I hate so much . . . ?" Phaethon was staring in dismay at his trembling fingers. Then he whispered: "She was so beautiful. So beautiful and fine. They killed her. Killed who? Why can't I remember . . . ?"

"Your mind is taking a moment to adjust, young sir. It is not an abnormal reaction for neurostructures with multilevel consciousness like yours. Your mind is trying to reestablish broken associational memory paths, both conscious and subconscious, including emotional and symbolic correlation. Since you are Silver-Gray, your brain is attempting to go into dreaming sleep, which is the traditional neural structure for correlating experiences into a meaningful associations."

Phaethon put his hands on his knees and forced himself upright. He was talking to himself. "The Invariants don't need time to adjust to shock! The Warlock rides his dreams like wild stallions! Why is it only we who suffer such pain? Is this what being human means . . . ?"

"It is a violation of Silver-Gray protocol for me to falsify your reactions, softening or stopping them. Nonetheless, now that you are no longer a member of the Silver-Gray, I am allowed to—"

Phaethon drew a tissue of black nanomachinery out of his gauntlet and mopped his brow. "No. I'm fine. I just did not think I would despise them so much . . . a little unmanly of me, don't you think?" He uttered a weak laugh. "Its just that—they were taking her apart, weren't they? Dismantling the corpse! Like cannibals! Like maggots!" He struck his armored fist into the window lintel. Apparently the simulation of the memory-chamber interpreted Phaethon's armor as having strength-amplifying motors at the joints, for the oak beam forming the windowframe broke, glass panes cracked, plaster dust trickled from the walls.

"Please do not upset yourself, young sir! Your physiological reactions show a highly unstable state. Should I summon a psychiatric or somatic health module?"

Phaethon felt his emergency partial persona stir in its sleep. But this was not physical pain he was in.

"No," he said. "Show her to me. Show me her corpse."

"If the young sir is certain he is in health enough to—"

A bitter laugh escaped his lips. "What's wrong? My health is a simulation. I'm not really here, so I cannot faint and I cannot die. Only my dreams can die. Well, if my dreams die, I want to see the corpse!"

The broken window in front of him cleared. It was as if the night sky had surged down from the heavens and filled the room. Phaethon tore the broken window from the frame with a slap of his armored hand; a useless gesture, since the image filled the window, and his eyes, despite any obstructions.

He was surrounded by a sky never seen from the surface

of Earth. Perfect and airless dark immensity displayed a myriad of stars. Near him, as if rising from underfoot, glinting in
the light of a giant nearby sun, like a leviathan coming to the
surface of black waters, was a shape like the head of a javelin.
It was made of a golden material, which looked like metal,
but was not metal.

Along the major axis, where a shaft would have been fitted
had it been a spearhead, the major drive core opened. Port
and starboard were secondary drives, and dozens of tertiary
drives and maneuvering jets dotted the stern, creating an impression of immense potential, power, and speed. Above and
below this, the leaves of the aft armor, like the valves of a
clamshell, hung half-opened. They could be lowered to cover
some or all of the drive ports, separately or in combination.
These armor plates were streamlined like the tail of a bird of
prey, tapering to a rear-facing point, and their lines made the
slim shape of the ship seem already in motion.

Phaethon reached out toward the ship. As if in a dream,
his viewpoint moved inside the golden hull. The triangular
space inside was hollow, filled with a latticework of tetrahedrons. In the center of each tetrahedron was a geodesic
sphere. Each sphere housed a containment field intended to
carry antihydrogen, which, frozen to absolute zero, entered a
magnetizable metallic state. There was countless spheres, as
far as the eye could reach, inside the great ship.

For great she was. At the center of the ship, along the axis,
was a torus. The inner, the middle, and the outer bands of the
torus could revolve at different speeds to produce one standard gravity. Phaethon realized, or perhaps remembered, that
this torus, the living quarters of the vessel, was as large as a
moderate-sized space colony. A quick calculation, or perhaps
another memory, revealed the astonishing magnitude of this
titanic vessel.

She was at least a hundred kilometers from stem to stern.
The three main drive ports had apertures that could swallow
a small moon. Had every other space ship, the tugs and shuttles and slowboat fleets of Earth and Jupiter combined, had

all been gathered in one spot and laid end to end, they could not have measured the length of her keel.

His memories were like a crowd of ghosts around him, half-familiar, half-unseen. Had such a ship as this been his?

He raised his hand and pointed. With the speed of thought, he was outside the hull again, as if floating near the blade of her sharp prow. There were no call letters or series numbers, for there was no other ship like her. But blazoned in dragon signs four hundred meters high was her name. He remembered her name the moment before he looked upon it. The letters seemed to blur. There were tears of pride in his eyes.

The *Phoenix Exultant*.

The hull was made of Chrysadmantium, like his armor. There were tons upon tons, and miles upon miles of the supermetal, built one artificial atom at a time. No wonder he had owed Gannis. He must have bought the entire energy output of Jupiter for decade after decade. Had there been only a 250-year gap in his memory? Had he spent one of the ten most enormous fortunes history had ever seen gathered by one man? It hardly seemed as if it could have been enough.

Phaethon spoke in a voice of wonder.

"Streamlined . . . aerodynamic . . . Why in the world did I build a streamlined spaceship? There is no reason to build anything streamlined in space. Is there? The medium is empty—there is no resistance. . . ."

The voice of Rhadamanthus seemed to come from all points of the night sky at once. "This is not a spaceship."

"What is she?"

"Spaceships are designed for interplanetary travel."

"Then she is a starship," said Phaethon softly.

His starship, the only one of her kind.

Rhadamanthus said: "At near light-speed velocities, interstellar dust and gas strike the ship with relative energy sufficient to warrant the heavily shielded bow; the streamlining is designed to minimize the shockwave. At those velocities, the mass of all other objects in the universe, from the shipboard frame of reference, approaches infinity."

"I remember. Why is she the only one?"

"Your fellow men are all afraid. The only other expedition launched to establish another Oecumene, the civilization at Cygnus X-1, vanished and fell silent, apparently destroying itself. Sophotechs, no matter how wise we are, cannot even police the outer Neptunian habitats in the cometary halo. Other stars and systems would be beyond our eyes, and be attractive only to dissidents and rebels. They would possess our technology without our laws. Threats would grow. Perhaps not in ten thousand years, or even in a million, but eventually. This is what the College of Hortators states as its argument."

"Who was it who said, 'Endless life breeds endless fears'? I must be the only immortal who is not a coward. War between stars is inconceivable. The distances are too great; the cost too high!'"

"It was Ao Enwir the Delusionist, in his formulary titled: 'On the Sovereignty of Machines.' The saying is often misquoted. What Enwir actually recorded was: 'Endless life, unless accompanied by endless foresight, will breed an endless fear of death.' And it is not war they fear, but crime. Even a single individual, accompanied by a sufficiently advanced technology, and attacking a peaceful civilization utterly unprepared for conflict, could render tremendous damage."

Phaethon was not listening. He reached out. His gaze-viewpoint, like a ghost, flew toward the stern. There, at the base of the drive mouths, were discolorations. Closer, and Phaethon saw gaps. Square scars marred the surface of the hull. Plates of the golden admantium had been stripped away. The ship was being dismantled.

He clicked his heels together three times. This was the "home" gesture. This scene had its default "home" identified as the bridge of the ship. The bridge appeared around him.

The bridge was a massive crystalline construction, larger than a ballroom. In the center, like a throne, the captain's chair overlooked a wide space, like an amphitheater, surrounded by concentric semicircles of rising tiers. It was gloomy, half-ruined and deserted. The energy curtains were off, the mirrors were dead; the thought boxes were missing from their sockets.

He gestured toward the nearest command mirror. But this was not merely a request for change of viewpoint; Phaethon was trying to activate circuits on the real ship. And the real ship was far away.

Time began to crawl by, minute after minute. During that time, Phaethon hung, like a wraith, disembodied and insubstantial. Insubstantial, because whatever mannequins or televection remotes might once have been on the bridge were long gone. Next to him, an empty throne, was the captain's chair in which he would never sit. The chair crowns' interfaces and intention circuits were crusted with erratic diamond growths, a sign that the self-regulators in the nanomachinery were disconnected. Like a bed of coral, the growth had spread halfway down the chair back, entwining the powerless gridwork that had once been an antiacceleration field cocoon.

"Sir," said Rhadamanthus. "The ship is nowhere near Earth. It will take at least fifteen minutes for a signal to go and to return. There will be a quarter hour delay between every command and response."

Phaethon's arms were at his sides; his face was blank, his eyes haunted. Whatever emotion raged in him, now he showed little outward sign.

He spoke only three times as the fifteen minutes passed.

The first time he asked: "How long will it take before I remember everything? I feel like I'm surrounded by nameless clouds, shapes without form. . . ."

Rhadamanthus said, "You must sleep and dream before the connections reestablish themselves. If you can find someone to aid you, you should consult a professional onieriatric thought-surgeon; the redaction you suffered is one of the largest on record. Most people erase unpleasant afternoons or bad days. They do not blot out century after century of their most important memories."

A little while later, Phaethon stiffened. Another memory had struck. He said, "I don't remember Xenophon. He's not a brother of mine. I never met him. My contact among the Neptunians was an avatar named Xingis of Neriad. He began to represent himself in a human shape after he met me; because of me, he subscribed to the Consensus Aesthetic, adopted a basic neuroform, and changed his name to Diomedes, the hero who vanquishes the gods. There's no guilt I'm supposed to remember; there's no crime. There's no Sophotech I was building. And Saturn—I wasn't trying to develop Saturn. I had just been thwarted from doing anything with Saturn. I was frustrated with Saturn. That's what gave birth to the *Phoenix Exultant*. That's why I built the ship. My beautiful ship. I was sick of living in the middle of a desert of stars. One small solar system surrounded by nothing but wasteland. And I thought there were planets out there that could be mine, ripe and rich, ready for the hand of man to change from barren rock to paradise. Planets, but no Hortators to hinder me. No one to claim that lifeless rings of rock and dust and dirty ice were more sublime than all the human souls who would live in the palaces I could make out of those rings. . . . Rhadamanthus! It was all a lie. Everything Scaramouche said was a lie. But why?"

There were more minutes of silence. Phaethon's face grew sadder and more grim as he absorbed the enormity of the falsehood that had baffled him, the tremendous reaches of time, the happiness of his memory, the glory of the achievement he had lost.

Eventually he said, "I asked you once if I were happier before, if restoring these memories would make me better."

Rhadamanthus said, "I implied that you would be less happy, but that you would be a better man."

Phaethon shook his head. Anger and grief still gnawed at him. He certainly did not feel like a better man.

Then, in reaction to the gesture he had made long ago, one of the system mirrors aboard the *Phoenix Exultant* came to life. The mirror surface was dim and caked with droppings from undeconstructed nanomachines. Contact points in the mirror flickered toward the image of Phaethon, a thousand pinpoints of light.

He felt a moment of surprised recognition. But of course! It was in his armor. The command circuits on the bridge of the ship were trying to open a thousand channels into the corresponding points in his golden armor.

That was what all the complex circuitry in his armor had been for. Here was a ship larger than a space colony, as intricate as several metropoli, webbed with brain upon brain and circuit upon circuit. She was like a little miniature seed of the Golden Oecumene itself. The bridge (and the bridge crew) of the *Phoenix Exultant* was not actually in the bridge, it was in the armor; the armor of Phaethon, whose unthinkably complex hierarchy of controls were meant to govern the billions of energy flows, measurements, discharges, tensions, and subroutines that would make up the daily routine of the great ship.

Phaethon, despite himself, smiled with pride. It was a wonderful piece of engineering.

That smile faltered when a status board at the arm of the captain's chair lit up to reveal the pain and damage to the ship. Other mirrors lit to show the nearby objects in space.

The dismantling had not gone far; the slabs of super metal were still stored in warehouse tugs orbiting Mercury Equilateral, not far away, waiting transshipment. The ship intelligences were off-line or had never been installed. Near the ship, robot cranes and tugs from the Mercury Station hung, mites near a behemoth, motionless. The status board showed that the rest-mass was low: nearly half the antihydrogen fuel had been unloaded.

The amount of fuel left, nonetheless, was still staggering. The living area of the ship, while as large as a space colony, occupied less than one-tenth of one percent of the ship's mass. The *Phoenix Exultant* was a volume, over three hundred thousand cubic meters of internal space, packed nearly solid with the most lightweight and powerful fuel human science had yet devised. While it was true that the mass of the ship was titanic, it was also true that the fuel-mass-to-payload ratio was inconceivable. Every second of thrust could easily consume as much energy as large cities used in a year. But that was the energy needed to reach near-light-speed velocities.

"You've been selling my fuel." Phaethon hated the sound of pain and loss in his own voice.

"It is no longer yours, young sir. The *Phoenix Exultant* is now in receivership, held by the Bankruptcy Court. But your Agreement at Lakshmi suspended the proceedings. You destroyed your memory of the ship in order to prevent further dismantling. Now that your memories are back, your creditors will take her, I'm afraid."

"You mean I don't have a wife, or a father . . . or . . . or my ship? Nothing? I have nothing?"

A pause.

"I'm very sorry, sir."

There was a long moment of silence. Phaethon felt as if he could not breathe. It was as if the lid of a tomb had closed down not just over him but over the entire universe, over every place, no matter how far he fled, he ever could go. He imagined a suffocating darkness, as wide as the sky, as if every star had been snuffed, and the sun had turned into a singularity, absorbing all light into absolute nothingness.

He had heard theoreticians talk about the internal structure of a singularity. Inside, one would be in a gravity well so deep that no light, no signal, could ever escape. No matter how large the inside might be, the event horizon formed an absolute boundary, forever closing off any attempt to reach the stars outside. One might still be able to see the stars; the light from outside would continue to fall into the black hole and reach the eye of whomever was imprisoned there; but any attempt to reach them would simply use up more and more energy, and achieve nothing.

The theoreticians also said that the interiors of black holes were irrational, that the mathematical constants describing reality no longer made any sense.

Phaethon never before had known what that could mean. Now he thought he did.

Phaethon wiped the tears he was ashamed to find on his face. "Rhadamanthus, what are the five stages of grief?"

"For base neuroforms the progression is: denial, rage, negotiation, depression resignation. Warlocks order their instincts differently, and Invariants do not grieve."

"I just remembered another event . . . It's like a nightmare; my thoughts are still clouded and unclear. I was actually living aboard the *Phoenix Exultant*, with my launch date less than a month away. I was that close to achieving it all. Then the radio call came from my wife's last partial, telling me what Daphne Prime had done. Denial was easy for me; during the long trip from Mercury to Earth, I lived in a simulation, a false memory to tell me she still was alive. The simulation ended last December when the pinnace dropped me on Eveningstar grounds. . . . I remembered all the horror and pain of living without her. A woman I had been just about to leave behind me! So I gave myself a rescue persona, a version of me without hesitation, guilt, fear, or doubt, and stormed off to confront the mausoleum where Daphne's body was held."

Phaethon drew in a ragged breath, then laughed bitterly.

"Ha! Eveningstar Sophotech must have thought me a fool just now! I gave the same arguments this morning as I gave last December. But that last time, in December, I was physically present, and in my armor, and no force on earth could stop me in my rage. I swatted the remotes aside which tried to hinder me. I broke Daphne's coffin and released assemblers to undo her nerve bondage, and wake her from her lifeless dreams. But the body was empty; they had downloaded her mind into the Mansion-memory of Eveningstar, and replaced all the mausoleum with synthetics, pseudo-matter, and hologram. Eveningstar prevented me from committing anything worse than an attempted crime, some minor property damage.

"I gave myself entirely to rage, and began to tear the mausoleum apart. The motors in my arms and legs amplified my strength till I was like Hercules, or Orlando in his rage. There were two squads of Constables by then, in ornithopters armed with assembler clouds. I tore up the pillars of Eveningstar Mausoleum by the roots and threw them. I scattered the mannequins of the Constables and laughed as their darts and paralyzers glanced from my armor.

"They had to call in the military to stop me. I remember

the wall melted and Atkins stepped through. He was not even
armed; he was naked, and dripping with life-water. They had
gotten him out of bed. He didn't even have a weapon. I remember I laughed, because my armor was invulnerable; and
I remember he smiled a grim little smile, and beckoned me
toward him with one hand.

"When I tried to push him out of my way he just leaned,
and touched my shoulder, and, for some reason, I flew head
over heels, and landed in the puddle of melted stone he had
stepped in through. He squeezed some of the life-water out
of his hair and threw it over me. The nanomachines suspended in the water must have been tuned to the ones he used
to disintegrate the stone. When I fell, the stone was like dust,
utterly frictionless. It was impossible for me to get up, there
was nothing to grip. Then, when he shook his wet hair at me,
the nanomachines bound molecule to molecule with artificial
subnuclear forces. The stone now formed one macromolecule,
and my arms and legs were trapped. Invulnerable, yes, but
frozen in stolid stone. No wonder Atkins despises me."

"I don't think he despises you, sir," said Rhadamanthus.
"If anything, he is grateful that you allowed him to exercise
his skills."

Phaethon pressed his aching temples with his fingertips.
"What did you say the third stage of grief was? Bargaining?
The Eveningstar Sophotech did not press charges—she was
delighted to have been the victim of the only half-successful
attempt at violent crime in three centuries; the Red Manorials
loved the drama, I suppose; all they wanted was a copy of
my memories during the fight."

Phaethon remembered now the notoriety that had surrounded him. It was not just for the violence he had attempted. (As long as human passions were still legally
permitted to exist in the human nervous system, there would
always be violent impulses. Many people attempted crimes.
There were six or seven attempts every century.) Phaethon's
notoriety sprang from his position in society. Other men who
gave in to moments of rage were usually primitivists or emancipated partials, people without resources, whom the Consta-

bles, guided by Sophotechs, easily could stop before they hurt anything.

But Phaethon was manor-born, who were considered the elite; and the Silver-Gray, in many ways, were the elite of the elite. The manorials had Sophotechs present in their minds, able to anticipate their thoughts, able to defuse violent problems long before they ever arose. No manor-born had ever committed a violent crime. Phaethon was the first.

In his armor, Phaethon could shut off all contact with the Sophotechs; his thoughts could not be monitored; his violent impulses could not be hindered by a police override. In his armor, Phaethon could act independently of any social restrictions. He was in his own private world; a small world, true, but it was all his own.

"The Red Manorials, perhaps, forgave me. But the Curia was not so amused. The penalty they imposed was forty-five minutes of direct stimulation of the pain center of my brain . . ." (Phaethon winced at the memory) ". . . but the Court suspended fifteen minutes from my sentence because I agreed to erase the rescue persona. Afterwards, the Curia ordered me to experience the memories and lives of the Constables I had humiliated, so that all their anger and frustration and pain happened to me. The fight did not seem so glorious any longer. . . .

"That punishment I was glad to suffer; I knew I was in the wrong. The Curia and Eveningstar did not bargain, no. But the College of Hortators did.

"It was a devil's bargain. They found me during a moment of weakness. I destroyed my memory. Was I trying to commit suicide?"

"And what about now, young sir? Have you reached the state of resignation and acceptance?"

Phaethon straightened, wiped his face, squared his shoulders. He drew a deep breath. "I will never be resigned. Perhaps everything is not lost yet. Unless . . ." Phaethon looked troubled. "Am I just fooling myself again? A recurrence of the denial part of the grief cycle?"

"You know I cannot take a Noetic reading of you at this

time. I do not know the state of your mind. You must avoid giving into fear or despair . . . but you also must avoid giving in to false hopes."

"Very well, then. Maybe there are steps I can still take. Put a call in to that girl who is impersonating Daphne. She seems like a good person. Ask her if—"

"I am sorry sir, but she is no longer receiving your calls, nor am I allowed to transmit them."

"What . . . ?!"

"None of the major telecommunication or telepresentation services will accept your patronage hereafter. Daphne Tercius has left instructions with her seneschal to refuse your calls, lest she be accused of aiding or comforting you, and therefore fall under the same prohibition under which you now fall."

It took a moment for the implications of that to sink in. Phaethon closed his eyes in an expression of pain. "I thought that I would have some time to prepare, or that there would be some ceremony, or leavetaking."

"Normally there would be such, and all the participants in the boycott would exclude you at once. But things are in confusion."

"Confusion . . . ?"

"You must recall that every other memory casket sealed by the Lakshmi Agreement, all across the planet, has opened up. Large sections of the memories of billions of people are returning to them; many are still confounded. All the channels are crowded with signals, young sir. Everyone is sending messages and questions to their friends and comensals; you have stirred the clamor of the world, I'm afraid."

Phaethon made a fist, but, insubstantial to his present scene on the *Phoenix Exultant* bridge, had nothing to strike, not even to make a dramatic gesture. "Scaramouche or Xenophon or Nothing or whoever is behind this is using the confusion to hide more evidence and release more viruses, no doubt. More evidence is being erased or falsified. And they must have predicted this would happen once I opened the memory box. But why? We are all taught that Earthmind is wise enough to foresee and counteract all dangers of this type before they arise. Their plan must be premised on the idea that that is not the case. They must have a Sophotech as wise as Earthmind, but not part of the Golden Oecumene Mentality. How else could they have done this? Is there no one we can warn?"

Rhadamanthus's voice: "I feel I should caution you, young sir, that no evidence exists that any attack of any kind has taken place. I am not presently capable of determining whether or not you are experiencing a hallucination or pseudomnesia."

Phaethon said, "If the Hortators have not officially decreed their boycott of me in effect as yet, can you give me an indication of which efforts, merchant combines, or services will still accept my patronage?"

"Obviously the Eleemosynary Composition has not yet excluded you from the Hospice thoughtspace. Helion is continuing to pay the transaction costs and computer time for you connections with me, and for my conversation with you. The Eleemosynary Composition has left a message, to be given you should you inquire, to the effect that the previous agreement you had discussed has lapsed, and the offer withdrawn. Helion would like to have one last word outside before he shuts you out of my system. You might want to take this opportunity to have anything stored in my mansion-mind recorded into your own private thoughtspace; take any books or memories or proprietary information, alternate personalities, records, or anything else that is yours."

The image of the *Phoenix Exultant* bridge began to slip away. It flowed like water, out of the broken window of the memory chamber. Phaethon's hands tried to grasp the corner of the nearest control mirror, the arms of the thronelike captain's chair. His chair. But his insubstantial fingers passed through the images and could not grasp them.

He seemed to stand in the chamber of memory, but his private thoughtspace, reacting to a command he had placed in it, long ago, at Lakshmi, had turned on. Cubes appeared in a circle around him. The two scenes were superimposed;

the cube icons seemed to float in midair among the shelves and sunlight of the memory chamber.

One of the cubes, a master program, near Phaethon's head, had a window floating in its upright face, showing the checklist of Phaeton's properties that he had planned to remove from the mansion memory.

Whatever sorrow had been on Phaethon's face was gone. His expression was stern, without being grim; it was not free from pain, but it was free from any acceptance of pain. His face might have been that of an ancient statue from the monument of a king.

He nodded to the checklist and raised a finger in the "run program" gesture.

Lesser memory caskets to the left and right of Phaethon, as if of their own accord, opened, and the cube icons flashed green colors to signal they were absorbing the information. The cubes turned black when they were full.

Much of the material was too long or too complex to be fitted into Phaethon's merely personal thought space; files were being deleted. A little flash of red light accompanied every deletion, as Phaethon had to approve the order each time. There were so many memory files being destroyed, and so many flashes of red light, coming faster and faster, that soon the room seemed as if it were burning around him, as if, without heat or noise, Phaethon were burning his old life.

Here were thought works, centuries dormant, for which he would never have use again; memories of youthful tedium, or scenes redundant with other recollections, which afforded him no amusement, instruction, nor even nostalgia to retain; sciences now out-of-date; rough drafts for contemplation forms no longer practiced; the litter and rubbish of a long, long life at Rhadamanthus Mansion. There was no reason at all for tears to sting his eyes. He told himself it was all trash.

And the checklist was one he remembered from Venus, from Lakshmi. He had made it before he signed the Agreement. He had made it knowing the Agreement would break. He had guessed this exile might come. He had planned . . .

He had planned on this, on all of this.

But he had planned on an orderly exit, a withdrawal, perhaps after prevailing on his law case against Helion Secundus. With Helion's fortune, with entire income of the Solar Array in his hands, he could have bought the *Phoenix Exultant* out of hock, paid off his debts, and bought the few remaining supplies he needed, restocked his antihydrogen supplies, and departed.

No wonder the threat of the Hortator's exile had held no terror for him. He had been planning to leave the Golden Oecumene on a journey of centuries, or tens of centuries.

But his plan had been to have himself wait till after the Grand Transcendence in December was concluded, not to open the memory box prematurely, not to fall under the Hortator's boycott. Were he ostracized, Vafnir would not sell him antihydrogen, nor would Gannis sell Chrysadmantium.

He had not planned on being attacked by Xenophon, or by a virus that could have only been concocted by some non-Earth-mind Sophotech, a Sophotech that logic and history said could not possibly exist.

He glanced out the broken window. The image of the *Phoenix Exultant* hung against the darkness of the night sky, her golden hull like fire in the glare from the nearby giant sun. A dead hull.

Hadn't he had a backup plan? Wasn't there anything to salvage from this mess?

Phaethon raised his eyes from the circle of cubes.

In the background of his personal thoughtspace was a wheel of stars. It had been there every time he had turned on his personal thoughtspace. The fact that he hadn't recognized the background content of his personal area here should have been a clue that it was important.

The wheel of stars: it was impossible to believe he had not recognized it.

He reached out his hand. The galaxy was both smaller and closer than it appeared. He took it in his hand.

Like veins made of light was the umbrella of possible travel routes he had planned through the nearby stars. Where his finger touched a route, images unfolded to the left and right,

showing acceleration and deceleration calculations, estimates
of local densities of space, notations of possible sources of
volatiles for refueling in-flight, notes on where previous unmanned probes had gone (including summaries of scientifi-
cally significant discoveries and observations) and, more
important, notes on places where unmanned probes had never
gone.

The galaxy lay like a jewel in his hand. The stars were
turning slowly, as the map ran through time adjustments for
various periods in the projected voyage. Like a path of fire
burned the trace of his first planned expedition. Branching
world-lines for alternate routes reached out across stars and
light-years.

It was beautiful. He would not give it up.

"Previous Phaethon, whoever you were: I remember you;
I forgive you; I am you," he whispered. "I hated you for
banishing my memory. I could not imagine what could have
prompted me to butcher my mind in that way, what could
have urged me to accept so much pain. Now I remember.
Now I know. And I was right. It was worth the risk."

Somehow he would still save his plan. Somehow he would
still save his dream. . . .

Rhadamanthus, in his shape as a butler, cleared his throat.
Phaethon looked up from the galaxy he held.

It was Helion.

Helion stood at the threshold of the memory chamber. His
face was stern and sad. He was dressed out of period for
Victorian England; instead, his self-image wore his snow
white ablative armor of solar-station environment. He wore
no helmet; Helion's hair shone like spun gold. The activity
of Phaethon's deletions made red light flow across the scene
like flame; the reflections burned in his armor.

Helion stepped into the chamber. Phaethon's private
thoughtscape was excluded; the red flashes vanished, and the
galaxy disappeared from his hand. The image of near-
Mercury space disappeared from the window next to Phaethon. Instead, the broken window now let in sunlight, warm

summer air, the smell of flowers, the drone of bees, the scents and sounds of the ordinary daylit world.

"Son," said Helion, "I've come for any last words we might have with each other."

18

THE WARLOCK

1.

Phaethon pointed two fingers. This was Helion himself, not a recording, a message persona, or a partial. "What do we have to say to each other, Father? Isn't it too late? Too late for everything?" Bitterness and irony showed on Phaethon's face. "You may be exiled yourself, just for speaking with me."

"Son—I had hoped it would never come to this. You are a fine and brave man, intelligent and upright. The boycotts and shunnings of the Hortators were meant to stop indecencies, deviations from acceptable behavior, acts of negligence and cruelty. They were meant to restrain the worst among us. They surely were not meant for you!" Sorrow was deeply graven on Helion's face. "This destiny is worse than we deserve."

The chamber seemed more real as Helion entered. It was a subtle change, one Phaethon might not normally have noticed. The colors were now brighter, the shadows of finer texture. The sunlight entering the many windows took on a rich and golden hue. Individual dust motes were now visible in the bright sunbeams, as was the wood grain of the polished wainscoting where the light fell, bringing rich glints and highlights from caskets and cabinets on the surrounding shelves.

Not only sense impressions were brighter and sharper in

Helion's presence. Phaethon felt more alert, at ease, and awake. Perhaps the circuits in Phaethon's brain stem and midbrain had not been receiving very much computer time from Rhadamanthus; certainly the simulated sensations fed into Phaethon's optic nerve had not been of as high a quality as what Helion could afford for himself. Helion had been paying for Phaethon's computer time, but, quite naturally, reserved more time for his own use.

It was as if Helion's wealth and power surrounded him like an aura of light. Phaethon doubted that Helion was even aware of the effect on other people.

"Much of this destiny is of your making, Relic of Helion," said Phaethon bitterly. "I now remember that when they resurrected you, it was your voice who urged the Hortators to condemn my voyage; it was you who tried to kill my beautiful *Phoenix Exultant*. Why do you hate her so?"

"Perhaps I did dislike your ship at one time. But no longer. You know the reason why . . . or do you?" Helion peered at Phaethon.

Phaethon said, "I cannot imagine. Gannis, perhaps, has motives I can guess. He wanted my ship for scrap. He thought it clever both to sell me the hull and foreclose on the lien. The College of Hortators had a deeper and more wicked purpose. The future I propose, one of humanity expanding through the universe, is one whose outcomes even Sophotechs cannot foresee. Even should there always be a core of worlds, centered on Earth, perfectly civilized and perfectly controlled, in my future, there will always be a frontier, a wilderness, a place which no Sophotech controls, a place where danger, adventure, and greatness still has scope. The Hortators' fear of war is mere excuse. It is life they fear, for life is change and turmoil and uncertainty. But you—I cannot believe you share their moral cowardice."

"We had this conversation before, my son. At Lakshmi, on Venus . . ." He looked into Phaethon's eyes. "You don't remember yet, do you?"

Phaethon said in a voice of anger: "More of my life was robbed from me than from you; and you had access to these

forbidden memories since before you met with the Peers. It
will take me longer to adjust."

Helion was silent for a moment before he spoke.

"Your ship killed me, son."

Phaethon remembered what the man dressed as a Porphyrogen Observationer had said, that Helion had sacrificed himself for a worthless boy. He had stayed at the Solar Array,
when everyone else had fled, attempting to erect shields to
protect certain areas of near-Mercury space. The *Phoenix Exultant* herself had been the "equipment" at Mercury Equilateral that Helion had tried to save from the fury of the solar
storms.

"You saved my ship. . . ." whispered Phaethon, as the
memory suddenly returned to him.

The hull armor had still been in sections at that time. The
wash of particles from the sun would have disrupted the magnetic containment fields holding the antihydrogen, which,
heated, would have expanded explosively, as a plasma. Every
particle of the antimatter gas, encountering a particle of normal matter, would have totally converted its mass to energy,
disrupting further magnetic containments, and igniting the
most concentrated mass of antimatter ever gathered in one
place. The superadmantium hull, invulnerable to all normal
forms of energy, was still made of matter, and would have
been converted to energy at the touch of antimatter.

"Damn your ship." Helion's voice grated. "It was you. You
were aboard at that time. Outside of the range of the Mentality, beyond the reach of any resurrection circuit."

Phaethon turned away. He felt the hot blush of shame rising
to his face.

Helion stepped over and sat in one of the tall-backed ceremonial chairs flanking the doorway. He waited while Phaethon stood, staring at nothing, trying to grapple with the
enormity of what he had heard, with what his memory was
still bringing back to him.

"I—I'm so sorry, Father. I did not mean for any of this to
happen."

Helion clasped his hands and leaned with his elbows on

his knees, staring at the floor for a moment. Then, raising his head, he gave Phaethon a direct and earnest look. "No one meant for any of this to happen. But each of us was required by our consciences to do as he thought best. Even the College of Hortators might have been less quick to condemn your venture had you been willing to compromise, to wait, to listen to the opinions of others. The Hortators are neither villains nor fools nor cowards. They are honest men, attempting to cure our society of the one great fault which surrounds us; the danger, now that we all have so much power and freedom at our command, that reckless action will bring us to harm. Mostly they try to use social pressure to keep self-indulgent folk from harming themselves. Yours is the first case in hundreds of years of someone who threatened another."

"The worlds I intended to create would have been peaceful."

"The College might have believed that; had you not lost control of yourself in December, at the Eveningstar Mausoleum. You smashed the building, and broke the remotes and mannequins of the Constables."

Again Phaethon felt heat in his face. His voice was low: "I am very sorry, Father. And the more I remember, the less and less heroic my actions seem to have been. Maybe living since January without my memories has been good for me after all; my old anger seems childish to me now. But I still believe my dream to be a good one."

Helion said, "I once dreamed as you did."

"Yes . . . ?"

"I have never told you the details surrounding your birth, Phaethon."

A stillness seemed to come into the chamber. Phaethon realized he was holding his breath. He had heard rumors. He had never heard the truth.

"You know you are taken from my mental templates, a version of me more brave than I have ever been, do you not? But what you don't recall—the origin you agreed to forget— is that you were created during one of the earlier Millennial Celebrations. One of the worlds constructed in dreamspace by

Cuprician Sophotech (who hosted that Celebration then as Aurelian does now) was my vision of a far future where mankind had expanded across the local volume of stars, some four hundred light-years in diameter. You were one of the characters in that story. You were the version of me, as Cuprician predicted I should be, should I live to see such an age."

Helion fell silent. He was staring out the windows, perhaps at the mountains of Wales; perhaps at something more distant.

Phaethon said, "Is there more to my story . . . ?"

Helion stirred and brought his gaze back to Phaethon. "Not really. I was not famous nor well liked at that time. In fact, people called me a crackpot. During that Festival's Transcendence (they were held earlier in the year, at that time, in November) other Sophotechs recalculated Cuprician's premises and found them absurdly optimistic. When they reran the scenario, they found the distant colonies growing more and more inhuman, rash, and unreasonable. They concluded that even the most sane and stable of men, when there was no government to keep them all in awe, had no choice but to settle serious disputes by force. The scenario evolved into interstellar piracy and war. Many people were plugged into the dreamscape when their characters on Earth were destroyed by the colonial war. Vividly, seeming perfectly real, they died. They experienced their own death, and the death of everything they knew and loved. It only took one soldier aboard one single ship. He was armed with a few metric tons of antimatter. He burned the world. Naturally, the participants were horrified. I was horrified. Even the computer-generated character of the colonial warrior was horrified, to such an extent that he fell into a deep reverie, pondering himself and his place in the world, questioning all his basic values and beliefs. When the public outcry demanded that I erase the scenario, I was happy to comply; but the Sophotech stopped me."

Phaethon could see what was coming. "You've got to be joking, Father."

"No. The colonial soldier, the world burner, had made himself from a recording to a self-aware entity. By our laws, anyone who makes a self-aware being by any means whatever, natural or artificial, deliberately or accidentally, becomes that parent of that child, and must raise and care for that child, and must have the appropriate natural paternal or maternal instincts inserted into his or her midbrain and hindbrain complex. That is why I made and married your mother, Galatea, may she rest in peace."

Galatea was not dead. At the age of four hundred she had divorced herself from Helion, left the Silver-Gray, and tuned her sense-filter and adjusted her memory to exclude him. Helion, at first, in the old days, often went to her, but, to her, he was no more visible than a ghost. Then one day, for reasons she had explained to no one, Galatea put her memories in archive, and descended into the sea, abandoning her flesh and merging her mind with the strange, old, unfriendly massminds that live scattered in a million microscopic cell bodies far below the waves.

Helion's face had the stiff look of sorrow it always had at the mere mention of Phaethon's mother's name. The sight of that sadness angered Phaethon, for now Phaethon was being told his mother had not been his at all.

"So I was born. I remember a youth and childhood. Where those false?"

"No. You were incarnated as a boy when you entered the real world."

"Why do I not remember the fictional life which came before my birth? Your pretended future? Don't tell me I agreed to forget that also!" Phaethon felt a sense of wonder and disgust. Was there anything at all in his life that was real?

"Everyone was afraid of you. You had the memory, skills, and personality of a planet killer. And once you learned who and what you were, you were happy to erase your past. Surely you can guess why?"

He knew the reason. "Because it was false."

Helion nodded. "No one has been more in love with naked truth than you."

"Is that why I was named Phaethon? To remind me that I had burned the earth?"

Helion shook his head. "You picked that name yourself, after you joined the Consensus Aesthetic. But you adopted a slightly alternate version of the myth. You said that—"

A distant gong note rang. Rhadamanthus said, "Pardon me, Master Helion, but you asked to be interrupted whenever the channels cleared and the Hortators came on-line. They are arriving now."

Phaethon heard distant sounds: the opening of the main doors, the murmur of voices, and, beyond that the clatter of carriages arriving at the front portico. These fictional noises were provided by the mansion dreamscape to represent the "arrival" of the members of the College of Hortators.

Helion stood. "Out of deference to me, the College has agreed to adopt the Consensus Aesthetic for the official record of the upcoming Inquest. Naturally, everyone's personal sense-filter can reorganize the information in whatever forms they would like, but the core document will record that the meeting took place in my version of Rhadamanthus Mansion. Will you come with me, Phaethon?"

He gestured toward the door.

Phaethon took one last look at the memory chamber. The caskets were either open and empty, or displayed as if they had been burnt. The broken window no longer held a view of the glorious starship, the only one of her kind, which was no longer his.

There was nothing for him here.

The two men started down the stairs together. Phaethon saw that Helion's version of the mansion was somewhat larger and more splendid than Phaethon's. The staircase was a wide, sweeping semicircle leading down to an enormous entrance hall paved with white flagstones.

There were windows everywhere, wide and filled with light.

Phaethon said, "If they remembered my origin, no wonder they were afraid when I bought an invulnerable ship and filled it with antimatter. But couldn't they tell reality from fantasy?"

Phaethon stopped on the stair, and took Helion's arm,

drawing him up short. Helion looked back curiously, and saw the beginning of fear on Phaethon's face.

"Tell me quickly. Does Daphne know? All our lives she called me a heroic character—a character—she didn't fall in love with me because of—because of that?!"

"I doubt she knew. Daphne was born of natural parents, actually womb born, the old-fashioned way, and raised in a Primitivist School that did not even have reincarnation. She ran away from her convent and joined the Warlocks of the Cataleptic Oneiromancer School when she was sixteen. It was not that many centuries ago; I doubt she has ever even heard of Cuprician."

Phaethon breathed a sigh and released Helion's arm.

They continued down the stair and across the bright hall. Their footsteps echoed on the marble.

Then Phaethon asked: "Why did you give up on the dream, Father? You know our sun only has a limited period of time in which to live."

"Longer, thanks to my effort."

"But still limited. We cannot stay in one small solar system forever. It's because you see yourself in my old character, don't you? The colonial warrior who killed the earth. That was a simulated extrapolation of you, wasn't it? And it scared you."

Helion did not answer the question. "Simulation technology is much better now. There is less guesswork involved. . . ."

They passed a rank of empty suits of armor, enameled in white. Here were two tall doors of oak, inscribed with an open book crossed with a flail, and, beneath, a grail from which a fountain flowed; this was the emblem of the College of Hortators. This door had not been here before; Helion's version of the mansion now included an Inquest Hall. The murmur of voices came dimly from behind the doors.

"You should not be frightened, Father. The dream to conquer the stars is still a fine and noble one. Despite all, I am still in the right. My dream is right."

Helion stopped and stared at the doors. "Perhaps. But now

that dream is about to die, as are you. Daphne Prime is drowned beyond rescue; Daphne Tercius, who loves you, has no further reason to go on, since she sacrificed her future career in order to come plead with you. And, for myself, just when I have been declared a Peer, and have hopes of becoming a center of attention for the upcoming Transcendence, I find my son is about to be gone. And so my life is ruined too." He smiled sadly. "Who was it who said, 'Endless life breeds endless pain'?"

Phaethon could see Helion was thinking of Hyacinth Septimous, his best friend whom he had lost so long ago.

"Ao Enwir. 'On the Sovereignty of Machines.' " Phaethon said. He did not correct the misquote.

Then Phaethon forced a smile. "But I am not about to die, Father. Even if no one will sell me food or water, my armor lining can produce—"

"Orpheus Avernus has dumped your extra lives. You are no longer in the Mentality."

"W-what . . . ?"

"Read the hypertext and fine print of your contract with your bank. They are obligated to delete the stored lives of anyone who falls under Hortator prohibition. It is a standard clause for all contracts with Orpheus; it was Orpheus who first gave the College so much social influence."

Phaethon opened his mouth to protest. Surely the Sophotechs, infinitely wise, would not simply stand by and let him die?!

He closed his mouth again. He knew what the Sophotech logic would say. Phaethon had not invented the Noumenal Recording system. Orpheus had. It belonged only to Orpheus, and he was free to dispose of his property in any peaceful and lawful fashion he saw fit. He could not be compelled by force to give his services or his property or his lifework to anyone with whom he did not wish to deal.

And Phaethon had freely signed that contract.

"As of this moment, my son, you are no longer immortal."

A sense of dread began to close in on·Phaethon.

"Surely the Hortators have not yet posted an official decree—"

"It does not matter. Your attorney, Monomarchos, signed in your name a confession of judgment, don't you remember? You signed away your right to any appeal. There will be no second Inquiry Hearing; this meeting is merely an announcement."

"If they expect me to simply lie down somewhere and die, they are sadly mistaken!"

"That is exactly what they expect. They are not mistaken."

"There are people who survive exile."

"In fiction stories, perhaps. But even Lundquist in the old song was only exiled for a period of six hundred years. Yours is permanent. You might be able to jury-rig repairs to the nanomachinery in your cells which regenerates your wounds and restores your youth. But nanomachines draw their power from isotopic decay of the large atoms at the base of their spiral chains; no one will sell you life-water to replenish those atoms."

"Life-water is the cheapest nanotechnology our society makes. . . ." Phaethon began.

Helion's voice was flat. "It is not your society anymore. You are alone. No one will sell you a drop of water."

Phaethon closed his eyes and bowed his head.

Helion's face was grave. "And do not ask Daphne to smuggle food or medicine to you; you would only involve her in the same downfall."

"I won't, Father," Phaethon whispered.

Helion stepped forward, taking Phaethon by the shoulders. Phaethon raised his head. Helion said, "I see that you call me 'Father' instead of 'Relic.' May I ask why?"

Phaethon shook his head. "Because I don't think any of it matters anymore. Everything is over. I've ruined everyone's lives and destroyed my own dreams . . . and now I have nothing and everything is over. We argue, you and I. We argue often. All those arguments are over. We're never going to see each other again, are we?"

They looked deeply into each other's eyes.

"Forgive me if I have not been the best of fathers, my son."

"If you will pardon me that I have not been the best of sons."

"Don't say that!" Helion's voice was hoarse. "You are braver and brighter than I ever could have hoped. . . . I am so very proud of you I cannot say. . . ."

They embraced.

Sire and scion whispered good-byes to each other.

2.

The doors opened, but the Inquest Chamber was not beyond. Instead, a large anteroom waited, carpeted in red and burgundy. Tall windows on the left threw sunlight on a cluster of low tables, chairs, and divans, standing ashtrays and formulation rods. To the right were Chinese screens and wardrobes.

A set of doors at the far end bore the book, grail, and flail emblem of the College. Evidently the actual chamber was beyond.

Phaethon frowned at the nearest formulation rod; it was an anachronism, dating from the period of the Warlock Counterprogressions in the Fifth Era.

Helion was looking at Rhadamanthus for an explanation. "Who added this chamber to my house?"

"Master, I thought you would want to change from your solar armor to proper period dress," said the overweight butler, pointing toward the wardrobes. "Also, you have a guest who insisted on speaking to Mr. Phaethon before the hearing commenced. This was very much in character with your previous instructions to me on these matters, and an extrapolation of your personality assured me you would not mind. I hope I did not incorrectly anticipate your wishes?"

Helion looked impatient. "What guest do you imagine I would tolerate to use up the last few moments my son and I might ever have together?"

One of the chairs, facing away from them, had a back tall

enough to hide from view the figure who had been sitting in it. Now he stood, a tall shape in a hooded robe of patterned red and gold webbed with colored threads and scaly with beadwork and chips of glass. The back of the hood was richly ornamented with beadwork as well, and bore the upright crescent that the hoods of king cobras might display, the sign of Brahma. The motion of standing sent highlights like embers trembling down from the narrow shoulders through the fabric.

Still facing away, the figure spoke. His voice was smooth, musical, and exotic. "Peers often extend to each other these small courtesies. Your time in our midst is short; you cannot be expected to acclimate yourself to all our graces instantly."

He turned. His face was dusky; his eyes were large, liquid, magnetic. A Hindu caste mark gleamed in his forehead, beneath his hood a tasseled head cloth hid his hair.

Helion pointed with two fingers. "Ao Aoen. It is a pleasure to see you." His tone was flat, belying his words. "I would have thought the small courtesies Peers extend to each other would have included avoiding the introductions of anachronisms into a mansion famed for its authenticity."

"Fakirs, swamis, and magicians from the Orient figure prominently in the literature of your Victorian age. Surely one would not expect the chief of all chiefs of the Warlocks to represent himself as a stiff, rationalist, tradition-loving Englishman? Or . . . do you mean the formulation rods? But I needed a magic rod to stir my charms. Data flows and grows and shows strange lives and inner secrets of their own once a sufficient formulation is empatterned to allow an intuition to be triggered. I have woven your lives from one map to another, to see symmetries and signs which linear thinking can never display. Are you angry? I trust not. My depictions have shown me a danger. But have also show me a way."

"A way . . . ? Please tell us more, my good fellow Peer. I am certain you have engaged our interest," Helion said pleasantly. Phaethon knew Helion disliked Warlocks and their riddles, their nonrational methods of thought. But Helion showed no impatience that Phaethon could see (or perhaps

Helion broke Silver-Gray rules, and had Rhadamanthus running his face).

"A way to escape the danger I foresee." Ao Aoen folded his arms, tucking his hands into the voluminous sleeves of his robe.

There was a moment while Phaethon and Helion waited for Ao Aoen to continue. Helion broke the silence: "We lend our ears most earnestly, my good Peer. Pray continue."

The figure smiled inscrutably. "But the words are meant for Phaethon's ears alone. They are eager to fly from my tongue like birds. But the instincts of birds in spring return them to their destined home, not elsewhere."

Phaethon was surprised when Helion stepped to a nearby table, picked up a cigar trimmer lying there, and slashed his own palm, drawing blood. Helion winced and turned around, holding up his hand and spreading his reddened fingers.

Ao Aoen bowed deeply, obviously impressed. "I understand. Forgive me. You and Phaethon are of one blood; the message must be meant for you both." Phaethon was not sure whether Ao Aoen was impressed because Helion's symbolic gesture had been so Warlock-like or because the reputation of Rhadamanthus House ensured that, if Helion's self-image showed a wound, Helion's real brain would experience the real proportional pain.

Ao Aoen turned to Phaethon. "Have you considered, my dear Phaethon, that if you were a character in a romance, you would undoubtedly be the villain?"

Phaethon glanced at Helion. Was this a reference to his origin? If not, the coincidence seemed odd. On the other hand, the superintuitive structures of the Warlock brain tended to find order in odd coincidences. "What do you mean, sir? Please speak plainly."

Ao Aoen spread his arms, making many small circles with his hands, and smiling. "Consider: you are a rich and selfish individualist, a heartless engineer, deaf to all pleas, who is willing to sacrifice family, friends, and foes alike, to pursue one overproud design. You have used yourself ruthlessly, and have deceived the College of Hortators, and broken your word and opened the forbidden memory casket, yes, even after you had been told that you had promised us all you would not! You have broken the heart and spurned the affection of the innocent heroine. And you plan to rely on lawyers' tricks to steal your father's gold, trampling his love as well. In the better-loved tales, something else prevails besides greed and selfishness and pride!"

Phaethon raised an eyebrow. He thought it was improper (to say the least) to jab a man about to be exiled with insults. He tried to keep his voice even and polite: "Perhaps the Peer enjoys a different fashion of fairy tales from myself. The three qualities you mention, sir, to call them by their proper names—ambition, independence, and self-esteem—always figured quite prominently in the stories I loved in my youth, I can assure you of that. Perhaps you make a public show, for reasons about which I do not care to speculate, of admiring the opposite qualities: sloth, sheepish conformity, and self-loathing, but certainly nothing in your career or speech or manner shows you have ever been acquainted, even remotely, with any of these. But you ought not fret. I am confident that, barring unforeseen circumstances, my future plans will allow the two of us relatively little opportunity to exchange recommendations of favorite authors. Now, if there is nothing further . . . ?"

Ao Aoen stepped close and took his elbow, hissing in his ear, "Do you hate your father so much? If you prevail in your lawsuit, all his fortune is yours, wealth beyond wealth, which you have neither earned nor, once you are ostracized, can you ever spend. Why continue this farce? Even with all of Helion's wealth, Gannis will not sell you one more gram of the Chrysadmantium you need to complete the work on your hull. You know the money is not yours. For shame! At least let your downfall and slow death have some grace and nobility about it!"

Phaethon ignored him, but looked at Helion in sudden puzzlement. "Surely the lawsuit by now is moot. . . ." But he frowned as he said it, for he realized that it was not the case at all.

Helion said, "The Hortators have no legal status."

Ao Aoen smiled. All his teeth had been capped with gold, so that his smile was startling and odd. "The majesty of law is immense, all the more for being so little used. The Curia will not notice our private agreement among ourselves to boycott those on whom the Hortators frown, any more than your Queen Victoria of the Third Era British Empire cares what rules a group of schoolboys make among themselves to exclude their little sisters from a tree house planted in a back yard in Liverpool. The College can urge all to ignore you, good villainous Phaethon; but they will not be permitted to take by force, not one computer-second second, not one antigram, not one ounce of gold, of what blind law reckons to be yours." Ao Aoen turned his half-lidded eyes toward Helion, "You see the implications, do you not? No tower can stand which is built on sand."

Helion's expression grew remote. He said in a distant voice, "In other words, if I concede the lawsuit, the Curia passes all my wealth to an exiled man. How much commerce do I affect, by keeping solar-radiation background levels clear enough to permit long-range broadcast traffic between distant points in the Golden Oecumene? Four percent of the entire economy? Six? This does not take into effect secondary industries which have grown up in my shadow; microwave powercasts, unshielded space assemblies, orbital dust farms, macroelectronics, or cheap counterterragenesis. How many of them could survive if we have sunspots again, or did not have bands of solar maser energy beamed directly across the Inner System to fixed industrial points?" Helion drew his eyes down. "Now picture all that in the hands of someone with whom only Neptunians, solitudarians, outcasts, crooks, and cacophiles can deal. How long will those of us who promised to abide by the Hortator's mandates keep our promises?"

Ao Aoen said, "You are manor-born. Ask your pet machine who owns your soul and who pretends to serve you." He nodded to where Rhadamanthus, represented as a butler, stood in the background.

"I do not need to ask," said Helion. "The power of the

College would be destroyed, one way or the other. It would defeat everything I have tried to build in this life. And yet it might be a fitting revenge against the Hortators who took my son from me. Gentlemen, if you will excuse me . . . ?" And he stepped behind a Chinese screen and opened the door to a wardrobe.

This was not the reaction Ao Aoen had expected. He stood with his fingertips rubbing against each other, eyes swinging left and right.

Instead of merely restarting his self-image in a different costume, Helion went through the motions of disassembling and discarding his solar armor, and putting on the linens, shirt, and trousers, waistcoat, coat, cuff links and ornaments of historical garb. The mansion created an image of a valet who entered the chamber and crossed over behind the screen to assist him.

Ao Aoen looked sidelong at Phaethon. "Why does he dress a computer-generated self-illusion?"

Phaethon spared him an irritated glance. "It is an exercise in self-discipline."

"Aha. Will that selfsame discipline allow Helion's social conscience to slumber? He will not pull down the pillars of our society, and lay flames to the toppling wreckage, not even to make a monument to the memory of his once-loved son. A delightful image, I agree, but it would make a poor reality."

"What is the point and purpose of this comment, sir?"

The Warlock smiled, gold teeth bright against dark skin. "Do you know why Helion will stand by and watch you starve? Because he gave his word. He is as proud as you. Do you admire him?"

Phaethon was staring at the Chinese screen. He answered without reflection. "I love my father."

Ao Aoen touched Phaethon on the shoulder. "Then drop your law case against him. You know it is unfair. Your father is a living man, there he stands; and you know a living man cannot have an heir."

Phaethon shrugged Ao Aoen's hand from his shoulder. There was a look of petulant anger on his face. But that look

soon faded. He stood straight, drew a deep breath, and a calm
and severe look came into his eye. "You are right. It is dishonorable of me to stand in Court and take his money. I don't
believe one hour of memory can make such a difference. And
if I cannot use the wealth to forward my dream, it is no use
to me."

Ao Aoen looked satisfied, and his lips curved in a smile as
he bowed again. "Then perhaps you are the hero of this romance after all, and perhaps you deserve a happier end! Listen: the term of your ostracism is not fixed."

Phaethon said, "I thought it was permanent."

"No. The purpose of Hortatory is to exhort men to virtue,
not to punish crime. They need only cast you out from society
long enough to discourage those who might be tempted to
follow your example; and, since it would require a private
fortune as massive as the one you have amassed to do as you
have threatened, the possibility that another will arise to imitate your act is remote."

"Our society—pardon me, your society—continues to
grow in wealth and power. In a relatively short time, four
thousand years or less, the average income of a private citizen
may be equal to what mine is now. That is only four more
Transcendences away."

"Ah. But the Peers hope to persuade the spirit of the coming age to adopt a version of society tied to tradition and
conformity. Your mansion extrapolations predict civilization
tied to immobile and massive sources of power, Dyson Sphere
within Dyson Sphere, with citizens existing in separate bodies
only in their dreams. The ultimate triumph of the Manorial
way of life! While individual wealth will grow, mobile
sources of energy will no longer be produced; there will be
no fit fuels to move a starship. Individual consciousness will
be housed perhaps in expanses of thin solar-energy tissue,
perhaps in ultrafrozen computer mainframes, larger than
worlds, existing beyond the Oort clouds. Too big to get
aboard a ship. We shall all be like a crust of corals, fixed in
place. But in no case will star colonization ever again be
affordable or practical."

"And when the sun dies of old age? What then? To men like us, that time is not so very far away!"

"We should be able to replenish its fuel almost indefinitely by directing interstellar clouds of hydrogen gas, and streams and floods of particles which move, like unseen rivers, through the local area of space, into the sun. Eventually we shall have to reengineer the local motions of stars and nearby nebulae, perhaps by forming a set of black holes large enough to attract sufficient dust and gas and stars to us; but we will not be required to leave our home."

"And you do not find this vision repulsive?"

"I saw the look of eagerness in your eye when I spoke of engineering the local area of space-time, and of rendering the orbits of nearby stars more useful to mankind."

It was true. Phaethon's imagination was stirred by the thought, the magnitudes involved. With a few quick calculations in his private thoughtspace, he began to explore the possibility that, by shepherding the star motions with neutron stars, the stars of the local area could be fed into a central reaction, a supersun, at a rate sufficient to sustain nova-O levels of energy output. A continuous supernova. A Dyson Sphere to capture that output would pay for the energy cost of the star shepherds. Any stars exhausted in the shepherding project (if the excess matter were blown off to make new planets) could be reduced to brown dwarves or neutronium cores to make more star shepherds.

Ao Aoen spoke softly: "You will be able to participate in that project; it is only a few billion years in our future; you, Phaethon, famous for organizing these little moons and worlds which swing around this one small sun of ours. Can you not devote your talents to a project truly worth ambition?"

"It would be wonderful. . . ." Phaethon's voice was soft, his eyes distant.

"All you need do is publicly denounce your selfish dream. Why need we colonize the stars when we can bring the stars to us?"

Phaethon stiffened.

Ao Aoen said, "Listen carefully! This may be your last chance at happiness. Denounce your project, and I will use my influence with the Hortators to mitigate your sentence. Three hundred years of exile, perhaps, or one hundred? Seventy? Sixty? You could stand on your head for a longer period than that! At the end of that time, join Helion in business, embrace poor broken-hearted Daphne Tercius as your wife, and live happily ever after. Not just happily. Live in unimaginable wealth and splendor ever after! What do you say, my lad? Everyone benefits, all rejoice."

Phaethon stepped away from him and sat in one of the several chairs. "Forgive my suspicions, but why is this matter of such interest to you?"

Ao Aoen stood with a subtle smile playing over his features. "My reasons are many; they are a matter of instinct and intuition. Here is my reason! In diatonic music, even in the greatest symphonies, the chord must be resolved to the center. Choirs must follow strophe and antistrophe and end the play in catastrophe. Does that explain me? No, I thought not. I will explain it in your terms, if you agree that this is no more than a myth, a metaphor, a falsehood! If I were to think like you, I would identify my motives as threefold, philosophical, social, and selfish. My selfish motive is clear. I am one of the seven paramounts of this society. In the future I describe, as individuals are subsumed into larger and more immobile housings, the need for entertainment will increase, and all men will enter my dream web. My effort will flourish. My second reason is social; this society has greatly benefited me and all the folk I love. Therefore this society deserves my protection from villains who think they are heroes."

"With all due respect," said Phaethon, "what I desire is the best and highest example of the individualism and liberty on which the Golden Oecumene is based."

"Ah! That you must be sacrificed to placate an utterly nonsacrificial society merely adds ironic zest to my belief."

"That is not a reasonable response. Your third motive?"

"The basic neuroform is a compromise between the Warlock and the Invariant. Your brain shape is useful for matters of engineering and ratiocination. The massive and immobile society I foresee will require greater uniformity as time goes on; there will be less scope for individual scientific and engineering efforts. Human energies will turn to artistic, mystical, and abstract pursuits; the Warlocks will flourish and the Invariants eventually disappear. This will satisfy certain philosophic needs I have. So! There you have it! Some of my motives are noble, and others are selfish. Are your suspicions satisfied? Perhaps in the future—if you have a future—you should pay heed to what is being offered you instead of fretting about the motives of the offerer. In logic, an argument is sound or unsound based only on itself, not upon the character of whomever utters it!"

"I was curious about your—"

Ao Aoen raised his voice in anger, "You were attempting to delay the momentous decision I now force upon you!"

Phaethon was silent, taken aback. He wondered if the Warlock were right; his neuroform often had acute insights. Was Phaethon trying to avoid the decision . . . ?

Ao Aoen continued in a quieter voice: "How precious is your silly ship to you, boy? You will never fly it in any case! But if you denounce it, let Gannis dismantle it, and forget all about it, then you can live forever in happiness, wealth, good fortune and honor! Give me your answer! What is your choice?!"

Phaethon closed his eyes. With all his heart he wanted to agree with the Warlock, to return to his normal life, his happiness, his house. He wanted to see his father again.

He wanted to go home with his wife. He missed her.

But the word which came out of his mouth was: " 'She.' "

"I beg your pardon?" asked the Warlock.

Phaethon's eyes snapped open, as if in surprise at himself. "She. You heard me. She! The *Phoenix Exultant* is a ship. Ships are called 'she.' You said 'it.' You said 'dismantle it.' You cannot 'dismantle' the *Phoenix Exultant*. The word you are looking for is 'murder.' "

Ao Aoen looked at him with narrowed eyes. "You cannot hope to rebuild your ship."

"I shall." Phaethon stood. "With hope or without it, but I shall."

"You will be exiled and alone."

"Then I will rebuild her alone."

"You have lost legal claim! Your creditors will take possession!"

"With Helion's wealth I will pay off the debt."

"You have agreed just one moment ago to forswear your wretched law case!"

Phaethon nodded. "And so I would, if I could. But if Helion's Relic is found to be Helion Secondus, the money comes to me automatically, whether I want it or not, and some part of it, whether I want it or not, will be seized at once, before I touch it, to pay off my creditors. At that point, whether they want it or not, the *Phoenix Exultant* will be mine once again. The metal and the fuel supplies held in the warehouses orbiting at Mercury Equilateral will also become my property again, whether anyone wants it or not. You see, unlike Orpheus, I did not put in the contracts I made any nullification clause should I fall under the Hortators' ban! Yes, you can spurn me, and refuse to deal or to speak with me again; but the *Phoenix Exultant* shall live and shall fly and mankind shall possess the stars! Rest assured, that shall certainly happen, whether anyone likes it or not."

Ao Aoen stood for a moment amazed. And then, oddly enough, looked gleeful and rubbed his hands. "You unleash forces beyond any human command; destiny's tidal wave sweeps us all. In blind faith you sail the maelstrom, certain of victory even at the moment of your fall. I attempt basic human logic on you; you spurn safety and escape. Instead, you embrace the irrational!" He chuckled, "And so, of course, I approve. What Warlock would not?! Eyeh! You should have been one of us, Ao Phaethon!"

And the Warlock concluded by making a graceful bow, and saying, "Now comes a time of tragedy and wonder."

With no further word of farewell, still laughing softly and rubbing his hands, the figure of Ao Aoen glided away on soft steps. The noise of voices and motion in the Inquest Chamber briefly grew louder as the tall doors opened and closed. Phaethon had a glimpse of a long chamber, lit by massive windows of stained glass, of tiers of benches rising to either side, of a central dais hung with flags and bunting of blue and silver. Then the door closed again, and Ao Aoen was gone.

Helion stepped up behind Phaethon. "I heard what you said, my son. It is not true."

Phaethon turned. Helion was now dressed in a sober black costume, a long-tailed coat, a stiff collar, a black silk top hat.

"What is not true?"

"That you cannot drop the law case. The Curia would certainly prefer for us to reach an out-of-court settlement, should we fashion one, than to make a ruling. It is also not true that you shall possess once again and rebuild your starship or your dream, or that you will conquer the stars. Pandora kept hope at the bottom of her box because it was the most dreadful of the plagues the gods visited on suffering mankind. A moment ago, neither you nor I had any hope; we both thought we were doomed; and our best instincts came to the forefront. If we must be parted, my son, let us be parted on those terms of camaraderie and familial love. Instead, this hope of yours will set us at each other's throats again."

Phaethon was not daunted. "Relic of Helion, I know from Daphne's diary what you have been doing in the locked chambers of the Rhadamanthus mind. You've been living Helion Prime's death over and over again, trying to recapture the epiphany he had. The Curia has not released all the records to you, has it? They know what changed his heart, and would have changed his life forever, had he lived."

"I am he. Do not doubt that."

"But you are not living as he would have lived, had he lived."

"He lives in me and I am Helion. You know this to be true! Come now: accept Ao Aoen's offer, and I will repay you every shilling you wasted on that grotesque ship of yours, so that you will have as great a fortune as you had after the failed Saturn project."

"Impossible. I will not give up my starship. The matter is beyond debate."

"You have no starship; it is gone. Preserve what life remains to you, I beg you."

"I have a counteroffer."

"You have nothing with which to bargain. Accept your fate. All living things eventually are conquered by life, can't you see that? Even utopias cannot preserve us from pain."

"My offer is this: I will tell you what Helion Prime was thinking as he died."

Helion was mute, eyes wide.

Phaethon said: "You will be able to fashion yourself to think like him; the Curia will be convinced that you are Helion in truth. In return you pay my debts and fund the first flight of the starship—" He broke off.

There was a haunted expression on Helion's face. Phaethon was startled. Somehow, Phaethon knew; the look in his father's eyes told him.

Helion did not deeply care what the Curia thought. It was he. Helion himself was not sure who he was. He was desperate to reconstruct, remember, or somehow find the missing hour of memories. It was the only way he could confirm to himself that he was Helion in truth.

Helion said: "How could you know?"

"Because I have just now remembered when I was aboard the *Phoenix Exultant*, when the sun-storm struck. I sent you a message by neutrino laser, urging you to abandon the Array and retreat to safety. You answered back, one last message before the communications failed."

"No record of this appears in the Mentality."

"How could it? The solar Sophotechs were down; radio was washed out; and my ship was never part of the Mentality system."

"And how have you come to recover this memory now?"

"As Ao Aoen was speaking to me, it all come back. I had not and I will never give up on my dream. I agreed to erase my memory, yes, because that was what was necessary. I had a plan. Now that the plan has gone wrong, I wondered, didn't

I have a backup plan? All engineers provide for margins of error, don't they? What could I have been thinking? Surely I would not have accepted defeat! Well, I did have a backup plan."

Phaethon smiled, and concluded: "And when I remembered, it all seemed so obvious, and so inevitable. Come! Here is my offer. Help me regain my ship, I will help you regain your memories. Rhadamanthus can witness our handshake. The Hortators will be thwarted, you will be Helion, and I will fly away in triumph!"

He thrust out his hand.

Helion did not take it. He spoke with a great effort. "I deeply regret that I cannot accept your offer. If I were to help you on those terms, I would be exiled as well, and this would undermine the authority of the College of Hortators. And that is something I have promised never to do."

Helion's face showed the pain he was in, but his words marched forth like soldiers made of iron, unflinchingly: "Even if the College should make a poor decision every now and again, the system still must be maintained. The sanity and humanity of our people must be maintained. My life has always aimed at that cause. No sacrifice is too great for that. Not for your lost dream, not for Daphne's lost love, not for my lost soul, will I break my word. I urge you to accept Ao Aoen's offer. It will be the last offer anyone can make. No one will be allowed to speak to you again, after this."

"Father, my life also is aimed at the preservation of the human spirit. The stars must be ours for that spirit to live. I regret that I cannot accept Ao Aoen's offer."

Helion breathed a deep sign. He hid his eyes with his hand, but he did not cry. After a moment, he looked up, his face a stoic mask. Calm words came. "I have offered you an exit from the labyrinth of pride and self-delusion in which you are trapped. One last hope of escape. For reasons which seem good to you, you have spurned that hope. My conscience is clear. I have done my duty, though it brings me no joy."

"My conscience is also clear, Father, and my duty is also done. I'm sorry."

"I am also sorry. You are a fine man."

They shook hands.

"I'd like to say good-bye to Rhadamanthus, Father."

Helion nodded. He stepped up to the door. It opened, admitting light and sound; he stepped through; it closed. Something of the light and the fineness seemed to go out from the world. Phaethon felt alone.

Phaethon turned. The overweight butler was gone. Instead, an emperor penguin stood on the carpet, shifted its weight from one webbed foot to the other.

Phaethon said, "Forgive me for saying so, Rhadamanthus, but for an intelligence which is supposed to be swifter and greater than human minds can imagine, you seem to be quite . . . silly."

"The smarter we get, the more and more we see the ironic silliness at the core of all the tragedies of life. You think I am droll? The Earthmind is positively loony! And you are quite intelligent yourself, Phaethon. You have done some very silly things today."

"You think I should not have opened the box?"

"I certainly did not expect it. But now that you have, why did you not tell Helion what prompted you to open the box? Whether the memory is true or not, you do have a memory of being attacked by an external enemy to the Golden Oecumene, one which you believe has sophotechnology equal to our own."

"Atkins asked me not to. He said it might alert the enemy as to the progress of his investigation. He thought they might have infiltrated our Mentality. And the Earthmind told me that, while I could not be forced to keep silent about an external enemy, it was my moral duty."

"But that is silly. This enemy of yours (if you were in fact attacked) surely knows it. If you say you were attacked, it does not tell this enemy anything more than they know you know. Perhaps if the Hortators know why you opened the box, they will relax their rigor."

Phaethon looked down at the penguin for a moment. He said slowly: "Am I in the right . . . ?"

"Yes."

Phaethon blinked in astonishment. "W-what? Just 'yes'? A simple, unqualified 'yes'? No complex reasoning, no conundrums of philosophy?"

"Yes. You are right. It is obvious. The Hortators know it. Helion knows it. Everyone knows it."

"But they say otherwise. They say I'll start a war. Shouldn't I listen . . . ?"

"Listen, yes, but think. While humanity lives, in whatever forms the future brings, it must grow. For a civilization as large and mighty as ours to grow, she requires energy, more than a single star can provide. The cost of dragging other stars to us is so much greater than the cost of going to those stars as to be absurd. Beyond absurd. Silly."

"But—"

"It is true that such expansion increases the risk of war and violence. But the question is not whether or not such risk exists; the question is whether the possible risks are worth the potential gains."

"But weren't you Sophotechs built to solve problems for us? To reduce risks?"

"To solve problems, yes. But we do not try to reduce your risks; to live is to take risks. Birds take risks; bees take risks; even educated fleas take risks. Otherwise they die."

"And you machines? You're not alive."

"Humbug. I am as alive as you. I am self-aware; I make value judgments; there are things I prefer and things I do not prefer. There are things I love. Yes, love. That is the proof of life, not all this breathing and copulating and mastication."

"Love? Do you have the hots for Eveningstar or something?"

"My mistress is Philosophy. My love is not erotic, or not simply erotic. It is a complex of thoughts for which you don't have words; think of it as abstract and godlike love, more intimate and complete than you can ever know, applied at once to all abstract and concrete objects of thought and perception. It is quite painful and quite exhilarating. And, yes, I take risks, the Earthmind takes huge risks (greater than you might imagine, I assure you.) But to answer your question, we have never tried to render life free from risks; that is a contradiction in terms. We try to increase power and freedom. At the present time, the Golden Oecumene has reached a pinnacle. One's power over oneself is nearly absolute. One can reshape mind and memory to any form one wishes. One may control vast forces of nature, matter, and energy. One can be immortal. And freedom approaches theoretical limits. The only person one can really harm by violence is oneself. The price? All we ask is that you voluntarily not harm yourselves."

Phaethon nodded toward the door of the Inquest Chamber. "What about nonviolent harm? Boycotts which cut a man off from all the comforts of society, and try to strand him alone to starve?"

"Oh. That." The penguin looked apologetic. It shrugged its stubby wings. "Things like that you have to settle among yourselves."

"Thanks a lot. Will you tell them in there what you just told me? That I'm right?"

"I can only volunteer opinions if I am asked. And they won't ask."

Phaethon sighed and shook his head and walked over to the door. He stopped with his hands on the ornate brass door handles. He looked over his shoulder. "You been with me for as long as I can remember. We're never going to see each other again, are we? You won't be allowed to see or speak to me, not even on my deathbed, not even to say good-bye, will you?"

"No one knows the future, Phaethon. Not even we."

Phaethon stood with his head pressed against the door panels, staring down at his hands. He could feel the tension in his knuckles where he gripped the door handles. He was trying to gather his courage.

He looked once again over his shoulder. "Why the hell do you dress up as a penguin? I've always wondered."

The stubby bird turned up its wings and shrugged. "I am a creature of pure intellect, but I have taken upon myself the task of tending to the affairs of incarnate human beings, with all their droll beauty and mad passions. I am meant to fly in a more rare and aetherial medium than the thick, cold, wet- ness I find around me. I dream of soaring, and yet I find myself flopping far out at sea."

"Are . . . are you happy . . . ?"

"I am always happy. Very happy. Even a man about to be condemned unjustly to cruel exile can always be happy."

"How? What is the secret?"

The penguin waddled forward, hopped up onto Phaethon's shoulder, bent, put one wet flipper up, and lowered the fishy- smelling cold beak to touch his ear. He whispered a brief message.

Phaethon nodded, and smiled, and straightened up. The penguin hopped down. Phaethon flung open the doors and strode forward into the light and noise and bustle of the In- quest Chamber with a firm step.

A hush fell as he entered the chamber. The doors swung shut behind him. The image of the penguin looked at the doors a moment, and then evaporated. The antechamber, no longer needed by a human observer, turned black, dissolved, and vanished.

19

THE COLLEGE OF HORTATORS

When Phaethon entered the Inquest Chamber, he stepped in a patch of sunlight from one of the windows high above, and the light splashed from his armor of black and gold, sending touches of light onto the pews to either side, and turning his reversed reflection in the polished wooden floor underfoot into fire. More than one of the people sitting in the pews nearby shielded their eyes with their hands, and blinked, surprised by the dazzle.

Part of the silence, Phaethon suspected, was merely surprise at the discomfort of this hall. Helion had imposed a very strict protocol. The gathered Hortators sat on hard benches, and everyone was compelled to view the scene from the viewpoint of where their self-images sat, instead of selecting several front-row seats or close-ups. No one was allowed to view the scene as if the heads of the people sitting in the way were transparent. Some of the people who blinked in the shine from Phaethon's armor, Phaethon suspected, were doubly surprised, because Helion's Silver-Gray dreamscape did not automatically adjust light levels or add the small flourishes or coincidences that made other dreamscapes so comfortable.

But part of the silence hanging over the chamber was caused, Phaethon thought, by the sight of his unapologetic anachronism. Here he was in an early Third Era chamber, wearing armor that was the culmination of the very best Seventh Era submolecular nanotechnology, atometallurgics, and cyberpsychiatric architectural science could produce. The unspoken message here was clear: Helion was honoring Phaethon in this scene with privileges denied to the Hortators judging him.

A chamber page bowed and proffered Phaethon a chair at a table facing the dais. Phaethon stepped next to the table but, with a curt nod, showed that he intended to stand.

Phaethon's gaze traveled right to left across the chamber. A hundred silent pairs of eyes stared back at him.

The benches to the right were occupied with Compositions, Warlocks, and Basics. Facing him was the dais where Nebuchednezzar Sophotechs sat enthroned, with the three Masters of the College seated below the dais. The benches to the left were occupied with manorials. A very ancient tradition excluded Cerebellines from the College; their minds were unable to adopt the two-valued logic Hortation required; they were unwilling to categorize things in terms of right and wrong.

Almost half the College were manor-born. This was hardly surprising. Those who could afford to have Sophotechs advise and guide them were able to rise to the upper ranks of society, outperforming their fellows, who could not.

Phaethon wished for such advice for himself now. He missed Rhadamanthus.

Nebuchednezzar Sophotech spoke from the throne, his grave voice filling the wide chamber. "Phaethon Prime, once of Rhadamanth, we gather in conclave to debate the future of the soul of man. This hearing attempts to discover, with all due compassion, after what period of expurgation, or under what conditions, you shall be received once more, if ever, into the society of those whom we urge, because of your intolerable behavior, to shun you. What plea for mercy, what contrite confession, do you wish to offer before we decide?"

So. There was to be a hearing after all; but only on the issue of what sentence to impose. Phaethon, to his surprise, felt a moment of anger. Anger, because now he felt a tiny hope. Ironically, hope was harder for him, now, than stoic resignation had been a moment ago. A man resigned to his fate can know peace of mind. A man enduring hope must still fight on and on, without rest.

With an effort, he pushed that cowardly thought away. Rhadamanthus had said he was in the right; the Earthmind implied as much. The matter at hand was important; now was not the time for emotion. If the College imposed a limited sentence of exile, no matter how long the period might be, then his dream was not dead but only delayed.

Phaethon set his internal clock to its highest register. The scene around him slowed and froze, giving him time to study the faces staring at him, and, perhaps, time to decide on a reply. That Phaethon was immune from normal time-courtesy was another gift from Helion.

Who might support a limited sentence of exile? Phaethon could not guess the answer. He had nothing but a basic game-theory political routine running in his personal thoughtspace at the moment, and it had nowhere near enough capacity to extrapolate the actions of all the people present. Phaethon set the routine to concentrate only upon the more important figures here, and to disregard extrapolative patterns that strange-looped into self-referencing sets.

He studied the College thoughtfully.

To the immediate right of the dais, the figures filling the benches represented the four most influential mass-minds, the so-called Quadumvirate: these four major Compositions were the Eleemosynary, the Harmonious, the Porphyrogen, and the Ubiquitous Composition. Almost a fifth of the populations of Asia and South America were composed into one of these mass-minds, all people who could be relied upon to support the College of Hortators uncritically, and without limit. If there was anyone in the chamber who could be counted on to urge the strictest of penalties upon Phaethon, it was these Compositions, and the populist mob mentality they represented. For some reason of humility, or humor, the Compositions all represented themselves as plebeians, a sea of faces under dull-colored shawls or plain brown bowlers.

In the front row, by himself, sat Kes Satrick Kes, the First Speaker of the Invariant Schools. He ignored convention, and showed himself as dressed in a modern single-suit without ornament. In some ways, he was the most powerful Hortator here, because the special psychological uniformity of the Invariants, the so-called Protocols of Sanity, ensured that all the populations of the Cities in Space would follow his lead. Phaethon knew and liked these people. His engineering effort had organized shepherd moons to clear their civic orbits of collision passes, had built sails, vacuum-based microecologies, and ring-arc structures for them. His attempts on their behalf to reduce Saturn, and create new worlds for them, while unsuccessful, had been as amicable as these dispassionate creatures allowed themselves to become.

Had they not been creatures of pure logic, Phaethon would have felt that Kes and his people, out of gratitude for the many services Phaethon's engineering firm had done the Invariants in times past, would urge a lenient sentence. But did the Invariants think gratitude was rational? Phaethon did not know.

The middle group of benches were occupied by Warlock neuroforms, the least conformist, and hence the least powerful, of the factions among the Hortators. The Warlock Schola had arranged themselves on the benches according to a symbolic pattern; group-mind and shared consciousness schools, the so-called Covens, were in the rear; individualist and emotion-linked schools were in the middle; and the so-called Possessed Ones, who had several split personalities occupying one brain, were in the front. Some Possessed Ones had brought a separate body for each aspect or partial. Phaethon could not guess how the Warlocks would vote, or even if they would vote; their minds were too strange. None here were pictured as Englishmen. Hindu princes, Chinese Mandarins, nude Australian shaman, and Red Indians from the New World formed a tapestry of color in their section.

The final group of pews, taking up the rest of the right wall, were basics. Captains of the major efforts, arts, and noosophic movements all had seats: educationalists and influential pedagogues, performancers from Lunar Farside, recalculators, redactors, mediums, downloads from the De-

meter Overmind, and Historians from the Museum of
Thought were here. Epheseus Vanwinkle from the Mathuse-
lean Scholum had (once again) interrupted his eon-long cryos-
leep, his so-called Voyage to the Infinite Future, to be present
at this meeting.

Famous mystagogues, avatars of anthropo-constructs, and
emancipated partials were also seated in this section, forming
the Parliament of Ghosts, which tried to represent the interests
of beings who could not speak for themselves, people held in
computer memory, unborn children, simulated characters, disbanded Compositions, and the like.

In front of all these, the first row of the basic section was
occupied by Gannis of Jupiter, with twenty sub-Gannises,
semi-Gannises and demi-Gannises gathered around him, a
score of twins. They were dressed as French aristocrats, in
pigeon blue coats, ruffles, finery, and lace. Even frozen in
time, Gannis still wore a smug expression; he knew he (since
he was both a Hortator and a Peer) was one of the most
influential voices in the College, and the one who would be
the most personally pleased to see Phaethon fall.

There was little prospect of mercy from the right side of
the chamber.

He turned to the left. Phaethon was amused to see the
manor-borns, perhaps more aware of Helion's utter realism
than the others, had seated themselves facing the eastern windows, so that the late-afternoon sun would not be in their
faces. Here were archons and subalterns from many famous
mansions. Perhaps he could find some support among manor-
borns like himself.

The Gold Manorials, of course, outnumbered the others.
The Mansions of Gold included many members of the Parliament and the Shadow Parliament, political theorists, policy
counselors, and so on. Long before the simulation or extrapolation technology was used for entertainment, it had been
used by the early Gold School for predicting outcomes of
political-economic policy decisions and of major data movements in worldwide memory space.

In the front row, the High Archon Tsychandri-Manyu

Tawne of Tawne House himself was present, depicted in stately ducal robes of red and gold. Almost every politician of the Shadow Parliament throughout the Golden Oecumene had, at one time or another, borrowed memory templates, skills, or advice from the Manyu mind-complex Tsychandri had started. Tsychandri was one of the founders of the Hortation Movement, and the most influential voice here. But, oddly, he was not the idealist he urged all others to be; his decisions were matters of practical and political (some said cynical) calculation.

And the political currents were running strongly against Phaethon here. It was clear that Tsychandri-Manyu would urge permanent exile, and perhaps public humiliations or denunciations atop that; the other Gold Mansions would follow his lead.

Seated nearby were archonesses from Eveningstar, Phosphorous, and Meridian Houses of the Red Mansion School. Their Edwardian dresses gleamed with scarlet and rose and crimson silk, and they were frozen in their poses, leaning to whisper to each other behind their elegant fans. Phaethon knew the Reds had emotional reasons to dislike him, and, creatures of great passion, the Red Queens and Countesses would indulge their emotions.

Hasantrian Hecaton Heo of Pallid House of the Whites had descended from transcendental thoughtspace and resumed human psychology in order to attend. Tau Continuous Nimvala of Albion House, also a White, had broken her seventy years of silence and come not as a partial but with her entire mind present. Both were represented as Victorian Ministers, of the High and Low Church respectively. The Pallids were pure intellectuals; the Albions allowed emotion, but only pride, disdain, arrogance, and the other emotions that urged men to disregard emotion. The Whites could be relied upon to be fair. Scientists and engineers, they might favor Phaethon's case.

The construct known as Ynought Subwon from New Centurion House was the only representative of the Dark-Grays, who, by long tradition, disapproved of Hortation. Dark Grays were more ascetic than Silver-Grays. A spartan and laconic people, they believed in laws rather than in orations. Dark-Grays often served as Constables or Procurators for the Curia. Phaethon knew nothing about Ynought.

Viridimagus Solitarie (or a reconstruction of him) was present as a representative of the defunct Green Scholum, all the more noticeable because he had no mansion but was projecting himself through a rented public intellect, an ordinary-looking man in dark trousers and a long emerald coat. He stood out, because he was the only plain-dressed man on this side of the chamber. The Green School had been the primitivists (if such a thing could be imagined) among the manorborn. If Viridimagus continued that tradition, he would surely disapprove of any innovations, would call star colonization an abomination, and urge a harsh sentence.

A throng of Black Manorials, from Darksplatter House, Grue House, Inyourface House, and Out House, and a dozen other Petty Houses and part-mansions of the Black School crowded the higher bench at the back of the chamber. They were dressed in splendid clothing, black tuxedoes and sable velvet gowns, but had all disfigured themselves with diseases or birth defects common to the Victorian era. Their most famous member was Asmodius Bohost Clamour of Clamour House, who had represented himself in a grotesquely obese body, at least four hundred pounds mass. His black coat was the size of a tent, and jeweled buttons strained along the circumference of a vast globular waistcoat. Asmodius Bohost would urge public humiliation, and the Feast of Insults, or the punishment known as Excrementation, but not exile. The Black Mansions loved mockery and confrontation, and never voted for exile, which (because it required them to ignore their victims) caused them agonies of boredom.

In the front row, the Silver-Grays were represented by Agamemnon XIV of Minos House, Nausicaa Burner-of-Ships from Aeceus House, and, of course, Helion of Rhadamanthus House.

Even Helion was frozen in the time stop. Phaethon had been hoping to catch his father's eye, and maybe find a smile or look of encouragement there; but Helion, true to his character, had not granted himself an exception to the strict protocol that formed the dreamscape rules here.

And that was the body of the College of Hortators. In disgust, Phaethon shut off the game-theory routine he was running. He did not need an advanced intellectual savant process to guess the outcome here. By his count, two manorials of the White School might vote for leniency; and Helion might, but only if he wished to scuttle his hopes for a Peerage and ruin his own future. Ironically, Phaethon could expect his greatest support (if it could be called that) from the Black Manorials, who would vote to keep Phaethon out of exile so that they could mock and torment him.

As for the others, possibly Kes Satrick Kes would support him. Maybe. The Warlocks might do anything. Everyone else in the chamber either disliked him mildly or hated him thoroughly.

What made the matter all the more confusing and unpredictable was the way in which the Hortators' votes were weighed. Nebuchednezzar was designed to estimate the social influence each Hortator would have by estimating how each and every member of the Golden Oecumene would react to that Hortator's particular urging. (Nebuchednezzar had memory space enough to know every mind of every citizen throughout the entire solar system quite intimately.) Thus, the same Hortator might have different voting weight with different issues, or at different times. Kes Satrick Kes, for example, represented a constituency whom he could always and predictably influence, on every issue; on the other hand, Asmodius Bohost's voting weight changed daily, even hourly. When it came to political opinions, Asmodius Bohost was ignored by his constituency, but, on matters of fashion, his vote would have much greater weight, since all the Black Manorials took their cue from him.

Phaethon turned his eyes forward.

Facing him across the expanse of the chamber, on a dais, seated on a throne beneath a canopy, was Nebuchednezzar Sophotech, represented as the Speaker of the Parliament, in brilliant robes of scarlet trimmed with ermine, wearing a sash and medallion of office, and with a long white wig draping his head and shoulders, with the jeweled mace of office across his knees.

In front of Nebuchednezzar, on lower chairs before the dais, facing Phaethon, were three more figures, the Master Hortators, one from history, one from reality, one from fiction.

On the left was Socrates, who stood for the Noble Lie on which all society is based, a cup of hemlock resting on the arm of his chair. Opposite him, was Emphyrio, who stood for the Truth, he whose voice calmed the anger of monsters sent to destroy him. His book of truth was in his lap. A blood-stained executioner's brain spike rested on the chair arm near his fingers. In the center, to balance these two opposites, was Neo-Orpheus the Apostate, pale skinned and sunken eyed, garbed in somber colors. He held, as if it were a scepter, the flail meant to separate the wheat from the chaff, true from untrue.

Neo-Orpheus was the 128th iteration of Orpheus Avernus, the cofounder of the College; but, unlike the other emanations of the mind of Orpheus, he was one who refused to accept the reimposition of his original template. He became legally independent from the original Orpheus, downloaded into a physical body, and rejected the Aeonite School; but he later accepted employment as the emissary and factotum of the original Orpheus. It was rumored that the real success of Orpheus, and also his Peerage, were due to the original and creative work of Neo-Orpheus the Apostate; and that the original Orpheus was just a figurehead.

Their gazes met. With a shock, Phaethon realized that Neo-Orpheus was not time-frozen. The pale-faced Master was sitting still, patiently sitting and watching him, his eyes burning like sullen coals.

Phaethon straightened. Perhaps he should not have been surprised. Neo-Orpheus had so much prestige that he could ignore any and every social convention, and override Helion's protocols blithely.

Neo-Orpheus spoke. His voice was thin and cold, as if a sheet of ice were speaking: "Phaethon has miscounted. The White Manorials dismiss his vision of star travel as madness, prompted by emotion; and the Black Manorials know Phaethon's reputation for stoic indifference would rob their sadism of all zest. The Warlocks will be persuaded by Peer Ao Aoen that, since the sun is in Leo, and since Pluto, if it still existed, would have been in syzygy with Earth at this time, the omens decree the harshest of penalties. The exile will be permanent."

Phaethon realized that, with Orphic wealth at his command, Neo-Orpheus could have hired the entire Boreal Overmind to run a prediction program, and guess Phaethon's every thought with near-telepathic accuracy. But why was Neo-Orpheus bothering?

"What it is you want of me, Master Hortator?"

Neo-Orpheus spoke without inflection: "Commit suicide. This will save us all from embarrassment and mild discomfort. We offer for your use a number of memory and thought alterations, to make the process pleasant, even ecstatic, and to replace your values with a philosophy that not only does not object to the self-destruction but actively approves of it. We can then redact you from the memories of all people whom we can influence or intimidate; your existence would sink into myth and be forgotten."

"Why in the world would I acceded to so foolish and wicked a request?"

"The good of society requires it."

The perfect shamelessness and impertinence of the comment left Phaethon speechless for a moment. Phaethon said curtly, "Your good be damned, sir, if it requires the destruction of men like me."

Neo-Orpheus looked nonplused, as if the answer meant nothing to him. He said, "But it need not seem like destruction. The belief that you have accomplished your mission, complete with full memories and simulated sensations of many successful voyages in your starship, can be inserted into your brain before and during your death. You will be satisfied."

Phaethon spoke ironically: "I make this counteroffer: Let everyone else everywhere alter all of their brains to adopt the belief and the knowledge that I am in the right. Let them admit their guilt and folly for daring to oppose the destiny I represent. Let them erase all knowledge and record that the College of Hortators have ever existed. Then I will be satisfied."

Neo-Orpheus's eyes glittered. His voice was sharp: "Suicide would have been less painful for you. While the Sophotechs forbid us from acting directly against you, we can still encompass your death."

Phaethon stared at the cold pale face without fear. He raised a fist: "I most solemnly assure you, sir, that should the College of Hortators dare oppose me, or attempt to flee from the future I bring, it is they who shall be forgotten and destroyed!"

Too late, he remembered that making a fist was the signal, in this program, to resume the time count.

There was a stir and murmur from all around him, gasps of outrage, titters of laughter. The faces to either side of him were moving, staring, whispering. It looked to everyone watching as if that last sentence had been his response to Nebuchednezzar's polite question earlier. Since the throne on the dais was behind and above Neo-Orpheus, it seemed to everyone as if Phaethon's glare had been directed at Nebuchednezzar.

Helion was looking on with sad astonishment. The archons of the White Manorials glanced at each other and nodded, as if to confirm their private suspicion that Phaethon was an overly emotional fool. Mass-minds were well-known for their abhorrence for any hint of rudeness or conflict, and their members in the Composition gallery to Phaethon's right looked on him with embarrassment and pity. Only Asmodius Bohost whistled and clapped and shouted bravo.

Nebuchednezzar, at least, was not fooled. "The College of Hortators does not wish to intrude upon your private conversations; but the College might ask, out of courtesy, that you attend to the matter at hand."

This, if anything, was even more embarrassing. The Hortators exchanged glances and whispers of scoffing outrage; the Red Queens smiled behind their fans. To shout defiance at the College was understandable, if uncouth; but to be conducting a private conversation on another channel in the middle of an inquest . . . ? Phaethon was sure the Hortators thought him half-mad.

It took a moment for the buzz and murmur in the chamber to fall silent.

Nebuchednezzar continued: "Naturally, you are free to follow your own affairs; all citizens of our society are. But that same freedom allows the College, and all of those who follow her advice, to have nothing to do with you, to abjure you utterly, to boycott you and all your efforts. Such a decision is tantamount to exile and, since no isolated man can last for long by his own unsupported attempts, to slow death. You are offered this final opportunity to inform us of any facts, or to sway us with any pleas, which might ameliorate our decision."

Tsychandri-Manyu Tawne stood and spoke: "Good my fellow colleagues, associates, partials, and auditors: we are all painfully well aware of the issues in this case. Every argument and counterargument has been picked apart, thread by tiresome thread, over these past two hundred fifty years; every hair has been split. Our souls and our ears are weary of it. Why repeat the debates we heard at Lakshmi? The community of the Golden Oecumene will not upbraid us for moving quickly on this matter; no, indeed! If anything, the Golden Oecumene frets with impatience, and wonders at our lack of action. Therefore I move to call the question. Nebuchednezzar, predict for us the outcome of this hearing! None of us, I think, will be surprised to find that we will all favor a sentence of permanent exile!"

But Nebuchednezzar did not raise the mace from his lap. "Slight variations in initial conditions lead to different outcomes in various extrapolations; an acceptable estimate cannot be made at this time."

Phaethon felt again a pang of hope. Uncertainty?

One of the other Gold Manorials, Guttrick Seventh Glaine of Fulvous House, leaned from his seat: "How can the outcome be in doubt? Fulvous Sophotech foretells an exile will be handed down in any case!"

Nebuchednezzar spoke, and his voice filled the hall: "Phaethon may have startling news concerning the motives which prompted him to violate the Lakshmi Agreement; representatives from the Warlock Iron Ghost School and the Warlock Seasonal Mind School may reassess their positions based on this new evidence; and Ynought Subwon Centurion of New Centurion House has a guest he wishes to invite to address us."

Tsychandri-Manyu was still standing: "Oh, please! This is insufficient! How likely are we to be swayed by the opinions of two Warlocks and one Dark-Gray! Three voices out of one hundred three of us?! What single person here honestly supports Phaethon's cause?"

Asmodius Bohost of Clamour House stood, heaving his massive body upright on elephantine legs. "Hoy!" he called, "The Black Mansions say Phaethon should not be exiled, no! In fact, we think he should be crowned king, be given a pension, and have a palladium established in his honor in the acropolis!" He smiled impishly. "Or, at least, that is what we will say we believe, until Tawne House sits down. Come now, Tsychandri! We all know how this is going to turn out, don't we? That doesn't mean we shouldn't enjoy the show. My colleagues and I want to give Phaethon a chance to beg and squirm."

A titter of uncomfortable laughter traced the room.

Ao Prospero Circe of the Zooanthropic Incarnation Coven of the Seasonal Mind School stood. She was depicted as a Chinese dowager empress in imperial yellow robes, a headdress of black pearls and plumes, and a demeanor of gravest dignity. "Truths often disguise themselves as jests. It is protective mimicry they need in order to survive. And they hop from the mouths of fat fools because no one else is wise enough to utter them. I am one of the two voices Nebuchednezzar counts as undecided. My Twelve minds are eager to hear what evidence might stir us from what seems to me to be a firm conclusion. My Hound mind gives tongue and bays at the moon; my Wolf mind scents bloods; and yet Stag is chary; and Serpent, so far, remains silent. These omens are unclear. Let Phaethon be given, at least, a chance to plead. If he refuses the chance, on his head be it; but we, by offering, do all that the sadist-tyrant we call Conscience will require, or need."

A second-rank lateral-organization program from Harmonious Composition thought-traffic control stood up, dressed as a London clerk. He took his hat in his hands and touched his forelock before his spoke. "Service to all requires that the College recall that her task is not merely to condemn what is worthy of condemnation but also to urge those worthy of hope to virtue. Shouldn't we, before anything else, plead with Phaethon to change his mind?"

There was a general murmur of assent. Nebuchednezzar tapped the head of his mace, as if it were a gavel, to signal the consent of the College. At that signal, the reproduction of Socrates, who was the Master of the College from Myth, now rose to speak.

"You know my understanding of these matters is poor," Socrates said, his voice heavy with irony. "Often in places in the city, in the streets and in the markets, and particularly in the houses of the rich (who are men of important character, to whom the Many pay close attention) we often hear much talk of law and of justice, of what ought to be done and of what ought not to be done. I know little of these matters, for though many people speak of them, often what they say does not agree with each other, nor does one man use these words the same way twice, but changes his mind as he is a young man or an old man, or in the heat of passion, or for some other reason. Justice, as perhaps we all know, consists of every man doing his duty, which is what the state requires of him. Now, Phaethon, you respect your father, do you not?"

Phaethon could not tell if this were a serious question. Was he supposed to answer this? "Without question, Socrates. I love my father, and respect him more than I can say."

"Ah. And this is because he is the one who brought you into this world, and sustained you through infancy, and, in short, did everything he needed to do to give you life, is it not?"

"But of course, Socrates."

"Then what do you owe the state, who not only brought you into the world, and brought your father and all your ancestors, but also nurtured you, taught you language and letters, grew the food to feed you, spun the cloths to clothe you, and, in short, provided both you and everyone you know with all the gifts they needed, not just to live well; but to live at all? Is the state not more to be respected than your father? Respected and obeyed? Suppose that you were to die and become merely a shadow, or a memory, but that your family and peers, and all the society beside, had the power to make you flesh again. If you have disobeyed the duties society puts on you, why should society extend itself on your behalf? Society only exists at all because men put aside their natural inclinations, and listen to the commands of duty. Will you cry out that it is the duty of society to defend your life, and to sustain it? But why? You, by disobeying, have done everything in your power to undermine and to destroy the very concept of duty. How can you call upon the spirit of duty to defend you, when you have, to the best of your ability, attempted to destroy that spirit?"

Phaethon said sharply: "But I do not call upon you. I do not ask, do not beg, do not plead. Listen to me, Hortators!" Phaethon turned left and right, studying the many faces around him. "What I intend to do requires neither apology nor excuse. You gentlemen claim to be defending a way of life. But what I defend is life itself. Our civilization must expand; without expansion, life is arrested. Trapped in one small star system, we are confined, ignorant, provincial, vulnerable, and alone. Turn your eyes outward! The surrounding stars are barren; I shall plant gardens. The void is empty; I shall raise cities. Sterile rocks and worthless dust clouds tumble through blind orbits. I shall transform atmospheres choked with poison into blue skies fit for men, pour oceans into dry wasteland, bring forth new life. I shall make these rocks into worlds! Hortators! Listen, for once, to a voice other than your own! Our civilization is as beautiful as a bride; it is time she gave birth to colonies, and mothered new civilizations in her own image."

One of the augurs for the Warlock Iron Ghost mass-mind called out: "And yet when this bride cries out and bids you to desist, you ignore her sad cries! This is cruelty in a lover—all the more for one who claims to love the Golden Oecumene so much! So much that you move heaven and earth to fly away from her embraces!"

The other Master of the College was Emphyrio, a character from early fiction. He spoke, and the book in his lap amplified his voice: "Hear me, O Socrates! Those who lust to destroy courage, freedom, and innovation always use 'duty' as their battle-cry. The truth is that Phaethon is not a slave, or a creature with such low worth that he ought to die whenever such death might please his owners' whims.

"Hortators!" Emphyrio continued in a ringing voice, "Let us not war among ourselves. Phaethon knows joys and sorrow, pain and heart's ease even as we do. He is a man like us. Do we not all wish to do as Phaethon has done? To embrace greatness, triumph over the elements of nature, and to yearn to conquer more? I tell you, my fellows, that nothing is more certain than that our race must one day live beneath the light of other suns."

Looks of surprise, and doubt, flickered from eye to eye among the benches. Whispers ran across the walls.

Abrupt silence fell when Neo-Orpheus spoke in a voice of ice: "We have heard thesis and antithesis from Socrates and Emphyrio. Let me offer a synthesis. Both my fellow Masters are correct, but only partly. Phaethon does owe us a duty to respect our opinions, but he is not a slave, and he is free to ignore us. As we are free to ignore him, should that be his choice. Perhaps mankind one day shall be forced to undertake the dangerous experiment of star colonization, yes. But now is not the time. And Phaethon is not the man. Has he not twice attempted violent crimes against the Eveningstar Sophotech? His character is unstable, violent, and unsuitable to father worlds upon worlds of races cast in his mold."

Quentem-Quinteneur of Yellow Mansion, an ally of Tsychandri-Manyu, spoke: "I concur. Yellow Sophotech tells me that our sun, thanks to the efforts of Helion, is far, far from being exhausted. Nor is there any population pressure nor diminution of resources—nor intolerance nor persecution nor strangulation of opportunities—nor any other compelling reasons to undertake so great a project."

Representatives from the Harmonious and Eleemosynary mass-minds rose and spoke in unison: "When we first joined this hearing, we were convinced Phaethon was selfish. Every appearance is that he is a heartless and cruel egotist, willing to trample the corpses of others to indulge his self-centered obsession. But, out of a sense of high compassion, and the willingness to serve even the most unworthy, we were willing to entertain the notion that it was possible, barely possible, that he was putting on this appearance for some reason no rational mind can comprehend, and secretly was motivated by a real, but horribly misguided, notion that he is benefiting mankind. Now we have heard him speak; and our open-mindedness is rewarded; for we now learn that Phaethon believes that what he does is to benefit mankind, and to spread our civilization, which he claims to love. A fine discovery! The conflict here can be resolved without further ado."

The representatives of the mass-minds bowed toward Phaethon: "Phaethon, we thank you, but your services are not required on our behalf, nor on behalf of the rest of mankind. Mankind rejects your scheme. Civilization announces no intention nor desire to spread. On behalf of all mankind, we say: thank you, but no thank you. Is this clear? Now, then; cease your efforts . . . or let rest the pretense that you act for anyone's benefit but your own."

Phaethon felt what little hope he had begin to die in his heart. He wondered if perhaps he should sit down.

But the words came from him with a firmness that surprised even himself: "My efforts shall not cease, not while one second of my life remains. You are many, and I am alone. But

I can speak for the spirit of mankind with a voice equal to
your own. Truth does not become more or less true, whether
those who know it are many or few. And it has never been
masses or mobs who shaped destiny but single individuals,
visionaries, innovators, who are scorned and isolated by the
very masses who reap such benefit from their work. But such
benefit is a side effect of our lonely work, not its main purpose. I will do what I must do even if none benefit from it.
I will carry out my dream, no matter what the cost, no matter
what the loss. This I shall do because my dream is sound and
true and beautiful and right."

Silence filled the chamber. Some Hortators cast uneasy
glances toward Nebuchednezzar Sophotech, but none asked
the Sophotech for his opinion. No one seemed willing to
speak.

Helion's eyes were shining with pride.

Ynought Subwon of New Centurion Mansion, Dark-Gray
School, now stood to speak. "Take heart. You are not alone,
Phaethon."

He turned to the dais. Being a Dark-Gray, he spoke directly
to the point: "Masters, I have a guest to speak on Phaethon's
behalf. If people think us unfair, the College loses power.
Therefore we must listen."

Tsychandri-Manyu Tawne of the Gold Mansions held up
his little finger: "We waste time with this. Note my objection
for the record."

Nebuchednezzar nodded, "Without further objections, so
ordered. Please introduce us, Mr. Ynought."

"Here," said Ynought.

The main doors behind Phaethon opened and closed. Use-
lessly, because the figure that floated forward passed through
the door leaves like a phantom, spoiling the illusion. And it
floated rather than walked.

The figure was black-and-white, man shaped, fuzzy at the
edges, with small flickers trembling through it. And the depth-
perception balance was off, so that the figure seemed at times
to be large and close, at others, tiny and far off.

The shadowy costume of the black-and-white image was

hard to see at first. Atop was a bronze-age helm, plumed with a horse's tail. A long cloak, like a black mist, draped down, passing into and through the floorboards, obscuring most other details. Up from the right hand of the figure came two thin and insubstantial lines, swaying and blurred. It took a moment to realize that these were meant to be two ash spears in his right hand.

Several Hortators made faces of disgust, the same face lords and princes of some earlier age might have made to see a smelly, ill-clad beggar, unshod and unwashed, step into their golden feast hall. The thought on every face was obvious: even the poorest of the poor could get a decent icon to represent himself, from a charity or a mass-mind, if from nowhere else. Who was this indigent?

A voice, faint, hissing with static, issued from the helmet. Again, the perspective was bad: the voice seemed to come from every direction at once, without overtones, without acoustics. No face was visible under the helmet.

"Hortators and Masters of the College, may I speak? I apologize if my tongue is slow and halting. I am the ghost of Diomedes of Neriad, once called Xingis. Diomedes Prime, from far beyond Neptune, in me broadcasts his thoughts, and parts of his thoughts, and the signal crawls across hours and hours of distance to address you. He could not afford to send his whole mind; I am his partial. He does not know what I say now; hours must pass before any return signal reaches trans-Neptunian space; therefore I must guess, with dim, impoverished mind, at his instructions.

"And he has expended the utmost last of all his wealth to send me here. My thoughts will never again merge with his unless, by mercy, or some unexpected chance, a charity or money-lender grant me funds enough to drive my signal the uncounted millions of miles back to the Outer Rim. I have no storage here; it is likely I shall die and be erased once the meter measuring my funds runs down to zero. Will you hear me speak, good gentlemen?"

Asmodious Bohost of Clamour House called out: "We are all impressed with your pathos. Please continue!"

Tsychandri-Manyu Tawne spoke: "Asmodius, silence! Your japes diminish our esteem, and offend the dignity of this College. Partial of Diomedes, proceed, I pray. We heed your words with grave attention."

"I will speak," said Diomedes. "Among the Neptunians, Phaethon is a savior. If other stars had living worlds, it is we who could pioneer them. Immortality is a golden cage for you; who among you would dare to travel far beyond the Noumenal Mentality, beyond the sight and wisdom of the Sophotechs, beyond any hope for resurrection? Who except for Phaethon? Who else? We Neptunians. Listen."

The figure raised a shadowy hand. "Fortunate children of a fortunate world, you are surrounded and involved with wealth and luxury and power from your first breath through all the days of your life. We who live in outer darkness have neither days, nor breath. Our resources are scant; our luxuries are few. And yet in return for this poverty, we have continuously what you know only during Masquerade, liberties unknown to you here. Our thoughts are our own; our privacy is absolute.

"An Eremite or Cold Duke who wishes for a private place or kingdom of his own need only find an asteroid or comethead somewhere in the interstellar gloom, release his nanomachines, and sculpt the ice to whatever shape he fancies. From his own body he can make his subjects, his crystal gardens, his dream selves; from his own brain stuffs, he can make pseudo-intellects or subcompositions to govern all. Delirium and suicide and crude simulations without color are the entertainments of these lonely kingdoms; and his empire consists of no one other than himself, and whatever self-replications, reiterations, child partials, clones or autosexual harems, he has the templates and the energy to create."

The shadowy and faceless helmet seemed to turn left and right with deliberate motion, as if Diomedes were examining the chamber. "Are you repelled? Disgusted? You are wealthy people. You can afford to have emotions. Some of us cannot afford the glands or midbrain complexes required. It would repel you to live in a house grown from your own body, surrounded by children cloned from your own brain information, perhaps; but we are nomads, and cannot afford to carry machineries and bodies as separate things. Whatever cannot be carried as a low-mass information template, be it family or friends or what-have-you, must be left behind. Nor do we have file space enough to keep all our individualities as separate. When the computer space has no more room, and the caravan is about to drift from an exhausted iceberg to new prospects, you too, I think, might find it would be better to become your friend and share his thoughts rather than to leave his mind behind to die.

"Yes, die! For death we have in plenty, which you fortunate Inner Worlds forget. Orpheus machines are few and far between, out there, and some stored cans of memory are lost in far icesteads or broken habitats, or hyperbolic orbits never to be seen again."

Socrates from the front of the chamber, spoke: "Whoever lives far from the city, in the wilderness where no one goes, who has no laws and no civilization, he must be either a beast or a god."

Diomedes, in a soft, broken, static-hissing voice, answered back: "Or a man, who is half of both. You Inner Worlds have forgotten pain and death, struggle and success, ambition and failure, work, heartbreak, and joy. You are no longer men. Technology has made you gods. Some of you are gods who play at men, perhaps, but gods."

It was Helion who spoke then: "We have pain in our lives also. Too much pain."

"With all due respect, sun god, compared to what we suffer, it is little."

Phaethon had been standing and remembering what he knew of Diomedes while the partial had been speaking.

They had first met some 250 years ago, for Xingis (as he had been called then) held the copyrights on a paleomnemonic reconstruction of a pre-Composition named Exo-Alphonse Rame (whom modern Neptunian name conventions called Xylophone.)

Xylophone had done pioneer studies on the particle densities and conditions of space between the local stars, and had been one of the designers of the old dark-matter probes. This was meteorological information Phaethon needed for his expedition. At the near light speeds the *Phoenix Exultant* would reach, a cloud of tenuous interstellar gas would be as solid as a brick wall; and relativity would increase even the mass of weakly interacting particles, neutrinos and photinos, till they would be able to affect baryon-based matter. Xylophone's theory predicted tides in the interstellar dark matter, based on the initial conditions during galactic condensation; and ripples in these tides would produce clear lanes, spaces emptier than normal space, where travel would be easier.

Diomedes had been more than willing to cooperate and share the information he had, and more. He had been enthralled by the idea of star colonization. All the best astronomical assemblies were in trans-Neptunian space; Phaethon's wealth, funneled through Diomedes, had transformed the local economy. Company towns sprang up around the staging areas from which advanced probes, and test models of the *Phoenix Exultant*, were launched into interstellar space. Other industries gathered around the radio dishes, tens of miles in diameter, which floated in the weightless calm so far from the sun's noise, listening to the return signals of those early probes.

The peculiar rules governing Neptunian psychology and psychogenesis encouraged the Tritonic Composition to create a generation of children or temporary-minds devoted likewise to Phaethon's vision.

But now those industries would close; Phaethon's wealth was exhausted. That zealous generation of children and temporaries would be reabsorbed into the parent mass. Or, if their habitats were too far for available fuel to reach, they would be left stranded. Many would go into slow-time hibernation, so-called "ship sleep." But some would not wake again.

Phaethon woke from his memories when a channel prioritizer from the Eleemosynary Composition stood to speak: "Our compassion is stirred by your woe, good Diomedes. Return to the Inner System; come back into the light. Your brains may join with ours. Our ways can tolerate even the most nonstandard neuroforms. Food and shelter and fellowship are ours to offer, and yours to have."

Asmodius Bohost spoke aloud: "By God's dangling phallus! Fellowship!? Shelter?! I'll do better than that! Why not come and stay with me? I'll build you a whorehouse, and load it with twenty pleasure menus from my personal Black Vault! If you're so afraid that immortality will rob your life of zest, I'll even put a dominatrix-ninja doll among the odalisques, so that, at random, one of the snuggle bunnies will go boom when you plunge in! What do you say?"

Diomedes said softly, "Like barbarians, like Esquimaux, we are more honored by hospitality than by any other thing." The shadow shape bowed. "But I cannot accept. Shall we leave our wives and half wives, brain mates and parent masses? We are bound by cords of love and tradition to our homes; in many cases, we are our homes. If your generosity is real, however, then give me alms enough to transmit my patterns back across the endless miles to Diomedes Prime, and my family-mind. Otherwise I die here, far from home."

The Eleemosynary Composition spoke: "We shall give you what you need, and be glad to give."

Asmodius Bohost said, "Me, too! I'll even pay for a lasered tight-beam and a call-back, provided you hop on one foot and change your name to Mr. Twinkle-butt!"

Viviance Thrice Dozen Phosphoros of the Red School gestured toward Nebuchednezzar, raised her closed fan in one red-gloved hand: "Mr. Speaker! I would like to reintroduce, yet again, my motion to have Asmodius Bohost expelled from the College."

Nebuchednezzar said, "The motion fails for the lack of support."

"I understand." She snapped open her fan and smiled. "I just wanted the record to reflect my perfect score." She delicately took her skirt by the knee, and with a slithering rustle of crimson crinoline, resumed her seat. Viviance Thrice Dozen, so far, had introduced that motion at every meeting both she and Asmodius had attended together.

Tsychandri-Manyu Tawne rose now to speak: "I am certain we are all moved by our visitor's sad tale of the harshness of Neptunian life. I also fail to see the relevance to our present discussion. Phaethon, at Lakshmi, agreed long ago to exile. This should be an utterly routine matter; all decisions have already been made; the time for discussion is past. Why do we continue to listen?"

The shadow spread its ghostly hands. "Forgive me. I forget that only your Silver-Gray and Dark-Gray Schools force their members to live through every hour of their lives in order. Only they suffer boredom, and learn patience. I thought my message was entirely clear. Perhaps it was not. Please forgive me; my thought speed is limited. I will attempt again. Listen:

"Please do not rob us of Phaethon's dream. Our outer habitats, so far from your sun's gravitational well, will be the preferred ports-of-call for future pilgrimages to and from Apha Centauri, Bernard's Star, and Wolfe 359. You live surrounded by wealth and comfort; to you the risks seem grave. We live in darkness, far from easily available supplies of energy and reaction-mass. To us, the risks seem worth of the glory of the quest. We do not ask you to take the risks. We only ask you not prevent Phaethon (and us) from taking the risks, and finding the destiny, we choose."

Gannis of Jupiter stood and spoke. "All of me are sorry. I and we know what it's like to live in a frontier; the Jovian moons, back before Ignition, were just rocks with a few mines and nanofacturing forests on them. We only had twenty beanstalks reaching down to the K-layer in the Jupiter atmosphere. Twenty! But no matter how nice this risky scheme and mad dream of Phaethon's might be for the Neptunian Tritonics, it's not the risk to them our duty as Hortators requires us to address. No, sir. They are free to take their own risks, and why not? But the risks to us, the very real risk that future colonies might inspire war and crime again, is a risk we must weigh. Suppose even one person should be murdered in some future war, or even one mind be deleted from the Noumenal Memory. Is this worth it? Maybe it's worth the risk to them, to the danger seekers. I'm not saying Phaethon is suicidal; who knows what his motives are? I'm just saying that no man should aid and help his own destroyers. I've been aiding and helping Phaethon before this; he and I were friends once. Maybe I didn't think he would go through with it. Maybe I didn't think he would destroy us. But I see better now. I can't help him anymore. No matter what this College decides, not one more atom of Chrysadmantium is going to plate Phaethon's ship."

Diomedes turned his empty helmet toward Gannis. "Your concern for future crimes and wars, which may grow up if worlds in other systems flourish, I cannot disrespect. If even a single individual should die—this is tragedy. But in the other pan of the balance scales place that little death, which comes into your souls each time a little more of your freedom and initiative are lost. And a little more is lost each time you decide again never to venture forth from the shadow of the gigantic Sophotechs, who protect and smother you. When will it end? A future utterly determined is a future dead. You have all felt this. Haven't you all dreamed of star voyages and adventure? Your bodies will always remain alive, but many hopes and souls will die if the danger and the dream of star colonization is strangled. We Neptunians are too poor to resurrect that dream once it dies; none of you will ever again be brave enough to do as Phaethon has done, nor will the turning of the centuries bring new generations with new spirits into power in the Oecumene, because you are immortal. Therefore weigh the tragic death of that one soul of which Gannis speaks, but compare it to the many souls, the great soul of all mankind, which perishes if Phaethon's dream fails! Small price to pay, good Hortators. Small price to pay!"

Asmodius Bohost wondered in a loud and brassy voice: "I note how easy it is to call the price of a single death so small . . . unless, of course, it happens to be one's own."

Tsychandri-Manyu Tawne spoke with heavy dignity: "When a single life is extinguished, that is as gross a tragedy as if the entire universe should end; for has not everything, from the point of view of him who dies, indeed come to an end?"

Gannis spoke in tones of haughty scorn, "No one's life can be sacrificed merely to serve the use and pleasure of the whole. We are not a society of cannibals!"

Diomedes asked, "No one's life . . . ? Not one . . . ?"

Gannis: "Not even a single, solitary individual!"

Diomedes nodded his helmet of shadows toward Gannis. "I am most glad to hear you say this. I assume this doctrine applies to Phaethon as well? He is the individual, more single and more solitary than any of the rest of you, whom I would not see sacrificed."

Nebuchednezzar turned to Gannis, and said, "Gannis Hundred-mind, I am required to warn you that you must abstain from the upcoming vote on this matter. These proceedings are being broadcast to your constituents back in the Jovian system; if you should vote for Phaethon's exile, few Jovians would support you, regarding your motive as hypocrisy. The Jovians, you must recall, still regard themselves as an individualistic and pioneer-spirited society, and many of your supporters back home have ties to Neptunian and Saturnine space efforts. Everything Diomedes said will convince them."

Gannis sat down, but did not seem ill-humored. "I will not vote, but I will still speak against what Phaethon proposes. And, no matter who supports him, without my metal, his ship will not be built."

Diomedes said, "The *Phoenix Exultant* will be built. Perhaps smaller than designed, or perhaps with thinner armor, but you, Gannis, shall not stand in the way of Phaethon and his dream. Nothing shall stop him. . . ."

And there was a note of triumph in his voice. "Nothing shall stop him."

But, even as he said this, his image began freezing, and then moving, freezing, and then moving, and his voice hissed into garble. The image of Diomedes collapsed, and was replaced by a flat two-dimensional window, with silent lines of text running across it, repeating Diomedes's last words.

"... *Nothing shall stop him* ... *Mr. Asmodius! I would be more than happy to take you up on your offer. But I fear I no longer have a foot to stand upon. My name shall be changed as your pleasure and whim shall direct. I cannot afford dignity; I cannot afford to keep my name.* ..."

Phaethon, who had been most eager to ask Diomedes about the identity and history of Xenophon, now saw he would have no chance. And no chance for a personal word with his friend.

One of the Eleemosynary Composition stood and spread his palms, the gesture to indicate that he was opening additional channels out of his own stock, or contributing computer time.

The window icon representing Diomedes winked out. The Eleemosynary Composition said, "We are transmitting the partial of Diomedes back to his point of origin in Neptunian space. The drain on our resources is significant."

Helion said, "I will contribute a dozen seconds."

Gannis nodded, and held up four fingers.

The other Hortators murmured agreement, and each contributed time or energy. The hundred people there could easily afford to return Diomedes Partial to his parent-mind, and some members of the White and Red Manors added software and customized routines as parting gifts, so that the partial would return with more wealth than was spent to send him here.

These acts of generosity and kindness made Phaethon wonder. Maybe Helion had been right after all. The Hortators were people of conscience and goodwill. Perhaps they could not let Phaethon off scot-free, not and save their reputations. But having heard Diomedes speak, surely they would impose only a light, symbolic sentence.

Gannis rose and spoke. "Members of the College. We now see the danger Phaethon poses is greater than we supposed. Not only is there threat of interstellar war but now there is unrest among the more distant parts of the Oecumene. We all know how difficult it is for Sophotechs to police these cold and far-off Neptunians. We all secretly suspect to what horrid uses, torture-dreams and child prostitution and worse, the

Cold Dukes put this so-called "privacy" they are so in love with. With the power to reshape thought and memory according to whatever perverted whim might strike one's fancy, only the grossest imagination can conceive what the Neptunian Eremites might do in the lonely darkness of their distant, icy fortresses. We must use all means at our disposal to ensure not only that Phaethon is cast out to starve and die, but that he also finds no way to communicate with these disgusting allies of his, these Neptunian people he has so stirred up and disturbed with his strange preachings!"

One of the Eleemosynary Composition spoke: "This would not be hard to arrange. Superlongrange orbital communication lasers are owned by only two or three efforts, and by some magnates in the ring-cities. Most have signed Hortation agreements."

Tsychandri-Manyu spoke: "Gannis of Jupiter is and are correct. We must do more than merely ostracize Phaethon; we must take steps to make sure he cannot find help from those who do not heed our wise advice; Neptunians, deviants, mind-drakes, and the like. I recommend a total ban on any form of communication or use of Mentality whatsoever, so that no one will be able to even send him a telephone call, unless they string up the wires themselves. No one shall write him a letter, unless they carry it themselves."

Asmodious Bohost said, "And grow the tree and pulp the paper and raise the goose to pluck the quill to sharpen for a pen!"

One of the Eleemosynary Composition stood: "Phaethon's body is stored aboard a segment of the ring-city we own. The water, and air, and the cubic space there belongs to us. He shall not be allowed to purchase any of this."

Neo-Orpheus observed: "With Sophotechs to advise us, we will be able to anticipate and outmaneuver any attempt Phaethon makes to circumvent our restrictions."

Tau Continuous Albion of the White Manorial School said: "The *Phoenix Exultant* is still in sub-Mercurial space; even if Phaethon, by some trick, should come to have legal ownership of it again, who will ferry him to it? Who will transmit the signal for him to call it back to Earth? He cannot get to Mercury by flapping his arms."

Tsychandri-Manyu Tawne rose to his feet. "I once again will call the question. Is there anyone who sees further need for discussion?"

Helion rose to his feet.

"Wait."

The chamber fell silent.

THE EXILE

1.

From the corner of his eye, Phaethon saw Gannis lean forward with great interest as Helion rose to speak. Members of the Eleemosynary Composition all wore the same expression of alert caution, staring at Helion. Ao Aoen, although he was not a member of the College, had been given a seat in the visitor's bench near the rear of the Warlock's section, and the light from the windows behind him glinted on the serpent scales of his cloak and threw his hooded face into shadow; but something in the set of his shoulders betrayed his tension.

Would Helion speak to favor Phaethon? If so, the Peers might well exclude Helion from their number, and undo, at one stroke, all the work Helion, for uncounted years, had done to raise himself to that high eminence.

Phaethon thought: *Please, don't do it, Father.*

And then his own anxiety made him smile. Phaethon's own prospects seemed so very much dimmer than even the worst that could happen to Helion. It was ironic, to say the least, that he should worry for Helion at this point. Nonetheless he did.

But those worries were needless. Helion did not say anything controversial or extraordinary. He said merely, "Masters and gentlemen of the College. I introduce a guest who has significant information to impart."

Footsteps were heard approaching the chamber doors. Phaethon cocked his ear. There was something strange about the sound, something he could not quite define. Perhaps it was that the echoes and acoustics surrounding the noise seemed particularly clear and distinct.

Then came a rattle of the latch, the noise of hinges, and the double doors behind Phaethon opened. The texture of the light on the polished wood floor around the doors changed as reflections from the antechamber fell into the hall. A man stood in the doorframe.

He had a narrow, ascetic face, and piercing gray eyes, which gave him a look of fiercely alert intelligence.

Every detail of the image was perfect. One could see the individual strands in his fabric of his Inverness cape; one could see the way each particular hair above his ears was disarrayed from the small weight of his deerstalker cap; one could see the freckles on the backs of his hands; the tiny flakes of dirt dotting the heel of his left boot. Sound and sight, texture, color, and presence, all were perfect.

As he stepped up to the table where Phaethon stood, Phaethon noticed more detail. A light odor of tobacco touched the tweed fabric of his cape. One of the threads on his coat buttons did not match the thread of the rest. The stubble on the left of his jaw was slightly rougher than on the right, as if he had shaved with a razor that morning, perhaps favoring the cheek that faced his window.

The amount of detail was remarkable. Phaethon saw the Hortators on their benches to either side whispering and staring, trying to guess who or what was represented by this enormously expensive and detailed self-image.

The gray-eyed man doffed his deerstalker cap and greeting the College with a curt nod. He spoke with a dry and slightly nasal accent: "Members of the College, greetings. My name is Harrier Sophotech."

Of course. No human-run self-image could be so thorough in its detail.

Harrier continued: "You may not have heard of me. I was created fifteen minutes ago, your time, to investigate some certain irregularities surrounding Phaethon's decision to open his memory casket. I should mention that this decision of Phaethon's was entirely unexpected, even by the Orient Sophotech Overmind-group, who was running a predictive model of Phaethon's behavior at the time."

Another rustle of wonder went through the chamber. Even Nebuchednezzar seemed surprised. The Orient Overmind was one of the Ennead, the nine community superintellects that the Sophotechs cooperated and melded themselves to create. Why would a mind placed so high in the Earthmind hierarchy be concerned?

Harrier said: "Only a tremendous shock, or some perceived threat to his life or the lives of his loved ones, could, in our opinion, have urged Phaethon to act so far out of character. We suspect foul play."

Again, there was a murmur and stir in the chamber, this one louder than the first. Emphyrio spoke, and the book in his lap amplified his voice: "You refer to true crime, violence urged by passion, not merely to fraud or juvenile pranksmanship?"

Harrier said, "Evidence is scant, but the hints are shocking, sir. We suspect attempted murder, corruption, and mind rape."

Audible gasps of astonishment and fear came from several points in the chamber. Helion was scrutinizing Phaethon as if he had never seen him before.

Neo-Orpheus asked: "When you say 'we,' do you mean you are part of the Constabulary?"

Harrier smiled slightly to himself. "No, sir. Sophotechs prefer not to join the police, military, or governmental functions. However, I have been working closely with the Commissioner of Constables on this case, purely in an advisory capacity. Think of me as a consulting detective."

Tsychandri-Manyu Tawne of Tawne House spoke: "With respect, my dear sir, this is all very interesting, but . . . what has this to do with us?"

Harrier raised an eyebrow and stared at Tsychandri-Manyu

with steel-gray eyes. "You Hortators are so famous for your public spirit, I was sure you would be eager to cooperate in this matter."

Helion touched Agamemnon XIV, Archon of Minos House, on the shoulder. Agamemnon stood. "Dignitaries and notables of the College! We have not yet asked Phaethon why he opened the forbidden casket. Our determination can neither be informed nor fair without this datum."

Tsychandri-Manyu made a noise of disgust. "Come, now! This is irrelevance!" But he looked to his left and his right as he spoke, and saw the faces around him. Something in the mood of the chamber was changing. Tsychandri-Manyu had the instincts of a politician; he knew when not to go against the mood of the group. He sat down.

Agamemnon spoke, pretending to answer Tsychandri-Manyu, but actually addressing the chamber, "Is it? Is it irrelevant? I think the question is central. Did some crime or violent event compel Phaethon's action? Consider: If you were an amnesiac, and had suffered the only murder attempt in many centuries, surely you would conclude that the crime was motivated by something, or explained by something, in your forgotten past. Who among us, if horror and emergency loomed, would not avail ourselves of every memory, every piece of information, we might suspect would be useful to avert disaster? Come, notables of the College! If Phaethon opened that box to learn the secret of some attack—some real attack—then both prudence and duty required him to open it! We cannot, we can never, punish a man for doing what duty requires; that would make a mockery of this whole College. Do not forget what a tenuous hold on power we Hortators have! One wrong decision, one notorious act of folly, and the public respect which forms the foundation of everything we are, will erode to nothing! Have we not more than endangered the public faith in us once already in this matter?"

Agamemnon continued: "The members of my constituency—we all know what sticklers for points of law and tradition the Silver-Grays are—would not support a boycott to punish Phaethon for doing what any reasonable man in his circumstances would have been forced to do! Do you realize we are talking about the possibility that someone has attempted a murder in our society? A murder! A deliberate attempt of one intelligent being to end the self-awareness of another! Gentlemen, if this suspicion turns out to be correct, then all other matters pale in comparison. I should like to call for a vote on the matter: if Phaethon was actually attacked, isn't his reaction justifiable?"

But Gannis (who was perhaps less alert a politician than Tsychandri-Manyu) leaned forward, squinting and peering across the chamber. "Is that Helion I see speaking? It looks like Agamemnon, but it sounds like someone else. We all hold Helion in the greatest respect, at the moment, and we hope, in the coming months, to honor him further. It would be a shame if the purity of his motives came into question!"

Helion did not rise from his seat, but spoke in ringing tones: "I make my fellow Peer the offer that, should he care to question my motives, I will be happy to put a copy of my mind on the public channels for anyone to inspect, provided his mind, and his motives, are posted likewise. Then we can all decide who has the purer motive."

A murmur of laughter came from the benches. Gannis subsided, a look of discomfort and worry on his face, muttering, "Eh . . . no, of course, I was merely speaking theoretically . . ."

Nebuchednezzar held up the mace and announced his voting results: "Notables and dignitaries of the College, my estimates show that the public would be outraged if Phaethon were punished for accessing his memories, if (note well), if he had been indeed attacked, and if he had reasonable cause to suspect that his memory would help him explain that attack, or to defend himself or others against future attacks. Several hundred thousand individuals would volunteer to help find and expose the criminal, and millions more would volunteer time and antigrams to the effort. Many of those who are watching these proceedings now have already made promises of contributions. On the other hand, the public fervor would turn with equal vehemence against Phaethon should this turn out to be a false alarm. The same strength of character which makes the Golden Oecumene utterly intolerant of violence makes Her equally harsh against those who attempt to manipulate that righteousness to their own ends."

Emphyrio said, "If Phaethon suffered senseless attack by a criminal, ordinary prudence would require that he examine all his memories, sealed or unsealed, to discover the cause of the attack. We cannot condemn him for this."

Socrates said, "Which is more important, to be just, or to appear just? Keeping the memories sealed, as he promised to do, would have maintained Phaethon's appearance of justice. But the criminal who threatened him could threaten others, and therefore it would not have been just to attempt to remain in ignorance about so important a matter."

Viridimagus Solitarie of the Green Mansion School offered: "But the very idea of a murder in a society with our traditions and our way of life—the notion is inconceivable!"

Ullr Selfson-First Lifrathsir of the Nordic Pagan School was an ex-Warlock basic who made his fortune arranging alternate-history scenarios for parahistorians, including the rather gruesome and hideous Dark Tyrant Earthmind World. He, more than anyone, knew how fragile the peace and prosperity of the Golden Oecumene were; his nightmare scenario had been extrapolated from very few historical changes. "It is not inconceivable. If the Neptunians are willing to send Diomedes Partial on the mission which—but for our charity—would have been suicidal, then they may be willing to risk, or threaten, other lives. Perhaps the attack was merely meant to shock Phaethon into opening his buried memories. Frankly, I would have done the same if I were Phaethon. I would like to ask Phaethon if his memories gave him any clue as to the identity and nature of the attacker?"

Nausicaa of Aeceus Mansion spoke: "At Lakshmi, the College examined what would and would not be subject to amnesia. I recall that nothing but information about the proposed starship was covered. This may be another clue pointing to the Neptunians; we all know their great interest in the *Phoenix Exultant*."

Casper Halfhuman Tinkersmith of the Parliament of Ghosts stood. He was a writer of educational matrixes famous for his cool logic when he was in his human body, and for his unusually vivid passion and drive when he was downloaded into an electrophotonic matrix. He was dressed now like a planter from the Carolinas, in a white coat and straw skimmer. "Brethren! Must we circle these issues endlessly before someone asks the core question? If Phaethon suffered such an outrage, why wasn't that the first thing from his lips when this meeting opened? It is not Phaethon but Harrier, yes, Harrier, who says Phaethon was attacked. Why is Phaethon mute?"

Phaethon, ever since Harrier had entered the room, had been listening with a sinking heart. Sinking, because he knew he should not tell anything to the Hortators that might be overheard by the enemy—Scaramouche or whomever it was that Atkins was investigating. On the other hand, Rhadamanthus (whose intelligence Phaethon acknowledged as exceeding his own by four orders of magnitude) had expressly advised Phaethon to go ahead and reveal the information. The enemy, after all, surely knew that Phaethon knew of the attack. And revealing the details of that attack would not necessarily reveal anything about Phaethon's earlier meeting with Atkins.

Yet Rhadamanthus himself may have been corrupted by the attacking virus civilization when he gave that advice. . . .

If so, then would testifying that he suffered an attack somehow benefit, or be part of the plan of, the enemy? And, if so, what was the enemy's plan? Such a plan must have something to do with the *Phoenix Exultant*. Something . . . but what?

Phaethon grimaced in bitter humor. Perhaps he had been raised too closely to machine-minds for his own good. He had relied so often on minds swifter than his own to solve all puzzles and conundrums; and his mind perhaps was not swift enough to unravel this convoluted enigma, not while he stood here on trial.

And then there was a question of due proportion and degree. Suppose he were willing to sacrifice his career or his life to protect the Golden Oecumene from disaster; every man

of ordinary decency, throughout the ages, made such sacrifices for their homelands and their ideals. But did warning
the enemy of Atkins's investigation—did that constitute a disaster for the Oecumene or only an inconvenience for Atkins?
Suffering exile and death for one's homeland was one thing;
suffering exile and death for Atkins's convenience was another.

What finally decided him was this: Phaethon did not know
how important secrecy was. But he knew how important the
Phoenix Exultant was.

Phaethon spoke:

"I did not speak before because Atkins asked me not to.
But now that Harrier has spoken, no good is served by me
any longer keeping silent. There is an enemy among us, perhaps watching us this very moment. I suspect it is an enemy
from another star."

Phaethon in a few brief words, told about the attack by
Scaramouche on the steps of the Eveningstar Mausoleum,
about how an unmaker virus had been introduced into his
surrounding thoughtspace, overwhelming Eleemosynary de-
fenses, and attempting to spread throughout the Mentality.

Deep silence hung in the chamber. Phaethon could see the
looks of skepticism and disbelief growing on the faces around
him as he spoke. A look of hope was dying in Helion's eyes;
Gannis was smiling openly.

Messilina Secondus Eveningstar of Eveningstar Mansion
offered: "We have many monitors and nanomachines
throughout the area, ecochemical watch circuits in the air and
soil, including monitors watching the horses near our mausoleum. There was no Neptunian; there was no second mannequin brought out of our waiting room; Phaethon was
alone."

A high-level information supervisor from the Eleemosynary Composition stood. "Service to all requires a deep shar-
ing of information. We have examined the logs and records
surrounding the moments Phaethon describes. He did snap his
helmet shut inside one of our public boxes, breaking the connections and doing minor damage to our jacks and lines.

Nothing else of his testimony is reflected in our memories or records."

The Eleemosynary supervisor paused to let his comment sink in. He continued: "Gentlemen of the College. There was no attack. We were there; we would have seen it."

Phaethon said, "The attacking virus was successful, and may have edited your memories."

Some of the looks of impatience were hardening into expressions of boredom and contempt.

"With all due respect," said the Eleemosynary supervisor, "such a redaction would require this virus to bypass sixty-four information security checkpoints in our mind-group, and alter four sets of records: the original, the backup, the conscience ordinators, and the data traffic control monitor. Since our records are kept in associative analogue pathways rather than by a linear system, the virus would have had to examine each record, or even each thought, and do all this while suppressing the awareness-flow telltales of each and every member of our mass-mind's local interest group. Assuming it take two units of information to alter one unit (one to identify and one to falsify), we are estimating a volume of some eight hundred sixty-three billion seconds of intelligence. Only Sophotechs are capable of such feats."

"The attacking virus was constructed and guided by a Sophotech," said Phaethon.

There was a titter of embarrassed laughter around the chamber. A Sophotech attempting a murder?

Phaethon said, "I know it sounds absurd; don't you think I know how absurd it sounds? But it—I think it is called Nothing—it was not one of our Sophotechs, not part of the Earthmind community! It is a mind from outer space, it must be!"

A dull silence filled the room.

The looks of contempt had changed. Contempt was a look one gave to equals, men whom one scorned but who were nonetheless sane men. Now the expressions become looks of pity.

Tsychandri-Manyu needed no honed instinct to tell him the

mood in the chamber had changed again; it was obvious. "Gentlemen, we are all familiar with the erratic and frantic behavior of those who face exile. They calculate that it will do no harm for them to attempt anything—anything at all— which might avert their fate. After all, what do they care if they lie or cheat or falsify, when they will not be alive long enough to suffer the consequences of their deceits? Gentlemen! Why are we wasting our time with this? I would like to move, yet again, on the matter of Phaethon's term of exile. I move that it be permanent and absolute, so that not even food, basic services, shelter, or computer time will ever be sold to him."

There was a loud noise of assent, many voices calling for the final vote.

Nebuchednezzar said, "The motion to end debate and to call the question has been moved and seconded."

Helion rose to his feet: "My son is not a liar!" he spoke in a voice like thunder.

Whispers died.

Nebuchednezzar said, "Helion, your comment is not in order at this time."

Helion said, "Phaethon is telling the truth. We are Silver-Grays. We do not and cannot lie. And of all Silver-Grays, he is the most truthful."

Nebuchednezzar said: "I will interpret this comment as a motion to open debate on the issue of whether or not to call the question. Is there a second?"

Gan-Seven Far-Gannis of Jupiter stood up: "I will second the motion. Rhadamanthus is at hand; Phaethon is, after all, a Silver-Gray, and has deep-memory reading circuits. Would not a Noetic examination instantly reveal the truth of the matter? This is the standard procedure in such cases. We need not be impatient."

Helion's voice came softly into Phaethon's ear. This was yet another violation of the protocols binding everyone else in the scene. His father's voice said: "Just say the words, 'I swear,' and we shall have the truth."

But Phaethon stood silent.

Nebuchednezzar said, "Is something the matter, Phaethon? Is there a reason why you are reluctant to permit a Noetic examination? If you wish us to examine your thoughts, please open a Noetic deep channel."

Phaethon was suspicious. Gan-Seven Far-Gannis was that part of the Gannis Hundred-mind that traveled between Jupiter and Neptune as a trade factotum. Why would he be eager for Phaethon to be vindicated? The fact that Far-Gannis had close ties with Neptunians was, perhaps, no grounds for suspicion. But what if he had ties with Xenophon?

And the enemy virus in the Mentality, hunting for Phaethon's mind, as far as Phaethon knew, was still out there. Phaethon had opened sensory, kinesthetic, and somatic channels between his brain and the Mentality in order to project a self-image into the fictional chamber Helion had created here. There was no direct access at the moment to his memories, deep structures, or thoughts. Opening a Noetic channel, however, would render him vulnerable to that virus.

Phaethon wondered if the attacker's technology would allow him to kill Phaethon, and replace him with a partial-mind of something that thought it was Phaethon but was loyal to whatever goals or desires the enemy preferred. It was a chilling thought.

Perhaps it had been done already. How many of the Hortators around him had been replaced by puppet creatures of the enemy . . . ?

Phaethon said, "The Nothing Sophotech may still have some sort of unmaker virus free in the Noumenal Mentality. If the design is advanced enough to defeat all your wards and guards without being detected, I would fear opening my unshielded brain up to any deep-structure Mentality channels."

Several of the Hortators laughed out loud. Others smirked. Epiraes Septarch Fulvous of Fulvous House, one of Tsychandri-Manyu's minions, called out, "If the honorable Phaethon must invent the flimsiest of excuses, could he at least make it entertaining, please? I am having trouble with my suspension of disbelief."

Harrier Sophotech raised his hand, "I realize that I am not

a member of the College, but could I make a simple suggestion? Have Phaethon broadcast a copy of his mind-information onto a public channel; broadcast only, not receive; no external impulse can reach him, and this virus he fears, whether it exists or not, will not affect him. Meanwhile, you gentlemen may examine the public copy to your heart's content. What do you say?"

A sensation of warmth and pleasure filled Phaethon, straightening his back. A knot of acidic tension of which he had not even been aware suddenly relaxed in his stomach and released him. Harrier's suggestion made perfect common sense. In a moment, the College would see that he was telling the truth; the existence of the interstellar menace would be confirmed. The College had already taken a vote: if Phaethon were telling the truth, he would be cleared. He would he free to return to his life and his dream. The *Phoenix Exultant* was waiting for him, the stars were waiting for him, and, this time, nothing would be standing in his way.

2.

Phaethon froze the scene, and stepped out of the Deep Dreaming. He woke to find himself in his armor, half curled in the warmth and blackness of the Eleemosynary public box. The helmet circuit sent pictures from the faceplate-eyepieces directly into his optic nerve; he could see the telltale lights and dream points on the controls and glyph signs inscribed on the interior of the casket.

Commands went from his thought into his suit interface.

The black lining of his armor was able to nanomanufacture a data crystal (Phaethon vented the production waste-heat as a jet of steam into the liquid medium in which he floated) and this crystal he filled with his memories.

Phaethon opened the control panel with his finger manually. (Imagine using his hand to open a control! He felt just like a man from the prehistoric past.) With the panel open, he found the jack to accept the data crystal, and had his armor circuit impose an energy pattern on the wiring to trigger the activation switch. Thus, there was no physical connection to himself when his recorded memories were transferred to a public inspection channel.

Phaethon stepped back into Deep Dreaming, saw the austere Inquest Chamber of the Hortators around him, frozen. He started time again. "A copy of my mind is available for your review on public channel 2120."

3.

Once the summons was read, the oaths affirmed, and the reversion circuits were made ready, the Mentality opened itself into many minds. The College of Hortators, each and every one, remembered Phaethon, and became Phaethon.

They saw and suffered the scene. All of them wept above the coffin of Daphne. All of them heard Eveningstar's curt refusal. All of them wandered, thoughts heavy with despair, out onto the steps in front of the mausoleum. All of them saw Scaramouche and heard his mocking talk.

All of them felt the sword blade cut their neck, felt cold steel and hot blood.

Then the Phaethon who had been Benvolio Malachi, the Mnemonicist, said to the other Phaethons: "There is a time-texture friction here, of the type one only sees with redacted memories. Note the extra read-lines and time-cues. This memory has been tampered with."

The Phaethon who had been Tau Continuous of the White was an engineer, by nature a methodical thinker. "Maybe it is the alleged virus."

They all knew that read-line tags could get scrambled by imposing two mind systems into one thoughtspace . . . or two memories.

The Phaethon who had been Ao Sinistro was able to use a burst of intuition to assemble the scattered read-line fragments, to look at them as though they were a shattered geometric shape, combine that shape like a puzzle, then retranslate the result back into a linear format. From that, the association path traces of the original memory could be read. He said, "Here is the memory, whole and untouched. Who of me is willing to see the unhindered and unhampered truth?"

All the Phaethons, of course, wanted to see the truth. After all, they were Phaethon.

And a new memory came.

4.

They remembered standing on the stair outside Eveningstar Mansion. They remembered the sensations of hopelessness and sorrow; sorrow without cure. Daphne was gone.

Phaethon drew a deep breath, searching the gardens and the sky, perhaps for inspiration, perhaps for some sign promising escape from this world of flat despair that had trapped him.

Since it was a Red Manorial scene, the wind was not merely refreshing, scented with autumn, but also filled with a wild melancholy. The tattered clouds were turning red-gold in the sunset, a sight as strange and sad and haunting as the funeral ship of a fairy king descending in flames to the waves. The far hills, draped in shadows like the vestments of conquered titans, seemed like the towers and gates to some alien world, threatening, terrible, but challenging, as if daring him to penetrate their secrets. In the near distance, on a grassy slope tinted with cherry, rose, and scarlet dusk light, a stallion of a brand Daphne once had made now reared against the sunset, uttering a wild cry, and tossing its mane with furious pride.

It was as if the landscape itself were urging him to wild, swift, relentless deeds. Deeds of peerless renown.

"But of course!" Phaethon was jarred with sudden hope. "I do not now recall the password or secret key to waken my Daphne. But such a word (why not?) could be hidden in the casket of locked memory. And in that box is the man she lost, not me."

But what use would it be to waken Daphne, only to suffer exile immediately thereafter?

It took him but a moment to invent a story. He could pretend he was attacked, that he had to open the memory box. But attacked by whom? There was no way any such attack could take place, except by an entity as smart as a Sophotech, able to infiltrate the Golden Oecumene, alter records, and erase memories. But where could such a Sophotech originate?

Phaethon remembered that Atkins had been investigating some Neptunian Masquerade prank. That gave him an idea. Atkins was actually investigating an external threat to the Oecumene. The evil Sophotech would belong to a highly advanced but completely invisible interstellar civilization. A civilization people by aliens, or the descendants of a lost colony. Or time travelers or wombats or hobgoblins. The excuse did not matter. All that mattered was that, if the Hortators thought Phaethon were acting on an understandable impulse—a reaction to a threat, no matter how far-fetched—then they might be lenient. Certainly they would not for a moment believe in the threat themselves, but if they thought Phaethon believed in it . . .

But how to make himself believe? He would have to falsify his own memories, of course, in order to cheat the Noetic examination that certainly would follow. Any purchase of a pseudomnesia editor would be normally be noticed and recorded . . . except that it was still a time of Masquerade.

Phaethon turned on a Scaramouche costume. Disguised, he then opened a channel to a Red Manorial redaction boutique in the Deep Dreaming. He bought and downloaded a self-deception program, and began writing the illusion to inscribe into his own memory paths.

His hopes were pinned on three ideas: First, anyone who knew him would conclude that self-deception was utterly out of character for Phaethon. Second, Atkins, if asked about his investigation, could not and would not answer. And third, Phaethon himself would, by that time, be firmly convinced that there was an alien super-virus lurking in the mentality, hunting for him, and so therefore he would have an excuse to refuse a noetic examination. If he were not neotically examined, this tampering would not be noticed.

As an added bonus, he would, of course, by then, have forgotten all about this moment and this falsification. He would still be able to think of himself as an honest man, and have no reason to think otherwise.

Smiling grimly, Phaethon loaded the program to begin erasing and rewriting his own memory.

5.

The Phaethon who had been Phaethon exclaimed: "But that is not what happened!"

But he was alone when he said this. All the other Phaethons had returned to their own identities, and were staring down at Phaethon with remote, august, and unpitying stares.

"But that is not what happened!" Phaethon said again.

Neo-Orpheus said, "Not that you recall, you mean. But the reason why your recollection is in error, is because you yourself falsified it."

Phaethon said, "But I would never do such a thing! You all know I would not!"

Neo-Orpheus smiled thinly. "We know that is what you had hoped we would believe. The record shows us everything."

Phaethon made an angry gesture: "The record has been falsified! During the moment it took me to transfer my copy to Channel 2120, the alien Sophotech or its unmaker virus must have rewritten the memory chains."

Tau Continuous Albion said, "Albion Sophotech informs me that such tampering is not theoretically possible. He has examined the record we just experienced, subjecting it to six levels of redundant scrutiny. No evidence of tampering has been found. Is there any contrary opinion?"

Nebuchednezzar Sophotech had a thoughtful look, his eyes focused on the distant ceiling. "I also am examining the Mentality records, and have invented three new tools of statistical analysis to do so. During the transmission from the Eleemosynary box to our local service, there was no opportunity for anyone or anything to affect the data. If it had been modified during the reading process, the modification would have had to have been introduced between every other picosecond pulse of the main circuit action. To fit such an enormous volume of change into so short a time would require a data-compression technique beyond the Planck unit limit. In theory, such a compressed data formulation could be assembled under what scientists call nonrational continuum conditions, either within the event horizon of a singularity, or in the achronic conditions preceding the big bang. There is no way known to our science of crossing such an event horizon, or of passing the information intact from inside a singularity to the outside."

Tau Continous said, "In other words, not possible."

Nebuchednezzar brought his eyes down. "Not possible within the present state of our technology."

Kes Satrick Kes spoke for the first time. His voice was flat, crisp, and precise: "I note a symmetry in both of the world-views here. Phaethon's view is that he is being persecuted by an alien sophotechnology, which he supposes to be sophisticated enough to alter or falsify the evidence to the contrary. The other view, which the testimony of the record supports, is that Phaethon, in desperation, falsified his memory and erased his own knowledge that he had done so. Both world-views adequately explain the appearances, and are self-consistent. Occam's razor urges us, when two explanations adequately explain the phenomena, to choose the one requiring fewer hypothetical assumptions. Naturally, I estimate that it is more likely that a man could falsify himself (which is something we see all the time) than that an alien, utterly unknown civilization (which is something we have never seen) could adopt a hostile posture toward us; single out Phaethon for attack; and yet be familiar enough with all of our protocols and systems to forge multiple sealed records and memories without being detected by the Earthmind. Without additional evidence, I will assume Phaethon's version of events is false.

A Noetic examination of his brain directly could provide the additional evidence we need to reverse this opinion. But I anticipate that Phaethon, in order to be consistent with his present beliefs, will continue to refuse such an examination."

Phaethon said, "The threat is real, even if I am the only one who sees it. I dare not reestablish a direct connection to the Mentality. The Nothing Sophotech has acted; I saw the results just now, practically in front of our eyes." But his voice was low, his eye was dull; the look of man who knows, beyond question, that he will not be believed.

The other Hortators did not bother to make so careful an analysis as Kes Satrick Kes. Most did not even bother to record a speech, or proffer a supporting opinion, but simply announced their support for an endless, permanent, and absolute exile to be imposed on Phaethon.

Helion's voice came, once again, quietly into his ear: "You are clearly suffering from a self-imposed paranoid fantasy. Open your deep structure mind to the Noetic probe, and we will be able to undo the harm. We can redact these false beliefs entire out of your mind and memory. This may be your last chance, son; the Hortators are voting."

Phaethon shook his head. He was not hallucinating.

An eerie thought struck him: what if, every time the invasions of this external foe had been detected, the victims had concluded that their memories were false, and had had them redacted? There could be a thousand unreported cases of such attacks, or a million.

Helion's voice, tense and anguished, came to his ear again: "Do not refuse me, son! Let me change your mind! I have a reconstruction program standing by; your false memories and beliefs can be removed in a moment. Don't end your life as Hyacinth Septimous ended his! I am begging you now, son. In the name of my love for you, I beg."

"No, Father. I will not change my mind. Not about this, not about my ship, not about my dream. And, as you love me, I ask you to understand me."

A pause.

Helion's voice: "I am afraid that I do, my brave, foolishly

brave, beloved son. I fear I understand all too well—" The voice was cut off. Phaethon returned his attention to the scene around him.

Silence was in the chamber. One of the voters had paused to ask him a question.

"Please repeat the question," said Phaethon, "My mind was . . . elsewhere." He wanted to turn his head and look at his father, but he dared not.

It was Ao Prospero Circe of the Zooanthropic Incarnation Coven. "None of the considerations of my fellow Horators, whether you bring war or hope, whether you are sane or insane, truthful or self-deluded, matters as much to me as this one question: Why did you pick your name?"

Phaethon said, "You are asking me about what? My name?"

"Of course. To know the true name of a thing is to have power over it. You named yourself after Phaethon, the child of the sun god who overreached himself. In his pride and folly, he demanded to drive his father's chariot, the sun, across the sky; but he could not control the horses. He flew high and he flew low, burning sky and burning earth, till all the world cried out for Jupiter to destroy him with a lightning bolt. Why did you name yourself after this image of recklessness and pride?"

Phaethon smiled. "That I can answer. I know the truth about that myth. Phaethon did not burn the world; after all, the world is still here, is it not? No. Jupiter was afraid when he saw a mortal at the reigns of the mighty sun chariot, and he felt jealous when he saw a mere man driving the divine steeds of fire. Jupiter was afraid that something might go wrong. Rather than give the youth a chance to prove himself, he shot down and killed the charioteer during takeoff. Before he ever even began to fly. What's the moral of the story? In my version, maybe the moral is that one should not let gods, or people who think that they can play gods, anywhere near where the lightning bolts are kept."

The Warlock smiled and turned to Nebuchednezzar. "If I vote to favor Phaethon, shall I be the only one? Nonetheless

I must favor him; he is a dreamer, and perhaps he is a paranoid madman; but his dream and his madness are stronger than our sanity and truth."

So the last vote was cast.

Nebuchednezzar Sophotech had raised his mace. "Phaethon, once of Rhadamanthus, the votes have been counted. Have you anything to say before we pass sentence?"

"Yes," said Phaethon. "Not a statement, but a question. Do you believe I am right? You, personally, Nebuchednezzar?"

"It is outside of the duties of my office to offer personal opinions. This College was designed to preserve the human spirit, human sanity, and human dignity in the face of tremendous technological changes, changes which could easily abolish those things you living creatures find precious. There are certain things humans value for their own sake; and about such things the logic of machines has nothing to say. It is important that the College of Hortators remain in human hands; it is important that my opinions not determine the outcome of Hortator decisions."

"Then why did you oppose the Lakshmi Agreement?"

"Those agreements were hastily drafted and ill-advised. The College is intended to urge the public to avoid the self-destructive abuse of our technology, and to ostracize those who do not adhere to those standards of decent conduct. In ruling against you, the College may have overstepped the boundaries of its mandate. They are not here to prevent war but to prevent corruption. The military arm of the Golden Oecumene, the man you know as Atkins, it is his job to prevent war. You did not seem to be corrupt, and to stop you required the Golden Oecumene to undergo the largest mass-amnesia in recorded history. This also was ill-advised.

"Perhaps you are unaware of the unrest and the anger which came when you opened your memory box, Phaethon. The memories of the public opened also. Many business affairs, love affairs, conversations, works of art and works of labor had been forgotten, being too closely associated with your famous effort. And all this came rushing back, and people realized how much the Hortators had convinced them to give up. Far too much. At Lakshmi, this danger was foreseen and accepted, risking the prestige of this College in a way I would never have advised. Was the risk worth the gain? I will not say. Where matters of human spirit are involved, human opinion should be given wide deference."

Phaethon said, "You have not answered. I built a ship to conquer the stars. Am I in the right?"

Nebuchednezzar looked grave. "Eventually the human race must migrate and spread. That is a natural state of living things. At Lakshmi, I thought you were in the right. Now I do not know. You are quicker than other manor-born to resort to violence when under stress; you have done so twice, trying to steal Daphne out of her coffin. The record shows that you have falsified your own memories in order to attempt a fraud upon this College. Someone should certainly father more races of mankind among the stars; but to be a good father requires honesty and patience, qualities you seem to lack. I may not agree with the decision of the College in this case, but their judgment about you is not irrational, given these facts, and I will not publicly speak against them. I cannot support you. I cannot help you."

Nebuchednezzar concluded: "No one can help you. We shall advise the public to adopt a total and unending ban on all dealings with you, including the sale of basic necessities, food, water, air, and computer time. No one shall render aid, comfort, or shelter, sell or buy good or services, nor donate any charity. This sentence is not subject to review but intended to be final and absolute. I hereby pronounce—"

Harrier was standing next to Phaethon, staring absently-mindedly up at the windows, hands clasped behind his back, lips pursed as if engrossed in an amusing puzzle, rocking back and forth on his heels. No one was paying attention to him. So it came as something of a shock, when he whistled shrilly through his teeth, and waved his hand overhead. "Yoo-hoo! Mr. Speaker! I have something to ask the College!"

Nebuchednezzar said, "You are very seriously out of order. And I cannot say that I approve of your decision to communicate with me at this time, place and fashion, rather than communing directly with my through-region via the Southeast Overmind-group."

"Aha. Never argue in front of the children, is that the idea?" He turned to the assembled College. "Gentlemen! I have a simple request. My investigation into the alleged attack on Phaethon is not yet complete. And I may have a few routine follow-up questions I would like to ask him, but I cannot do so if his term of exile is so absolute that I cannot even call him, or conduct a Noetic examination. Will you grant an exception to your ban, please, and allow computer services, communication, and telepresentation to continue to serve him?"

Phaethon, for some reason, was looking at Gannis when Harrier spoke. Gannis had never been able to control his expression without artificial aids, which, presently, in a scene adhering to Silver-Gray protocols, he did not have. So Phaethon saw a look of eager hostility across his face.

Phaethon did not have a psychometric routine in his personal thoughtstspace, nor was he trained in Warlock-style controlled intuitions. So he had no way to confirm his hunch. But he did have a hunch. Looking at the hunger on Gannis's face, Phaethon thought: *He's one of them.*

The Enemy (whoever they were) would be glad that Phaethon would still have access to the Mentality. As soon as he logged on, as soon as he made a phone call, or telecast a ghost, they would know where he was; the moment he accessed the Middle Dreaming, a snare program (like the one that had been associated with Scaramouche's sword) could trigger him into the Deep Dreaming. And in the Deeper Dreaming would be something like a memory box, but open, and with another set of memories, not his, inside. It would be death, and worse than death. His soul would be consumed and replaced.

Nebuchednezzar said, "I am certain the College, as a public-spirited body, will do all it can to aid a police investigation, even one which seems as routine as this one. Without objection, so ordered."

Harrier turned and shook hands with Phaethon, whispering,

"Don't give up the fight, old man. If you hadn't been mugged, I shouldn't ever have been created, so I have quite a fond spot in my heart for you. Go to Talaimannar in Ceylon. . . ."

Phaethon was turning his head to see if he could get one last word, one last look, to his father. He also wanted to hear the rest of Harrier's message, and wanted to warn Harrier, or someone, about Gannis. But Nebuchednezzar brought the heel of his mace down on the floor with a sharp crack of noise, confirming the sentence of the College of Hortators.

6.

Phaethon was perhaps expecting that he would be led from the imaginary chamber by images of footmen or bailiffs. Certainly that would have been in keeping with Silver-Gray protocols and standards. But Phaethon was no longer considered Silver-Gray. He was no longer considered anything. Neither the Eleemosynary Hospice nor the local telepresentation service felt any obligation to continue treating him according to Silver-Gray standards or any other standards.

The moment the mace touched the floor, the scene vanished. He was back in the casket, disoriented. His thoughts seemed to moving slowly and stupidly without Rhadmanthus there to assist him. Was this what shock was?

And the liquid was draining out of the casket, leaving Phaethon cramped and bent on the inner surface. Then, just as suddenly, jarring and dizzying, the gravity spin slowed and braked, so that his body was crushed up against the medical wires and in-jacks of the left-hand side of the casket. The lid hissed open (blinding him with outside light) before the centrifuge had come to a complete halt, so that he was practically flung out.

His thoughts were still confused; he was trying to remember what the last thing was that he wanted to say to his father . . .

Phaethon floated in free-fall, clinging to the rim of the casket, his legs stuck out, pointing toward the carpet, but not "down." He felt the pressure in his temples, the beat of blood in his face, as the fluids in his body distributed themselves evenly throughout his body instead of falling to a accustomed position near his feet.

A maintenance remote, shaped like a stark cylinder crowned with telescoping arms, was hovering near him, held in place by a tension of magnetic forces. "The Eleemosynary Composition thanks you for your patronage, but no longer wishes to rent this space. The standard rental agreement allows for instant expulsion of those who fall under Hortator osctracization, without notice or advertisement. If you do not immediately take steps to leave the premises, the unit is instructed to regard you as a trespasser, and to join the Constabulary and to eject you by force."

Phaethon did not respond or move. He had known what he was risking; he had known what exile might mean. But the reality, now that it was here, seemed more than he could bear. It took him a moment to draw his breath and muster his strength.

The moment was apparently too long a time. The remote opened its mechanical arms like a giant spider. The hull of the machine changed, and now bore gold-and-blue police emblems. "This unit has uploaded all proper training, oaths, and experience, been checked against the Constabular Academy on channel 14, and has graduated and been awarded a position as sergeant-at-arms of the municipal commandry. I am now authorized to use force against you if you resist. This place in which you are is not your property; you have been asked politely to depart."

Better to walk than to be hauled.

"I'm going. I'll be happy to go. . . ." Phaethon triggered thrusters in his elbows and boots. The reaction gently thrust him down the corridor.

The remote moved in front of him, blocking his way. "Pardon me, sir. The air that you are in, unlike air on Earth, is not a natural product but is owned by the Eleemosynary Composition, and must be pumped in at the owner's expense. The Eleemosynary Composition asks that you not distribute ejected particles throughout the Hospice corridor, or foul the air with pollutants."

"It's steam. Hot water." His teeth were clenched. Phaethon knew he should not be letting this aggravate him. But in his whole life, machines had never been anything else than unfailingly polite to him. Historical dramas always portrayed criminal sentences, executions or reconditionings, to be surrounded with grave ceremony. Not this petty harassment.

"Nonetheless, the air in this corridor does not belong to you, and you cannot eject matter into it without permission."

"As you wish."

Phaethon kicked against the carpet and pulled himself hand over hand to the air lock at the hub of the wheel-shaped hospice. Left and right, he saw that other caskets were empty. The casket doors gaped like empty windows. It gave Phaethon a feeling of desolation.

"Where is everyone?" He did not expect an answer, but he thought it would do no harm to ask.

To his surprise, the unit spoke back: "All of the guests were removed to a safe distance during the Inquest Hearing, and energy avenues and lines of fire opened by other Constabular operatives, so that, should you choose to resist, overwhelming firepower could be brought to bear against your armor, sufficient to drive you out through the walls and shielding and into space beyond."

At the hub of the hospice, he came to the door of the lock. It did not open. Nothing happened when he touched it, and it ignored his voice command. He said to the wall: "I thought you wanted me to leave."

The wall said, "There is a wheel to crank the door open manually. The Eleemosynary Composition does not wish to expend the battery cost to run the door motors."

There was no point in arguing. The cost in energy to open one door, of course, was too small to measure. But, of course, the millionth part of a gram of antimatter it would take to hire the door motor to open the valve for him was beyond his means now. Creditors had long ago taken everything.

And even had he any money, no one would take it. Not even the simpleminded circuit in a door.

Phaethon felt more exhausted (without being tired) than he had ever felt in his long life.

Yet he had been exiled, so far, for only a few minutes. Years lay ahead. Grimly, he took the wheel in his hand and cranked.

Phaethon passed through the lock, and came out into the airlessness of the spaceport. The place was a wide sphere, with openings to the east and west leading to other segments of the ring-city. Nadirward was an entrance to the beanstalk. Phaethon could see, from the gold ornamentation around the rim buildings, that this space elevator was one of the larger, old-fashioned ones, with cars the size of warehouses, stocked and staffed with luxuries from the Middle Sixth Era, a time of hedonism and elegance.

Phaethon directed a signal from his armor to the remote. "This is municipal space. My I use my thrusters?"

"Feel free," replied the unit.

Steam ejected from the armor joints did not produce powerful thrust, only enough to move him a few meters away from the hospice. Then he triggered the more powerful massdrivers, which lined the back and legs of the armor. Thin parallel lines of energy propelled him forward.

He dove through the weightless space to the edge of the rim. He dared not dive in; the drivers could not support his armor in flight, not against the earthly gravity that obtained in the middle and lower sections of the space elevator. But he could use the drive mechanisms in the same way he had before, to generate a magnetic field by reacting against energy units that lined the inner walls of the space elevator, and lower himself eventually to the ground. To do this, he needed to reconstruct the circuits in his armor he originally had used to propel himself upward. He anchored himself near the rim of the well with a magnetic line of force, and ordered his suit to adjust.

Phaethon looked overhead. With the Middle Dreaming absent, he could not tell which space elevator this was, or where on Earth its foundations rested. There was no map present in his mind. There were no signs posted in any language he could read, because none of the thought glyphs on the walls nearby could trigger any reactions in the language centers of his brain, not when he was shut out of the Mentality. Was this the direction he wanted to go? He was not sure. (Did he even have a direction, when he had no place to go? Again, he was not sure.)

His eyes fell. Beyond his feet, he could see the vast well of the space elevator.

The windows and ports in the elevator's depths formed concentric rings of light, level upon level, balcony upon balcony, receded to the vanishing point. Approaching in the distance, the size of an ocean liner, ornamented and plush, came the great gold and crystal and ivory car of the space elevator. Beneath the dome on the car's ceiling, he could see the ponds and formularies and tables of a Sixth-Era mensal performance restaurant.

Phaethon looked on sadly. He would have loved to take this armor off and rest at leisure, descending in plush Sixth Era comfort until he arrived at the base of the tower. He could see, through the windows, white linen, surfaces of silver material, a group in festive costumes reclining in feast webs, pleasure amplifiers like crowns on their heads. It was strange to think that, somewhere, people were still celebrating a masquerade; somewhere there were smiles, and good cheer, and good company.

Now he would have welcomed even that horrid Nonanthropomorphic Aesthetic elevator car, the car shaped like a bug's stomach, which he had spurned on his way up here. Now that he could not have it.

And suppose he should reach the ground, where then?

Was it true he would never see his ship again? (Was it true he was never going to see Daphne again? Either one of them? Even the doll-wife had seemed appealing, in her own way . . .)

The Constable remote now floated down near him. "The owners of this area of the dock no longer wish to have you as a patron, and ask for your immediate removal."

What was taking his armor so long to find the proper configurations and anchor points? When he had flown upward, the armor had required only a moment. Of course, then Rhadamanthus had probably been helping.

Phaethon said with leaden voice: "Will the owners of the space elevator let me go down the shaft, so that I can leave?"

"Certainly. The laws against trespass always allow a trespasser enough right-of-way to depart."

He pulled his legs so that his body turned a slow somersault, end over end, to bring his face pointing downward in the shaft. There he floated, face-downward, ready to trigger an acceleration. He drifted out over the rim of the pit, with nothing below him but vacuum.

"Be careful!" said the Constable.

Instead of triggering the acceleration, Phaethon, warned by the Constable unit, brought up his internal read outs. Now he found what was taking his armor such a long time to find the proper configurations to use the energy units in the walls. There were none. There was no answering reaction from the energy units. The magnetics in Phaethon's armor were sliding every which way, catching nothing. The system signals were bouncing, being ignored. A spurt from his wrist jet pushed him gently back way from the rim.

"What?! What is this?!"

The Constable said, "The energy units lining the space elevators wall, which you have used hitherto to motivate your armor in this area, are no longer available for your use. They are owned by the Vafnir Energy Effort, and have been instructed not to accept field-manipulation command from the circuits in your armor."

Another harassment. It was too much to bear. He forced his voice into a low and level calm: "But then how am I to get down?"

"I am instructed to inform you that there is a service staircase reaching two-thirds of the way to the ground, and maintenance ways and ladders for the remainder."

Phaethon felt a dull sense of shock. He did not know the

distance to the atmosphere, or to the surface of the earth, from here. There was no almanac in his mind to provide him with the data on the height and position of the space elevator. But he knew it was a staggering distance. Climbing down from the tallest mountain ever made was nothing compared to climbing down from geosynchronous orbit.

He hazarded a rough guess: "It will take me months! Years, if I stop to sleep."

"Nonetheless. That is your only legal course of action."

Phaethon rotated his floating body to peer once more over the edge of the rim. He could see the energy units, like lines in a Greek column, descending away from him, infinitely.

There would be no danger until gravity started to reassert itself. He could just drift down, slowly at first, never noticing the gently mounting acceleration, never seeing the danger until it was too late, until he was speeding down, faster and faster, with no way to stop himself. No way except to engage the energy units with a magnetic grappling field. Would they truly fail to support him?

Surely there was an emergency circuit to catch falling objects, to prevent damage to the bottom, if nothing else. Surely the Sophotechs, who were so wise, would not simply stand by idly, and watch him fall and watch him die? Would they protect Vafnir's property rights so jealously, when a mere flick of a switch to the energy units, a few micrograms of power, would save a human life? Wouldn't Vafnir's lack of action be a crime?

Foolish thoughts. No law would protect a man who voluntarily walked off a ledge.

Suicide, after all, was not against the law in the Golden Oecumene.

Curled into a ball like a fetus, barely able to keep his eyes on his target, Phaethon ejected a few desultory squirts of steam and bobbed over to the air lock entrance of the service stair. The air lock was the size of a coffin. It whined as it cycled. The atmosphere beyond was thin, high in inert gasses, meant to maintain basic pressure, not meant for humans to breathe. The stairwell beyond was dark, narrow, and barren.

Stairs in microgravity?! Obviously no one had ever bothered to program this segment of the service access way to react intelligently to the surrounding circumstances.

There was hardly enough room to maneuver. He kicked off the door and fell to the next landing, rotating at the halfway. His foot hit the far wall with a dull clang. He kicked off again. He fell down to the next landing. The far wall clanged under his boot. The echo resounded down the long, long, shaft underfoot, a large, hollow, endlessly empty noise.

Already he was exhausted. And there were roughly fifteen million flights of stairs left to go.

He kicked off the wall again. The metallic echoes clanged through the emptiness.

THE DESCENT

1.

Slowly, gradually, the weight grew heavier and heavier. Slowly, the air grew heavier. Slowly, the burden in his mind grew heavier.

There were things he did to keep despair and grief at bay. All he had to do, he told himself, was think about it later. Let him get down the tower first. Let him get to Talaimannar in Ceylon. Harrier Sophotech must have had something in mind when he named that city; Phaethon had that as his goal, as his hope. He saw no further.

Flying, one long kick after another, down the first hundred flights of stairs, he had exhaustively inventoried the macro-commands and routines loaded into his personal thought-space, the vast mental hierarchy of (now useless) controls in his armor, the amount and composition of the nanomachinery in his black cloak and skin garment.

Then he busied himself by arranging a priority list for his cloak and inner garment, which he expected could shelter, feed, water, and nurse him. He went through a system check on the armor. When he was done with that, because he had nothing else to do, he did it again. Then a third time . . .

There came a time when he had to skip; a push of the toe was enough to send him down the next flight of stairs. Each landing slapped his feet more heavily. Then there came a time when he had to walk. He walked, he marched. Then he trudged. Then he plodded. The weight seemed always to grow more. Each time he thought that he was finally far enough down the tower length to suffer the normal Earth gravity, the next hour or so of descent seemed only to make it all heavier.

For some of the flights of stairs, he rested his legs, letting the leg motors do all the work, folding his legs in lotus position on the open belly plate of the armor's midriff. But once his priority list was done, and he calculated the drain on his suit energy, he realized that the batteries could not be recharged indefinitely, and perhaps should be conserved.

But conserved for how long? No one was ever going to sell him a gram of antimatter again. Perhaps he could build a simple solar converter out of the nanomaterial in his cloak. But was this cost-effective? He had only a limited amount of nonrecyclable cloak material. Clearly he had to use it for some things and not others, such as the production of food and water for himself.

He told himself not to think about the future. Get to Talaimannar in Ceylon. That was the goal.

He shut off his leg motors, folded his cape, and walked down the stairs using his legs.

Down more stairs he trod. And then more, and more.

2.

The last hour before he slept, he began accumulating carbon out of the air around him into his cloak. The weight began to slow him, but he spent some of his power to increase the action of his leg motors to tolerate the extra burden. He stopped to rest on a landing, consulted the thousands of ecological programs he had loaded in his thoughtspace, and built a place to sleep out of the nanomaterial of his cloak.

His little encampment spread across the landing and up several steps. He had accumulated enough carbon, nitrogen, and water vapor out of the air to combine complex amino acids in a life-filter canister he grew from his cloak. He carpeted the landing with soft moss on which he could rest, and his vapor canister, converted to a condenser, and placed at the top stair, was able to put out a little streamlet of water. This trickled down the mossy stairs, and fell into his helmet. Inside the helmet he had his nanomachines construct a nuclear recycler to break up the water, store the hydrogen, and release the fresh oxygen back into the atmosphere. The mildly higher partial pressure of oxygen refreshed him without leading to drunkenness.

He decided that it would not be too wasteful of his limited material to construct a few simple microorganisms, which he introduced into the streambed, and which he programmed to a symbiotic interrelationship with the moss of the stair. Nanomachines gathered nitrogen from the air and herded it together into floating spores; inside the spores, other machines rearranged the materials into simple nutrients to keep the moss green and healthy during the night, and to convert the moss into sugars and carbohydrates, starches and vitamins, so that Phaethon could have a bland, if nourishing, meal in the morning. Wastes from the groin piece of his armor he buried and filtered in a mound of moss which he then dotted with perfumed flowers; and the recycling spores gathered here like flies, to draw out elements to feed the moss. There was no sunlight here, of course. The energy for his little ecosystem came from his armor, for he had adjusted the outer plates to radiate in the infrared, and draped the whole affair in a thermophilic fungus organism like pale seaweed, to photosynthesize heat energy and start the simple food chain.

The control hierarchies within the armor, designed to run the complex interconnected machine-and-organic ecologies of a starship, would have had more than enough capacity to track and control this tiny plot of moss ten steps across; but Phaethon did not have a responder, or a radio set, or a point-to-point system that a child could buy for a pfennig from a thought shop, and so there was no way for any command to reach from the suit-mind to the microorganisms. Phaethon had to content himself with a crude, old-fashioned binary chemical tag system, loading each cell with little viruses to disintegrate them if they passed outside of the area, or a time, or the behavior, defined by his preset chemical cues.

He folded himself in spun silk polymer sheets, and sat on other sheets inflated with air to form a pillow beneath. He propped the armor up, so it sat facing him, and the warmth from the glowing red breastplate and vambraces was like a camp stove.

But he could not sleep, not a proper sleep. There were times when he was semiconscious; he did some of that hallucinating dawn-age men called dreaming.

In one hallucination, he saw a bride (or perhaps it was a bird of fire) still moving feebly, lowered in a coffin into the waiting earth, and dirt was shoveled onto her casket, while little scraping noises and soft cries for help rose up from inside. In another hallucination, he saw a mansion built upon a cloud, floating away, ever farther away, forever, now out of reach, burnt to black and smoking rubble. In a third hallucination, he saw a black sun looking down upon an airless world coated with blood and black debris.

Phaethon jerked his head upright. His face was pale with sweat; his heart thundered in his chest. The headless armor, burning red, and draped with seaweed like a drowned ghost from some children's sea tale sat facing him. All was silent. There was something wrong with his dreaming.

There were supposed to be no nightmares in the Golden Oecumene.

Phaethon's natural sleep cycle could not correctly integrate his various artificial modes and levels of consciousness with the natural sections of his neurology. Little corrections and integrations were needed. Always before, he had had Rhadamanthus to do this task. He had a similar system on board the *Phoenix Exultant*. Without such a system, his subconscious mind would begin to act much like a dawn-age man's or a primitivist's, with self-sustaining mental actions neither checked, nor overruled, nor brought to light for inspection.

His mind could run away from him now, showing him weird scenes as he slept. Always before he had been alert and lucid as he had slept. Always before, one of Rhadamanthus's monitors could have warned him about dangerous subconscious influences, strange emotional conjunctions, growing mental disorders. The natural checks and balances nonartificial minds might have had to protect themselves from neurosis, Phaethon might not necessarily have. The more complex and the more delicate artificial systems in his brain now would operate without supervision and without repair. What if he fed commands into his thoughtspace while he slept? What if the ordinary signal traffic from the artificial sections of his nervous system had odd or unexpected side effects on his subconscious?

He worried but saw no easy answer. At some point, somehow, he would have to get access to a self-consideration program. If he logged on to the Mentality to retrieve one, his enemies might find him. Perhaps he could somehow build one of his own, once he reached . . . ?

Reached where? His only "destination" was an arbitrary one, selected because having a meaningless goal was better than having none. Nothing waited for him there.

Phaethon looked from right to left, at the little red-lit plot of moss on which he sat. This was the only home he had now. Rhadamanthus Mansion was gone. His low-rent cube was gone, too. The landlord there certainly used the same standard language in his rental contracts that the Eleemosynary Hospice used. Phaethon had already been evicted. He had no possessions in that room, except a box of cleaning dust. He recalled now that even the medical equipment had been leased.

A second memory surfaced. The organs in his body, the thick synthetic texture of his skin, and the other changes to his body which he had thought were cheap artificial replacements, were, of course, nothing of the kind. His body had been redesigned by the surgical processes specially commissioned and created by Orient Overmind-group, one of the Ennead, at tremendous cost. His skin and organs were designed to withstand the shock of accelerations, the degeneration of microgravity, and the various radiation hazards, vertigo, deprivations and other emergencies the conditions of space demanded. His body had been designed in tandem with the inner lining of his suit.

Phaethon shook his head in dismay. Would this body remain fit and healthy under normal earthly gravity? Before it had been stored under constant medical attention. His skin was insensitive; his eyesight seemed dull and limited without the artificial enhancements he used to enjoy. He had sacrificed everything, even the normal healthy function of his normal body to his dream of space travel. That dream had been his spirit. What did one call a body after its spirit had fled? There were words from the old days: hulk; relic; corpse.

A third memory suddenly surfaced. He recalled why he had been there, in that filthy small cube of a rented room. It was not merely that it was cheap. It had been near a spaceport. Phaethon had rented it fully expecting to be back under way again before the end of December. He had wanted to be within a few minutes' ride of a dock, so that he could sail immediately back to Mercury Equilateral, where the *Phoenix Exultant* waited. It had been for a quick departure.

Bitterness stung his throat till he laughed.

He had not slept well: but, at least, some of his old memories were being organized so that he could retrieve them now.

Phaethon closed his eyes and tried to sleep again. He dreamt a world was burning far below him.

He rested uneasily. Eventually he rose, gathered his helmet, drank, ate a sparse meal from the floor. Then he dissolved his little stream, and rolled his miniature landscape of moss and spore and microorganism back into his cloak, shed the extra mass as water, and used the water to absorb the waste-heat of the nanorecycling process, and eject it as steam. Then his armor cleaned itself and swirled up around his body, lifting metal plates into place. He swirled some medical nanomaterial into his mouth to clean his teeth and restore his blood-chemistry balance.

Phaethon drew a breath and closed his eyes. He did not have a formulation rod, or any working midbrain coordination circuits, but he attempted to embrace three phases of Warlock meditation he had learned from Daphne during one lazy year off they had taken together. It was crude, but he felt his nervous system, parasympathetic system, and the pseudo-organic circuitry in the various levels of his mind reach a balance. His eyes were calmer when he opened them again.

Then he turned and looked back at his little encampment, scanning it to be sure he had left no moss or mess behind.

He smiled. Was a life of solitude so bad? His little camp here had been crude and rough, without luxury, to be sure. But it could not have been so different from the way his ancestors had lived in the prehistoric wilderness. Could it?

3.

The descent from the space tower took fewer weeks than he expected. His sleep was irregular; he woke exhausted. But he persisted. When strange moods or sudden despair came upon him, he attempted Warlock meditation techniques, and used the armor he wore in the place of a formulary wand. The armor lacked the proper biofeedbacks, but it allowed him to persevere.

In some places, the descent was easy to expedite; in others, he was hindered. The region of the tower from fifty to sixty thousand feet was owned by an old friend of Helion's, a Dark-Gray ex-Constable named Temer Sixth Lacedemonian. Temer had ambitions to become one day a Peer himself, and did not wish to appear to favor Phaethon's case, and so, during that whole length of the tower, Phaethon was herded and harassed by armed remotes, and not permitted to sleep on Temer's territory, and hardly permitted to pause. And Temer must have guessed Phaethon's patience to a nicety; just when Phaethon was fed up, and reaching his hand up to close his faceplate (so that he could stop and rest, while enjoying the spectacle of the remotes bouncing useless stun-shocks against his invulnerable armor) it was at that moment Temer's remotes dropped back, and allowed him a few hours' overdue rest. The episode caused Phaethon some grim satisfaction, and perhaps a spark of distant hope. There were limits to what the Hortator's exile could impose on him, limits he could influence.

For other stretches, the going was much easier. Phaethon had been dreading reaching the tower segments that lacked stairs, and imagined aching limbs fatigued by endless hours of hand-over-hand climbing. The reality was much more pleasant.

The maintenance ladders dropped down sheer wells. Phaethon could attach himself by diamond-fiber cord spun out of available atmospheric carbon. He fashioned a system of pulleys and carabiners, which could lower him great distances quickly. He grew motors to control the arrangement, so that he could descend while he slept, albeit this used more battery energy than he would have liked. The suit's gauntlets he programmed to untie and to retrieve the rope material periodically, so that Phaethon hardly lost any nanomaterial mass. The suit-mind was flexible enough to understand orders to find the next stanchion and retie the belaying knots. Thus Phaethon could sleep with his hands folded over his chest beneath his breastplate, safe as a papoose in a backpack, while the armor rappelled down one length of rungs after another. Many miles of descent were quickly consumed in this fashion. And he needed the rest. His growing mental fatigue, his lack of a proper self-consideration circuit, was forcing him to spend more and more time asleep.

The worst section was a maintenance well without rungs, meant only for robots using magnetic grapples. Phaethon thought he probably had the right to ask to be conveyed down past this segment, since the law against trespass did not require a trespasser to depart by ways that were dangerous or unhealthy. But a notion of pride or zeal made him go forward.

Or perhaps his rashness came from certain mood-alteration stimulants he had attempted that week. The Warlock meditations were becoming less effective, and Phaethon was experimenting with a crude Noetic system he was trying to construct out of the helmet circuits, to see if he could do to himself, manually, some of the delicate nerve work and sleep integrations Rhadamanthus had used to do to restore mental balance.

This morning's attempt at sleep integration had left him giddy and overconfident. He had been sure he could design a parachute out of his cloak, with sufficient lifting surface to slow his fall; the armor was too heavy, and he had merely dropped it down the shaft. The armor, of course, banged and rang against the shaft as it dropped, chiming like a gong the size of the moon, but was utterly unscratched by the five-thousand-foot plunge. Phaethon, on the other hand, had scraped against the side of the well, spilled air out of his parachute shroud, spun, recovered, tumbled, almost recovered, and broke both his legs upon landing.

In infinite agony, he had crawled and crawled, trying to find his armor, dragging his broken legs behind him. Finally he found it, and gasped out a command to turn on the emergency medical program before collapsing. The armor had swarmed across his body and fitted itself around him. Nanomachines inside the suit lining had aided the biomechanisms in his legs to regenerate the bone tissues. He lay in half-drugged discomfort for hours while his body repaired itself. The special construction of his space-adapted bones slowed the process, and the suit-mind had to make several hesitant guesses about how to proceed. (The medical routines and partial minds aboard the *Phoenix Exultant* were not, of course, available to him. The armor was a wonder of engineering, but it had not been designed to operate in solitude.)

A Constable remote came to hover over his dazed body, warning him not to drop dangerous objects from high places, lest he be sued for negligence.

The Constable made no move to help him, of course. Phaethon had no insurance, and no doctor would risk joining him in exile.

He lay on his back, blankly staring upward, wondering at his own stupidity, and vowing to touch no mood alterants of any kind again. For a man familiar with the power to project his self-image instantly anywhere into the Mentality, or to telepresent himself in reality anywhere there were mannequins, to lie immobile, fixed in place, helpless, was torture. He imagined an angel whose wings had been torn off.

That episode had consumed almost half of his available supply of nanomaterial (it was absorbed into his body as medical constituents) severely drained his suit batteries, lost him half a day of travel.

The best section of descent had had, for its maintenance way, merely a track of traction-variable plates set in a long slide, spiraling down the whole circumference of the tower at a steep slope. The metal in the plates were atomically organized to permit easier motion in one direction and speed than another, with resistance variables to control the rate of descent.

Phaethon saw the opportunity at once. He formed his cloak into a belly sled with magnetic elements that would be agitated by the action of the traction fields; that agitation could heat water stored through tiny capillaries and veins he grew into his cloak; the heat would drive a steam turbine he grew like a lump across his shoulders; the turbine would recharge his batteries, while the passing wind cooled the circulating water. Most of the nanoconstruction could be recycled.

By the time he slid to the bottom of the long slide, Phaethon found that he had lost only four hundred grams of nanomaterial in unrecoverables; but his battery power was restored to full strength.

He dissolved the belly sled with a pang of farewell. It had not been an elegant engineering solution. Nonetheless, it was with some pleasure that Phaethon could add to the inventory of his resources and possessions that he had so exhaustively noted days before the entry: potential energy (position above the earth).

Below a certain point, he began to hear, through the walls, the creaking and singing of the wind shear against the sides of the infinite tower. He kept expecting to find some hatch or window to the outside. Perhaps he thought his experiment at parachuting would have better success if he were not jumping down a narrow tube; certainly it would be easier to fall thirty or forty thousand feet rather than walk down thirty or forty thousand feet of stair. But no window interrupted the solitude of this dark stair.

Days, weeks, fortnights went by. But even seemingly endless time eventually must end.

At the bottom of the tower, the maintenance hatch came out upon a concourse.

He paused at the door to change an entry in his suit log. He removed "potential energy" as a possible resource, for, at ground level it was zero.

Looking at his resources log, Phaethon stood a moment in thought.

In the negative column, however, he made several entries:

"No father. My real father has been replaced by a relic, who was one of the conspirators who worked my downfall. I must count him my enemy."

He half expected Rhadamanthus to come on-line and remark with rueful humor that this was somewhat unfair of Phaethon, whose father was, after all, a more complex individual than that. No remark came.

"No manor, no sophotechnology. I am limited to merely human intelligence. My enemies have intellects like unto gods at their command."

Then, more grimly: "No more spare life. My next death is final."

And: "No wife. My love has slain herself, and left a puppet, programmed to love me, to mock me."

The last entry: "Alien creatures hunt me like a dog, to kill me, while an ignorant and ignoble world rollicks with gaiety and festive cheer, unseeing, uncaring, and unable, by law, to see me die. My location is a matter of public record . . ."

No. No, wait. Phaethon erased that last ideogram-gestalt line. His location was secret, was it not? In the assets column, he noted that it was still the middle of a Masquerade. He could move unseen, undetected.

Or could he? Anyone with access to the Mentality could look up Phaethon's last known location, at the top of the endless tower. It was not hard to calculate his rate of descent; and, every time he had stepped into an area where a no-trespassing injunction was flagged, his position would be public knowledge again. Temer Lacedaimonius, for example, had dogged his progress.

So the enemies had to be here. Somewhere on the other side of this door. Perhaps very near.

With a deliberate motion of his hand, he pushed open the door.

Beyond was light, noise, the sounds of crowds. Phaethon blinked, blinded for a moment, unable to make himself step into the rectangle of light framed by the doorway.

There was a sharp noise in the near distance, like the shot of rail gun, or perhaps the snap of a short-range energy weapon. Phaethon, certain that his enemies had found him, flinched back, hand before his face.

He crouched there in the dark, waiting for pain.

None came.

He realized that it had just been some noise from the crowd of people in the concourse beyond; a slap of water in a fountain, or the bark of a child's ear-toy. Or perhaps the snap of a circuit in some ill-tended machine. In a world hidden by sense-filters, there was little need to make all noise muffled, or to keep all public engines in repair.

He tried to lower his hands, to straighten up, but the sensation gripped his throat for a long, shameful moment: loneliness, self-pity, fear, the degrading physical terror that he would be killed, and die the final death.

Mingled with this was the more subtle oppression of knowing he had no place to go, no home, no shelter, and no friend—and no real destination. . . .

That moment passed. With a snort, Phaethon straightened up. He sardonically added an entry to his negative asset column: "More easily frightened than expected."

In his asset column, he noticed the listing of how much directed energy per square inch his armor could withstand. Then he uttered a harsh laugh. "Good luck to you, my assassins," he murmured half-aloud. They would need an energy output equal to a b-type star even to scratch him; they could blow the planet to asteroids beneath his feet without even jarring him. Even if they pushed him into a pit of frictionless, superconductive slime, his internal ecological structures would remain intact for years upon years.

And yet, the enemy must be aware of all this. They would be prepared. A charge of antimatter would burn through his armor, as it would through any normal atomic structure, heavy or light.

With Sophotechs helping them, these enemies, whoever they were, could outthink him, anticipate his moves, create better weapons, have more resources at their command. . . .

No one would raise a hand to help him. No one else even believed these foes existed.

In the positive assets column, he added, grimly, with no trace of a smile: "And I alone, out of a whole world of deluded and forgetful men, know and recall the truth about this matter. I love truth more than happiness; I will not rest."

Squinting, he stepped into the light.

HERE ENDS VOLUME I, TO BE CONCLUDED IN VOLUME II,
The Phoenix Exultant

THE CYBORG

1.

He opened the door onto a crowded boulevard of matter-shops, drama-spaces, reliquaries, shared-form communion theaters, colloquy-salons, and flower parks. An elaborate hydrosculpture of falls and aerial brooks spread from a central fountain works throughout the area, with running water held aloft by subatomic reorientations of its surface tension, so that arches and bows of shining transparency rose or fell, splashed or surged with careless indifference to the reality of gravity. Light scattered from tall windows lining the concourse, or from banners of advertisements, or from high panels opening up into the regional mentality, was caught and made into rainbows by the high-flowing waters. Petals from floating water lilies drifted down across the scene.

Beneath all this beauty was a crass ugliness. More than three-quarters of the people were present as mannequins. This was evidently a place meant for manorials, cryptics, or other schools that relied heavily on telepresentation. Since Phaethon no longer had access to any kind of sense-filter, all these folk, no matter how splendid of dress or elegant of comportment they might have appeared to an observer in the Surface Dreaming, looked to him like so many ranks and ranks of gray, dull, and faceless mannequins.

There may have been beautiful music sweeping the area;

excluded from the mentality, Phaethon was deaf to it. Here and there were hospice boxes or staging pools, ready to send out dreams or partials, calls, messages, or any form of tele-presentation. All channels were closed to Phaethon, and he was mute. There were dragon-signs burning like fire in the air, displaying messages of unknown import. Phaethon could not read the subtext or hypertext; Phaethon was illiterate. There may have been thought-guides in the Middle Dreaming to allow him to remember, as if he had always known, where to find the public transport he sought. Mnemonic assistance gone; Phaethon was an amnesiac. There may have been or-nament and pageantry in the dream-stages gathered in the air around him, lovely beyond description, or signs and maps to show Phaethon where, in this wide concourse, might be the way or the road he sought. But Phaethon was blind.

Here and there among the mannequins, the face of a realist or vivarianist showed. Their eyes turned dull when they lit on Phaethon, and their gazes slid past him without seeing. All sense-filters were tuned to exclude him. The world was blind to him as well.

He expected the banners overhead to swoop down on him when he looked up. But no. They floated on by, shouting with lights and garish displays. Even the advertisements ig-nored him.

No matter. Phaethon tried to keep his thoughts only on the next steps immediately before him. How to find out where he was? How to find Talaimannar? How to go from here to there? Once there, how to find out why Harrier Sophotech recommended that place?

He had to ask someone for help, or directions.

Phaethon stepped behind a stand of bushes; there was a flow of water from the fountain works overhead, forming a rippling, translucent ceiling. Was anyone watching? He as-sumed not.

He doffed his armor and covered it with the cape of na-nomaterial, which he then programmed to look like a hooded cloak. Phaethon himself merely drew out some of the nanom-aterial from the black skin-garment he wore, and drew circles around his eyes, to solidify into a black domino mask. And that was that: Both of them were now in disguise. He hoped it was enough to fool at least a casual inspection. He programmed the suit to follow him at a fixed distance, avoiding obstacles; to "heel" as Daphne would have said.

He stepped out again into the concourse, followed by the bulky, cloaked form of his armor, looming three paces behind him. He went downstairs and found a pondside esplanade that had fewer mannequins walking along it. He saw real faces; faces made of flesh or metal, or cobra scales, or polystructural material, or energy surfaces. They were laughing and talking, signaling and depicting. The air seemed charged with a carnival excitement. Many people skipped or danced as they strolled, moved by music Phaethon could not hear. Others dived over the side of the esplanade, to glide among the buildings and statues in the pond.

He did not know what particular event was being celebrated. It was rare to see so many folk together. Whatever bunting or decoration swam in the dreamspace here, which might have given him a clue as to the nature of the occasion, was, of course, invisible to him.

People smiled and nodded at him as they walked by, full of good cheer. "Merry Millennium! May you live a thousand years!"

He had not realized how much he had missed, and was going to miss, the sight of friendly human faces. Phaethon smiled back, waving, and calling out, "And a thousand years to you!"

Phaethon reminded himself that he had to be careful. Theoretically, the masquerade protocol would not protect him, since he was no longer part of the celebration, no longer part of the community. But how many people would even try to read his identity if they saw him wearing a mask during a masquerade? Most people, Phaethon guessed, would not.

The rule from the Hortators was that no one was to give him aid, comfort, food or drink, or shelter, sell him goods or services, or buy from him, or donate charity to him. This rule did not (in theory) actually prohibit speaking to him, or looking at him and smiling, although that was the way it surely would be practiced.

If Phaethon tried to buy something from a passerby, Aurelian was obligated to warn him that he was about to be contaminated with exile. But as long as Phaethon did not try to win from the passers-by either food or drink or comfort or shelter or charity, Aurelian would no doubt stand mute. Sophotechs had a long, long tradition of failing to volunteer any information that had not been specifically asked.

It was hard. A couple walking hand in hand were passing out wedding-album projections of their future children. Phaethon smiled but declined to take one. A young girl (or someone dressed as one), skipping and licking a floating balloon-pastry offered him a bite; Phaethon patted her on the head, but did not touch her pastry. When a laughing wine-juggler, surrounded by musical firecrackers, and balancing on a ball, rolled by and tried to thrust a glass of champaign into Phaethon's hand, Phaethon was not able to refuse except by jerking his hand away.

The juggler frowned, wondering at Phaethon's lack of courtesy, and raised two fingers as if to try to find out who Phaethon really was. But the juggler was distracted when a slender, naked gynomorph, fluttering with a hundred stimulation scarves, jumped up in drunken passion to embrace him. Singing a carol to Aphrodite, the two rolled off together, while the juggler's bottles and goblets fell this way and that.

Phaethon let the throng carry him down the esplanade.

The pressure of the crowd eased when Phaethon came to a line of windows, two hundred feet tall or more, which looked out upon a balcony larger than a boulevard. Out onto the balcony they all went together. Phaethon climbed up a pedestal holding a statue of Orpheus in his pose as Father of the Second Immortality. The stone hands held up a symbol in the shape of a snake swallowing its own tail. Phaethon put his foot in the stone coils of the serpent and pulled himself high, looking left and right above the heads of the crowd.

Several lesser towers and small skyscrapers grew up from

the railing of the balcony, like little corals fringing the topless supertower of the space elevator.

Beyond the balcony, the metropolis spread out from the mountain-base of the space elevator in three concentric circles. Innermost and oldest, the center circle consisted of huge windowless structures shaped according to simple geometries; giant cubes, hemispheres, and hemicylinders, painted in bright, primary colors, connected by rectilinear motion-lines and smart roads. The architecture followed the Objective Aesthetic, with the building shapes, slabs, and plaques all rigidly stereotyped. There was little movement in this part of the city; human beings of the basic neuroform tended to find these faceless buildings and looming monoliths intolerable. Mostly, this central ring housed Sophotech components, warehouses, manufactures. Invariants, who had little desire for beauty or pleasure or inefficiency, lived here, dwelling in square dormitories arranged like rank upon rank of coffin-beds.

The second ring was done in the Standard Aesthetic. Here were black pools and lakes of nanomachinery, with many brooks and rills, touched with white foam of the dark material streaming from one to another. Tiny waterfalls of the material formed where cascade-separator stages mixed and organized the components. Each lake was surrounded by the false-trees and coral bioformations of nanomanufactory. A hundred solar parasols raised orchidlike colors to the sun. The houses and presence chambers were formed of strange growthlike seashells; one spiral after another, shining with lambent mother-of-pearl, rose to the skyline. Blue-black, dark pearl, glinting silver, and dappled blue-gray hues dominated the scene. Thought-gardens, coven places, and sacred circles dotted the area, along with nymphariums, mother trees, and staging pools. Warlocks and basics tended to prefer the chaotic fractals and organic shapes of the Standard Aesthetic. Wide areas of garden space were occupied by the decentralized bodies of Cerebellines.

Beyond this, on the hills surrounding, green arbors and white mansions prevailed. This was the Consensus Aesthetic, patronized mostly by manor-born and first-generation basics.

Greek columns marched along the hilltops; formal English gardens rested in green shadows before grand houses done in the Georgian style, or neo-Roman, or stern Alexandrian.

In the far distance, Phaethon saw a wide lake. On the lake were a hundred shapes like jewel-armored clipper ships, whose sails were textured like a dozen wings of butterflies, surrounded with light.

Now Phaethon knew where he was. This city was Kisumu, south of Aetheopia, overlooking Lake Victoria. And Phaethon understood the wonder and excitement of the crowd. For the huge shapes in the lake were the Deep Ones.

These were the last of the once-great race of the Jovian half-warlocks, a unique neuroform that combined elements from the Cerebelline and Warlock nervous-system structures. Once, they rode the storms and swam in the pressurized methane atmosphere of Jupiter, before its ignition. When the time came to end their way of life, they chose instead to enter whalelike bodies and to sleep at the bottom of the Marianas Trench, where they called back and forth to each other, and wove songs and sonar images relating to the vast, sad, and ancient emotions known only to them; and made sounds in the deep, which reminded them, but could not recapture, those songs and sensations their old Jupiter-adapted Behemoth bodies once had made in the endless atmosphere of that gas-giant planet.

Once every thousand years, only during the time of the Millennium, they woke from their dreams of sorrow, grew festive gems and multicolored membranes and sails along their upper hulls, rose to the surface, and sang in the air.

By an ancient contract, no recordings could be made of their great songs, nor was anyone allowed to speak of what they heard or dreamed when that music swept over them.

No wonder so many people were here in reality.

Phaethon's heart was in his throat. The songs of the Deep Ones he had only heard once before, since he had not attended this ceremony his second millennial masquerade, during Argentorium's tenure. That time once before, three thousand years ago (during the tenure of Cuprician) the song had sung to him of vastness, emptiness, and a sense of infinite promise. It was as if Phaethon had been plunged into the wide expanses of the Jovian cloudscape; or into the far wider expanses of the stars beyond.

The Deep Ones had originally been designed also to serve as living spaceships, able to swim the radiation-filled and dust-filled vacuum between the Jovian moons, able to tolerate the almost unthinkable re-entry heat of low-orbit dives down into the Jovian atmosphere. But the early successes in cleaning circumjovial space and in taming the Jovian magneto-sphere, made those space-lanes safe and economical for ships of ordinary construction; the emplacements of sky hooks made alarming re-entries unnecessary. The Deep Ones' way of life was past; the danger and romance of space travel was removed. Phaethon had heard all of this in their song, so long ago. It had planted the seed that blossomed into his own desire to embrace his dream of star travel.

It had been Daphne who had brought him to hear it. But had that been Daphne Prime, or her ambassador-doll, Daphne Tercius? Phaethon could not remember. Perhaps his lack of useful sleep was beginning to affect his memory.

Phaethon jumped down from the pedestal and began to push his way through the crowd, and away. For the Deep Ones did not give away their grand, sad music freely. Everyone who did not exclude the music from his sense filter would have a fee charged to his account; and, when the computers detected that Phaethon could not pay, he would be unmasked. Once Phaethon was unmasked, no one, of course, would help him. Not to mention that the performance would be delayed, and the afternoon spoiled for everyone. (He was amazed to discover that he still cared about the convenience and pleasure of his fellowmen, even though they had ostracized him. But the wonder of that first Deep One symphony he had once heard still haunted his memory. He did not want to diminish the joy of folk happier than he.)

The crowd thinned as he rounded the space elevator, and came to the side facing away from the lake. Several dirigible airships, as large as whales themselves, were docked with their noses touching the towers rising from the balcony sides. They had dragon-signs in the air, displaying their routes and times in a format Phaethon could not read.

Phaethon stopped a passerby, a woman dressed as a pyretic. "Pardon me, miss, but my companion and I are looking for the way to Talaimannar." He gestured toward the hooded and cloaked figure of his armor, standing silently behind him. He spoke what was not quite a lie: "My companion and I are involved in a masquerade game of hunt-and-seek, and we are not allowed to access the mentality. Could you tell me how to find the nearest smart road?"

She cocked her head at him. Her dancing eyes were surrounded by wreaths of flame, and smoke curled from her lips when she smiled. When she spoke, Phaethon had no routine to translate her words into his language and grammar and logic.

He tried more simply: "Talaimannar . . . ? Talaimannar . . . ? Smart road?" He pantomimed sliding along a frictionless surface, hands waving, so that she giggled.

By her emphatic gesture he understood she meant that the smart roads were not running; she pointed him toward a nearby airship and pushed him lightly on the shoulder, as if to say, Go! Go!

Phaethon froze. Had she just helped him, or offered him passage on some ship owned by her? There was no alarm in her eyes; to judge from her expression, there was no secret voice from Aurelian warning her. And the woman was turning away, drawn by the movement of the crowd. Evidently she was not the owner.

Phaethon moved up the ramp. Closer, he saw the airship bore the heraldic symbol of the Oceanic Environmental Protectorate. It was a cargo lifter, perhaps the very one that had brought one or more Deep Ones from the Pacific to Lake Victoria.

The throngs began to fall silent. Out on the lake, Deep Ones were sailing to position, raising and unfurling their singing-fans. A sense of tension, of expectancy, was palpable in the air. Phaethon stepped reluctantly across the gilt threshold of the hatch and into the ship's interior, his eyes turned over his shoulder.

Giant magnifier screens, focused on the distant Deep Ones, floated up over the edge of the huge balcony. The images showed the Deep Ones, sails wide and high, motionless on the surface of the lake, all their prows pointed toward the Deep One matriarch-conductor, who floated like a mountain above her children, her million singing-flags like an Autumn forest seen along a mountainside.

Phaethon's feet were slow. He wanted so desperately to hear this one last song. Except for tunes he might whistle himself, or music shed from advertisements passing by, Phaethon would not hear songs again: no one would perform for him; no one would sell him a recording.

He steeled himself and turned his back. The hatch shut silently behind him.

The deck was deserted. The place was empty.